Martha

A FAMILY SAGA

ELLE B. HESS

PipStones

PipStones

PipStones Publishing
P.O. Box 4507
Fort Walton Beach, Florida 32549
www.pipstones.com

Martha: A Family Saga
Copyright ©2026 by Lynne Hess
Published by PipStones, LLC.

Author, Elle B. Hess
Editors: Abigail Turner, Deborah Hoffman, and Elizabeth Omoh
Cover Illustrator: Robert Sauber

Library of Congress Control Number: 2025927679
Copyright ©2026; Published in 2026

ISBN-13: 979-8-9932579-4-5, Ebook
ISBN-13: 979-8-9932579-5-2, Paperback
ISBN-13:979-8-9932579-6-9, Hardback

For Worldwide Distribution.
Printed in The United States of America.

Dedicated To:

My Mother, Martha LeClerc-Bilyeu
Born the 11th of August 1921 & Died the 17th of April 2007

I Finally Understand...

A Woman's Soul

Maybe my mom wasn't always
exhausted from doing so much...

Maybe she was exhausted from feeling so much. The weight of love,
worry, sacrifice, and the endless thoughts that never let her rest. I get it
now. Motherhood isn't just about what we do; it's about everything we
carry in our hearts.

No wonder she was tired...
No wonder I am, too.

- Author Unknown

Table of Contents

Introduction

When I was a child, my mother was my idol. She was definitely my favorite person. In my eyes, she was perfect... until I was old enough to know better. Eventually, I learned that there are no perfect moms. Then again, there are no perfect daughters.

I think mothers, for the most part, are heroes. Especially the single moms, because I believe they have the most difficult job. I truly don't know how they do it. My mom was technically a "single mom." My dad was a merchant seaman who was gone ninety percent of the time. When he was home, our household fell into total turmoil—three girls, including my older sister and me, who all of a sudden had to deal with a man who had no idea how to be around the female gender, let alone be a father.

After all, he spent his days on a ship with a bunch of men. There were no women in sight. We didn't know how to handle him, and he certainly didn't know how to handle us either.

This is the story of two moms: one is an example of mental illness and poor choices, and the other is an overcomer. *Martha* is a story of regrets and triumphs, a story of choices.

Every living being has a mother. It is one of the only things that all species have in common. Webster's Dictionary defines a Mother as, "A female parent." The Urban Dictionary definition of Mother is, "The woman who loves you unconditionally from birth. The one who puts her kids before herself and the one you can count on above all else."

In my opinion, both Webster's and the Urban Dictionary are epic fails when it comes to its definition! Actually, mothers are entirely too complicated to define. It leaves us on a journey to figure out this amazing being, the one we call mom, or mother, or mama.

I started this project almost fifteen years after my mother, whose name was Martha, had died. I was going through some of her things (which I had stored at my house), and inside her high school yearbook, I found her father's obituary. I was shocked to read that my mother, her three siblings, and her mother were not mentioned. I read it several times to be sure I hadn't missed anything. At this, I sat back and thought about how sad that was. The absence of my mother's name made it painfully clear: he hadn't acknowledged her as his daughter, and the rest of the family hadn't either. Imagine, as a daughter, having that knowledge. He died when she was just a young child.

Then I looked through her yearbook. She graduated from Lewiston High School, Class of 1940. Undoubtedly, she was part of the "greatest generation." There were hand-penned notations next to the names of classmates, many of which read, "killed in action."

Next to my mother's beautiful picture, it read...

"Pep is Marty's outstanding characteristic. Tall and lithe, she is a good basketball player and a graceful dancer. As sketching greatly interests her, who knows, here may be a future designer!"

It made me sad that I had no idea. Why didn't I know who my mother really was? It seemed that the Martha of 1940 died when she became a wife and mother. It was then that I decided to write a book in honor of my mother and her memory. Although this book is loosely based on my mom's early history, much of it is a stretch of imagination about how my mother might have liked her life to be after her early struggles. I have tried to honor her by writing a book that would make her smile and bring her delight.

Martha is a historical fiction, family saga set in Canada and the New England states from the early 1930s through the 1940s. It follows three generations and is full of hope, love, sadness, loss, and the ability to overcome adversity. Martha struggles with severe anxiety and low self-esteem. Eventually, with the help of a sport that she found a deep passion for and the love of an amazing man, she was able to rise above.

As I have written this from the heart, I hope you will enjoy it. It is also my desire that mothers and daughters alike will remember that life is short and see the need to love one another. There are no perfect mothers, and there are no perfect daughters. Grace is the key to maintaining a great relationship! Give each other grace, and try to create a life with no regrets.

Prologue

Have you ever wondered what would have happened if you had made different decisions at the important crossroads of your life? What if you took a different path? Have you ever had that little voice in your ear telling you, *No, don't do it,* but you ignored it?

This is that kind of story: a "what if?" story. There are a lot of "what ifs" in here. The truth is, every decision has consequences. For me, the consequences were fatal. I can think of at least half a dozen decisions that ultimately caused my death.

In stories like this, it is hard to decide where to start. But I think I'll start in 1929. It's not the beginning of the story, but it's not the end either. I think the middle is a good place. Along the way, I will fill you in on the beginning, but someone else will have to tell you the ending...

It was exactly 7:00 a.m. when I heard a knock on the door. They found me. It was something I had been dreading. Since that knock, I've wondered many times what my life would have been like if they hadn't.

In 1928, my husband was killed in an automobile accident. I guess the fact that we were in the process of getting a divorce plays an important role in the overall message. My in-laws didn't like the stigma of divorce, so they were trying to have our marriage annulled. This put the whole process in limbo. I'm pretty sure the fact that we had four kids did not help them with their pleas to the Catholic Church.

While Richard was alive, I had separated from him and moved from New Hampshire to Maine. Luckily, I had a friend with some connections, and so I was able to get work as a nurse's aide at the hospital in Lewiston. While it wasn't exactly a glamorous work, it gave me a steady paycheck.

With my husband's death, I became a widow instead of a divorcee. The LeBlancs—my in-laws—were staunch Catholics, and they didn't believe in divorce. From what I can gather by people's reactions, either everyone is Catholic, or everyone hates divorce. Anyway, now it didn't matter because Richard was gone, and instead of being divorced, I was now widowed—a much more acceptable title for a young woman with four children. I thought that all the court proceedings would end, but my in-laws were a very bitter, angry bunch, with a lot of money to hire attorneys and investigators, even if it was the beginning of the Great Depression. The Depression didn't seem to have any effect on them.

Now, they were trying to take away my four children: Claire-6, Martha-5, Diane-3, and Ricky-2. In reality, they only really cared about Claire and Martha. They alleged that I was an unfit mother and did not have the financial means to support my children. They were not wrong. Well, I mean, they were not wrong about my financial situation, but the fact that they moved all of Richard's and my assets into their accounts didn't help my cause.

Richard worked for the railroad. The only thing that they couldn't take was his pension, which had an early death clause and a good-sized life insurance policy for which I was the beneficiary. Richard's mom had all this tied up in court. I couldn't afford an attorney, so I was on my own. Moving to Maine, I had my friend, Jean, watch the kids for very little pay while I worked. She had a young one of her own and said she was happy for her son to have some other kids to play with. I was born in Canada, the seventh of nine children, so I understood this.

All Richard's friends were in New Hampshire and were afraid of the LeBlancs, so I knew they would be of no help.

The LeBlanc's lawyer showed up on my doorstep and presented me with some papers to sign. He said if I signed over my rights to Claire and Martha, my in-laws would release the hold they had on the life insurance. And I could still keep the younger children.

"This will make you a very wealthy woman," he sputtered. "Remember, we are in the Great Depression." I read the documents very slowly. I was burning with anger, and I knew I was not going to sign anything. But I wanted to compose myself before I told him to shove it. I said it in as nice a way as I could, but he still called me a nasty name and said that I was making a big mistake. "See you in court!" spouted the snotty attorney.

I'm sure if my mom knew what was going on in my life, she would've blamed me. She always seemed to blame me for everything. If I had been smart, I would have taken back my maiden name, and then they might not have found me so easily. By the way, my name is Imogene Dionne. As the story unfolds, I become Imogene LeBlanc.

CHAPTER 1

Signs

Richard and I met at a huge, fancy railroad gala. We immediately hit it off. Young and innocent, without any "real-world" experience, I had hardly even dated before I met him. At just eighteen, I had come to New Hampshire for one goal —to go to nursing school. People often told me I wasn't bad looking, and Richard was a shameless flirt, and handsome too. He was tall and well-built with brown eyes and curly brown hair.

It was the Golden Age for rail travel, and I was excited to be included in such a fancy event. He shamelessly approached me while I sat there terrified and all alone, as my "date" had abandoned me. The first words he spoke to me were, "Well, well, what's a beautiful girl like you doing sitting over here all alone?" I was tongue-tied and had no response. He went on to tell me that I needed to loosen up a bit. "I'll go and get you a drink. Don't move, beautiful. I'll be right back."

As I sat waiting for him to return (and I didn't even know his name yet), I was thinking how confusing the gala was to me. All the top railroad brass were there, dressed to the nines. There were politicians and local celebrities who mingled about. In all honesty, it was such a merry event, but for such a tragedy.

Before I arrived, I had asked my date what the gala was for. He proceeded to tell me that it was in remembrance of the *1920 Bellows Falls Vermont Train Wreck*. The host of the gala was the father of one of the men killed in the accident. He went on to tell me the crash occurred because the southbound train misread the posted train order. They thought it said Bartonsville instead of Bellows Falls. Instead of waiting at Bartonsville like they were supposed to, they continued to proceed, colliding at Williams River with a northbound train. At least ten people were killed, including the host's son. I thought it was kind of strange to celebrate such a tragic event.

When Richard returned with my drink, he introduced himself as Richard LeBlanc II. I was happy someone noticed me, especially someone as handsome and debonair as Richard LeBlanc. Since I had arrived, I had been planted in the same spot, like a scared little doe. Numerous female railroad employees interrupted us at the gathering to try to garner Richard's attention. I don't even know if Richard had a date that night. He certainly had a lot of attention from all the women, though.

Tasting the drink Richard brought me caused me to nearly choke. "What is this?" I asked, slightly coughing. Richard laughed and promptly pulled out a flask he had hidden in his jacket. Now this was 1922. Prohibition had begun in 1920. I had never had alcohol before, but I wanted to impress, so regardless of the taste, I continued to "nurse my drink."

As Richard and I sat talking, I asked him if he thought it was strange to hold a celebration commemorating such a sad event. He paused for a moment, then said that he hadn't really thought about it that way before. He continued on and gave me a history lesson on train accidents. He said that 1918 had been a very tragic time period for the rail industry. Apparently, there had been two really horrific rail accidents that year. The first one was in July. It was referred to as "The Great Train Wreck." There were 101 people killed in a head-on collision at "Dutchman's Curve." That is where two passenger trains collided at high speed in Nashville, Tennessee.

Richard was very animated and knowledgeable in relating the details. In that accident, the signal tower operator was at fault. He had given a green light to both trains when one should have been red. Besides the one hundred and one people killed, there were one hundred and seventy-one people injured. I was mesmerized by his storytelling. He was obviously well-versed in train wrecks. Maybe this was an omen of things to come.

"What was the other wreck?" I asked.

To which he responded, "Have you not heard anything about these accidents? Where are you from anyway?"

"Well, I'm from Canada, but I have been here for a year."

Nodding his head, Richard went on to tell me about the *Malbone Street Wreck*. "It happened in Brooklyn, New York, on November 1, 1918. One hundred and two people died, and one hundred people were injured in that one. The train derailed and smashed into a concrete wall in the Malbone Street Tunnel. It was traveling too fast. If you want my opinion, the engineer was much too inexperienced. He should never have been at the controls of that train. Of course, I don't want to besmirch his name, as he was one of the people who died," he said solemnly.

Richard continued to entertain me with interesting stories for the rest of the night. He was a very good storyteller. With every word and sip, he became increasingly more handsome to me. He was also a great dancer. He expertly guided me around the room. Despite his being familiar with everyone, his attention was solely on me. He made me feel special. I hadn't felt like that for a long time. Maybe not ever. He was handsome, funny, and smart. What more could a girl want?

At the end of the night, we left in Richard's really fancy Dodge Roadster and headed to my apartment. That in itself was more of a risk than I had taken since I left Canada to attend school.

He was a perfect gentleman. He didn't try to kiss me or touch me, but he did ask if he could see me again. The nice man that he was, made sure I got into my apartment safely that evening...

And that was how Richard and I began.

After six months of indulging in fine dining at places I would never have been able to afford on my own, he finally convinced me to "make love." I was a virgin, and the experience was awful! I cried, and Richard consoled me. Two months later, I found out I was pregnant. Two weeks after that, we were married. I know! I know! It all happened too fast.

There were several red flags that I should have picked up on while we were dating. First, I never met Richard's family and was never taken to his house. Next, Richard had a flask everywhere we went. Lastly, days would go by without a word from him. One time, two weeks went by. You would have thought that bells would go off... screaming danger, danger... but I was in love.

When Richard found out I was pregnant, he turned green. "We will work it out... but I have to go now," he said before stepping out that day. A week went by without a word... then two weeks. I cried until I was sick. I was sure that I would never hear from him again. Just when I was about to call my parents, he showed up on my doorstep with a ring and flowers. He got down on one knee and proposed. I didn't hesitate to say yes. I was so thankful that I didn't have to call my parents.

"Go put on your best dress. We are going to do it now!"

"Get married now? Right now?" I asked.

"Yes. Why not? It's as good a time as any," he responded with a mischievous smile plastered on his face.

So, off we went to the Justice of the Peace. Our witnesses were strangers whom we pulled off the street. It wasn't fancy, but I didn't care; I was in heaven. I was just so happy that he hadn't abandoned me. I really didn't know anyone in Manchester. I came here for schooling purposes. I worked hard and studied even harder. I didn't have time for friendships.

Shortly after the ceremony, Richard suggested we travel to Boston for our honeymoon. The idea again took me by surprise. "I can't go on a honeymoon. I have to go to school on Monday," I protested.

He demanded, "Forget school. You just quit."

"No, I don't want to quit school."

"Well, you're pregnant *and* married now. You don't have a choice. You have to."

And that was the end of that. Off we went to Boston. I told you I was naïve.

For our honeymoon, we stayed at Boston's Beacon Hotel. It was luxury at its finest. Leather couches in the lobby, and beautiful marble floors. Taffeta curtains that went from ceiling to floor. It was beyond elegant. There was painted art on the ceiling, which was amplified by huge, crystal chandeliers. Yep! Art on the ceiling. I had never seen anything like it.

Our room had a tub that was bigger than my kitchen. The bed was huge, and the mattress felt like we were lying on a cloud. I had no idea how anyone could afford this, let alone someone who worked for the railroad, but Richard told me not to worry about it. We stayed for four nights. There were a lot of fancy meals and room service. We made love every morning and every afternoon, and he assured me every time that having sex is not going to hurt the baby. I was nervous about that. Richard drank heavily every night, and I was amazed at how little the alcohol affected him.

When it was time to go back to Manchester, I asked, "Where are we going to live?"

Richard said, "At my house, of course." I was relieved because I thought he was going to say we were staying with his parents, whom I still had not met.

Then I thought, *Maybe his house is his parents' house.* Little did I know.

When we pulled onto "his" property, I was astounded. He lived in a mansion. I knew he had money, but this was more than I had ever suspected.

"Before we step out, Immy..." That's what he called me. It was a name I would grow to hate. "I need to tell you something: I still live with my parents."

"I figured," I responded, and Richard immediately heaved a sigh of relief.

And actually, I understood as soon as we pulled up. After all, Richard said he was twenty-two years old. No one twenty-two years old could afford this.

"Let me ask you something, Richard. Do your parents know that we are married, and do they know that I am going to have a baby?" There was a very uncomfortable silence. "Oh, geez," I said as I realized the mess I was currently in.

So, that was how my relationship with the LeBlanc family began.

Richard got our bags out of the car, and we walked up the driveway hand in hand. Hugging me, he said, "Don't worry, Immy. They are going to love you just as much as I do. We can leave the bags here. We have people who will bring them up."

People? Wow! As we walked up, I began to tremble. I came from a modest family with nine kids. My only thought was that I would never fit into the family. *They are going to hate me...* And boy, was I right!

Walking into the sprawling LeBlanc home felt like we were walking back into the Beacon Hotel. In front of me was a wide sweeping staircase that seemed to go on forever. The floors were made of white marble, and there was a huge table in the foyer that had a gigantic fresh flower arrangement on it. The primary colors in the home were white and various hues of purple. It was absolutely stunning. Greeting us was a middle-aged man, who I later learned was the butler. Yes, they had a butler. I was speechless. I honestly could not catch my breath.

"Hi, Wilson. Please bring our luggage in and take it to my room. By the way, this is Imogene, my new bride. Where is my mom?"

"Your mother is outside in the garden." Wilson was looking at me with raised eyebrows and what I took to be a look full of sympathy and horror.

Richard grabbed my hand and led me through a huge, beautiful kitchen that opened up to a magnificent garden. It was full of flowers. The smell was so intoxicating and wonderful that I almost couldn't breathe. His mom, who was a dark-haired, tall, slim, stunning woman, was down on the ground pulling weeds and watering her beautiful flowers. She stood up and spotted me, smiled and said, "Well, who is this lovely girl, Richard?" I think that was the last nice thing she ever said to me or about me.

Richard didn't break the news slowly or gently. He simply blurted out, "Mom, this is Imogene, my new bride." At that point, his mother promptly fainted. He hadn't even told her I was pregnant yet, and she was already out cold on the ground. It could not have been handled any worse.

When Mrs. LeBlanc (Barbara) recovered, she demanded to speak with Richard in private. She also requested that Wilson call Mr. LeBlanc (another Richard) and ask him to come home at once. Richard asked Ruth, the maid, to show me to his room. I spent the next four hours crying, alone in Richard's bedroom. It was a huge room with a gigantic private bath. Very comfortable, but not for a scared, pregnant, newlywed who had just met someone who obviously hated her—a mother-in-law, to be exact. When Richard finally came upstairs, he said, "See, I told you we would work it out."

I should have seen the signs. Was he nuts... or was I?

CHAPTER 2
Wake-Up Call

It was 1925. I found out that Richard had been married before. No children from that one. Her name was Elise, and she apparently escaped the home with nothing but the clothes on her back. They had been married for two years, and Richard was twenty-four at the time. His parents were able to have that marriage annulled. Remember, Richard said he was twenty-two when we met. Turns out he was twenty-eight.

I discovered Elise completely by accident. I had gone to the library to apply for a card, but when I filled out the paperwork, the woman behind the desk told me I already had one. When questioned, she told me that Elise LeBlanc, who lives at 311 Uptown Lane—my address— was issued a card several years ago, and it had become inactive. The librarian was kind enough to offer a free reactivation. I explained that I was not Elise; I was Imogene LeBlanc...

"Oh, she must be your sister. Do you want to reactivate her card?" I declined, but I couldn't figure out who Elise was. By this time, I knew everyone in the family, and there was no Elise. The only sister Richard had was named Claire (who our oldest daughter was named after). She lived in Boston, and we had met only once. The LeBlancs rarely spoke of her.

By this time, Richard and I had been married for three years and had two children. Life wasn't great, but it was the life that I was willing to live. My mom always used to say, "You made your bed, now lie in it." And so, I was making the best of it.

When I got home from the library, I asked Barbara who Elise was. Very matter-of-factly, she said that she was Richard's first wife. I was dumbfounded. Barbara went on to say, "Yes, she was worse than you, but not nearly as much trouble." When I asked her what happened to her, she quickly said, "Ask Richard."

Barbara was in our marriage more than I was. She wanted to make every decision in our lives. She wanted to "mother" my children. She even told Richard what to wear, what to say, and what to do in every situation. To my disbelief, he always listened and obeyed. It was ridiculous. She tried to bully me like she did him, but I was too strong-willed. I might have been young and naive when we first got married, but I had grown up since then. Two kids will mature you really quickly. Barbara criticized everything I did. I was lazy. I was fat. The children weren't being taken care of properly. She hated my taste in clothing. The list goes on and on. Richard never stood up to her, and he never stood up for me. If I complained to him about it, he would dismiss me and say, "She's my mom. Just ignore it."

Claire and Martha were good babies. They couldn't be more different. Claire looked like me: blonde with blue eyes. A beautiful baby who was mild-mannered and easy to parent. Martha looked like the LeBlanc family. She had brown-hair and brown eyes. Her skin was olive like her dad's. Also, a beautiful baby, but fussy. She never seemed to be comfortable or content. Most of the time, I couldn't figure out why she was crying. Barbara used this against me, and spouted things at me like, "I don't know why you had two children so close together. You are not a rabbit, you know. You have no idea how to be a mother. You don't have a clue how to make your own children happy." Her constant criticism made me doubt myself. Maybe she was right. Maybe I wasn't cut out for motherhood.

As Claire and Martha got older, their stark differences continued. My mother-in-law wanted so badly to be their "mom." She just took over. I don't even know how it happened, but she definitely was parenting my children. Claire and Martha loved her, and she doted on them. Knowing Barbara, I was really surprised that she didn't favor Martha over Claire because of how much she looked like the LeBlancs and how much Claire looked like me. Claire was a very easy child to love. I think God worked it out that way. I think that if Martha looked like me, Barbara would have been as mean to her as she was to me.

Anyway, life went on. Richard continued to be a "player." He would come stumbling in at odd hours of the night. I had no idea where he went or who he was with after work. I asked about it a few times, and his response was, "I work hard. You lack nothing. Stop complaining, Immy. If I want to go out and blow off a little steam after work, I will. Where I go and who I go with is none of your business." I found it amazing that he was always able to get up for work in the morning. He actually never missed a day.

After we had Martha, our sex life was nonexistent, which was fine with me. Richard was not a very gentle, patient, or considerate lover. He was all about his needs and satisfaction. It had nothing to do with me and my needs. Richard had quite a strong libido, so I figured he was probably getting satisfied elsewhere.

Two years after Martha was born, surprise, surprise, I was pregnant again. I swear we had had sex once since Martha, and now here I was—pregnant.

Maybe I am a rabbit after all. The one time we did have sex, Richard was so drunk he probably didn't remember it. I'm not gonna go so far as to say he raped me, but I was an unwilling participant at best. I waited as long as I could before announcing the "good" news. To my surprise, Richard was actually happy. Richard's mom said, "Well, maybe you'll have a boy this time."

Six months later, Diane was born. So much for having a boy. Diane looked like me. Another beautiful baby. She was not as easy as Claire, but not as difficult as Martha. Richard became very sweet to me and the children. He told me that he was not disappointed with another girl. He said, "I love being surrounded by girls. Besides, I already know what to do with a girl. I would have to learn how to take care of a boy." He really could be pretty charming when he wanted to be. His mother, of course, acted like I had failed again. Her comment was, "I should have known."

In the weeks after Diane was born, Richard came home early. He had dinner with the family and spent time with Claire and Martha. I'm pretty sure he stopped drinking altogether. I thought maybe this would work out after all. I talked to Richard about moving out of his parents' house. He was totally against that and took a hard stand. He said we could not do it without his parents' help. He made a good salary, but not one that would keep us the way we were accustomed to. I told him I could go back to work, and he asked if I was crazy.

"Three little kids!" he blurted. "How on earth will you go back to work? No one is going to hire you!"

I didn't care about material things. I was raised poor and didn't mind going without. Apparently, he did.

One night before bed, I finally asked Richard who Elise was. Well, that turned out to be a huge mistake. Richard went into a rage. He snarled out his complaints, "I heard you were asking my mom about her. She is gone, and I don't want to hear her name ever again." This further piqued my curiosity.

Ruth, the LeBlancs' maid, had been with them for twenty years. She was always kind to me, and I felt like she had sympathy for me because of the way Barbara treated me. We both liked to read, so we shared and compared books. I often got books from the library for her, and we would discuss them. We both enjoyed history, suspense, and historical fiction. As I didn't have any friends, I enjoyed and treasured

Ruth's company, even though she was at least twenty years older than me.

One day, when we were home alone with the girls, I asked Ruth about Elise. She became really nervous and told me she wasn't allowed to talk about it.

"It's okay. I know about her. Richard told me everything." I lied.

"Do you know where she is now?" I asked.

"I heard Elise went back to Maine," Ruth nervously responded.

"Interesting! I have some friends in Maine. Where in Maine?" I probed further.

"I'm not exactly sure, but I think it is somewhere near Lewiston or Portland," Ruth responded as she tried to distance herself from the conversation we were having that day, so as to avoid further questions.

Richard's "new leaf" didn't last long. He started back to his old ways a few months after Diane was born. Unfortunately, I was with child again. I really did think that every time we were intimate, I got pregnant. Richard wasn't that happy this time. He accused me of purposely getting pregnant. His mom did the same. She claimed I was running around with other men. Richard did not disagree. I don't know when they thought I had an opportunity to see other men when I had two toddlers and a baby to look after. Besides, I was barely out of Barbara's sight. For me, this was the last straw. I could not live like this anymore.

I had no money and no connections. My family already disowned me after they found out I got pregnant, which was before I married. They were Catholic too. I was on my own. I had no idea what I was going to do. At one point, I thought about fleeing, running away to somewhere I couldn't be found. But I didn't have any money to do this, and how do you flee when you are pregnant and have three little kids? Friends suggested I just give up the kids and turn them over to these awful people! For me, that would never be an option.

Finally, I had managed to squirrel away some money in anticipation of an escape. Mr. and Mrs. LeBlanc were going to some sort of convention in New York City. They would be gone for five days. Richard was back to drinking and carousing. He would leave the house by 7:00 a.m. and would not return until around midnight. This was a daily occurrence. So, the day after the LeBlancs left for their trip, I loaded up the girls and walked out the door. Ruth knew I was leaving and, even though she was scared of the LeBlancs, she had her husband pick us up. He met us down the road so the rest of the help wouldn't see us. Then, he took us to the train station. From there, I bought a ticket to Lewiston. Ironic that Richard's first wife, Elise, had ended up somewhere in Maine, too.

My friend from nursing school, Jean, lived in Lewiston and gave us shelter until we could get on our feet. Jean was a nurse supervisor at a local hospital. She got me a job there. As her title allowed, she was able to make our schedules work so that she could help with the girls. Diane was only six months old, and Claire and Martha were toddlers. It was very difficult for all of us, including poor, dear Jean. We lived with Jean for over a year. She was there with me when I delivered little Ricky. I'm not sure why I decided on the name Ricky. I'm sure some psychologist could figure that out. In any event, I will never forget everything that Jean did for the four of us.

After I left New Hampshire, I don't think Richard even bothered to look for us. If he did, he never found us. It wasn't until he died that his parents located us. They hired investigators. And it was then that I found out that Richard was dead. I didn't even have time to decide how I felt about that. I mean, he was my husband, the father of my children, but now these people (Richard's parents) were trying to take away my children.

By this time, I was living in my own small apartment. Martha and Claire were both in school. Diane was three, and Ricky was two. The hospital was paying for me to go to nursing school, and we were doing okay. Another nurse's aide, Rita, moved in with us to help with rent and childcare. Working full-time, being a mom to small children, and going to school was rough, but we were getting by.

After the Leblancs found me, they continually harassed me. There had been several instances within the last year where men, whom I assume to be attorneys, had come to try to intimidate me. Barbara desperately wanted my girls. I couldn't afford an attorney, and I had no idea what my rights were. The LeBlancs tried to have me declared unfit as a mother. I'm sure if I were still in New Hampshire, they would have been able to take the children. Maine was a different story. They had no connections in Maine, and I had friends here. Every time we went to court, I represented myself. The only thing that saved me was the overwhelming support I was getting from my friends. The court ruled that just because I was poor didn't mean I was an unfit mom. But the LeBlancs just kept bringing me back to court.

Finally, one day I just walked into an attorney's office in town with Diane and Ricky by my side. I spoke to the lady up front and told her my predicament. She was very nice and told me to take a seat and wait. After what seemed like an eternity, they called me back to an office. There, a man who looked to be around sixty years old greeted me warmly. "Mrs. LeBlanc, so glad you came," he said. He continued by stating that he was well aware of my situation and advised that I let "Barbara and Richard" take custody of the children. He said that we could negotiate a settlement with them, and I could be well taken care of for the rest of my life, if I would only sign over the children to "Barbara and Richard." As the meeting continued, it became more and more obvious that this attorney knew my in-laws personally. As I was about to leave, he remarked that I was being quite silly and foolish for insisting on my stance. He added, "You are fighting a losing battle. Good luck."

I left the office with tears in my eyes, and the receptionist ran out after me. She handed me a piece of paper and whispered that I should call the contact on the paper. Sympathetically, she mentioned that she had young children, too, and hoped he could help me.

"Good luck. I'll be praying for you," she said with a look full of compassion.

I folded the paper and tucked it into my pocket.

So, there I was in 1929—a widow with four children under the age of seven, being sued by my in-laws. The divorce was never finalized because Richard and his parents wanted custody of the three girls. They did not want Ricky (Richard III), because they insisted that he was not Richard's child.

That was ludicrous. He looked exactly like his father. I had fled before he was born, so in their minds, he couldn't possibly be Richard's, and my calling him Ricky instead of Richard was more proof that he wasn't theirs. They weren't that interested in Diane either. Diane had been just an infant when I left their home. They didn't really have a connection with her, but I guessed that they kept her in the lawsuit as a bargaining tool.

I was under no illusion that this was going to be an easy or short fight. My in-laws were rich, well-connected, and ruthless. They were the driving force behind the break-up of our marriage. Granted, there were many other issues, though—Richard's drinking, womanizing, and lying were just a few.

I felt a little tug to pull out the paper from my pocket. Peeling it open and written in beautifully scripted handwriting, it read, **Tweet Martin**, and there was an address, **777 Main Street**. It was very close to where I was standing. It was on the same street, but about two blocks down. *Tweet? Whoever heard of such a name?* But I was desperate. I had a few hours left before getting Claire and Martha from school, so I decided to give it a try. I thought that maybe there was hope.

Reaching the front building, I felt refreshed, but scared. The place was small, old, and a bit run-down. There was a sign out front needing a good paint job. It was so faded and washed out that it was barely readable:

Edward "Tweet" Martin
Attorney at Law

I entered the office, which was understated but neat. The furniture was sparse: two chairs, an end table, a coffee table, and a large desk. The rug was the most beautiful thing in the office, full of brilliantly bright colors of blues, oranges, and greens. The walls had a picture of Abraham Lincoln hanging there and were painted a soft blue. Several nicely framed diplomas were displayed behind a reception desk. It seemed Mr. Martin attended the University of Maine and Boston University.

There was no one up front, but there was a bell on the desk with a sign that said, Ring For Service, so I followed suit.

"Come on back. I'm in the second office," hollers a pleasant voice.

I walked back with the kids hanging behind, and there he was, Tweet Martin, sitting at a desk, eating a sandwich and drinking a soda pop. I looked at the clock and realized it certainly was lunchtime. Of course, then both of the children started fussing.

Mr. Martin was an interesting-looking man. I would say he was handsome, in a very different sort of way. He had red hair and brilliant green eyes and looked to be in his early thirties. He stood up when I came through the door and had a tall and lanky appearance. I am 5'9", so when I say tall, I was guessing that he was well over 6 feet. Maybe 6'2" or 6'3". He was dressed in a blue button-down shirt that looked like it could use a good ironing. It was open at the collar and lacked a tie. He greeted me with an extended hand and said, "You must be Mrs. LeBlanc. And these must be your children. I'm Tweet Martin."

I immediately grew suspicious. "How do you know who I am?" I queried.

"Donna from the Black Law Firm called and said she gave you my name and address. Donna is my sister. Have a seat and tell me what's going on." He extended his hand toward a weathered, emerald-green chair with brass rivets.

As I explained my problems, he listened very closely. No interruptions and no emotions about it, one way or the other. When the kids started fussing, it didn't seem to bother him. He bent down and asked if it was okay to hold Diane, who had gotten a bit antsy. He was immediately likable. When I was finished, he asked if I had been served with a lawsuit or had been given any paperwork. I showed him the agreement that my in-laws wanted me to sign.

He read it over carefully, looked up with surprise, and said, "You have four children? Wow. How can I help you?"

I told him that we had been to court several times, but I didn't have any paperwork from that. "I just wanted to be left alone to raise my children in peace and want whatever money is due me to help with the children's care." I explained to him that I didn't have any money to pay him. He said he wasn't worried about that. What he was worried about was the fact that the LeBlancs wanted the children and were making some pretty strong allegations of "unfitness" on my part.

"It says here that Richard LeBlanc is the father of your four children. Is that correct?

"I'm surprised it says four. The LeBlancs have always contended that little Ricky was not Richard's child."

"And he is deceased?"

"Yes."

"Has anyone from the state contacted you?"

"No one has."

"Okay. That's good. They are alleging that you are living in unsanitary and unfit conditions. They claim that you cannot feed or support the children and that you leave them unattended."

"I live in a two-bedroom apartment that I share with another nurse's aide. She helps with the rent and does some babysitting for me."

"So, you are working? Who cares for the children when you are at work?"

"I work and take some classes in the hopes of becoming a nurse. My roommate, Rita, or my friend, Jean, helps me most of the time."

"How are you paying for your schooling?"

"The hospital pays for my classes under the agreement that I work there for two years after I get my nurse's license."

"Do you ever leave the children alone?"

"No."

"Where are your other two children now?"

"Oh my gosh! I have to go. I have to get them from school."

Mr. Martin asked how he could contact me, and I gave him my address and the community phone number for our apartment complex. He said he would be in touch.

When I got home with the kids, there was a man with a summons at my door. I was to appear in court the next day... and I was to bring the children. Since I was scheduled to work the next day, this was going to be a problem. I frantically called Jean.

She was able to work the schedule so I could get off and agreed to come with me to court. Next, I called Tweet Martin. When I told him I was expected to be in court the next day at 10:00 a.m. with the children, he asked me to come to his office first thing the next day. He wanted to look at the paperwork and accompany me to court.

CHAPTER 3
Meet Tweet

"Tweet, thank goodness you answered. When are you gonna get a secretary?"

"Sis, why are you whispering?"

"Tweet, just listen please."

"Okay, shoot."

"There is a young mother I gave your info to. Please help her if she contacts you. She has four kids and is in a bind. Imogene LeBlanc is her name."

"But Donna, that sounds complicated. I don't know if I can get wrapped up in something like that right now."

"Tweet, you know why you do what you do."

"Donna, who's that? I hear someone in the background."

"Gotta go!" Click.

Hmm, she's right, I do know why. She knows me too well.
Tweet stares out the window as he reminds himself why he does what he does...

Being a lawyer runs in my veins, which most of my clients know. My father was a lawyer, as was his father before him. Dad always said, "There will always be disagreements among men. You will always have a steady flow of cash. It's good work." So, there was never any question what I was going to do when I grew up. Dad practiced mostly property law. He advised me to find something more interesting. When I told him that I wanted to help people, he laughed. "There is no money in that," he said. He suggested that I find an area of the law that was more lucrative and "help" people on the side. Not bad advice, really. In Lewiston, I became known as the "marital dispute attorney." There was only money in this if the client hiring me had money. Otherwise, it wasn't profitable. I had some rich clients. Most of them just paid me to draw up paperwork and/or to figure out a way for them to get out of their marriages without going broke. I worked closely with private investigators. Often, it was a matter of following people to see what kind of dirt we could uncover. Sometimes it was very interesting work. Other times, it was just plain sad.

My mom died of cancer when I was fourteen years old. She had struggled with it for over two years before it finally caught up with her. She was a wonderful woman whom everyone loved, and Dad never remarried. After her death, my older sister, Donna, was pretty much in charge. She was sixteen when it happened. My dad did the best he could, trying to raise two teenagers on his own. He was a very patient and kind father. He wanted his children to be happy and tried to make our home a safe and pleasant place. Mom had been a great cook, and she taught Donna how to make a few of our favorite recipes before she passed away. Donna wasn't a replacement for that role, but she did her best.

She also started working at Dad's law firm. She enjoyed the work, and when she graduated from high school, even though she graduated at number two in her class, she decided that she wouldn't go to college. This was the norm for girls back then. Instead of college, she stayed in Lewiston, living at home, and continued to work at Dad's office. She was a pretty girl and had many dates during this period. But never anyone special, until Phillip Beck came along. Donna and Phillip started dating and were married less than a year later. Five years later, with two miscarriages behind her, Donna finally had twin boys (Benjamin and Robert). Donna was twenty-eight and Phillip was thirty, and he was a police officer. Donna came back to the office soon after she had the boys. Dad just set up a nursery in one of the offices and life went on. Phillip was at the office regularly, and he and Donna were a great match. He was a laid-back Irish-Catholic boy, and my dad loved him so much, which is why he allowed them to live there.

Donna pretty much wore the pants. She was used to being in charge at our house, and Phillip didn't seem to mind her taking the helm of their family.

I graduated from high school with honors and headed off to the University of Maine in Orono. College was easy, and I had a lot of fun. Girls were interested in me, and I was interested in them. Most of the girls I dated wanted to get serious too fast. I didn't. None of my relationships lasted more than a few months.

Upon graduating with my degree in pre-law, I immediately moved to Boston to attend Boston University. Law school was a bit harder than college, and I really had to study to make good grades. I joined the law review, which left me with little time to socialize. There weren't any girls in my class at law school, but there were a few in the undergraduate programs at BU. I dated a few times, but nothing really serious. Like I said, I just didn't have time.

After law school, I passed the bar exam and officially became a lawyer. I started practicing law with my dad, but still felt like a kid under him. He really wanted me to take over and continue doing property law; however, I wasn't interested. I moved out of the house and out of the practice after one year. Dad wasn't mad; he understood. Donna stayed on as his assistant until he died very suddenly of heart failure.

He just had his 70th birthday the day before he passed. A lawyer named Samuel Black bought his office and his practice on the next day. He kept Donna on as his assistant. Donna and Phillip inherited the house, and I inherited the money. Dad had substantial savings. Donna and I had agreed to this before our father died. We were both happy with the deal... it was just sad to lose Dad.

The money he left me enabled me to do a lot of pro-bono work. I have especially helped the homeless population in Lewiston. You would think that if you were homeless, you would move somewhere warm. It amazes me that Lewiston, Maine, has so many homeless people. In any event, if I felt someone was not being treated fairly and they couldn't afford to hire me, I would usually take on their case for free or in exchange for a barter. One woman I helped cleaned my apartment every week for six months. I kind of missed that after she stopped, so I hired her.

I have thought about buying a house and upgrading my office, but I just don't see the need to, yet. Besides, like I said, I do a lot of pro bono work. A mortgage and debt might not allow me to do that.

When Imogene LeBlanc came into my office, I immediately knew I had to help her. My sister knew a little bit about the situation. The in-laws had contacted her boss, Samuel Black, for some legal advice about this situation. When Mrs. LeBlanc filled me in on all the details, I knew she was going to get a bad deal. Although I didn't know her in-laws, I certainly knew people like them. They were bullies. People with money, who didn't mind throwing their weight around to get what they wanted. I was actually surprised that they hadn't already proceeded with their plans. It was obvious they wanted Mrs. LeBlanc's children, and I was compelled to do something.

On Wednesday, October 2, 1929, Mrs. LeBlanc, her four children, and her friend Jean were in my office promptly at 9:00 a.m. Her in-laws, Mr. and Mrs. Richard LeBlanc, were seeking custody of her two oldest children, Claire and Martha. They alleged that Imogene LeBlanc was an unfit mother and did not have the means to take care of these children. They claimed the children were hungry, and no one was around to watch them most of the time. The lawyer who would be standing in court for them that day was none other than Samuel Black. I was dumbfounded. This was surely unethical on the part of Attorney Black.

Imogene asked that I call her by her first name, and I told her to call me Tweet. She was in tears, so I tried to reassure her. However, I was worried. The judge who was to preside over this matter was a great friend of Samuel Black. I didn't tell Imogene this.

We left my office and walked the block to the courthouse—all seven of us. I couldn't believe that the court was requesting that all of the children be present. What was the point of that? One thing I noticed immediately was how well-behaved the children were. They were dressed appropriately, and the two older girls had very nice manners. All of the children seemed to be functioning at age level or above. The oldest daughter, Claire, seemed to be particularly smart and happy. She appeared to watch over the younger children. Martha was quiet and more solemn, but she answered questions appropriately and also seemed to be pretty smart. The younger two, Diane and Ricky, seemed like typical toddlers.

Staring at the courtroom door, I worked a game plan. I asked Jean if she wouldn't mind staying in the hall with the children. I really didn't see the need for them to be in the courtroom while the adults argued about what was going to happen with them. Imogene looked like a scared child. Despite her height and a rough go of it, she looked much younger than her twenty-five years.

Imogene and I walked in together. Samuel Black was already there with another attorney whom I didn't recognize. I assumed he was an attorney from New Hampshire. Imogene's in-laws were not present. The judge had not entered the courtroom yet. Samuel Black looked very startled when he saw me. He whispered something to the other attorney, and they both looked at us. I think they just expected Imogene would be alone. "Hi, Samuel," I said.

"Well, well, well, if it isn't the illustrious Tweet Martin."

Just then, the bailiff asked for order in the court and for us to stand. Judge Simon DePaus entered the courtroom. Judge DePaus was a well-respected jurist who had been a judge long before I had been an attorney. My father always had great respect for him.

"You may be seated," said Judge DePaus.

"I understand we are here to discuss the possible removal of four children from the care of their mother due to unfitness." Mr. Martin, I don't see you listed on any of the pleadings. Am I to presume that you are representing the mother... a Mrs. Imogene LeBlanc?" as the judge thumbs through the paperwork. "Is that correct?"

"Yes, Your Honor. I will be representing Mrs. Imogene LeBlanc."

"Mr. Black, you are representing Mr. and Mrs. Richard LeBlanc, along with attorney Pile from New Hampshire? Is that correct?"

"Yes, Your Honor. That is correct. However, we are asking that only the two oldest children, Claire and Martha, be placed in the custody of Mr. and Mrs. LeBlanc. The two younger children are not a part of this lawsuit."

"Mr. Martin, I don't see an answer from you to the allegations in the suit."

"No, Your Honor. I just received a copy of this lawsuit this morning. Mrs. LeBlanc was not served with the suit until yesterday afternoon. That said, we object to the removal of any of the children. The allegations in the suit are unfounded. If Mrs. LeBlanc is an unfit mother, why wouldn't the LeBlancs want all four children removed from her custody?"

"That is a valid point, Mr. Black." Judge DePaus's face expresses concern. His eyebrow raises, and he faces his attention toward Mr. Black.

"Your Honor, the LeBlancs feel that if Imogene only had the two younger children, she might be able to get by. They are willing to let her try."

Shocked, I stood up quickly and said, "Willing to let her try? That is certainly big of them. These are her children. As much as the elder LeBlancs wish Claire and Martha were their children, they are not. There is no basis for this lawsuit. Mrs. LeBlanc is handling her responsibilities just fine. The children are well-fed and clothed. They live in an apartment, and the two older girls are enrolled in school. Mrs. LeBlanc has friends who help with the children when needed. She is employed as a nurse's aide at the hospital and is studying to become a registered nurse. This lawsuit is simply an attempt to steal these children from their mother."

"Mr. Martin, it sounds like Mrs. LeBlanc has a lot on her plate. How can she be employed and go to school and still take care of four children?" the judge asked.

"Her employment and schooling are both part-time, and as I said, she has friends who help out when needed."

Imogene sat very quietly without showing any emotion during this exchange until the judge turned to her and asked her if she wanted to say anything. At this point, she started to sob. She told the judge that she loved her children very much and was doing the best that she could for them. She went on to say that she didn't understand why the LeBlancs were harassing her.

Finally, after more questioning of Imogene about the living situation, Judge DePaus asked where the children were right now. Over my objection, he asked that they be escorted into the courtroom.

Jean entered the courtroom with the four children, and the judge looked them over. The only questions that he asked each of them were, "What is your name, and how old are you?" Claire answered first in a strong, pleasant voice. After Claire, each of the other children answered in turn. Even little Ricky was clear and precise. When they were through, the judge dismissed them back to the hallway.

"Mr. Black, based on what I have seen today, I don't see any basis for your request. However, I would like the court to assign a worker to do a report for me. I will arrange for one of the workers to come out, visit the home, and interview the children. After I receive their report, we will reconvene for a final ruling. Until then, this court is adjourned."

Immediately, Samuel Black strolls up to Imogene to tell her that this would never be over. She would never win against the LeBlancs. He said she would walk away with nothing. No children and no money.

I told Imogene to wait for me outside.

"Listen, Samuel, I'm pretty sure you are in violation of ethics already. Did Mrs. LeBlanc come to your office yesterday and discuss this case with you? I know she did. That is unethical, and I am going to make a motion to have you removed from the case. In the meantime, don't speak to my client. Anything you have to say goes through me."

"Okay, Tweet. Whatever you say. I'm just being realistic. Your client doesn't have a chance in hell of winning this case. The LeBlancs have unlimited resources, and they plan to use them."

"When did you become such a money-hungry ass, Samuel? Was it before or after you fell off the wagon? Or maybe it was before you went on the wagon. You know as well as I do that this case has no merit. The young woman is being harassed by your clients, who want to rip her family apart. They might have that kind of pull in New Hampshire, but the name LeBlanc means nothing here."

"Listen, Tweet, we all know you are a big bleeding heart, so we will see how it goes. The LeBlanc name might not have any pull here, but the color green is the same here as it is in New Hampshire. Your client is quite a good-looking woman. I hope she makes it worth your while because she doesn't have any money." At that, Samuel Black and the attorney from New Hampshire began to laugh and walked out of the courthouse.

I was burning mad, and I felt that this was going to be the start of a long war that nobody was going to win, particularly the children.

When I got back to my office, I immediately filed a petition to remove Samuel Black from the case, citing a conflict of interest. It was really an easy rule. Samuel should never have talked to Imogene about her case. That little meeting made him ineligible to represent the LeBlancs. I had no doubt that Samuel Black would deny that he met with Imogene. Normally, it would have been her word against his. This time, though, my sister was a witness. Another big problem. I knew that if Donna were to side with me, she would most likely lose her job. Getting by on a policeman's salary would be tight.

I didn't want to alarm my client, but I was skeptical about the court appointing someone to conduct a home visit and assessment. I knew that the judge and Samuel Black ran with the movers and shakers of Lewiston. I, on the other hand, was not part of the "group." I had no doubt that money talked, even in Lewiston.

The next day, I personally went to the courthouse to file my petition. I hoped that Samuel Black would file his own paperwork requesting to be released as counsel for the LeBlancs. That is what he should have done, but I doubted that he would.

I wanted to see Imogene's apartment, where the children slept, and also meet the roommate. Imogene was working and wouldn't be home until 4:00 p.m. from her class at the college. I told her I would be there before 5:00 p.m. In the meantime, I knew I needed to dig for a little information on the LeBlancs.

A friend from law school just happened to live and practice law in Manchester. I put in a call to him. We had been on the law review together and socialized from time to time. As soon as he picked up the phone, we made some small talk, and then I got to the point. Dave said that he knew of the LeBlancs but didn't know them personally. He said that their son had recently been killed in a car accident. He mentioned that the younger Richard was a real partier. He was known to "drink and carouse."

I asked if he knew that Richard was married. He said that yes, he knew and had actually met his first wife on several occasions. He had heard that he had remarried and had a bunch of kids, but he had never met the second wife. "The first wife was really nice. I think her name was Elise. She was pretty, but very shy and quiet. Then one day she simply disappeared. I hear now they are trying to get the second marriage annulled, too."

I asked what he thought about the parents. "I really haven't been around them enough to give you an opinion. I know that they pull a lot of weight around here. They have a lot of money and are not shy about flaunting it."

Dave said that he heard Mrs. LeBlanc was devastated by her son's death. He also heard that she was trying to take the grandchildren away from their mother. "Word on the street is she will do whatever is necessary to get those kids."

"What about an attorney named William Pile?"

"Bill Pile is a lap dog for the LeBlancs. I'm pretty sure they are his only clients. I know he got their son out of a lot of crap."

"Is he a good attorney?"

"I guess he knows the law pretty well. Like I said, he is a lap dog for the LeBlancs."

CHAPTER 4
Unwelcomed Guests

I arrived at Imogene's house just before 5:00 p.m., and she was just arriving home. We walked into the house together. Jean was there with the children. Rita, Imogene's roommate, was not home yet. The children were excited to see their mom. They were all over her, showering her with kisses and hugs. Little Ricky, in particular, was giddy to see her. Jean looked exhausted, and so did Imogene. Even in her exhaustion, Imogene took time to hug and love on each of the kids.

As we were coming into the living area, there was a strange woman sitting on the sofa. Jean introduced her as Ms. Holmes, a worker from the court. She said she was there to inspect the home situation. Ms. Holmes looked exactly like you would picture someone who does home inspections. She had her slightly graying hair in a tight bun and was dressed in a very conservative plaid skirt and white blouse. Her expression was stoic, but she looked like she had just swallowed a lemon. I would guess her to be in her mid-to-late forties. A short, stalky woman who wore no make-up. She wasted no time on pleasantries, immediately asking in a very judgemental tone, "Is this your usual time to return home to your children?"

I couldn't believe it. This was one day after our hearing. No notice was given. The woman just showed up. Jean said she had been there questioning the children since around 4:00 p.m. The judge obviously wanted this done quickly, but I found this to be highly inappropriate and unfair.

At the beginning of the questioning, I tried interjecting and explained, "This was not a good time." I continued, "Mrs. LeBlanc is just getting home from a day of work and wants to take care of her children." I told her to make an appointment, and we would be happy to see her and answer any questions she might have. Ms. Holmes wanted to know who I was. You could tell by her tone who she thought I was. However, when I explained that I was Mrs. LeBlanc's attorney, she backed down and, to her credit, said that she understood and asked when it would be a good time to come back. After conferring with Imogene, we agreed that Saturday at 3:00 p.m. would work. This was a Thursday, so that was two days away.

As Ms. Holmes was leaving, Imogene's roommate, Rita, was entering the home. She was curious to find out what was going on.

After the woman left, we all sat down at the table and ate. Jean had prepared hot dogs and beans with corn on the cob. I didn't eat much, and neither did Imogene. I could tell that she was rather rattled by Ms. Holmes' invasion. I asked Jean what kind of questions the woman asked the children.

"She asked lots of questions about who lived here and who came to visit. I think she was fishing to see if Imogene had many male visitors. Whenever I tried to answer anything, she told me that she wanted the children's answers, not mine."

"What did the children say?"

"They told the truth. Rita lives here, and the only other visitor is me. She wanted to know what the kids had for breakfast in the mornings and dinner at night."

"What did they say to that?"

"Cereal in the morning and different things for dinner like hot dogs and stuff."

"She asked Claire if she was ever hungry, and Claire said, 'Yes, I'm always hungry.'"

Claire pipes up, "Well, I am always hungry. That's because I have a hollow leg." We all chuckled at that.

"She asked if they were ever left alone, and they said no."

Claire spoke up again and said, "That lady wanted to know how old I was and told me I was very smart."

Martha says, pouting, "She didn't say I was smart."

"Did she ask Diane or Ricky anything?"

"No."

After the dinner dishes were cleared, Jean and Rita bathed the kids and put them to bed so Imogene and I could talk.

"Imogene, you seem very sad and distracted."

"Of course, I am. I am going to lose my children."

"So, you have no faith in my abilities to handle your case?"

"I didn't say that. I'm sure you are a great lawyer, but my in-laws are formidable. They have an endless supply of money and a huge circle of friends in high places. They are nasty people, or at least my mother-in-law is. They don't care who they crush in the process of getting what they want."

"Imogene, this is not New Hampshire. This is Lewiston, Maine. They don't have the same resources here as they do down there."

"What about their attorney, Samuel Black? He seems pretty connected."

She had a point there, but I told her not to worry about that. I told her I had just as many connections as he did. It was just a little white lie!

"Listen, on Saturday, just be yourself. Just tell the truth and go about your normal routine. I'll be here by 2:30 p.m. and will stay the whole time Ms. Holmes is here. She seems pretty businesslike. I think she will play it straight."

"I'm off on Saturday and will pretty much be on my own. Rita and Jean both work." I said that was even better. "Ms. Holmes will get to see you and the children interacting without any other distractions. Is there anything that you feel like I need to know before Saturday?"

"No, I guess not. Do I need to prepare the kids?"

"What do you mean, prepare?"

"Like, should I practice answering questions with them?"

"No. Just let them know that Ms. Holmes will be returning, and she might ask them more questions. Tell them to tell the truth. Unless, of course, you think there is something to hide."

"No. What you see is what you get. Nothing to hide here."

"Good! Imogene, do you have any family you can reach out to?"

"I have lots of family. Unfortunately, they are all in Canada. We don't have much contact."

After I left, I called my sister. "Do you know a woman named Ms. Holmes? May Holmes, who does home studies for the court?"

"Yes. I know of her. I don't personally know her, but our office has dealt with her before."

"What is she like?"

"She's okay. Very efficient. I've never had a problem with her."

"Does she usually side with Samuel?"

"Yes. Usually, she agrees with our side of things. Why?"

"She has been assigned to the Imogene LeBlanc case."

"Oh, Tweet, there is something you need to know about her. She is related to Herbert Holmes."

"The Herbert Holmes who ran for Senate last year against Frederick Hale?"

"Yes." Donna said she thought they were first cousins, but she wasn't sure. She did say they seemed quite close.

I knew that Samuel Black had donated huge amounts to Herbert

Holmes's election campaign and was pretty friendly with his family. With a little digging, I found out that the judge had also donated to his campaign. The fact that Herbert Holmes was soundly defeated by a seventy to thirty percent margin by Frederick Hale was not relevant. This was not good. I had to get Ms. Holmes removed from the case.

I spent the rest of the night drawing up an emergency motion to not only have Ms. Holmes removed, but to have the judge recused from the case also. Now I was asking for a new judge and a new case worker. I had already filed a motion to have Samuel Black removed. I wanted the motions heard the next day, which would be a Friday, and most judges didn't work on Fridays.

As soon as the courthouse opened its doors Friday morning, I was there to file my motion. One of the clerks who was working told me he would try to get the motion in front of the judge, but he couldn't assure me that it would get done. He said he didn't know if the judge would be in or not. I asked him to call Judge DePaus's secretary and find out.

Finally, about mid-morning, I heard from the clerk. He said, "The judge asked me to call you and tell you he would hear your motion on Monday at 10:00 a.m. His secretary is calling all the other parties involved. He said that he has informed Samuel Black and Ms. Holmes of your motion. Nothing will happen over the weekend."

Imogene was working on Friday, but she didn't have her class. She would be picking the girls up from school at 2:00 p.m. and would be home by 2:30 p.m. Rita had the two other children until she got home. I couldn't believe how complicated their schedules were. I just didn't know how they kept track of it all. I arrived at Imogene's apartment at exactly 2:30 p.m. She was already home and playing with the children. Rita was getting ready to go to her job. The apartment was clean and organized. The kids were clean and seemed content. Imogene looked happy, but looked surprised and worried when she saw me at her door.

"Oh no. What's wrong?"

"Can I come in?"

"Of course. What's going on? I didn't expect to see you until tomorrow."

"Well, sorry to disappoint you," I said playfully.

"I didn't mean I wasn't happy to see you. You are always welcome."

I informed Imogene about my findings regarding the judge and the case worker, and I explained my motion to have them both removed from her case. I explained that we were required to be in court on Monday at 10:00 a.m. and that the home visit had been cancelled for now.

"Tweet, I have to work on Monday. I can't take time off." After thinking for a moment, I told her she didn't have to be there. I told her I would handle the case.

"I want to be there. This is my life we are talking about. I know you can handle it, but I don't want the judge to think I don't care. Maybe I can switch shifts with someone."

In reality, it was definitely better if Imogene attended the hearing. I could see Samuel Black making a big show of the fact that my client wasn't there.

"If you can find someone and be there, that would be great. If not, I will handle it." Imogene asked what all this would mean for her and the kids. I told her that it would delay any kind of ruling, but in the end, it would have a fairer and hopefully more favorable ruling.

"What are the possibilities for an outcome?"

"The judge assigned will have to review all that has transpired so far. Then he will schedule another hearing. He will probably also want a home evaluation."

"So we have to start all over?"

"I'm afraid so."

Imogene wanted to know what could happen after that. I told her that the judge could throw out her in-laws' motion to remove the children, or he could proceed with a trial to determine if removal is warranted.

"Tweet, do you think the new judge will remove Samuel Black from the case?"

"I don't even know that we will get a new judge yet. Judge DePaus might throw out my motion, and we would proceed as is. I don't think that will happen because the conflicts are blatant. If we get a new judge, yes, I do think he will remove Samuel Black."

"If you can be in court on Monday, I will see you at 9:30 a.m. at my office. We can walk to the courthouse together. No need to bring the children. Enjoy your weekend and do not fret. If you can't be there, I will let you know what happens."

As we sat there thinking, Claire came over and sat next to me. She was a really beautiful child. Looks a lot like her mom.

"Mr. Tweet, are you my mom's boyfriend?"

"Oh, my goodness!" said Imogene as she turned red as a tomato. I snickered and told Claire I was her mom's lawyer.

"Well, I don't even know what that is, but I think you should be her boyfriend instead. You are pretty handsome and very nice."

Martha chimed in, "Yes, and we need a new dad. Ours up and died."

I could not help but smile. These were some very cute kids. Just as I was preparing to get up and leave, little Ricky climbed on my lap and cooed at me. Diane just sat in a corner of the room smiling.

"I am so sorry, Tweet." Imogene grabbed Ricky and told the girls, "Mr. Tweet has to leave now."

When she said Mr. Tweet, Martha laughed and said, "That is a funny name. Why is that your name?"

I explained that my real name was Edward, but everyone called me Tweet.

"Why?" asked Martha.

"When I was a kid in school, I started making bird sounds in class one day. Like this..." I made the sound. "Apparently, I am pretty good at it, and everyone thought it was a real bird. It drove the teacher crazy. She couldn't figure out where the sound was coming from and had everyone looking all over for the bird. She finally couldn't take it anymore and evacuated the class until the bird could be found. Well, obviously, the bird was never found, but the rest of the kids in the class knew it was me. Ever since then, they called me Tweet."

Before I left, Martha said, "I want to hear you tweet again."

Imogene said with a chuckle, "Great story. You know those kids are all going to be tweeting the rest of the night. Thanks!"

"They are great kids, Imogene. You are doing a wonderful job with them. When we get a new judge, I am going to make a motion that you and your husband's assets be freed up so you can claim what is rightfully yours. Do you know how much money the pension provides or how much the life insurance is?"

"I don't know. I just know that it is there, and it should go to me and the kids."

"Okay. I'm going to see what I can find out between now and Monday."

Donna was there waiting for me at my office.

"I got fired, Tweet." She raised two briefcases in the air and shrugged her shoulders.

"I guess Samuel got my motions?"

"Yep. He suggested that I find another job, as you and he were at odds. He also accused me of feeding you information and clients."

"Did you deny it?"

"Well, yes, I didn't feed you any confidential information about anyone. Everything I told you was a matter of record, but he overheard our phone conversation when I was talking to you about Imogene."

"Well, Donna, guess what? I just happen to need a secretary."

"I was hoping you would say that. When do I start?"

"Right now, if that works for you."

This was the first time I ever had a secretary, and I was thrilled that it was my sister. She knew as much about the law as I did.

CHAPTER 5
Living Witness

On Monday morning, Imogene was in my office at 9:30 sharp. She was dressed up and looked very pretty. Her hair was tied back in a ponytail, and her makeup was understated but pretty. She wore a cute powder-blue dress that highlighted her slim figure. It was paired with tasteful, low-heeled, black pumps. Imogene was tall and very slender. Looking at her, no one would guess she had birthed four children.

Donna greeted Imogene with a hug and a cup of coffee. She told her that she was now working with me and would be helping with her case.

Imogene immediately looked less stressed. My sister had a way of doing that to people. As we were leaving the office, I asked my sister to look into Imogene's husband's pension and life insurance. I also asked her to find out what she could about Richard LeBlanc's first wife.

Walking to the courthouse, Imogene had all kinds of questions. She mostly wanted to know if I thought my motions would make the judge and his cronies mad. I explained that this was nothing personal. It was business. She asked if my sister had been fired because of her. I explained that my sister didn't do anything wrong, and it was going to work out better for all of us this way.

When we arrived, Samuel Black and Ms. Holmes were already there. They had their heads together and gave us a brief, cursory look. Samuel actually looked tired and old today. He was probably worried about what he was going to do now that he had lost the best secretary in Lewiston. Ms. Holmes looked like she did on Thursday—all business!

At exactly 10:00 a.m., Judge DePaus entered the courtroom. He looked serious. After formalities, he said that he had my motions and was ready to rule on all three of them, so he saw no need for testimony.

"As to the first motion, that Counselor Black be removed from the case for conflict of interest, I rule in favor of Attorney Martin and his client. I find the fact that Mr. Black spoke to the plaintiffs and/or their attorney and then agreed to meet with Mrs. LeBlanc to be a conflict. Mr. Black, you should have immediately told Mrs. LeBlanc that you could not speak to her. Counselor Black, you are excused.

"As to the second motion that Ms. Holmes be replaced with another case worker, I find there is no evidence that her relationship to Herbert Holmes in any way would cloud her judgement. I have worked with Ms. Holmes for many years and have never found her to be anything but fair and professional. Mr. Martin, Lewiston is not that big. If I took everyone off a case because of who they know or who they are related to, we would not have anyone to take any cases.

"I am denying the third motion as well. Attorney Martin cites the fact that I gave money to Herbert Holmes's political campaign as a valid reason to have me removed. I'm not sure what that has to do with this case. If you had really done your homework, Mr. Martin, you would have found that I also gave money to his opponent, Frederick Hale. I am more than capable of being fair and unbiased in this case. Court is adjourned."

Judge DePaus pipes up again, "Wait, there is one more thing... I still want that home study as soon as possible. Please work out the details with each other before you leave the building. That's all."

Ms. Holmes immediately came over and asked when we could set up the home visit. Imogene said that she was off on Wednesday. The visit was set for Wednesday at 2:30 p.m. Ms. Holmes wanted all the children to be home, so the visit was set for after school.

"Ms. Holmes, I hope that I didn't upset you with my motion?" I asked, wanting to clear the air.

"Of course not, I realize that you have a job to do. I hope you realize that I have my job to do, too. I'm just glad the judge has faith in me," replied Ms. Holmes, her tone reassuring.

The hearing took less than thirty minutes, and Imogene immediately rushed off to work. Before she left, I told her I would be there for the home visit on Wednesday.

When I arrived at my office, Donna said the only thing that she was able to find out about the railroad pension was that it wasn't government-funded. It was a private pension and wasn't very stable. She said that she called the railroad and was told that she would need a court order to get information about an individual account or employee. Donna said she wasn't able to find out anything about the life insurance. She needed more information to proceed. I suggested that if Imogene reached out, since she is the pension's beneficiary, they would have to provide her with the necessary information.

"What about Elise LeBlanc?"

"Now that is an interesting one. I'm still digging, but I'm pretty sure, if it's her, she lives in Booth Bay Harbor. She is married to a lobsterman named John Pine.

"Do you have an address?"

"103 Bay Court."

"You feel like going for a ride?"

Concerned, she asked, "Now? Who's going to answer the phone and keep the office going?"

"The same people who kept it going before you got here on Monday. No one!" I laughed.

"Tweet, don't you have any other clients?"

"I've got plenty of clients and they know how I work, so don't worry about it."

"I'm just worried about how you're going to pay me." She chuckled.

"Pay! You expect to get paid?"

"Ha! Ha! Very funny."

The almost three-hour drive to Booth Bay Harbor consisted mainly of Donna drilling me about Imogene. She went on and on about how nice and pretty she is. She asked about the children. I was sure she was going to try to play matchmaker.

"You know she's Catholic, Tweet?"

"Listen, Donna, Imogene is a client and nothing more. She is a great gal who is being railroaded and bullied by her former in-laws. I want to help her. Can we end the match making please?"

"Well, I'm just saying, Dad would approve."

"Okay, listen, Donna, when we get there, I am going to need you to take the lead with Richard's ex-wife. I have a hunch that she won't be happy to see us, and she might be more willing to talk to another woman than a man."

"What kinds of things do you want me to ask her?"

"I want to know about her marriage to Richard LeBlanc, and I especially want to know about the in-laws and her experience with them."

Booth Bay Harbor used to be a sleepy little fishing village that began thriving at the turn of the century. Lobstering and fishing had always been its main sources of income. Tourism was just starting to take over the area. There were a lot of small inns and bed and breakfast places springing up. The population consisted of mostly the working class. The residents who did have money didn't flaunt it.

The house at 103 Bay Court was a modest, two-story, well-kept, single-family home across the street from the water with a large, detached garage. Unfortunately, no one was home. The mailbox said Pine on it. Tweet and Donna were quite sure that Donna had the right Elise. She said she had called the Manchester Post Office and was told that Elise LeBlanc's forwarding address was in Lewiston. When she contacted the Lewiston Post Office, they told her that Ms. LeBlanc had been forwarded to Booth Bay Harbor. The Postmaster for the Booth Bay Post Office informed her of the new name and new address.

"Donna, was it really that easy? Who did you say you were?"

"A long-lost sister. I said we had been separated after our mother died, and we were put in orphanages."

"My, my, aren't you a little storyteller."

She laughed. "It worked, didn't it?"

After we waited for over an hour, and just as we were getting ready to give up, we saw a woman walking up from the beach. It was just after 2:30 p.m.

The woman was tall and slender with a sun hat shading her long, dark hair. She wore brown clam diggers, a shirt that said "Lobster," and was holding her shoes while walking barefoot. When she saw us, she smiled for just a second and then, as if she remembered something, her expression changed and she hesitated in her approach. I immediately told Donna to take the lead, which she did by walking to meet Elise.

Donna said, "Hi. Are you Elise Pine?"

Full of suspicion, Elise answered, "Who is asking?"

"I'm Donna Beck, and this is my brother Edward Martin. Do you think we could have a word with you about Richard LeBlanc?"

"Richard LeBlanc? What do you want to know about him? I heard he died last year. I haven't had any contact with him for years before that."

"We are trying to help his wife, Imogene. Her in-laws, Barbara and Richard, are trying to take her children away, and they are withholding her inheritance."

"Listen, I don't know anything about any of that, and I really don't want to get involved." The woman began fidgeting and twiddling her fingers together. You could tell that Elise was very nervous and getting ready to turn us away. I asked her if she had children, and she said, "Yes, two boys."

"I'm Tweet Martin. I'm an attorney from Lewiston, and I represent Ms. LeBlanc. I'm sure you know how difficult the LeBlancs are. They are trying to intimidate and bully their daughter-in-law. She has four children and is working like crazy to try to keep them."

"Four children! Wow! I can't believe that anyone would have four children with that man!"

"They have accused her of being an unfit mother. She has to work extra to support them because they refuse to give her funds that are rightfully hers. As a mother, please put yourself in her place. We just want to ask a few questions."

"Mr. Martin, I can certainly sympathize, but I really can't get involved. The only thing I can tell you is that Barbara LeBlanc is a very evil woman. Her husband just goes along with whatever she demands. That woman cannot be reasoned with. She will make that poor woman's life a living hell if she can. My best advice is for Imogene LeBlanc to move away and give no forwarding address. I was lucky that I didn't have children with Barbara's son. I'm sure that if I did, I wouldn't have gotten out of that situation so easily. They were able to have the Catholic Church annul our marriage. Imogene and Richard's marriage was the best thing that happened to me. I was essentially off the hook after that. I'm sorry for her. I really am, but there is nothing I can do to help."

"Ma'am, was Richard abusive to you?"

"Not physically, but let's just say the apple didn't fall too far from the tree when it came to Richard and his mother. Richard was a bully just like her. I left there with nothing but the clothes on my back and a bruised ego that took years to heal. Richard and his mother had me believing that I was good for nothing. The fact that I couldn't conceive a child was a daily disappointment to them."

"Yet, you were able to conceive two children since then?"

"They are my stepchildren, which is neither here nor there. I love them as my own. Their mother died while giving birth to the youngest. Look, I have a great life now. I try to forget about that part of my life and those people. I have a wonderful husband and wonderful kids. Like I said, I wish I could help, but I don't want to get dragged back into that family's issues."

"Is Richard Sr. someone who can be reasoned with?"

"Not as long as that woman is alive. He listens and does anything she says. In the end, he was just as mean to me as she was. Now, I really have to go. My kids and husband will be home soon, and I've got chores and dinner. I'm sorry I can't be more helpful. I will pray for that poor woman and her children."

As she was turning away, she added, "The only thing I will say is that the worst thing that could ever happen to those kids is that they be placed with the LeBlancs."

I gave Elise my business card and asked her to call me if she thought of anything else that could help us.

The drive back to Lewiston was quiet. But finally, Donna broke the silence. "Those LeBlancs must be something else. Elise seemed really frightened to even discuss them. I think something really bad happened to her."

"Do you know Elise's maiden name?"

She replied, "Sorento or Mangionie or Rossi or something like that."

"Well, now," I laughed. "Those names are nothing alike. Can you narrow it down some?"

"I just remember it's an Italian name," laughed Donna.

I made a mental note to find out when we got home. The rest of the ride home, we talked about Donna's twin sons, Benjamin and Robert, and her husband, Phillip. I asked what Phillip thought about her working for me.

"Ha! He is thrilled... as long as you can pay me. He said he never liked Samuel Black. Thought he was an ass."

"You wanna get paid? Ha! Ha! I thought we were family."

"Very funny. When is pay day anyway?"

"Will the first of every month work?"

"Yes, how much?"

"I'll pay you whatever Samuel was paying."

"It's a deal."

CHAPTER 6

The Pine Family

Elise and Richard Leblanc were married for a little less than three years, and had met at the Catholic Church. The priest was actually the one who introduced them. Elise was working as a nanny for a prominent Manchester family. The senior LeBlanc and the father of the children that Elise was nannying were big golf buddies. Less than four months after their first date, they were married. The talk in the town was that the LeBlancs wanted to get Richard married so he would settle down. He was a wild one.

In the beginning, things seemed to be working out. Elise was a quiet, shy, demure woman, and that seemed to fit what the family wanted. Soon, though, they began pushing for Elise to have a baby. When it became evident that Elise was barren, the marriage was over. At least this was the word on the street.

Elise met John Pine through her sister, Daniella. John's first wife died during childbirth, leaving John with two-year-old Isaac and a newborn, Johnathan. John Pine and Daniella's husband, Ross, were not only brothers but they were also business partners. A very close-knit, Irish Catholic family. John and Ross's mom, Jana, lived in the same house where John and Ross grew up. The sons built homes for their families on each side of Jana's.

John came from a large Irish Catholic family, and Elise came from an Italian Catholic one. After her experience with the LeBlancs, Elise wanted nothing more to do with Catholicism, so she and John began attending a small Protestant church right around the corner from their house. Her sister, Daniella, and her husband, Ross, eventually joined them, and so did John's mom and sister.

The family had been lobstering their whole life. John and Ross had a younger sister named Margie who had Down Syndrome. She lived with their mom, Jana, and was a joy to everyone she met. Margie and Elise had an immediate bond.

BACK IN BOOTH BAY HARBOR

After Tweet and Donna had left, Margie came running over to Elise's house with her dog, Hardy. He was happily pouncing behind her. Margie was so curious about the people who had just been there. "Who were those people?" she asked.

Margie was pretty high-functioning and extremely social. Sometimes her speech was difficult to understand because of her stutter, and she wasn't quick in her reaction to questions. Margie never went anywhere without her best friend, Hardy—a sweet, beautiful black Labrador.

"They were just some people who were asking about others I used to know."

"What people did you used to know? What did you tell them?"

"Okay, Ms. Nosey Nellie. It is none of your business."

"My name's not Nellie. Why won't you tell me?"

"It was a long time ago, and you don't know the people."

"Was it about those horrible LeBlancs? I heard the guy say that name. I have heard my mom talk about them. She said they were not very nice to you."

Just then, John and the boys pulled up. *Saved by the bell*, or so Elise thought. They ran directly down to the beach like they usually did, but John, of course, stopped to talk to Margie. Hardy scampered quickly after the boys.

"Hey, Margie, what's going on with you, girl?"

"John, I need my hug first."

John always said Margie was the best hugger ever, which was true.

"Some people were here asking Elise a bunch of questions about those awful LeBlanc people."

"Oh really," he said with raised eyebrows.

Elise looked at John sheepishly and told him she would tell him all about it later.

"Now, Miss Nosey Nellie, I think your mom is calling you."

"I told you my name is not Nellie, and Mom isn't calling, but I do have to go because I have to help her with dinner. I love you, Elise." After a big hug, Margie hollers for Hardy, and they both dash home.

John Pine couldn't be more different from Richard LeBlanc. John was a good Christian man. He didn't drink other than a casual beer now and then. He didn't play around. He never once raised his voice to Elise or the boys. He was a hard-working, nice, steady man who thought family was everything. He never looked for or caused trouble, and everyone seemed to love him. Life was good for Elise with John Pine.

"So, what's this about the LeBlancs?"

"Some attorney from Lewiston and his sister came by today. He is representing Richard's second wife. His parents are trying to take her kids away."

"Not surprising. Those people have no soul. What did they want with you?"

"Just information. They wanted to know what life was like with the LeBlancs."

"What did you tell them?"

"I said I didn't want to get involved. I told them that those people were evil, and I was lucky to get away when I did. I basically told them I couldn't help them."

"Whoa, you said you couldn't help? What kind of help were they looking for?"

"I don't really know. I think they just wanted any dirt I could give them."

"Well, did you tell them that they locked you in a room for a week and mentally abused you throughout the time you were married to that bastard? Did you tell them that you fell down the stairs trying to get away from their drunk son and that the fall left you barren after you miscarried their grandson?"

"I only told them it was awful, but I didn't go into details."

"Listen, if we can help that poor woman, we need to do it. There is no way that Barbara LeBlanc should ever be allowed to have any children placed in her care. They hold themselves out to be "Good Catholics." But we all know that they control the Catholic Church in Manchester because they pay them off. Those people will find a way to take those children away from their mother, and in my opinion, people like that need to be stopped. How many children are we talking about?"

"Four! But I think the lawyer said the LeBlancs only want the two oldest."

"Four kids? Wow! What was she thinking, having four kids with Richard LeBlanc?"

"That's funny, I said the same thing."

"What are they saying? What is the reason they want to take the kids?"

"He said that the LeBlancs are saying she is unfit. They say she can't financially support four kids... well, and a bunch of other stuff. I don't know what all."

"Elise, we need to pray about this. I know you're scared. I know you don't want to get involved, but it might be the right thing to do. This could have been you. Put yourself in her place. You don't have to be afraid of those people anymore. There is nothing that they can do to you. They already did their damage. Let's think about it and pray about it over the weekend. Did the attorney tell you how to contact him?"

"Yes, he gave me his business card," I said, handing him the card.

"Tweet Martin? Interesting."

That night before bed, John and Elise held hands and prayed for God's wisdom. They prayed for Imogene LeBlanc and her children, asking the Lord to watch over them and guide them in making good decisions. They prayed for Tweet Martin and his sister, asking God to give them wisdom and insight on how to help Imogene.

Bringing the prayers to a close, John said, "Lord, we don't know Imogene LeBlanc, but we know how mean and spiteful Barbara and Richard LeBlanc can be. We pray that your arm of protection will be on Imogene and her children. Please help us decide what to do. In Jesus' name. Amen!"

The next day, John and Elise's lives went on as normal. John went to work. The boys went to school. Elise stayed home and could not think of anything but Imogene LeBlanc and her children. She felt like God was tugging at her heart. She knew that she couldn't just sit by and let bad things happen, but she was scared. The LeBlancs had ruined her for a time. Elise did not want to let that negativity back into her now wonderful life and beautiful family. She was sure John didn't quite grasp the severity of the situation and the fact that it could be even worse.

At mid-morning, while Elise was hanging some clothes on the line —it's a messy job when you're lobstering—Margie and Hardy stopped by for a visit. They pretty much dropped by every day to chat. Elise usually looked forward to their visits because Margie was such a character, and she always made her laugh. Today, however, Elise was so preoccupied with the LeBlancs that she wasn't in the mood for entertaining or small talk. Margie was smarter than anyone gave her credit for. She was very intuitive. She knew something was eating at Elise and wanted to know what.

"Elise, why are you so sad?"

"I'm not sad, honey. I just have a lot on my mind."

"It's about those awful people again, isn't it? Momma always says, 'You got to give your cares to Jesus.' She says, 'Worrying is like a rocking chair. It's a lot of work, but it doesn't get you anywhere. A day of worry is harder than a week of work.' Yep, that's what Mom says!"

"Okay, okay," I said laughingly, "I get the point."

"Well, Mom is pretty smart, you know."

"Yes, she is."

"I think you're pretty smart, too, Margie. You always know just what to say to make me laugh and forget my cares."

"Let me know if you want to talk about it, Elise. Mom says I am a good listener. I gotta go now because the lady who bakes the pies for the church is coming over, and I don't want to miss her. She always brings me samples."

A few hours later, my mother-in-law, Jana, came around to bring me some of her homemade cobbler. It was always John's favorite. Margie was right, my mother-in-law was a very smart lady. I loved her like a mother. We sat down to some tea and cobbler and had a nice little chat.

At the end of their teatime, Jana said that she would support John and Elise in anything that they decided to do. Hugging her, she let Elise know that she had a strong family and no one was going to pull it apart, no matter what. She, like John, suggested that they pray about it. That was years of wisdom speaking.

"Listen, Elise, I don't know all that happened when you were with that family in Manchester, but I know that it broke you for a time.

When we met, you were so timid and self-doubting. You could hardly look anyone in the eye. Look at you now! You are a wonderful wife to our son and mother to our grandchildren. We couldn't ask for anyone better. If that poor young woman, Imogene, had been through even half of what you went through, she would be a wreck—plus four kids? She probably needs all the friends, support, and help she can get. I know you went through a lot, but imagine how bad it would have been if you had children to protect along the way."

After much thought, prayer (and a lot of urging from other parties), Elise eventually told John that they should help Imogene. She said she was scared but thought it was the right thing to do.

"I knew you would want to help. I'll call Tweet Martin tomorrow." John embraces Elise and brushes her hair from her cheek. Elise immediately felt safe and knew she was making the right decision.

CHAPTER 7
Visits

On Wednesday at 2:30 p.m. sharp, Ms. Holmes showed up at Imogene's apartment. I was already there, and all the kids were home. She was immediately "all business." There were no niceties. Ms. Holmes walked around to each room and gave them the once-over. She then proceeded to grill Imogene about who slept where, her schedule, and what she did with her free time. Even though Imogene was a wreck, she answered each question calmly and politely.

"Free time. I don't have much free time. When I am free, I am with my children."

"What do you and the children do?"

"We play. We read. We go to the playground. The two older girls have chores that they do."

"What kind of chores?"

"They make their beds. They sweep. Claire helps me cook sometimes. Both Claire and Martha help with Diane and Ricky."

"Who stays with the children while you are working and going to school?"

"My roommate, Rita, and my friend, Jean."

"Are there any other people who stay here?"

"No."

While Imogene was being peppered with questions, the children were playing with some blocks and dolls. They were having a good time laughing and running around, and didn't seem to be paying too much attention to the adults. They were being typical children, and I couldn't help but smile.

Ms. Holmes asked if she could speak to the children privately. To this, I piped up and said, "No. Anything you have to say to them can be said in front of their mother and me."

At that, Ms. Holmes called Claire over to her.

"Hi Claire. Do you remember me?"

"Yes, I do remember you. You are that lady from the court."

Pointing to me, Ms. Holmes asked Claire if she knew me. "Yes, that is Mr. Tweet. He is my mom's lawyer."

"Wow! Lawyer! That is a pretty big word. Do you know what it means?"

"No. I just know it means that he isn't her boyfriend."

"Did your mom tell you to say that?"

"Well, she tells me every time I ask her if he is her boyfriend that he is not her boyfriend. He is her lawyer."

"Why do you ask her if he is her boyfriend?"

"Because he is nice and my mommy likes him, and he likes her, so I think he should be her boyfriend."

"Has anyone other than Rita ever spent the night here?"

"Yes. Jean and her son have stayed here a few times."

"The last time I was here, you said that you sometimes are hungry. Are you still hungry sometimes?"

"NO. I said I was ALWAYS hungry, and, yes, I still am."

At this point, Ms. Holmes pulled out a book. She asked Claire if she could read.

"Yes," Claire replies confidently.

Interrupting, I asked to see the book before she gave it to Claire. It was a standard Dick and Jane book, so I gave the book to Claire. Ms. Holmes asked her to read it, and Claire read the first few pages perfectly.

Next, Ms. Holmes called Martha over. Martha was a little more shy and tentative. She went directly to her mother and sat on her lap. Ms. Holmes said that it was fine for her to sit on her mom's lap while talking to her.

"Martha, do you know who I am?"

"The court lady?"

"I am Ms. Holmes, and yes, I am from the court. How old are you, Martha?"

"I am five."

"Are you in school?"

"Yes, I am in kindergarten."

"What school do you go to?"

"The little red school around the corner. My sister Claire goes there too, but she is in a different class."

"Do you like school?"

"No! I don't like school. Claire likes it, but I don't."

"Do you have friends in your class?"

"Not really. No one is my friend," Imogene interrupted and said that wasn't true. Firmly, Ms. Holmes directed Imogene not to interject. She said she wanted to hear from the children, not her.

Martha went on to say, "Claire has friends in her class, but no one wants to be my friend. It's okay though, 'cause I don't really need friends."

"Are you lonely sometimes?"

"No. I have Claire, Diane, Ricky, and Mommy."

"Do you like your teacher?"

"I like her, but I don't think she likes me."

"What is her name?"

"I forgot."

"What do you like to do at home?"

"Play. I like to play."

While Martha was being questioned, I could tell that Imogene was getting more and more anxious and upset.

Next, Ms. Holmes pulled out the same book she had given to Claire. Martha did well reading it also, although not as confidently.

Pointing to me, Ms. Holmes asked if Martha knew who I was. For the first time in the interview, Martha smiled and said, "That is Mr. Tweet, and someday I hope he will be my daddy."

"Okay, Ms. Holmes, I think you have asked enough questions about me. An hour has passed, and if you have anything else, I suggest you get on with it," I told her firmly.

"No. I think I am done for now. Thank you for letting me come. I will write up my report to the court and make sure you get a copy."

After Ms. Holmes left, Imogene broke down in sobs. She said she wasn't crying because of Ms. Holmes. She was upset because of Martha and her answers to some of the questions.

"I don't know why Martha is so unhappy. I try everything to make her feel loved. Claire has even expressed concern about Martha. She said that she sometimes hears her crying at night. She also told me that Martha plays by herself at school. She just doesn't seem to have any friends."

My heart was hurting for Imogene. She was doing everything she could to be a good mom and provide a nice life for herself and her family. I hated that everything was so hard for her.

When I got back to the office, there was a message that John Pine had called. I immediately called him back. Mr. Pine said that Elise was ready to help in any way she could.

"The LeBlancs made my wife's life a living hell when she was married to their son. She is terrified of them and what they will do to her if they find out that she is helping you. That said, we both think that it is the right thing to do."

"Mr. Pine, would it be okay if I come by tomorrow?"

"Please, call me John. I want to be with Elise and support her when you talk to her, so it will have to be late in the day, after I have finished work. Say around 3:00 p.m.? A lobsterman's day starts early and ends early. I should be home and cleaned up by then."

I hadn't even met this man yet, but I already like him.

At 3:05 p.m. the next day, I pulled into the Pines' driveway. It was already almost dark and freezing cold. Luckily, there was no snow on the menu. Our winter has been relatively mild so far. There was smoke coming from the modest home's chimney, and the front porch light was on, as well as most of the lamps in the house. I knocked on Elise and John Pine's door, and a healthy-looking, young boy answered. He called for his parents, and then he and another younger boy left the house and ran next door. I assumed these were John's sons.

I was greeted by a big, tall, and jolly John Pine. When I say big, I don't mean heavy. He was a very well-proportioned and burly man. Inviting me in, he gave me a hardy handshake with a calloused, working man's hand and a broad smile. As I had predicted, I immediately liked him.

I had not been in the house the other day. Entering, I found it to be so cozy and inviting, and I immediately felt at home. I could smell something wonderful cooking on the stove. John called Elise, and she came from the kitchen. Definitely not as welcoming as her husband, but nice all the same.

"Hello, Mr. Martin. I hope you haven't eaten. Dinner will be ready shortly," said Elise. I responded that I hadn't, but hoped that they hadn't gone through too much trouble. I actually was extremely hungry, and the sweet aroma wafting from the kitchen wasn't helping matters.

"I hope you like lobster. Elise made lobster stew and fresh biscuits. You won't find a better cook than Elise," John added.

"That sounds fabulous!"

With that, we headed to the kitchen, where the table was set for three. John offered me a beer, which I eagerly accepted, and we sat down to a wonderful meal. Before we ate, John blessed the food and asked the Lord for wisdom in dealing with the difficult situation. I could tell that this was a regular part of their mealtime.

"You know, being a bachelor, I don't often get home-cooked meals. Let alone a meal this good. I sure do appreciate it," I said as I carefully slurped the succulent warmth from the spoon.

We made some small talk and then got down to business. John did most of the talking, with Elise only occasionally adding and correcting. John told me about the abuse that Elise endured, and I could see the tears in both John's and Elise's eyes. Particularly, the time that Elise fell down the stairs. Apparently, she was pregnant and lost the baby. The doctors told Elise that she would never be able to conceive after that.

"She fell because she was trying to get away from Richard. He was drunk and was trying to rape her. She was four months pregnant. After that, the LeBlancs wanted her gone. If she couldn't provide grandchildren, she wasn't needed. She left with nothing but the clothes on her back. The LeBlancs were actually able to bribe the Catholic Church into an annulment."

Driving home from the Pines' house, I was burning mad. *How do people get away with acting like this?* It made me, more than ever, want to take those people down and get Imogene away from them for good. I had initially hoped that we could reason with them and provide a visitation schedule for the children and them. *Not now!* Now I didn't want them to ever have any contact with Imogene or the children! *This is WAR!*

Elise, with encouragement from John, said that she would make herself available if I needed her to come to Lewiston and testify against the LeBlancs, but I could tell that she was extremely frightened.

I couldn't believe that someone like Richard LeBlanc could manage to find and marry two such fine women. How had they ever gotten woven into the LeBlanc web?

CHAPTER 8

The Court Speaks

Weeks went by with no word from the court or Ms. Holmes. With the holidays approaching, it was clear that the courts would likely shut down for the season. I mentioned to Imogene that I doubted anything would move forward until after New Year's Day. Thanksgiving came and went... no word. But then, just before Christmas, there was an emergency motion made by the LeBlancs and their attorney. They wanted Claire and Martha to visit them over Christmas. The hearing was scheduled for Thursday, December 19. This was Monday, December 16.

Imogene was distraught.

"Imogene, relax. There is no reason for the judge to grant this motion."

They were requesting the children from December 20 to January 2. I asked the court to provide me with a copy of Ms. Holmes's "home study." I also objected to the short notice of the hearing and made a motion that the hearing be pushed back to December 23 to give us time to answer the request. My motion for a delay was denied.

On Wednesday, December 18, the judge's secretary called to tell me I could pick up Ms. Holmes's study at the clerk's office in the courthouse. She also informed me that Judge DePaus was ill and would not be the judge for this hearing. Instead, we would be in front of Judge Gill. This was bad news. Judge Gill was a crusty old jurist who mainly presided over family court issues. I had been before him many times and personally thought he should have retired years ago. His hearing was bad. His eyesight was bad, and his memory was worse.

Ms. Holmes's assessment was pretty standard. The only concern she had was for Martha:

"These children are well-loved. They have everything that they need. They are not neglected in any way. Claire is very smart and seems to be very mature and self-assured. Martha is also very smart. However, she seems to suffer from low self-esteem. Imogene LeBlanc appears to be a loving, concerned, and caring mother. I do not recommend any change in the placement of the children. That said, I do recommend and think that visitation with the grandparents would be beneficial to all. I have interviewed Barbara and Richard LeBlanc. They have expressed sorrow at not being a part of their grandchildren's lives. They tragically lost their son in an automobile accident, and this is the only connection that they have left to him. Having more people loving them can only be beneficial for Claire and Martha."

Those last few lines were the clincher. I was pretty sure the LeBlancs would get some kind of visitation.

On Thursday, December 19, we sat waiting for our case to be called. Richard and Barbara LeBlanc, looking very smug, were there with their attorney, as was Ms. Holmes. Imogene was a wreck, and I didn't have any words to console her. I had already warned her that the court might grant the motion. She sat beside me with a stoic expression, one she had perfected to the point where it seemed completely natural. I gently reminded her that it was okay to express her emotions. I suggested that perhaps this would help put a stop to the LeBlancs' relentless push for custody of the children.

"You always said that they were nice to the children. It was you that they hated and abused," I said gently.

"You just don't understand. No one seems to understand. The LeBlancs will never give up. I may have said they were nice to Claire and Martha, but that was when they were just toddlers. The children are older now. They have a will of their own. Barbara does not like anyone to go against what she says. When someone does, they feel her wrath. I do not want them around my children for even an hour, let alone weeks at a stretch. I am worried that if they take them to New Hampshire, I will never get them back," Imogene said, her eyes glistening with unshed tears.

I didn't want to tell her, but I was worried about the same thing.

Finally, the clerk said, "All rise for the court, the Honorable Horace Gill is presiding."

"You may be seated," said Judge Gill. The judge looked even older than the last time I saw him. He looked tired.

"I understand we are here today under a motion for grandparent visitation made by attorney Pile for the plaintiffs, Mr. and Mrs. Richard LeBlanc. Is that correct?"

"Yes, Your Honor. I am Attorney Pile, and I am representing the LeBlancs."

"Mr. Martin, am I to understand that you are representing Ms. Imogene LeBlanc and you are objecting to the visitation?"

"Yes, Your Honor. We are objecting."

"On what grounds is your objection, Counselor?"

"As I have written in my brief, the LeBlancs have been tormenting my client for over a year. They have been trying to take Ms. LeBlanc's children from her, and have filed numerous petitions with the court that are inflammatory and frivolous in nature. They do not like Imogene LeBlanc, and we are fearful as to what they will fill the children's heads with. We also feel that if the LeBlancs are permitted to take the children back to New Hampshire, they will not bring them back."

"Attorney Pile, do you have anything to say about these allegations?"

"Mr. Martin is grasping at straws. There is no reason or evidence that any of these alleged problems will take place. Mr. and Mrs. LeBlanc simply want to spend some time with their granddaughters. Based on the information from Ms. Holmes's home study, the Leblancs plan to drop their custody suit against Imogene LeBlanc. Their son died tragically last year, and the LeBlancs want a relationship with his children. As a grandfather yourself, I'm sure you can understand."

I quickly rose to my feet, "Objection, Your Honor. That last statement is highly uncalled for."

"Sustained. Mr. Pile, you know better than to bring my personal life into this," said Judge Gill, looking impatient and irritated.

"I'm sorry, Your Honor."

Judge Gill went on to say, "I have read the home assessment made by Ms. Holmes. She seems to think that visitation is a good idea. Based on what I have filtered through, I am going to allow visitation. However, I think the children need to be home with their mother and other siblings for Christmas. I will grant visitation from Friday, December 27, to Friday, January 3."

At this pronouncement, Imogene broke down completely. Every pent-up emotion came loose. She slumped at the table, sobbing uncontrollably. I looked over at the LeBlancs and saw a sly, ugly smirk on Barbara's face. As soon as she realized I was looking, she shifted her eyes away.

Judge Gill went on to say that he wanted Ms. Holmes to coordinate visitation. He mandated that it was up to the LeBlancs to pick up the children and to ensure that they were back in Imogene's custody by 5:00 p.m. on January 3.

Imogene looked at me and pleaded, "Do something. Please don't let this happen."

"Your Honor, I want the record to reflect that we highly object to all of this. We do not trust the LeBlancs. We want a home study done of their home before the children are forced to spend any time there," I forcefully said.

Ms. Holmes immediately responded, "Your Honor, if I may, I have a home study of the LeBlanc home, too. Mr. Martin is welcome to a copy of it. The LeBlanc home scored very high. It is a safe and appropriate environment for the girls."

Grasping, I said, "Then, I request a psychological evaluation of the LeBlancs and Claire and Martha LeBlanc to see what the long-term effects of visitation might be."

"Mr. Martin, this is a one-week visit. I hardly think a psychological evaluation will be necessary. My ruling stands. Ms. Imogene LeBlanc will make the children available to their grandparents starting at 12:00 noon on December 27 through 5:00 p.m. on January 3. Ms. Holmes will coordinate. This court is adjourned." Boom!!! The gavel resounded loudly through Imogene's ears—a sound that would haunt her forever.

Outside, it was just beginning to snow. I asked Imogene to come back to my office so we could discuss the proceedings.

Angrily, she said, "Why? What is there to discuss? You said that you would protect me! You said that the judge wouldn't let the children go to Barbara's house for Christmas. All lies! You just let it happen. You think that this will make it better? You think that the LeBlancs will settle for visitation rights? You have no idea who you are dealing with!"

"Imogene, I have no control over the judge. Judge DePaus was sick, so we got Judge Gill. If Judge DePaus had been there, I don't think he would have granted visitation." I knew, though, that this was all questionable. Ms. Holmes's recommendations were pretty straightforward. Probably any judge would have ruled in favor of the LeBlancs.

"I appreciate everything that you have done for me, Tweet, but I think you are out of your league. I am not turning over Claire and Martha now or ever."

"It's a court order, Imogene. If you don't turn over the kids on December 27, you will go to jail."

"Then I'll go to jail."

"Great, and then what happens to your children? You are not thinking rationally, Immy?"

"Immy? I hate that name. Don't call me that ever again! You obviously don't know or understand me at all. I trusted you. I relied on you to protect me from exactly what is happening now. They can't put me in jail if they can't find me." At that, she spun around and stalked away.

Shocked, I just stood there for a moment. This was a side of Imogene I had not seen before.

CHAPTER 9
Road Home

IMOGENE:

I couldn't believe that this was happening. I headed home in tears. The snow was coming down pretty heavily now. Looked like we were going to have a white Christmas. It was December 19. I had less than ten days to figure out what I was going to do. I started weighing my options. I could run. I could disappear. I still had my family in Canada. Maybe they would help me. How was I going to get myself and four young children to Canada, and what would the Canadian courts do if I violated an American court order? I needed help!

School was out for the holidays, so the kids were home with Rita. When I came in the door, they ran toward me with arms open as always. I had told them that we would put up the small Christmas tree that we had gotten the night before, so they were excited. I, on the other hand, could not get into the Christmas spirit. I told Rita about what happened at the court, and she was as incredulous as I was.

"What are you going to do, Imogene?"

"I don't know yet. But I am not giving over Claire and Martha."

"I'll be here to help in any way I can."

"Thanks. I know you will."

"Maybe if you sleep on it, your mind will be clearer tomorrow."

Sleep is the last thing on my mind, I thought. My mind was reeling. I was so upset it almost made me sick.

After we decorated our tiny Christmas tree, the kids wanted to go out and play in the snow. It was coming down more briskly. I bundled them all up, and we went outside to make a snowman. They were having such a fun time. Even Martha was visibly enjoying herself. She started throwing snowballs at me, and Rita and all the rest of the kids joined in. For a few minutes, I was able to forget about our problems, and then Claire began to play pretend.

"I want to name our snowman Tweet."

This brought all the memories of the horrible predicament I was in back to me. I felt terrible about the way things went down and how I spoke to Tweet. He, after all, was only trying to help.

Martha said, "Me too. I want to name him Tweet, because we like him and wish he were here."

"I wish he were here too," I said as I fixed their knit hats and mittens.

The next morning, my mind was made up. I was going to Canada. I didn't have a lot of money, but I had enough for bus tickets for me and the kids. Diane and Ricky didn't incur any costs because of their age. So, I only needed three tickets. Rita said she would help me, too.

"I have some savings that I can part with. It will be my Christmas present to you and the kids," Rita sadly expressed as I hugged her and thanked her profusely for her kindness. We planned on leaving on December 22. That was only two days away.

I had the bus schedule. The bus for Montreal left at 6:00 p.m. on the 22nd. I packed one bag for the five of us. We had only the clothes we were wearing and an extra outfit for each of us, along with a few essentials. I had escaped before with nothing, and I would do it again.

The bus station was a few miles from our apartment. Rita had a friend with a car who agreed to get us to the station. After many hugs and tears from Rita and Jean, we left our apartment at 5:00 p.m. on the 22nd. We got our tickets and boarded the bus. It had us arriving in Montreal at 7:00 a.m. on December 24, Christmas Eve.

My parents lived just outside the city. They had no idea we were coming, and I had no idea how I would get from the bus station to their house. It was about a twenty-minute car ride. I hadn't seen or heard from anyone in my family since just after I married Richard, and that conversation with my mom was not a pleasant one. I was scared. I didn't know if they would turn me and the kids away. My mother was a hard woman.

When the kids asked where we were headed, I told them that we were going to spend Christmas in Canada with my family. They were excited to be going on a bus and experiencing a new adventure. The kids slept most of the way to Montreal. The bus was practically empty, and the ride was uneventful. I had packed some snacks for us, and they appeared content. It seemed like the bus stopped at every town we passed. When we arrived at the border, an officer boarded the bus. The kids were asleep. He came down the aisle and asked for my paperwork. Luckily, I was still a Canadian citizen. He wanted to know what was bringing me to Montreal. With the way he ogled me, I wasn't sure if this was a security question or a personal one. When I said family, he didn't probe further, and the bus continued on.

I had never felt so alone. Here I was with four kids, running away from my husband's family into the arms of my family. One that I had not seen or heard from in years. I had no idea how they would welcome me. Maybe they wouldn't welcome me at all. I was afraid. While my children slept, I quietly wept as my mind reeled through everything that had transpired over the last six years. I just felt totally defeated.

It had snowed off and on the whole trip. Traveling through the night, everything looked beautiful. It was certainly a stark contrast to how I felt. As December 22 turned to December 23, I gave myself a pep talk.

"I can do this. My family would help. Mom and Dad would open up their home and their hearts to me and my children."

I had no idea where my brothers and sisters were. I only knew that my sister Claudette had become a nun and was stationed at a convent somewhere in Canada.

We finally pulled into Montreal Station at about 8:15 a.m. on Christmas Eve. We were a tad late because of the weather on the roads. I shuffled the kids off the bus and into the station. Since it was December 24, it was crowded with people waiting to board buses for the holidays. I asked an attendant for the best way to get to my destination, Blainsville, a small town northwest of Montreal. That's where my parents lived and where I was born and raised.

"The only way to get there is by car. Unless, of course, you are willing to walk." He laughed. When he realized I was not laughing and saw that I had four small kids with me, his smile faded, and he said, "Wait here a minute. I might know someone who can help you."

A few minutes later, he returned with another man. This man introduced himself as Gus Jenkins. He said he worked at the bus station and lived in Blainsville.

"What is in Blainsville for you?" he asked.

"I have a family there. The Dionne family."

"The Dionnes? Michael and Michelle Dionne? You're one of their youngins? Which one are you? I know they had a boatload of kids."

"I'm Imogene."

"And all these children are yours?" My affirmative nod was met with a whistle from him. Then he said, "I get off work in about an hour. Do you have much luggage?"

"None really."

"Okay. We can squeeze into my truck if you don't mind some of the kids riding in the back. It's pretty cold, but I have some blankets we can use."

Of course, all of the conversation was in French. Most Canadians spoke both French and English. Mr. Jenkins did not. I was surprised I remembered the language that well.

On the ride to Blainsville, I probed Mr. Jenkins for information about my family. He told me that my mother had died earlier that year. He apologized for breaking the news, thinking I already knew. He said my dad still lived in the same house where I grew up, and one of my sisters, but he wasn't sure which one lived somewhere close by. He didn't have any other information as to where any of my other siblings were.

As we approached my old house, I grew increasingly anxious and started rubbing my sweating hands together. The fact that my mother had died was very disturbing. I always thought of her as the strong one. I didn't know what to expect from my dad, who, for much of my childhood, was quiet and solemn; never mean or anything of that sort. He just didn't show much emotion or interest in us kids. He was a man of few words. My mom ran the house and the family, and he worked 60-hour weeks to put food on the table.

Mr. Jenkins pulled in the driveway and asked if I would be okay. I said yes and gathered the children from the truck. I felt so stupid standing at the front door waiting for someone to open it. I'm pretty sure this was the first time I had ever knocked on this front door. After all, I grew up here. Even though I hadn't been home in years, I felt like this was still my home.

After what seemed like an eternity, my father finally opened the door, and Mr. Jenkins pulled away. I was glad that he wasn't going to witness this reunion because I had no idea how it was going to go.

Dad looked so much older than I remembered. He had always been a fairly large man. He was an outdoorsman, a logger by profession, so he was built very sturdily when he was younger. I got my height from him. He was 6'2". The man who now stood at the door was old and stooped; his hair was completely gray. All the time spent outdoors in the sun and other harsh elements was etched deeply in the lines of his face. A wave of sadness and guilt surged through my body.

My father looked at me and said, "Can I help you with something?"

He didn't recognize me. Had I really changed that much? Maybe I had. Perhaps, I had changed as much to him as he had to me.

Claire looked at me questioningly. "Mom, is that our grandpa?"

"Dad, it's me, Imogene. I'm sorry to surprise you like this, but I didn't have any way to reach you. And nowhere else to go."

"Imogene? My goodness. What are you doing here? Are these children all yours?" My poor dad looked confused and distressed as he scratched his head.

"Can we come in? It's pretty cold out here." At this point, I was not worried he would say no. I could see the compassion in his eyes, and his face drooped slightly with concern.

"Yes. Yes, of course, please come in. How did you get here?"

"We took a bus from Lewiston, and Mr. Jenkins from the bus station gave us a ride from there."

My dad began to whistle and said, "It sounds like you have had a long few days."

Ricky spoke up next. "I am hungry," to which all of the kids proclaimed, "Me too!" Dad and I looked at each other and couldn't help but smile as he led us to the kitchen.

Dad didn't have much, but the kids gobbled down some leftover pasta that Dad heated on the stove. They acted like they hadn't eaten in weeks.

While the kids ate, Dad and I talked. "I heard about mom. I am so sorry, Dad. I wish I had known that she was sick. I would have come home sooner."

"She wasn't sick. As far as we know, anyway. She just went to bed one night and never woke up. They say it was her heart."

"Oh, wow. I'm so sorry." And I truly was. I felt so mad at myself for not being a better, more attentive daughter.

"I know that you and your mom didn't see eye-to-eye for a while, but your mother loved you. I'm pretty sure she had some regrets about your last conversation... And look at all these beautiful children. Your mother would have loved them too." He had a tenderness to his voice as he gave me a hug.

My father and I got "caught up" on my brothers and sisters. Well, caught up might not be the right term. Dad said that he didn't hear from any of them much, except Claudette (the nun), and my sister, Rose, who lived in Montreal. He said Rose was married to an accountant and didn't have any children. It was hard for me to be in judgement of my siblings. I had done exactly what they did... forgotten all about the fact that I had aging parents. I had my regrets.

"Rose stops by now and then to check on me. She's pretty busy, though. Her husband and his family are some high society people. They don't have a whole lot of time for the likes of me."

"Listen, Dad, I'm kinda in a jam. Can the kids and I stay here with you for a few days or maybe at least through Christmas and New Year's?"

"Sure. I have plenty of room and would love the company. What kind of a jam are you in? Marriage problems?"

"My husband died in a car accident last year."

"I'm so sorry. I had no idea. Wow, leaving you with four kids? How on earth have you survived?" Dad asked, shaking his head.

I wasn't ready to tell my dad all my problems and secrets yet, so I just told him it has been rough.

It was amazing how little my childhood home had changed. I felt like I was stepping back in time. My dad took me to my old bedroom, which I had shared with three of my sisters, and it was exactly how I remembered it.

Sunny yellow blankets still adorned each bed. Such a contrast to the gloom of the Canadian winters. It brought back some good memories of my childhood. I began to plan the bed situation. *I will sleep here with Diane and Ricky. Claire and Martha will sleep in the room next to us.*

My dad asked, "Where is your luggage?"

"I only came with a little bag that I had packed with essentials and a few Christmas presents for the kids. That's all."

My dad immediately looked very sad. "Everything is closed for the holidays, so we will have to make do with what we have. After Christmas, we will have to go to town to buy some stuff," Dad said apologetically.

The house had no Christmas tree or anything else to celebrate the holiday. This was Christmas Eve, which of course meant Christmas was tomorrow. It made me sad that there were no trees or decorations in sight. I couldn't help but remember how important Christmas always had been to my dad.

After putting my kids to bed, Dad and I sat out in the kitchen and talked at length. I narrated all that had happened in my life, and he wept for me and hugged me. I had never seen him show any emotion when I was growing up. Mom was usually the emotional one, and Dad just went along. I was so touched by his empathy, it again made me sorry for not having made more of an effort as a daughter to stay in touch.

"Dad, do you think maybe we could find a tree to put up for the kids? They don't understand what's going on, and being kids, they are still excited for Christmas. They don't require a lot, and I did pack a few little gifts for them, but a tree would make them happy."

At that, in the middle of the night, we were out in the yard to cut down a tree.

The next morning, the kids were giddy with excitement over the tree and the fact that it was Christmas. We took out our old decorations from when I was a kid and began decorating. It brought back so many great memories for me. I wanted my kids to have the same fun memories as they grew up, too. Hopefully, this will be one of them. We sang and we danced. Martha wanted hot chocolate. Luckily, Dad had the ingredients, so we stirred up a batch. We played in the snow, and I felt like Dad was really enjoying it all too.

Ricky was happy to have a man around for a change. He followed my dad everywhere and kept asking, "What are you doing now? Why? Why are you doing that?" It was funny, and it warmed my heart to watch it. I thought of Richard and how sad it was that he would never get to enjoy time with his son. I was glad that my dad was able to have this experience.

The scene outside was beautiful. The snow had created a thick blanket over everything. We lived in the country, so there were no vehicles driving by, and there was no noise. The tracks that Mr. Jenkins' truck had made the day before were covered by new snow. Peace was imminent. I had not felt so relaxed and happy in a long time. I was looking forward to spending the holidays here with my dad and my kids. I was so grateful that he was so welcoming. Not only welcoming, but genuinely happy to have us. That night before bed, Dad did what he always did on Christmas when I was growing up. He got out the Bible and read the Christmas story. I couldn't help but smile. It actually was one of the best Christmases I could remember. All of the kids were in good spirits and happy that we were together, and I didn't have to work. We had certainly settled in with Dad. He told us to stay as long as we liked.

"Honestly, Imogene, I was so lonely before you and the kids got here, I didn't know what to do with myself. Now I feel like I have a purpose. I love having you here and wish you would stay forever." He had said this with tears in his eyes, as we all planned to retire to bed.

December 27 came and went. I couldn't help but think about the fact that the LeBlancs were supposed to take Claire and Martha on that day. I wondered what was happening in Lewiston and prayed that all my problems had just disappeared.

I also couldn't help but think about Tweet Martin. I'm sure he was taking the brunt of the anger from the LeBlancs and the judge. I hated that I had caused him so much trouble. Tweet was a great guy. Under different circumstances, I would have been very interested in him romantically. Let's face it, though, I have a lot of "baggage." A woman with four kids and legal problems is not much of a catch. I probably will have my regrets. I already did.

My dad was a good Christian man. He read the Bible daily and sang all the hymns. Martha, in particular, was a good singer, and she loved to sing with her grandpa. Every day, Martha and Dad sang "Jesus Loves Me" together.

Dad and she spent a lot of time together. It was obvious that Martha loved her grandfather, as all the kids did. But Dad seemed to realize that Martha needed more attention and positive, quality time than the others, and he eagerly provided it. On Sundays, Dad always gathered us around and told a story from the Bible. We didn't really have a church that was close enough for us to get to easily, so we had church right there at the house. All of the kids seemed to drink up the stories. Both Ricky and Martha asked a lot of questions. Dad seemed to know all the answers, and I was learning again too.

Meanwhile, back in Lewiston, Tweet was handling all the turmoil as best he could.

CHAPTER 10
Upside Down

TWEET:

I could not believe that Imogene was so angry with me. I had done everything I could to help protect her and her kids from the LeBlancs. Things just kept going against her. Maybe if I gave her a few days, she would calm down and listen to reason. At least I hoped so.

My sister encouraged me to reach out to Imogene.

"She needs a friend, Tweet... not just an attorney. You can't blame her for being upset. From what we know of the history of her and the LeBlancs, it is very dark. She doesn't trust them, and I don't blame her." I knew that Donna really liked Imogene and felt a lot of sorrow over how things had turned out.

I tried to call Imogene several times to no avail. Finally, on Christmas Eve, I went to her apartment with gifts for the kids. When I knocked, Rita answered the door with a scared look on her face, and I knew immediately there was something wrong.

"Where are Imogene and the kids?"

"They aren't here," said Rita. From the way she said it, I knew she was hiding something. After some prodding, Rita admitted that Imogene and the kids were "gone," as she put it.

"Gone where?" My voice was panicked.

"I can't tell you that. Imogene swore me to secrecy. She is gone and is not coming back, and the fact of the matter is, I don't really know exactly where she went. I can tell you she was very determined in her quest to escape."

"Oh no! Rita, do you know how much trouble she can be in? She has to have Claire and Martha back here by the 27th. She is under a court order to hand the kids over to the LeBlancs!" I exclaimed loudly, followed by a sigh.

"That's exactly why she is gone. She was not going to hand them over. She knows that if she does, she will never get them back."

"Well, if she doesn't, she is going to jail. Then all the kids will be placed in someone else's custody. Most likely the LeBlancs'. You have to tell me where she is," I said angrily.

"I'm sorry, Tweet. I know you mean well, but I can't. I promised."

"Please, Rita, get in touch with her and beg her to come home. The courts don't take contempt lightly."

"I have no idea how to reach her. She did not tell me exactly where she was going. I just know she is not coming back."

After it was obvious that Rita couldn't help me, I left and hurried to Jean's apartment. *Maybe she can tell me where Imogene and the kids are.* I was so disappointed and frustrated. I couldn't believe that Imogene was so desperate to do this. Jean took the same stance as Rita. They had circled the wagons in a misguided attempt at protecting their friend and her children. I had a pretty good idea that Imogene had left the country for Canada. Her family was there, and she was still a Canadian citizen. I knew that she came from a place outside of Montreal but had no real idea of exactly where. I also had no idea how long she had been gone.

I went back to the office and called Donna. She was at home since the office was closed for the holidays, but she agreed to come in and find out anything she could about Imogene's family in Canada. We knew that her maiden name was Dionne. We knew that she had a bunch of brothers and sisters, but the only thing we knew about them was that one was a nun. Donna seemed to remember her name being Claudette, Claudette Dionne.

On December 27, just as I had dreaded, my phone rang. Ms. Holmes was on the line.

"Mr. Martin, your client, Imogene LeBlanc, and her children were supposed to meet at the courthouse this afternoon for the transfer of Claire and Martha for visitation with the LeBlancs. They never arrived. Do you know where they are?"

"I'm sorry Ms. Holmes, Ms. LeBlanc fired me after the last hearing. I have no idea where she might be."

"She is violating a court order, and the judge said he is issuing an arrest warrant for her. I would advise that if you know of her whereabouts, you should tell her to come back immediately. If she does, they may have some mercy for her," she firmly said.

"I really wish I could help Ms. Holmes, but I have no idea where they are. If she contacts me, I'll let you know." It was true. I had no idea where Imogene and the children were. At this point, I was glad I didn't.

The next day, my brother-in-law, Phillip, showed up at my apartment. He said that the whole police force was looking for Imogene. The LeBlancs were claiming that she kidnapped their grandchildren and wanted her criminally prosecuted.

"Those people are crazy. They want your head, too. They think you helped her abscond with the children. They are also threatening Rita and Jean. Do you know where she is, Tweet?" Phillip asked as he settled into the couch directly opposite me. Usually, Phillip was a laidback, calm person, but right now he seemed distressed.

"No. I don't know. I'm pretty sure she is not in Lewiston, so tell your chief not to waste his manpower looking for her." A few minutes after Phillip arrived, Rita and Jean showed up.

"Tweet, they are going to throw us in jail if we don't tell them where Imogene is. Can they do that? I mean, the truth is, we don't really know exactly where she is," Rita asked, expressing concern.

"No. They can't throw you in jail. Don't tell them anything. Tell them to talk to me. Tell them that I am your attorney."

"Are you? Are you our attorney?" Jean piped in. Both of them seemed stressed out and beside themselves.

"I am now. You don't have to tell them anything. If they threaten you, tell them you will file charges of harassment." I tried to reassure them as best as I could. They had been good friends to Imogene, and I hated that they were so worried.

Rita and Jean knew where she was. I was almost positive she was in Canada. This was actually a brilliant move on her part. The long arm of the law would have to overstretch to get her to answer any charges from here. She was either a pretty smart gal, a pretty desperate one, or both.

Later that day, the LeBlancs showed up at my office. They were very upset but said that they would overlook everything if I would just produce the children. I told them I didn't know where they were, and they left. But of course, before they left, Mrs. LeBlanc had to get in one more barb. She told me she would see that I lost my license to practice law.

"You are a liar, and I will ruin you!" she roared and stormed out of my office.

Soon after, my sister stepped into my office. With worry written all over her face, she asked, "What are you going to do?"

"Nothing," I said. "Imogene made her choices. Whether they be good or bad, she did what she thought she had to do to protect her children. I just hope it works out for her."

"Tweet, are you telling me you feel nothing for that woman? Was she just a client to you? You can't be serious! I saw the way you looked at her. I saw the way you acted when she was around. You can't just go on and forget about her!"

"What do you want me to do, Donna? The less I know, the better for both of us."

"Well, Tweet, I doubt that the LeBlancs are going to just give up. They will continue to pursue her and her children... and they will find her. You know that, don't you!" she said with raised eyebrows.

"Probably so. When that happens, I will be here for her. Right now, she might have a little happiness until everything blows up," and somehow I knew it would.

IMOGENE:

I was so happy to be away from all the turmoil with the LeBlancs. Christmas was so fun. As I entered the New Year, I had to start thinking about the future. The girls needed to be in school. I had no income and needed a job. So far, my dad has been great about every-thing. He said not to worry about getting a job. He was happy to have me and the children with him. Ricky was his little shadow, and they enjoyed each other's company. Dad said he had enough money and a pension to take care of us all. He was so great with all the children. I was so proud to watch how wonderful and patient he was with them. Since the LeBlancs cared so little about me as a daughter-in-law, they didn't try to get to know me. So, they really had no idea where I was from or anything else about my past. Thank goodness! They only knew I was from Canada, but Canada is a big place. Maybe they would just give up their quest for my children.

The girls started school in January and seemed to be enjoying it. The school was much smaller than the one in Lewiston. Claire and Martha were in the same class, which was great. The school grades were different here since the whole school went from Kindergarten to 12th grade, and there was a total of just twenty-five students. The girls' teacher was Miss Par. She was young and not married. There were seven kids in her class, ranging from ages five to ten, with Martha being the youngest. Every day, Claire and Martha came home excited to tell me about what happened at school. They loved Miss Par. She was their new idol. At school, they primarily spoke French. The girls picked it up quickly. It helped that I spoke French frequently when we were in the States. I had never seen Martha so happy.

In March, I had a meeting with Miss Par to see how the girls were doing. She raved about both girls, and she spoke about how both of them were a great joy to teach. She commended their smartness and their eagerness to learn. In her words, "I wish all my students were as well-behaved and as smart as they are."

I was so proud of them. I also enjoyed staying home with Diane and Ricky. I cooked and cleaned for Dad and the kids. I could not have been happier. I thought and worried about the LeBlancs less as the days passed by.

My dad's 75th birthday was in April. He actually looked younger than he did when we first arrived. He was healthy—both in mind and body. I really think he had been so lonely before we came that it had made him look ten years older than he was. It was as if he'd been dying of loneliness. My sister, Rose, came for his birthday. Although I don't think she knew we were there, she didn't seem surprised to see us. Rose arrived in a pretty fancy car, and she looked beautiful.

"Imogene, what on earth?" she asked with surprise.

The girls were at school, but Diane and Ricky were home.

"Who are these beautiful children? Are they yours? You must tell me all about your life. Where have you been and what have you been up to for the last ten years?" She bombarded me with so many questions all at once. I became a little bit guarded.

I felt very uncomfortable for some reason I couldn't put my finger on. I didn't want to share anything with Rose. She didn't seem to be the same Rose I grew up with. I don't know if it was the airs that she put on, or just the fact that we were now strangers, but I didn't trust my sister. I didn't share any intimate information with her. I didn't tell her about the LeBlancs. I told her my husband had died, but that was it. When Claire and Martha got home from school, I felt even more uncomfortable. Rose's questions to them were concerning. After some time, she left, and I was happy when she did.

My dad blurted out, "Well, that was strange." I wasn't sure what my dad's statement meant at the time, but I, too, thought the whole interaction was odd.

He told me Rose was married into a very rich and influential family in Montreal. Her husband was the latest patriarch of the largest accounting and finance firm in Canada. Their clients stretched across Canada and into the United States. Her husband's father, George Morin, had founded the firm twenty years earlier. By then, bells and whistles were going off in my head—the LeBlancs were in the accounting business, too.

After he retired, Rose's husband (George Jr.), took over. They were politically connected and very involved in Montreal's largest and most influential Catholic Church. *Sounds familiar*, I thought. The Catholic Church ran Montreal, and the Morin family apparently ran the Catholic Church. Of course, I had no idea about any of this at the time.

A few weeks went by. I had decided to stay with my dad as long as I could. He wasn't in any hurry to get rid of us, and the kids loved being settled in with him. Life was better than it had been in a long, long time. I had practically forgotten about my sister and her odd visit, and then... my life was turned upside down again.

Claire and Martha always got home from school at the same time every day. There was a little van that transported them the five miles to school each way. This day, they didn't arrive. Instead, Miss Par arrived on our doorstep. She was in tears. Miss Par said that some woman came and got Claire and Martha from school. The woman claimed to be with the court. She showed papers signed by a judge giving her permission to take the children.

"Where? Where did she take them?" I pleaded.

"I don't know. I don't know. She just gave me this paper and told me to give it to you. I am so sorry. There was nothing I could do. Claire and Martha were so upset. It was a big commotion. I just didn't know what to do. I couldn't believe it."

The paper contained the address and phone number of a convent in Montreal. I immediately broke down and sobbed. Dad was there to catch me when I fell to the ground. I didn't know what to do. How had this happened? The LeBlancs were obviously behind this. Why? Why? Why was this happening to us?

I was beside myself. The girls had been taken. I called the phone number and was told I had violated a court order in Lewiston. The man on the phone expressed that if I tried to get Claire and Martha back, I would be thrown in jail. He said there was a hearing in the Queen's court in five days, and I had to be there.

I immediately called Tweet. I told him where I was, and he said he would come in time for the hearing. He urged me not to talk to anyone. "Wait for me to get there. If anyone wants anything, including information, you tell them to talk to your attorney when I arrive."

Claire's Journal

THE CONVENT

OUR FIRST DAY:

When the woman came to the school to take us, Martha and I were frightened. Mom had told us never to go anywhere with strangers. She said that if anyone we didn't recognize ever claimed they wanted to pick us up from school, we shouldn't trust them. She said we should tell the teacher right away. Miss Par was there when the lady came. She tried to help us. She tried to tell everyone that they needed to speak to our mother, but they wouldn't listen. The woman told us her name, but I don't remember it, and she put us in a car with much struggle from both Martha and me. There was a man driving, and the woman told us they were taking us to a new school. Martha got very angry and started yelling at them.

She told them that we didn't want to go to a new school. And that we wanted our mom and our grandpa. Then she started crying really hard. I tried to tell her it would be okay. It was hard because I didn't really believe that it would be.

We drove for a long time. When we got to our "new school," it was dark outside. The lady and the man woke us out of a dead sleep, took us by our hands, and walked us up a steep walkway. The school looked like the church we had attended a long time ago in New Hampshire. It was big and very dark. Martha and I were both scared, but that fear was overridden by our hunger. As soon as we walked a little distance, Martha began sobbing and calling for mommy.

She kept saying she was hungry and that she wanted her mommy. She also kept asking where we were. The woman told her to be quiet several times. I tried to help Martha, but I was too tired, scared, and hungry too.

When we finally got up the big hill, there was a gate with a bell. The man who had driven us rang the bell, spoke to the gate, and it opened.

Another woman dressed in black and white came out to greet us. She was really old and didn't speak any English. I know how to speak some French, so I understood what they were saying. I don't think they thought I could speak or understand French. The lady in black and white was angry. She wanted to know why we were so late. But then she ordered, "Never mind, just give me the children." She was scary.

At that point, the two people who drove us here turned around and left. We followed the lady in black and white (who we later learned was a nun) into the school. She was Sister Margaret. She didn't say much, just led us to a room with twin beds. She gave us some night-clothes and in French she told us to go to sleep.

Martha immediately cried that she was hungry and couldn't sleep. Sister Margaret told us she would be right back and left. A few minutes later, she returned with some cheese, bread, and water, and again very firmly told us to go to sleep. So here we were, just me and my sister. I told Martha that at least we had each other. We made a promise that we would look after each other no matter what. I promised that I would never leave Martha, and she promised me the same. Then we cried ourselves to sleep, clinging to each other in one of the twin beds.

THREE YEARS LATER:

Martha and I are still here at the "orphan home." That's what the older girls here call it. The nuns say it's a convent. Our mom sends us pictures, letters, and goodies from time to time, although sometimes the nuns would take the goodies for themselves. It seems so long ago that we were with my mom and grandpa, and I can hardly remember what they look like. I don't remember Diane and Ricky much either.

I've adjusted pretty well and don't think things are too bad here. I've made some friends and enjoyed the classes. Most of the girls are nice, but Martha is still very unhappy. She cries herself to sleep every night. The other girls pick on her because she is an easy target. One girl named Jennifer is particularly mean. She told Martha that our mom doesn't want us. She told her, "Nobody loves you, Martha. Even your sister doesn't like you." Jennifer is older, and I heard that she has been here the longest of all the girls. Maybe that's why she is so mean and unhappy. I was frightened of Jennifer myself. I did object when I heard her tell Martha that even I didn't like her. I told her to stop lying and picking on my sister. She just laughed. After the first night, we were moved to what they call a dormitory. There are twenty-two of us in one large room, with ten bunk beds and no privacy. The two oldest girls have their own bed with a curtain around it.

My best friend is Tricia. She is a year older than I am. She came to the convent just a few days after Martha and me. Tricia's parents died in a fatal car accident. She cried all through her first week here. I tried to console her because the nuns just ignored her. I thought that was so mean. Now Tricia is hoping someone will adopt her.

I really don't know why Martha and I are here. Most of the other girls' parents are dead or can't take care of them anymore. Our mom wants us home with her, but she says the courts are keeping her from us. I don't think any of it is fair. I think my grandmother is behind it all, but I'm not allowed to ask questions, and when I do, I am scolded. It is all so unfair.

A few weeks ago, a new nun came to see us. She said her name was Sister Claudette and she was our mom's sister. Martha begged her to rescue us. "Please, can you please get us out of here and back to our mom?" Sister Claudette promised us that she would try. When I asked her why we were here, she said things were complicated between my mom and my grandma. Sister Claudette said that everyone wanted what was best for us, but no one could agree about what that was.

I told her that I wish they would ask us. Then we can tell them that we want to go home.

Sister Claudette told me that sometimes kids are smarter than adults. Sister Claudette stayed at our convent for a few days and then had to go back to her home convent. She promised that she would not forget about us, and that she would try to visit again soon. I wished she could have stayed with us. She was the nicest nun we had ever met.

The day that we were taken from our school and brought here was the last day we saw our mom or grandpa. Mom said there is a court order that she was not allowed to see us. She says grandma is stopping her, but grandma isn't allowed to see us either. Basically, we have no one but each other.

Martha and I deal with things in two entirely different ways. I am a pleaser. I don't like to make anyone mad. Martha can be an instigator and doesn't care who she makes mad. I've tried to tell her to try to "get along" and not make "waves," but she just can't do it. One day, she put dead bugs in Sister Henrietta's soup. Sister Henrietta ate almost the whole bowl before she found them. Boy, was she mad! One of the other girls told on Martha, and the punishment she got from that was brutal. Sister Margarita removed her from the cafeteria, and she got a pretty bad beating afterwards. She couldn't sit down for a week and had to go without eating for two whole days. I tried to sneak her some crackers, and when I got caught, I had to go without dinner that night, too.

Another time, Martha had worms. She actually had worms coming out of her bottom. She was always squirming around and could not sit still. The nuns were always yelling at her for squirming. And when she told them that something was wrong and that she was itchy "down there", they ignored her. So, during chapel one morning, she put some of the worms she had collected on the altar and decided to have a worm race. Some of the girls were actually betting on which worm would win the race.

Many of the other girls started screaming in horror, and others were laughing. This was during Chapel, mind you. The nuns were furious and removed Martha from the Chapel. Martha stood up to them and told them that's why she couldn't keep still because they were in her bottom. After another beating, Martha was sent to the infirmary. They treated her with some medicine and put her in confine-ment so none of the other girls would get worms. I'm pretty sure Martha had those worms for a while before the intervention. So, if they were contagious, we all would have had them.

When she was allowed to come back to the dorm, some of the girls called her "Wormy." All of this just made Martha more defiant. After that, the nuns and some of the girls treated Martha horribly. The nuns looked for any little thing to blame her for, and some of the girls teased her unmercifully. Martha was targeted by the nuns, and they actually encouraged some of the girls to be mean to her.

Martha was punished daily for one reason or another. I wasn't happy about this, so one day I called Martha aside to have a conversa-tion with her about the entire issue. I asked Martha why she didn't just do what the nuns asked. I didn't understand why she had to fight everything. She looked at me and said she hated them, that they had ruined our lives.

I told her it didn't matter. I begged her to just go along, to make things easier. That's what I did—survived quietly. But she shook her head.

She told me she couldn't and said that nothing would change. She's still here and would continue to have all that anger inside. Said she would probably explode. She said she wished she were more like me and realized that she wasn't. I didn't know what to say. I wanted peace; she wanted justice. Martha swore she would find a way to escape.

One day, Martha had just dealt with enough from Jennifer, as she would not let her be. She just kept teasing her and calling her "Wormy." She went further to call Martha ugly and gross.

I constantly asked Jennifer to leave my sister alone, and she always laughed it off. The next thing I see is Martha dragging Jennifer's toothbrush through the toilet. A few days later, Jennifer fell very ill. She was throwing up everywhere and had diarrhea. Jennifer spent a week in the infirmary. When she came back, Martha whispered to her, with a sly look on her face, "If you don't leave me alone, I will make you sick again." Jennifer looked terrified. I think she believed her, and she left Martha alone after that. I truly believe that the tables had turned, and Jennifer was really afraid of Martha for a change, and it was great to see.

Sometimes a girl would vanish from the home. Tricia believes they are being adopted. After one leaves, another one is there to replace them.

Martha and I kept hoping and praying that our mom would come and get us. One day, Martha told me she was done praying. She said there was no one up there listening, and that she doesn't believe in God anymore.

I told her that she was going to go to hell for saying that, and she angrily screamed, "This is hell! We are already here!" I really had nothing to say to that.

Our Aunt, Sister Claudette, never came back to see us. I was beginning to think that Martha was right; there was no God hearing our prayers.

CHAPTER 12
Betrayals

IMOGENE:

Two days after the girls had been taken, Tweet was at my door. I had never been so happy to see anyone in my life. Throwing my arms around him, I hugged him and wouldn't let go. He hugged me just as hard in return. When I finally let go, I broke down, tears spilling down my face. Not once did Tweet blame me or say anything to indicate that he was mad at me for leaving as I had done; instead, he promised to always be present to help and support me in any way he could.

"Imogene, I don't know how the court can do this for something that happened in the States. It sounds like someone is pulling some strings. Obviously, the LeBlancs were able to find you. They must have some connections here in Canada. Who knows about your situation besides your father?"

"No one. Well, I mean, my sister, Rose, came to visit us for Dad's birthday. I didn't tell her much, but her visit was very strange."

"When you say strange, what do you mean? Could Rose have any connections to the LeBlancs?"

"I don't know. I mean, her husband's family has a large accounting firm in Montreal. They do business all over Canada and sometimes in the United States."

"Wait! Isn't that what the LeBlancs do? Accounting?" Tweet said incredulously.

Shaking my head, I reluctantly reply, "Yes. But I don't think my sister would betray me like that."

My dad chimed in sadly, "Well, I wouldn't put it past her."

Tweet, looking concerned, said, "She didn't have to betray you. All she had to do was mention you to her husband or anyone else in his family, and the snowball begins. If I were a betting man, I would bet that your sister was the catalyst for all of this. It could be an innocent mistake on her part, but we will find out on Monday. In the meantime, I have to research Canadian law."

Dad loved Tweet Martin. I later found out that they had many conversations about me and the possibility of a relationship between the two of us. Dad told Tweet that I was a lot like my mother.

"Imogene is a tough one, just like her mother. If I hadn't pursued a relationship with her mom, I would still be a single man. If you are interested in Imogene, you'd better let her know it in a strong way."

Smiling, Tweet said, "What makes you think I am interested in Imogene as anything other than a client, Michael?"

"Oh, come on, Tweet. It's all over your face. No one travels to another country to help just a client. I'm just saying that Imogene can be hard and stubborn. She hates rejection and will never make the first move. Particularly after what happened with her ex-husband."

"Your daughter has far too many problems to get involved with anyone right now. Maybe after all this is over, I can consider a relationship with her. Believe me, I like her a lot, but now is not the time."

When we went to court that Monday, I found out just how much influence my sister's husband's family had. They were obviously running the show. The Court refused to recognize Tweet as my lawyer. The judge said that he had no "standing" with the court.

"Mr. Martin, you are lucky I did not throw you and your client in jail. It is obvious you were in cahoots with Ms. LeBlanc to disobey a court order. The children will remain in the custody of St. Benedict's Convent until this matter is sorted."

Tweet rose to object, but the judge cut him off. "One more word, Mr. Martin, and I will have you jailed today."

I opened my mouth to protest, but the judge turned his glare toward me. "Ms. LeBlanc, don't test me. You should be ashamed of yourself. When a judge issues an order, you cannot simply run away. You are a disgraceful example for your children, and if you utter another word, you will never see them again."

My in-laws (Barbara and Richard) were present in the courtroom along with my sister and her husband's family. They were all obviously pretty chummy, not only with each other, but with the court personnel. The smirk on Barbara's face showed a winning smile. She looked so proud of herself with her head pointed up. I would have hit her if I could. My sister just sat there. She wouldn't look at me. When we were leaving, I called out to her, and she ignored me. If Dad had been there, he would have been horrified by her behavior, or perhaps not. After all, he did say that he wouldn't be surprised if she was involved. I guess Tweet was right; she was the reason we found ourselves in that position.

I left the courthouse heartbroken. A wave of defeat and hopelessness washed over me. I couldn't shake the thought that poor Claire and Martha were completely in the dark about what was unfolding. Through no fault of their own, their lives were being interrupted in the most horrible way. I can only imagine what they were thinking and feeling. I'm sure they were scared and confused. I could only hope and pray that they were being taken care of. Were they warm, did they have enough food, and did they have a bed to sleep in? All of these things were going through my mind. It was unbearable.

On the way back to Dad's house, Tweet said that we had to hire a

Canadian attorney. He said that the court would not allow him to represent me because he was not licensed in Canada.

"Hire an attorney?" I asked in desperation. "I don't have any money to hire an attorney. How am I supposed to do that?"

"Sometimes attorneys will work for free."

"You mean like you?"

"Yes. They call it pro bono work in the States. I'm sure they have something like that here in Canada. When we get back to your dad's, I will make some phone calls and see what we can do."

Tweet settled in with us for the time being. He stayed in Claire and Martha's room. We had a lot of issues to discuss and phone calls to make. Tweet was very focused on getting an attorney. I don't know how many he called, but finally after two days, Tweet proudly announced, "Come on, I found an attorney. We are meeting him at his office in Montreal in two hours." Thankfully, Dad was there to watch Diane and Ricky again.

I was worried about Dad. I could tell that all this turmoil was taking a toll on him. When I told him that Rose was behind all this, he wasn't surprised. That didn't mean he wasn't disappointed.

Shaking his head, Dad said, "I knew something was off with her when she came on my birthday. Something just didn't seem right. Why on earth would she do this to her own sister? I've always said money changes people," he said as he reached forward to console me with a hug.

On the way to Montreal, Tweet explained how he had called a number of attorneys, and when he explained the situation, they had wished him good luck. According to them, the Morin family is a force to be reckoned with, and they wanted no part of it. But he eventually found Attorney Harold Carr. Although Carr was hesitant, he agreed to take up the case.

After a little bit of directional effort—it seemed both of us didn't know north from south—we finally found the office of Harold Carr. The office was very nice and homey. There was not a lot of ostentatiousness or pomp. I immediately felt comfortable. We were greeted by Mr. Carr's secretary, Eve—a small, nice-looking woman who welcomed us warmly. Later, we determined she was Mr. Carr's wife. She showed us back to a large office that looked to be a mess. There were what appeared to be files and law books everywhere. Even though the door was a bit ajar, Eve knocked. A soft but firm voice came from behind the mountain of Manila files.

"What are you knocking for? Come in, come in," he snickered.

Looking over the piles on the desk, Eve says, "A Mr. Martin, from the United States, and his client, Ms. LeBlanc, are here to see you."

Mr. Carr, who was a short, stocky man of about 5'6", stood up from his desk and gave us a huge smile. He appeared to be a few years older than Tweet. He was prematurely balding with a really likable face and a paunch that showed his affection for food.

"It's a pleasure. Come on in and don't mind the mess." He moved some papers off two chairs and told us to have a seat. After a few pleasantries, Mr. Carr got right to the point. It was obvious that Tweet had briefed him on the situation. "Mr. Martin, I don't think you know how influential the Morin family is in these parts. They run a lot of the businesses around here. I've heard that they control the Catholic Church and, therefore, the courts. Not a good family to be on the wrong side of. Even so, I've read the paperwork that you sent, and I am willing to help."

"That is wonderful!" exclaimed Tweet.

"Well, don't get too excited. When I say I'm willing to help, I mean I am willing to assist you. I can help you maneuver the Canadian judicial system. I can inform you about court procedures and specific laws that address this kind of issue. I can go on record and go to court as Ms. LeBlanc's attorney. What I can't do is devote all my time to this case. Litigation is expensive and time-consuming. Ms. LeBlanc will have to pay any court and out-of-pocket expenses. I've agreed to help because I hate to see anyone bullied, and that is what is happening here."

"We completely understand all of that. What do you advise as our first step?"

"The first step is to register me as the Attorney of Record. I can file that motion today. After that, you have to tell me what you want and how you would like to proceed. Be warned that this could be a long process. The Morins and the LeBlancs could keep this case tied up for years. Her Majesty's Court does not move as quickly as the courts in the United States. Canada doesn't give anyone the right to a speedy trial, and my experience is that when kids are involved, the courts move even slower."

"Well, can I see my girls?" I looked at Mr. Carr with tears in my eyes.

Compassionate, yet honest, he answers with a sigh, "We can try to request that, but I doubt they will grant it. They will say that you would likely try to take them. They will say that you ran away with them before and are not to be trusted."

"Mr. Carr, Harold, can you help me file a motion for visitation and then another motion to have this case dismissed? Do the Canadian Courts even have any standing for a violation of a court order case in the States?" Tweet asked.

"Do they have standing? You're kidding, right?" laughed Mr. Carr. "I don't mean to sound harsh, but you are in Canada. Here, the Courts have standing in all things on Canadian soil. This case is being filed by the LeBlancs. The fact that Imogene—do you mind if I call you Imogene?—fled to Canada is relevant to her fitness as a mother. These are the arguments that are and will be made, Mr. Martin. The fact that you have two very influential families with unlimited resources will be a huge mountain to climb. Like I said, this could go on for a very long time. Don't kid yourself into thinking this will be easily resolved."

"But my children are in a strange place with strange people and God only knows what they're being told," I pleaded.

"Ms. LeBlanc, I'm pretty sure we could resolve this case tomorrow if you give Mr. and Mrs. George LeBlanc custody of Claire and... let's see here..." He brings the paper closer to the end of his nose. "Martha, is it? The LeBlancs aren't strangers to them, but from what I know, though, I think that your girls are probably better off at St. Benedict's, don't you?" He stares at me over his glasses.

"Yes," I said defeatedly.

"Okay. I will get the motions filed. I will ask the court for visitation and also ask for a dismissal. We will see what happens, but don't get your hopes up. As soon as I hear anything, I will let you know."

Tweet had gone back to Lewiston after staying with me and Dad for a few more days. Several weeks went by before Mr. Carr finally called and asked me to come to his office. The news was not good...

"Ms. LeBlanc, I'm afraid at this point there is nothing that I can do. Your in-laws have made it impossible for me to get you visitation. The Court has labeled you a criminal for absconding with the children and fleeing the law in the United States. The one thing that I have been able to do is stop the LeBlancs from taking the children back to New Hampshire. For the time being, we are in limbo, and Claire and Martha will have to stay at St. Benedict's."

"What about visitation?"

"The court feels that this would just upset the girls and make it more difficult for them to settle in. I know it sounds dumb. Sometimes the court is dumb. Believe me, I have full sympathy for you. I have children myself and can only imagine what you are going through."

"What should I do now?" I asked defeatedly. I so wished that Tweet Martin was there with me to help me through this newest disappointment.

"Is there anyone that you know who has any pull with the courts or the Catholic Church?"

"I have a sister who is a nun."

That was how my sister Claudette became involved. When I got back home, I told Dad what had happened. He was distressed. Dad contacted Claudette to let her know what was going on, and she got permission to visit the girls. After her visit, she called me and told me that they were doing fine.

According to Claudette, the girls were in good health. "They asked about you and said they wanted to come home," she told me. Unfortunately, there is nothing I can do. I asked the nuns at St. Benedict's to please watch over them. The nuns said that Martha can be a handful, but Claire is an angel. I will try to get permission to visit again soon." While it wasn't the most uplifting news, at least I took comfort in knowing they were okay.

Dad died not long after we reconnected with Claudette. I was afraid that this would happen. I could tell that Dad's health was failing, and I just knew it was because of all the turmoil I had brought upon him. I was left to take care of the burial arrangements on my own. My sister, Rose, didn't come to pay respects or otherwise inquire after me or my dad. Neither did any of my other brothers and sisters, for that matter. It was pretty sad. Only Claudette called to sympathize with me and check how I was faring. Dad left everything he had to me. Now I was on my own. Little Ricky took my dad's passing the hardest. He and Dad had grown very close over the past several years. Dad was a big help with the kids. I couldn't help but wish he had been such a presence when I was growing up.

I was busy trying to take care of Diane and Ricky and trying to figure out what to do with everything else. I hadn't forgotten about Claire and Martha, but I had reconciled to the fact that there was nothing I could do. I still wrote them letters regularly. I would hear from Tweet Martin often, but I was still waiting for the phone call telling me my girls were coming home.

I started working as a home health aide, taking care of Mr. Jenkins's wife, Liza. Mr. Jenkins was the man who drove me home from the bus station the very first day I got to Canada. His wife was sickly and needed someone to be there while he was at work. She was a wonderful, warm, caring woman whom I was growing very close to. My relationship with my own mother was never that close. Liza was everything that my mother was not. Life was busy, so the time devoted to thinking about Claire and Martha diminished drastically.

Mr. and Mrs. Jenkins had a son named George. I remembered him from when I was growing up, even though he was a few years older than me. He was pretty cute back then. Now he was married and had a daughter of his own who was nine years old. George came over to visit his mother regularly. Over time, George and I grew fond of each other. One thing led to another, and we started to have a relationship. I knew it was wrong. But George was a big, strong, handsome man, and I was lonely and starved for the affection of a man. He was great company and made me feel beautiful, smart, and appreciated. I hadn't felt like that, well, since forever.

Mr. and Mrs. Jenkins had no idea what was going on between me and their son. To be honest, I had no idea what was going on either. George was just fun to be around, and I felt safe with him. I knew there was no future there. George was married, and he let me know that he would never leave his wife and daughter. He told me he loved me but would honor his marriage vows. I was pretty sure I loved him. Liza was growing weaker and slept for a good amount of time. This gave George and me plenty of time to get to know each other intimately.

One day out of the blue, I came home from work and found Tweet Martin on my doorstep.

"Tweet, what are you doing here?" I asked in surprise.

"Well, it's nice to see you too, Imogene."

"I didn't mean it that way. Of course, I'm happy to see you. Just... surprised, that's all."

Before I could catch my breath at the surprise of seeing him, Tweet broke the news about Barbara LeBlanc's demise.

"The girls are being released from St. Benedict's and are coming home."

I was dumbfounded. "You're kidding, right? Barbara is dead? How? When?"

"I don't know any details. I just know that she died, and Mr. LeBlanc has dropped his actions with the court here. Mr. Carr called and said that Claire and Martha would be remanded to my custody tomorrow. I have to go and pick them up."

"Your custody? What about me? I want to pick them up!"

"The court order, for some reason, prohibits that. It specifically says that you are not to pick them up from St. Benedict's." Just another stab by the LeBlancs. I wasn't going to argue, though. I was just happy they were coming home. At least I thought I was happy.

"There is something else," said Tweet. "Mr. LeBlanc has also released the hold on your husband's life insurance proceeds. I have a check here for $1000."

"One thousand dollars? That's all?" My dad had left me $2,000 cash, and the house, which I didn't want to sell, was worth about $4,000. Another $1,000 would sure help, but I had thought it was more.

"What about Richard's pension?" I asked incredulously.

"There is no pension. It was underfunded and is now bankrupt. Imogene, $1,000 is not a bad inheritance. It should help with many bills. You own this house free and clear. What other bills do you have?"

"Well, now I am going to have two other mouths to feed. I don't know! I guess I'll be fine. I just thought the life insurance policy was more, and I was hoping for a pension."

Changing the subject, Tweet asked, "Are you thinking about coming back to Lewiston?"

"I don't know. Maybe. But not right now."

"You have friends in Lewiston. Who do you have here?"

"I said I would think about it!" I snapped. In the back of my mind, I was actually thinking about George Jenkins.

After a tense night between us, Tweet left the next morning to go and pick up the girls at the convent.

My relationship with Tweet was complicated. There were many undertones that suggested a future for us. But whenever we got to the point of something physical, something got in the way. I'm pretty sure Tweet would have been all in if I had given him any indication that I was interested, but I just wasn't.

It wasn't that I didn't find him attractive. He was a nice-looking man. If I had to analyze my feelings, I would say that Tweet was just too nice. That sounds crazy, but it was true. I really felt like I didn't deserve anyone as nice as him. All our communication was initiated by him... except, of course, when I really needed him. He checked on me regularly and was always willing to help in any way he could.

Sometimes I wished he would just go away and leave me alone, because Tweet always made me see how selfish and foolish I was. This may have been why I couldn't be with him. He was everything that I was not. He knew too much about my past and my flaws. In the back of my mind, I wanted to be left alone. I mean, really alone. No kids and no Tweet. I felt robbed of my life. My whole life, I had longed to be a nurse. I had dreamed about it, but because of my own stupid decisions, that was never going to happen. All I did now was work for the Jenkins, take care of the kids, and regret not spending my life with George Jenkins. Now, two more kids were being added to the mix. I just didn't know how I was going to cope. Besides all that, I was so nervous. I had no idea how Claire and Martha would react to me. When they left, they were five and six years old. Now they were ten and eleven.

I told Diane and Ricky that their sisters were coming home. They were both so excited. They acted like I had told them that Santa Claus was coming. I wished I had the same excitement. I was just unsettled by it all. It wasn't the most ideal or appropriate feeling for a mother to have. I had gotten into a routine here. I was used to having just two kids. They were now in school. I enjoyed my freedom, as little as it was. It wasn't that I didn't want them to come home, but I really felt like I should be more excited and happy. My life had been in such turmoil about the girls when they were with me, and I found myself grappling with an overwhelming sense of resentment, even though I knew it wasn't their fault. I needed to push through that feeling. After all, they were just kids. The thought of how to manage all of this was daunting, and I had no idea where to start.

When the girls got here, I couldn't recognize them. They were so grown. In my mind, I still pictured them as younger—much younger. They didn't seem like my children. They were crying, and so was I. Ricky and Diane looked scared. They just stood there, watching the little reunion playing out in their presence. Finally, Ricky ran over and gave Martha a hug. As soon as that happened, Diane was on top of Claire with hugs and kisses. Now it was me who was just standing there. Finally, Tweet said, "I think this calls for a group hug." We all gathered around and hugged each other.

"Ricky and Diane, these are your sisters, Claire and Martha." "We know that, Mom," Ricky responded, giggling.

Martha finally broke the silence by saying she was very hungry and wanted to know what was for dinner. Tweet said, "I'm pretty hungry myself. What is for dinner?"

"Dinner. Oh, my goodness, I forgot about dinner. With all the excitement of you coming home, I totally forgot."

Tweet laughed and said that he would take us all out. "Let me get the bags out of the car."

When he brought out the bags, I was dumbfounded. Claire and

Martha each had one little bag. It contained just the basics. This was five years of their life stuffed into one tiny bag. That made me very sad.

Tweet took us to a little diner, aptly named Ton Meres. Ton Meres means Your Mothers in French. It was just a few miles from the house and the only game in town. Nothing fancy, just good ole home cooking.

As soon as I took a seat at the restaurant, I spotted George dining with his family. Ricky pointed excitedly, "Mom, there's George!" and quickly dashed over to join him at the table where he was sitting with his wife and daughter. Diane followed right behind him. Meanwhile, I just stood there, frozen in place.

"Who is that?" asked Tweet.

"Oh, that is Mr. and Mrs. Jenkins' son, George."

"Funny, you never mentioned that they had a son."

"Why would I?"

"The better question is, why wouldn't you?"

George promptly came over to our table to say hello. His wife and daughter waved cheerfully from their seats.

"Imogene, it's so good to see you." Speaking about Claire and Martha, he curiously asked, "Who are these lovely ladies?"

"These are my daughters, Claire and Martha, and this is my attorney, Tweet Martin."

"Claire and Martha! Oh, my goodness. Did they just get home? I can't believe it. Why didn't you tell me they were coming home? What wonderful news!" I immediately remember telling George all about the girls and their situation.

"I didn't know they were coming until yesterday. Tweet came all the way from Lewiston to give me the news, and he picked them up today."

"So nice to meet you, Tweet. I'm George Jenkins. You certainly do go above and beyond for your clients. That's a long way to come."

"Imogene is a special client, and I have known the girls since they were just toddlers. I consider them family."

"Is that so? Well, it is all really wonderful. I won't keep you from your celebration. You will have to tell me all about what happened later, Imogene. Nice you meet you, Tweet."

"You as well, George."

"Will you be staying in Canada for a while, Tweet?" George asked curiously.

"I'm not really sure yet. If I do, I'm sure I will see you around."

After we got back to the house and the kids were all settled in bed, Tweet looked at me with crossed arms and huffed, "Your attorney? Is that all I am?"

"What are you talking about?"

"That was how you introduced me to George Jenkins. Your attorney."

"Of course, that's not all you are to me. You know that."

"No, Imogene. I don't know that. You introduced me to George as your attorney."

Innocently, I said, "You are my attorney. How else should I have introduced you? What did you want me to say?"

"I wanted you to say this is my good, long-time friend. I wanted you to say, this is someone who has always been there for me. Someone whom I love and appreciate very much. Someone with whom I hope to have a future. But that would be a lie! Wouldn't it!" he said angrily as his voice was rising.

"Tweet, you know how I feel about you."

"Do I? I don't think I do. Why don't you tell me, Imogene?"

The silence that followed seemed to be for an eternity. It was deafening. I could actually hear my heart beating in my chest. Each breath from Tweet resounded louder each time. It was one of the most uncomfortable moments of my life.

"Maybe it's like your dad told me. Perhaps I should start by sharing how I feel. Is that what you require?"

"Tweet, don't do this."

"Do what? Tell you that I love you and have loved you almost since the first day I met you. Tell you that I want to marry you and take you and the kids back to Lewiston with me. Tell you I love the kids and would do anything for them and you. Is that what I shouldn't do?"

I closed my eyes, overwhelmed. "Tweet."

His voice was agitated. "I see. I get it now. Imogene, are you having an affair with George Jenkins?"

"An affair?" I shouted.

"Never mind. I know the answer. Do you love him? Never mind again. The answer to that doesn't matter, because it is obvious you don't love me. I don't know how I got this all so wrong."

"Tweet, I do love you. Just not in the way that you want."

"That's helpful. That makes me feel better. Thanks. What is it, Imogene? What exactly are you looking for? You obviously are not looking for a long-term, secure relationship if you are having affairs with married men."

"Affairs? Married men? It's only one affair with one man, Tweet, and he happens to be a loving, caring, and thoughtful man."

"Does his wife think so, too? Does she know about you? Has he promised to leave his family for you? If he has, he is lying. Imogene, I don't know how you got to be so cold and callous. Even toward your children, you are distant and hard. Your dad said that your mother was a cold, hard, and bitter woman. Looks like you took after her. I will be leaving first thing in the morning. I am exhausted, and I want to say goodbye to the kids, or I would leave tonight."

"I'm sorry, Tweet. I really am. I do love you, and I hate that I have hurt you. Please stay a few more days."

"Good night, Imogene," he said as he settled in on the couch.

The next morning was very emotional for all of us. The kids didn't want Tweet to leave and asked him when he was coming back. He said he didn't know. He told them that he loved them all and asked them to take care of their mom. They were all crying. I couldn't help but think they must have heard at least some of last night's argument.

"Your mom knows how to reach me if any of you need me." At the time, I didn't know it, but Tweet had given Claire a card with his contact information on it.

"Good luck, Imogene. I will still be there if you need anything for the kids. You know how to reach me. I will pray that you make some good decisions for all of you."

And just like that, he vanished. I had an awful feeling in the pit of my stomach that I had just made the worst mistake of my life. The last ten years of my life were playing out in my mind. How had I gotten here? How?

I had sparked the relationship with George Jenkins fairly soon after I began working at his parents' home. Gus Jenkins, George's father, was gone most of the day. Liza was pretty much bed-bound. Her mind was clear, but her body was shut down. My duty was to keep her company and take care of her physical needs. She enjoyed me reading to her and telling her about Diane and Ricky. I also cooked meals, did light cleaning, and helped exercise her legs and arms. It was necessary to turn her over in the bed so she wouldn't get bed sores. Emptying her bedpan and sponge bathing her several times a week were also on the list of my duties. She was a lovely woman who always treated me with kindness. She slept quite a bit, so I often had the house to myself.

I met George the second week that I was there. He dropped by to visit his mom. He was a tall, dark, and handsome man, and there was an immediate attraction between us. I could tell he felt it as much as I did. I knew he was married and had a daughter. His mom had already told me all about her son and his family.

After that first meeting, George's visits to his mom became more frequent, at least three times a week. I couldn't help but think that they became more frequent because of me. When his mom slept, we visited with each other. Everything happened so quickly. One day, I just threw myself into his arms and kissed him. That same day, it progressed from kissing to lovemaking in the Jenkins' guest bedroom. I definitely initiated it, but he was more than a willing partner. I think I was so starved for male attention and affection that I just couldn't help myself.

Honestly, it felt like I had known George my whole life. I had not been with a man since Richard. Sex with Richard was good in the beginning, but never great. I guess the main reason I stuck around was that I was in love with him—young and naive, I suppose. But with George, it wasn't just good, it was wonderful. I became insatiable. When I wasn't with George, all I could think of was him. He was slow, tender, and caring in a way that deeply touched me. He always checked in to see how I was doing and asked what he could do to make me feel good. Richard, in contrast, was more of a "wam-bam thank you ma'am" type of lover. Whenever Liza interrupted us with calls for assistance, George never got irritated by it. I, on the other hand, just wanted to steal more time with him.

Some days, Mrs. Jenkins stayed awake the whole time. On those days, George stayed by his mom's bed and visited with her instead of me. I couldn't help but become resentful. Liza was getting in the way, and I was jealous. Horrible of me to feel that way, I know. It was because I was in love with George and selfishly wanted as much time with him as possible.

There were several times that George became irritated with my attitude towards his mom. "Imogene, I come here to see my mom. I don't know how much longer she will be around, but if she is awake and wants to talk, that is what I am going to do," he said angrily. "I'm sorry if you don't like it. Maybe we should just stop what we are doing. Maybe I shouldn't come when you are here."

"Surely you don't mean that, George."

"I don't want that, but if my time with my mom makes you unhappy, then maybe that would be best."

"I'm sorry, George. You are right. It's just that we get so little time together. I miss you, and then you come, and I still don't get to spend much time with you."

"I know, Darling, and I'm sorry."

Our relationship continued.

One day, while I was at the Jenkins house, George's wife and daughter showed up. I had never met them before. They came to see Mrs. Jenkins. George never really talked about his wife. He never said what kind of relationship they had or didn't have. I never asked, either. When I met her, I realized that Patricia was a lovely woman. I had not expected that.

Patricia was very sweet and very attractive. Physically, we looked nothing alike. She was small and petite with dark hair and blue eyes. Patricia dressed very stylishly and was very well put together. Her skin was flawless, and her voice was soft and sweet. Not overly sweet, though. I couldn't help but like her. For this, I hated her.

She and her daughter, Jane, came into the house singing. Patricia said she had heard a lot about me and was thrilled to finally meet me. She thanked me for taking such great care of Liza.

"I know that Mr. and Mrs. Jenkins and George think very highly of you. We are all so thankful that you are available to watch over and take care of George's mom. You know, I am a firm believer that the Lord puts people in our path for a reason. God sent you to us." With that, she gave me a very warm hug, which left me feeling awful.

Jane was a shy and quiet girl who always smiled. She and her mom seemed to have a very loving relationship. It was obvious that Liza adored them. That first time, they brought some homemade chocolate chip cookies and stayed to visit for about an hour or so. It was George's usual day to visit, but Patricia said he wouldn't be able to make it that day. When I inquired why, she said, "Oh, I don't know, something has come up at his work."

After that, George's wife and daughter visited more frequently and stayed longer. George's visits became less and less frequent. When I questioned George about it, he got irritated and his response was, "It's life, Imogene. I have some work responsibilities that I can't ignore right now. Besides, Patricia and Jane want to spend time with Mom because they realize she is failing and might not be around much longer."

I felt that George was pushing me away.

The night at the diner was the first time I had seen George with his wife and daughter. It was obvious that they were a happy and loving family. What on earth was I thinking?

Tweet leaving made me feel really sad. It was like losing my best friend. Claire and Martha's homecoming didn't feel like a joyful event anymore. Even though I longed for it, now that it had finally arrived, I felt nervous and anxious. When I saw George again, I asked him about him and his wife.

Sighing, he asked, "What exactly do you want to know, Imogene?"

"Are you in love with your wife? Are you intimate with her and with me? What are your long-term plans, George?"

"I have never lied to you or misled you, Imogene. Yes, I love my wife, and yes, I am still intimate with Patricia. She is my wife after all."

"Does she know about me? What exactly have you told her about us?"

"Imogene, what is this all about? Is this about this so-called "attorney," Tweet? Has he instigated this? I love my wife. I never plan on leaving her. If you got the impression that this was anything other than a little roll around once or twice a week, then that is on you. I never said anything to make you think I was in it for anything but a little fun. I like you, Imogene. You're a lot of fun, but this is getting a little too complicated for me. I think maybe we need to stop seeing each other."

At this point, I was burning with anger. "A little roll around? Is that what you said? I think you are right, George! Your wife is a very nice lady. I feel sorry for her being married to a lying cheat like you. She and Jane deserve better. I wonder what she would think if she knew about us."

"Is that a threat?"

Our voices had risen, and Liza was listening. "George and Imogene, I need to speak with you, please," Liza said very firmly.

And just like that, Liza fired me.

"You are no longer welcome in this home. As for you, George—I am ashamed of you. I am praying that Patricia can forgive you when she finds out. Now, both of you get out!"

As we were leaving, George turned to me and said, "You aren't going to tell Patricia, are you?"

"I haven't decided yet."

"I wouldn't do that if I were you."

"Are you threatening me now?" To this, George just gave a little smirk. "Goodbye, George. Go home to your wonderful wife and daughter. Maybe you can somehow make it up to them. I thought I was in love with you, but it turns out I was in love with someone who doesn't even exist. Have a nice life."

I knew I wasn't going to tell Patricia. My actions had already hurt her enough. I prayed that George had learned a lesson and wouldn't stray again. Later, I learned that Patricia had taken over Liza's care. When she asked about me, they told her that I needed to be with my children now that Claire and Martha were home.

I still thought about George but realized what a fool I had been. Poor little, gullible Imogene, taken in again by a man. I was done with men.

CHAPTER 13

Claire's Journal

THE AFTERMATH

THE DAY THAT CHANGED OUR LIVES:

We had been at the convent for over four years when one day, one of the Sisters told me and Martha to come to the Mother Superior's office. We had never been summoned there before. I was now eleven and Martha was ten. The summons to the Mother Superior's office had both of us scared and on edge. Were we getting in trouble?

When we got to the office, a man was waiting for us. He looked familiar to me, but I didn't recognize him. He asked us if we remembered him. Martha and I both shook our heads no. Grinning, he told us his name was Tweet, Tweet Martin, and asked again if we remembered him.

Martha, wincing her eyes, immediately said, "Yes. I remember you. You are the nice man who was friends with our mother. Can I hear you tweet like a bird?"

He laughed and began tweeting. At this, we all laughed and both Martha and I advanced to him and gave him a hug, which was returned in the warmest way.

"What are you doing here?" beamed Martha. "I hope you have come to get us out of here," she said hopefully.

"I am here to take you home," he answered. The nuns are packing your things. Your mother is waiting for you at home," he said with a huge grin on his face and a huge, warm hug.

We later found out that Tweet had a court order, but one of the terms of our "release" was that our mother could not come to the convent. Martha and I were so excited. We couldn't believe that we were finally going home, but we were confused as to why our mother was not allowed to come and get us. Court stuff, I guess. We never did understand that.

The ride home was pretty quiet. We were nervous, and Tweet seemed nervous too. But Tweet Martin was the kind of adult who made you feel safe and comfortable. Even though I slept most of the way home, it seemed like it took forever to get there. When we pulled up in front of the house, it looked a little familiar, but we had been away for so long and had lived there for such a short time that we could hardly remember anything. I was very nervous. This is something Martha and I had wished for since we were dropped off in the middle of the night in that strange place, but I was still apprehensive.

Mom came out to greet us. Two kids were swaying on the porch swing, soaking up the warm July evening. We assumed they were Diane and Ricky, but we had no recognition of them. They looked nothing like we remembered. When we left, Diane was a toddler and Ricky was barely two. Now they were kids. We could tell that they didn't remember us either.

Mom broke down in tears when she saw us. She looked much older than I remembered. Her hair had some gray in it, and there were lines on her face that weren't present before. Her eyes were sad and didn't have much life in them. She hugged us, but the hug felt so tentative. Mom's greeting was so confusing for me. It didn't feel genuine. Tweet Martin's approach to us when he arrived at the convent felt much warmer. By now, Martha and I were both crying too.

It was a few days before we finally found out why we were put into that horrible convent. In addition, we discovered that our beloved grandpa had died. This news made us sad because, although we only knew him for a short time, Martha and I both had fond memories of him. It also turned out that our dad's mom had died too. We had no memories of her. We did know, however, that she was the one who put us in the convent. Her passing was the reason we were finally allowed to come home. For us, there was no sorrow there for her.

LIFE AFTER THE CONVENT:

Martha and I were enrolled in our old school. There were so many rumors going around about who we were and where we had been. Mom said, "It's none of their business. Just tell them you were at boarding school." So that was what we said. One of the good things that came out of the convent was that we got a high-quality education. Martha and I were far and away the smartest kids in the school. Even kids in the upper grades weren't as smart as we were. The teacher we had before, Ms. Par, was no longer there. Our new teacher was Ms. Copper. She was nice and paid special attention to us. I'm pretty sure she knew what had happened in our past.

Martha continued to struggle with fitting in. I tried to help her, but she told me to stop.

She kept assuring me that she knew what I was trying to do. "Listen, Claire, I know what you are trying to do. I am fine. You need to make your own friends. Don't feel like you need to include me in everything. To be honest, it is exhausting."

So, I made my own way. Martha stayed home a lot. When there were parties or dances (which were seldom since we lived out in the middle of nowhere), she declined to come. Mother was not very sympathetic to her. She constantly berated her and asked her why she couldn't be more like me. As the years passed, my mom's contempt for

Martha became more apparent. Even Diane and Ricky noticed. It felt like we were back in the convent, and Martha was being targeted by the mean girls. Except now it was our mother targeting her.

Ricky was really curious as to why our mom treated Martha in such a demeaning way, but I told him I had no clue, and he shouldn't worry his head about it. All of a sudden, Diane chimed in while we were discussing it and said it was because Martha is difficult: that mom always told her that not only was Martha difficult, but that Martha reminded her of our grandmom—the one who tried to take us from her.

I was taken aback that Mom would have such a conversation with little Daine. I probed further to know what Mom had said concerning Martha, and Diane continued to say Mom told her Martha was born unhappy. After hearing all of these things, I pleaded with Diane to never mention what Mom had said to Martha or anyone else, hoping she could keep a lid on it.

Wow! Just wow. A lot was making sense now. I know Mom hated our dad's mom. I don't remember what she looked like, but apparently, Martha looked like her. I couldn't believe that our mother would talk about Martha like that, and to Diane no less. At this point, I was fifteen. Martha was fourteen. Diane was twelve and Ricky was eleven. I just thought everything about this was wrong.

Since Martha and I returned from the convent, our mother had been pretty aloof. It didn't seem like she wanted us there. We never had any time with her... with just her. When we were all home, she had us doing chores or homework. It was as if we were a bother. Diane was her favorite. There was no denying that. They always had little secrets going on.

Martha and I were in the room one day when she broke the silence and asked me if I thought Mom wished we had stayed in the convent.

I wasn't shocked by the question, because secretly I had been asking myself the same. The mom that I remembered was not this mom. She does not seem happy and rarely wants to spend time with us. At one point, she actually said that children are meant to be seen, not heard.

Catching myself in my thoughts, I responded, "Of course not!"

We never had any good discussions about what was going on in our lives. Mom never asked about school or about our friends. Basically, we came home from school, did our homework, ate dinner, and went to our rooms. Dinner was a quiet affair. I specifically remember one night sitting down to eat and Ricky saying, "Well, I had a really crummy day today."

As I probed to find out what happened during his day, Mom told us to be quiet and eat our dinner. I looked at Ricky and saw the hurt in his eyes. They were brimming with tears that I could tell he was holding back. My heart broke for him. Later, I found out that some older kid at school was teasing Ricky. I tried to talk to Mom about it, but she didn't want to hear any of it.

After we were home from the convent for a few months, I asked Mom about Tweet Martin. She got angry and said that Tweet went back to the United States. "He had a job to do. His job with us was over. We won't be seeing Tweet Martin anymore."

I had secretly hoped that Mom and Tweet would get married and we would all live happily ever after. I thought Tweet could bring some normalcy into our lives. Even though I already knew things had gone south between them (I had heard the argument they had the night before he left). So, I couldn't help but shed more than a few tears over it. It felt as if someone had died, a grief that came from watching my dreams fade away.

One day, Martha stayed home from school because she was sick with some kind of stomach bug. None of us knew what Mom did all day. A lot of times, when we got home, Mom wasn't there. When we got home that day, I asked Martha if she knew where Mom was. She weakly said, "I don't know. I haven't seen her since this morning."

Martha looked pretty bad. She said she had been throwing up all day. I got her some water and crackers and then sat with her until she fell asleep. I thought it was pretty sad that my mom was gone all day when she had a sick kid at home. After she finally arrived home, I defiantly asked her where she had been.

"It's none of your business where I go."

"But Martha is sick. She might have needed you," I said angrily.

"Listen, Missy, where I go and what I do is none of your business. You are the kid, and I am the mom. You don't ask me questions. I ask you questions. Besides, Martha is always whining and complaining about something."

"If you're the mom, maybe you should start acting like a mom then." It was the first time I had ever talked back to my mother. And she slapped me hard across the face for it. I went to our room crying. Mother never checked on either of us that night. The next morning, we got up and went to school. Martha was still weak from being sick, but she said she was fine. Mom acted like nothing ever happened.

Prior to leaving St. Benedict's, I had started menstruating for the first time. The nuns had thrown some supplies at me, saying, "Welcome to womanhood. You can thank Eve." At first, I didn't know who they were talking about. Then I realized they were talking about Eve from the Garden of Eden. Some of the older girls helped me figure it all out. I thought I was dying, but they assured me that it was all normal. Luckily, Martha had learned from my experience and knew what was happening when she started menstruating a few months after we returned home. When that happened, my mom casually told me to handle it as she didn't have the empathy and patience to listen to Martha's whining. Martha had really bad cramps. Mom told her to stop being such a baby and directed me to give her some aspirin.

Martha started withdrawing as time went by. She loved to read and constantly had her head in a book. The kids at school treated Martha well. They were never mean, but she still didn't have any friends. I overheard a few girls talking one day, and they said she was "strange." The reality was she wasn't strange. She just didn't seem to want any friends. She was happy to be alone.

One day after school, Mom and Martha got into a big fight. Mom was in the mood to instigate. I don't know what had happened that day, but it was obvious that she was going to take her anger, or her hurt, or whatever it was, out on Martha. I just didn't understand my mom. This was the beginning of Martha's attempts at running away. I think that if Mom had taken that first time seriously and tried to improve her relationship with us, our lives would have been different.

After that day, Martha ran away from home a few times. She never went far and always came back. When I would try to talk to Martha about what was happening, she would just say that Mom didn't like her. That she would have been better off staying in the convent. I tried to talk to Mom about these things, but she would just shrug me off. As we grew older, the situation improved a bit. We could take care of ourselves better and didn't really need Mom. She liked that, and so did we.

When Martha was just shy of fifteen, she and Mom got in a huge fight. Mom wanted to know why Martha was always hanging around the house. She told Martha that she didn't have any friends because she was not "likable." Martha turned around, got in Mom's face, and said, "I guess you have the same problem. Where are all your friends, Imogene?" Although Martha had stood up to Mom before, this was definitely the first time she called her by her first name. Mom smacked Martha hard across the face, and Martha almost smacked her back. Thankfully, she restrained herself.

"You know what, Mom, I'll be fifteen next week. You probably didn't even remember that, since your kid's birthdays don't seem to be a big deal to you. Anyway, don't worry about celebrating this year because I am leaving. You don't have to worry about me anymore!"

"I've heard that before, Martha. Grow up and stop being so childish."

"I'm sorry that I have been such a disappointment and burden to you," Martha said as she turned and stormed out. I tried to convince Martha not to leave, but she was determined. "I'm going, and this time I am not coming back," she said as she counted the money she had been saving.

I gave her all the money that I had and the card that Tweet Martin had given me the last time we saw him. I knew that if she could get to Lewiston, Tweet would help her. Martha left that same afternoon with just the clothes on her back, the little bit of money I had given her (along with some money she had saved), and Tweet Martin's card in her pocket.

At first, Diane and Ricky seemed basically unaffected by the turmoil between Mom and Martha; however, as Ricky got older, he started to look more and more like our dad. He and Martha definitely had the LeBlanc gene more than Diane and me. We looked like our mom. The more Ricky grew to look physically like Dad, the more I saw Mom's attitude towards him change. Ricky was a sweet boy. He was popular in school, and the girls loved him. Mom said many times, "You are just like your father. Such a charmer. You don't fool me one bit, Ricky LeBlanc."

My mom could be pretty hurtful when she wanted to be, and it seemed she chose to do so more and more frequently. Ricky told me that most of the time when Mom was mad or mean, he didn't even know what he had done wrong. I tried to tell him to ignore it. But she was his mom, and he was desperate for her love and approval. Unlike Martha, who was defiant and more rebellious, Ricky was a people pleaser. It felt like he had become the new focus of her harshness, yet he did everything he could to avoid upsetting her.

A few months after Martha left, our mom walked out the door with just the clothes on her back and probably some cash and never returned. I was sixteen, and all of a sudden, I was in charge of my younger sister and brother. She left nothing except a piece of paper with Tweet Martin's contact information on it and an envelope with some cash.

The note read:

I AM SORRY.
TWEET MARTIN WILL HELP YOU.

THANKS,
MOM!

CHAPTER 14

Open Arms

TWEET MARTIN:

When I got back to Lewiston, my sister was eager to know what had transpired. As I made my way home, I replayed the events in my mind, feeling increasingly distraught. Still, I knew I had to pull myself together. My sister was a worrier, and I didn't want her fretting over me.

As soon as I walked in the door, Donna eagerly inquired if Imogene and the kids were coming back to Lewiston. Hesitantly, I told her that Imogene wanted to stay in Canada.

"What? Tweet, why don't you admit that you are in love with that woman and get her down here? I know that if she knew how you felt, she would be here in a minute. You are so stubborn," she said, shaking her head.

Firmly, I replied, "Actually, Donna, I told Imogene exactly how I felt and asked her to marry me. I told her I wanted to take care of her and the kids. I told her I had been in love with her almost since the day we met, but she said she is not interested."

"What? You are lying. I saw the way she used to look at you. There is no way this can be true. Did you tell her you love the kids?"

"Yes, but apparently, she is in love with someone else. Unfortunately for her, that person is not available. He is married. Obviously, Imogene doesn't make very good choices as far as men are concerned."

With tears in her eyes and a sorrowful look, Donna said, "I'm so sorry, Tweet. She is missing out on a great guy. That's for sure. Do you think the kids will be okay? How were Claire and Martha when you picked them up?"

"They were happy to be leaving the convent, but they seemed a little confused. They didn't remember me initially until I started talking to them about some things we had done in the past. I tweeted for them and then they remembered." I couldn't help but smile at the memory.

"Did Imogene go with you to pick them up?"

"No. The court order specifically forbade her from coming. I had to go alone."

"That's odd, but maybe not. Maybe they know something that we don't. Was she happy to see them when they got home?"

I shook my head, "Donna, the whole thing was strange. When I told her they were coming home, she seemed ecstatic. Thinking back, though, it seemed she was more interested in the money she was or wasn't getting from the insurance than she was about the girls coming home. When they got home, she actually seemed distant and aloof. I don't know what goes through her mind."

Hugging me, Donna said, "It all sounds very strange. I am so sorry, Tweet."

It was a difficult year for me. I couldn't stop thinking about Imogene and the kids. I knew that even if Imogene changed her mind, we could never make it work. She was not the person I thought she was. I was particularly worried about the kids, but Donna kept telling me to snap out of it. She was constantly trying to fix me up with other women. I could only laugh.

A year had gone by, and one evening I came home from a hunting trip with friends, only to find out that big John Pine had tragically been killed in a boating accident.

John and I had stayed in touch over the years, so when his wife, Elise, reached out for guidance on some legal advice, I felt the weight of the situation. My sister informed her that I would get in touch once I was back in Lewiston. I was so distressed by John's death that I needed a few days to gather myself before making the journey to Booth Bay Harbor.

JOHN AND ELISE'S HOUSE:

It was with trepidation that I pulled into the Pines' driveway. I said a little prayer before I got out of the car. Everything looked exactly as I remembered it. Such a beautiful area. The Pine home was still so warm and homey. It looked like there was a fresh coat of paint on it—a beautiful and inviting yellow. I knocked on the door, and Elise answered. She seemed surprised to see me. The boys were at school. Margie, Elise's sister-in-law, who has Down Syndrome, was there with Elise.

I immediately felt the absence of John. He was a big teddy bear of a man who was kind and well-loved by his family. Even though I had only met John in person a few times, I considered him to be a friend. I could see that Elise's countenance was down. She was obviously very sad. Sweet Margie greeted me with a big hug. She said, "My brother, John, is dead. He won't be coming home today. Mom says he is with Jesus in heaven."

"I'm sure your mom is exactly right. John is with Jesus, and you will see him again one day."

"Hey, that's what Mom said too."

Elise invited me to come into the kitchen while she asked Margie to stay back and play with the dog. "Do you want anything to drink?" Elise asked.

"I'm fine. Thank you. My sister, Donna, told me you called and wanted to get some legal advice. I am so sorry about John." I told her that I thought John was a really wonderful man, and I meant it in every sense. "Do you want to talk about what happened?"

"Well, that's the thing, I don't really know what happened. That day, John left for his normal workday on the water. His brother was sick, so John was on his own. The day was a little cloudy, and the water was choppy, but it wasn't something that John hadn't dealt with a million times before. This time, though, he just never came home. Two days later, they found his boat back in a marsh, destroyed. It had obviously been in some kind of accident. They still haven't found John." At this, she started to cry. I reached out to put my hand on hers in a bid to console her. I said, "I am truly sorry. Are they still searching for him? Could John still be alive somewhere?"

"I wish I could say yes to both of those questions, but no. They have stopped searching, and I don't think John is still alive. Based on the condition of the boat, his survival would be a miracle. Besides, if he were alive, he would be home."

"How can I help you? Anything you need, I will do."

"There are two things going on. One is that since they didn't find John, they are not going to be paying out on his life insurance policy. They say they won't pay until John has been missing for two years."

"Who says that? The insurance company?"

"Yes."

"How much insurance are we talking about?"

"I have the policy right here. If I read it right, he has $15,000 coverage, which doubles if he is killed in an accident. Right now, I have no other income. We have some savings, but I am going through that quickly. John's mom has been helping us. However, I fear that she may not be able to continue. The truth is, before the accident, we were helping her and Margie. They don't have much savings and will need it to survive themselves."

"Do you mind if I take this policy with me when I leave? What about the boat?"

"John's brother had it towed to the docks. It's a total loss."

"Was the boat insured?"

"Yes. The money hasn't come through yet, but since it was John and Ross's livelihood, we expect to get about $5,000. Which will be invested in another boat."

"How are the boys holding up?"

At this, Elise looked very concerned. "They are devastated. Luckily, I adopted them when John and I got married. Not that any of the family would cause any problems with that. John's family is really close. I consider them my family, too. Honestly, I don't know what I would do without the boys."

"Were there any other boats damaged that night?"

"None that have been discovered or reported, but we know there is a boat out there somewhere that hit John's boat. There is no way that it didn't have significant damage. The police have just given up on investigating it. They said accidents happen, and that this was an accident."

"I'm pretty sure that if it were just an accident, the other people involved would have called for help. It all sounds very strange. Do you know anyone in the police department?"

"John's brother, Ross, has some connections, but right now they are playing dumb."

"Maybe I'll stop into the station on my way home. I'll see what I can find out. It just seems that they would want to find out what happened."

"I would really love for you to talk to John's brother. He might be able to give you some insight."

Elise, Margie, and I decided to walk two houses over to where Ross and Elise's sister, Daniella, lived. Another cozy little house that looked well-loved. With a big smile, Daniella opened the door, and I thought I was looking at Elise. They could pass as twins because they looked so much alike. Daniella hugged Margie and invited us in. Margie made the introductions, and then she and Hardy bounced off to the kitchen to get a snack. I couldn't help but smile at her childlike manner and ability to find happiness in almost everything.

As soon as we settled in, Daniella told us that Ross wasn't home. She told us that he was working on a friend's boat, but he would be home shortly. Elise told Daniella about what we had discussed, and she agreed that everything was strange.

"Personally, I think that the police or the coast guard are covering up something. Either that, or the other boat sank and everyone on board died too. The thing about that is that no one else has been reported missing. No missing boats either."

Just then, a big teddy bear of a man walked in. Once again, just like Elise and Daniella, I felt I was looking at a mirror image of John Pine. It was as if I were looking at a ghost. Ross Pine, though a little older, looked exactly like his brother. It really was mind-boggling. With Elise and Daniella looking so much alike and John and Ross looking like twins, it was all a bit too strange. Ross had a strong handshake and an imposing, jovial voice, just as I remembered John's voice to be. Like John, I immediately liked Ross.

"You must be the illustrious Tweet Martin. I am Ross Pine."

At that, Daniella exited to the kitchen and brought back two beers. I told Ross how sorry I was about John and then filled him in on what I already knew.

"What is your take on all this, Ross?"

"You know, I just don't know what to think. One of my best friends is a policeman. He has been extremely close-mouthed about it all. The whole thing has affected our friendship. He told me not to ask him anything about it again. He was John's friend too. I would have thought that he would do anything to help us solve this mystery," he said incredulously.

"What about the Coast Guard? How are they involved?"

"Well, that's the thing, the police say the Coast Guard is handling the investigation, and the Coast Guard says the police are handling it. Consequently, no one is handling it. Poor Elise can't get the life insurance payout because they haven't found John's body. The insurance on the boat should come through pretty soon, but until it does, I'm working for others."

"So, no one is looking for John?"

"No one except friends and family. You know, I feel so guilty. I should have been on the boat with John that day. I was sick, and John told me to stay home. John said jokingly that day, 'Do you want both of us to be sick? I don't want your nasty germs!' If I had been on the boat, the accident probably would never have happened."

"Stop beating yourself up, Ross," interjected Daniella. "You can't be too sure. If you had been on that boat, you might both be missing."

"No! One of us would have been on lookout when we were retrieving traps. We would have seen the other boat and been able to get out of the way. There is no question about that. I think what happened is that John was retrieving a trap or traps, and another boat slammed into him before he could react. That put him over the edge and in the water. He probably hit his head and drowned."

"Wouldn't he have heard another boat coming? I mean, boats are pretty loud, aren't they?"

"Sure, but he wouldn't have worried about it because he would have assumed they saw him. By the time he realized what was happening, it probably was too late."

"What is the name of your friend at the police department?"

"Jim Boone. The department is small. It only has three officers. The chief is Larry Kline. He is Jim's boss."

"Do you mind if I stop over there on my way back to Lewiston?"

"No. I don't mind at all. I would appreciate it. Hopefully, you will be able to get further than I did with them."

During our discussion, I could see Elise looking out the window, as if she were waiting for someone. Finally, she exclaims, "Oh, there go the boys. I'd better get home. Thanks, Tweet, for all your help. Don't forget to stop by and pick up that copy of the insurance policy before you leave." At that, she hurried out, and Margie and Hardy were not far behind.

After they left, Ross and Daniella told me that Elise was taking all of this very hard.

"We were actually afraid for a little while that she was suicidal. She had such a rough time before John. He was her rock and anchor. It has gotten a little better, but there are still days she won't leave her bedroom. Thank God for Margie and the boys. Margie has been so wonderful. The boys have taken it hard, but I think that they realize that Elise needs them to be strong."

"I'm going to look into the insurance. Since this is a case where it is fairly obvious that the insured is deceased, I think we can obtain payment now. The insurance for the boat should not be a problem. Have you filed the claim?"

"Yes, the claim is filed. They said it would take four to six weeks for the money to come through."

As I prepared to take my leave, I told Ross I would also stop by the police department on my way home.

"I just am really curious as to what they will say. Here is my card. Call me anytime. I will be in touch soon to let you know what I find out."

After stopping by to get the insurance policy from Elise, I proceeded to the police department. Booth Bay Harbor is small, so the police department was just a mile or so inland. When I say police department, I am talking about a one-room office with a desk and a prison cell in the middle. Luckily, the Chief, Larry Kline, was at the desk, and there was no one currently in the jail cell. I introduced myself to Chief Kline, and he was cordial but guarded.

Leaning back in his chair with his arms crossed and his feet propped up on the desk, Chief Kline said, "Mr. Martin, I'm afraid that I can't enlighten you about the John Pine investigation as it is still ongoing."

As non-confrontationally as possible, I said, "Ross Pine says that there is no investigation going on because no one wants to take responsibility for it. He said the Coast Guard says that you guys are in charge, and you guys say they are in charge. Can you at least tell me who is heading it up?"

"We are working together," he stated matter-of-factly.

"The problem that we are having, Chief, is that Elise Pine cannot collect on her husband's insurance until a body is found. Is anyone looking for the body?"

This seemed to soften him a little. "We are still searching. To be honest, John's body may never be found. Lots of big predators in that water. At this point, I would imagine that they have fed off John and there is nothing left to find."

"Are you sure John is dead?"

"As sure as we can be without a body. John was a hard-working, stand-up guy. He loved his wife and his family. There is no indication that he simply left. The boat was destroyed. Anyone who sees it can assume that it was rammed by something, and John went overboard. John grew up in Booth Bay Harbor and was a strong swimmer. If he were alive, he would be home by now." At this point, realizing that I was not a threat to his credibility, Chief Kline was warming up to me and was willing to share a bit more information.

My wheels were spinning. "Chief, you said, "rammed by something?"

"Yes, but please call me Larry. One of the theories suggests that the boat was rammed by a whale or a shark. There are lots of huge whales and sharks all over these waters. Right now, we really don't know what happened and may never find out."

"Let me ask you this, Larry, would you be willing to sign a document that attests to the fact that John Pine is deceased?"

Shaking his head, the chief said, "Oh, I have to think about that. I don't actually know he is dead, but the probability is high. I would have to read it over carefully before I put my signature to it."

"That's fair. I should be back this way in a few days. I may bring one by for you to look at."

"Mr. Martin, everyone here in Booth Bay is so sorry about John. We are sad to see Elise and the boys having to go through all this. The Pine families are all good, decent, Christian folks who have been in these parts for many years. One of my deputies was a good friend of John and is a good friend of Ross. His family goes to church with them. I think all of this has put a rift in their friendship. Deputy Boone doesn't know anything. I hope that Ross can ease up on him."

"Thanks. I'll relay that information to Ross. Hopefully, I will see you in a few days. Oh, before I go, do you think the Coast Guard has any information that you don't?"

"No. They are too busy trying to catch pirates," he laughed. "Between you and me, although it is not official, this case is pretty much ours."

It was late when I arrived back in Lewiston. I was exhausted. I decided to follow up on the insurance the following day. When I reviewed the insurance paperwork, it was all pretty standard. Like most insurance policies, the wording was vague to serve the insurer and the insurer's interest. Insurance policies rarely make it easy for the insured to file claims. Sure enough, in this policy, there was a disappearance clause that said, "...unless there is irrefutable evidence that the policyholder was deceased, the insurance proceeds would not be paid." However, it went on to say that if, after two years, there is no evidence that the insured is still living, the proceeds "may be paid."

"May be paid! Oh wow!" The insurance company could still get out of paying even after two years. With that in mind, I drew up a statement letter in the hope that Larry Kline would sign it.

A few days later, I headed back to Booth Bay Harbor. When I got there, I went to the police station immediately. Larry Kline was in the same spot I saw him last. He stood up as I approached and put out his hand. We shook, and he said, "Mr. Martin, I have some interesting information for you." He seemed giddy to tell me.

He had my attention. "Really, what might that be?"

"We had another boating accident that can't be explained. Another fisherman is missing."

"Wow. Did you find the boat?"

"We found his boat, but not any people. Same thing! The boat is heavily damaged, and the fisherman is nowhere in sight."

"Where did you find the boat? Was it near the area where John Pine's boat was found?"

"Yes. About a mile north. It is really strange. The boat was a little bigger than John's boat. Again, just like in John's case, there was only one person on board. Unfortunately, he wasn't reported missing for a few days. This makes the investigation harder. The man, Bill Seger, doesn't have many people who keep track of him. He wasn't married and had no kids. He enjoyed drinking and occasionally went on benders. When he wasn't where he was supposed to be, nobody was worried. Finally, the people who own the marina called to report him missing. As soon as the call came in, I thought of John and his boat."

"WOW! Well, Larry, what are you thinking?"

"After looking at the boat, I think his boat was attacked by a great white, and he became shark bait. We have a few great whites that make this water their home. I think that is what happened to John, too. At this point, I think we have a rogue great white. If we don't find him, there will be more attacks."

After we spoke for a few more minutes, I asked Larry about signing the statement testifying that John was most probably dead. Larry reviewed it and signed it, saying, "Elise deserves to be paid this money. I would bet my ass, excuse my language, that he is dead and will testify to that if asked."

I thanked him. We shook hands, and I was on my way to talk to Elise. Elise was thrilled that the chief signed the statement. "Do you think the insurance company will accept it?"

"I do. But I could be wrong. I will send it today." After, Elise hugged me and kissed my cheek. She immediately stepped back in horror, saying, "Oh my! I am so sorry."

I smiled, "What are you sorry about, Elise? You have nothing to apologize for. I am happy that I could help you and happy that you are happy and excited," and I was. Elise was a great gal. No pretensions, no games. I really liked her and the rest of the Pine family a lot.

Finally, after several months, John Pine's death was ruled an accident. They never did recover his body. Everyone involved thought it was a shark. Nothing could prove it, but there had been two more mysterious boating accidents and deaths in waters around Booth Bay after John's disappearance. They never did find the suspected predator. Ross said, It probably moved on to other waters. Sure enough, about six months later, there were a series of similar incidents off the coast of Bar Harbor.

Elise was able to get the insurance payout pretty quickly after I sent the signed statement to the insurance company.

I traveled back and forth from Lewiston to Booth Bay many times that year to visit Elise and her family. About a year after John died,

Elise and I got married, with blessings from both sides. My sister loved Elise, and so did I. I was commuting back and forth from Lewiston to Booth Bay. I opened a law office in Booth Bay Harbor, but I still had business in Lewiston. I usually spend two days a week at my office in Lewiston and the rest of the time in Booth Bay Harbor. I loved it there—so laid back. Not nearly the hustle and bustle of Lewiston.

One night, about a year after Elise and I married, I arrived in Lewiston to find my brother-in-law, Phillip, waiting for me. I had given up my apartment and was staying with Donna, Phillip, and their twins (Robert and Benjamin) when I was in Lewiston, and it seemed to be working out well.

"Tweet, I got a disturbing phone call from a lawman up north. He said that there was a girl in the hospital up in Bar Harbor. She had your name and contact information in her pocket," Phillip said.

"My name? Why? Who is it?"

"They are not sure. It appears that she tried to kill herself. Actually, she did a pretty good job of it. If some man hadn't come to rescue her, she would have died. She stabbed herself in the side."

"Good Lord! Did they give you any sort of description of her? I don't know anyone in Bar Harbor."

"Just that she is a young girl, about ten or eleven years old. The officer said she is going to survive. She didn't hit any large organs or vessels, but she is unconscious and has been since they brought her in."

"How do they know she stabbed herself? Maybe someone stabbed her?"

"The knife was still in her hand and in her side. Tweet, could this be one of Imogene's girls?"

"Ten or eleven is young. Imogene's two oldest would be fifteen and sixteen. I guess it could be the youngest Diane, maybe, but I think she is even older than that. Did they give any kind of physical description? Hair color or anything?"

"They said she was very small, with brown eyes and brown hair."

"That's not Diane, but it could be Martha. Except Martha would be at least fifteen by now, not ten or eleven."

"They want you to go up there."

A day later, after letting Elise know what was happening, I was standing at the bedside of Martha LeBlanc. She looked so small and pitiful, I barely recognized her. When I arrived, she was just waking up. The doctors said that she had lost a lot of blood and would need to stay in the hospital for a few days to regain her strength. Other than that, she would physically be okay. Mentally was a different story.

The police had a lot of questions. I provided the information that I had then. I instructed them on how to contact Imogene. They left only to return later to say, "The woman you told us about said that she doesn't know this girl."

A social worker interviewed me. She asked how I knew Martha. I told her that Martha's mother had some legal trouble in the past that I had helped her with.

"Why would the child's mother say she doesn't know her?" she probed further.

"Imogene LeBlanc has some issues. I'm not really sure what is going on, but I can assure you that Martha is her daughter."

The doctor on call asked to speak to me in his office, where he expressed great concern. "I've seen cases like this before, and I don't think this was just a call for help. Given the circumstances, I am certain that Martha truly wanted to die. The knife wound missed some vital organs by a millimeter, and when Martha was brought into the hospital, she was very close to death." The doctor said, "Some people don't believe in miracles, but I do. To me, the fact that she survived is a miracle."

Two days later, Martha was way better, and she was released to me.

Upon leaving the hospital, the social worker told me to be very careful, as Martha is still very troubled.

I didn't press Martha for details of how she got to where she was. I felt like she wasn't strong enough physically or mentally yet. One thing was sure: she had been through a lot. She had told the police that she truly did try to kill herself. Thankfully, Martha remembered who I was, and she was happy to see me. I knew eventually she would talk to me. Right now, I just wanted her to feel safe and loved. I could not believe that Imogene had let this happen.

When I got back to Lewiston, I went to my sister's house. I explained to Donna what was going on, and she was very emotional about what had happened to poor Martha. With tears in her eyes, Donna embraced Martha protectively. I could tell Martha was still very scared and tentative. She didn't remember Donna and seemed to tense at Donna's embrace.

Fearfully, Martha said that she was willing to stay with Donna and Phillip until everything was straightened out. Donna and Phillip had plenty of room for her. My nephews, Ben and Robert, were a little older than Martha and seemed unfazed by the whole thing. Thanks to our dad, the house was a large, four-bedroom. Donna got Martha settled in the guest room, and she seemed completely exhausted. When Donna checked on her thirty minutes later, she was fast asleep. After everyone was settled, I called Elise to fill her in on the latest development. Donna asked if I was going to call Imogene.

"I haven't decided yet."

"Oh, Tweet, you have to call her. What about the other kids? They might be in danger."

"I was hoping you would call her."

"Me? No! Imogene barely knows me, and I obviously don't know her. How any mother can find out that their child is hurt and lying in the hospital and then deny knowing the child is absolutely beyond me. No, Tweet. You have to call her."

Defeatedly, I agreed, "Okay, okay! Tomorrow I'll try to find out what happened from Martha and go from there."

"I bet that girl hasn't slept in a real bed in a while. Where are her clothes and other personal things?"

"I took her out of the hospital with what she had when she was admitted. I guess we will have to go shopping."

The next morning, after everyone had gone about their business, Donna came downstairs, and we picked up our conversation from where we had left it the previous day.

"Listen, Tweet, Phillip is at work, and the boys are at baseball. While you talk to Martha, why don't you let me go get some things for her? Your office can take care of itself today. I'm better at picking out girl things than you anyway."

Martha came downstairs a few minutes later, and I was grateful that Donna was still around. She fixed Martha breakfast and explained that she was going to get a few things that Martha might need. She promptly gathered her things and was out the door.

After some prodding, Martha told me her sad story. She said that after she left Canada, she spent a lot of time on the streets. Luckily for her, it was summer. She walked most of the way, but Claire had given her some money, so she was able to take a bus over the border into the United States. She had been living in northern Maine since her arrival. I couldn't decipher when exactly she arrived or where she stayed. Although she didn't say it, I think she was basically living on the streets. Eventually, a man befriended her. He took her in and let her sleep on his couch. Without her going into detail, I surmised that he tried to rape her. That was when she took to the streets again and tried to kill herself.

"Tweet, I had nowhere to go. I had no more money and was

desperate. My mother didn't want me. My father is dead. I had no friends. What was I supposed to do?"

"Martha, why didn't you try to call me? They said you had my phone number in your pocket," I sympathetically asked.

"I was scared."

"I am so sorry you had to endure all of this. What happened between you and your mom?"

"My mom was mean to me. It was obvious that she didn't want me around. I just got tired of it. Being around her was almost as bad as being in the orphanage. No, actually, I think it was worse. At least at the orphanage, there was no one who was supposed to love me. If your mom doesn't love you, then no one will. That is exactly how I felt."

"Oh, Martha, I am so sorry. You are loved here. You can stay here as long as you want."

Then, realization hit me in the face. It would be a long and arduous road to recovery. Maybe not physically, but certainly mentally. Martha looked like she was about ten years old rather than fifteen. She was so frail and thin. Her skin was sallow, and her lips were blue. She was wasting away. She looked as scared of life as a new kitten without a mother.

CHAPTER 15

Martha's Journal

REFLECTIONS

L ife is sad. People are disappointing. Some say that your first memories mold the rest of your life. My first memories are of my mom and my dad fighting. I remember my mom saying that she should never have had us, and I remember my dad telling her she was right, that she wasn't cut out for motherhood. I remember my grandmother telling me that my mom was not a good mother. I remember my mom constantly telling me I needed to be more like Claire. She was right. I wanted to be more like Claire. Claire was the happy, pretty, and compliant one. She looked like my mom, who was a beautiful woman, while I looked like my dad and grandmom. Very dark features.

My dad was a handsome man, but I don't think that it translated well for a girl. My mom always told me I looked like the LeBlancs. She would say that, and in the same breath, she would call them the horrible LeBlancs. I always felt unloved. I always felt awkward. I never felt like I fit in anywhere. I really don't know what I would have done if I didn't have Claire. I don't have many good childhood memories.

I don't really remember much about living in Lewiston. The one thing I do remember is Tweet Martin. He was so nice. I wanted him to be my daddy. I actually thought it was going to happen, too. I had often fantasized about it. We were going to live in a nice house, where Mom would act like a real mom would, and Tweet would become the father I had always wished for. Then all of a sudden, we left. I was too young to understand what was happening. I knew there was a problem with my grandparents. But that was all I knew.

I don't remember the bus ride to Canada, but I remember being so hungry. I remember Mom looking scared, and this made me even more scared. When I asked what was happening, she just told me not to worry. I do remember arriving at my grandpa's house. I have very good memories of him. He was the dad I had longed for. I was so happy to finally be settled.

Grandpa played and talked with me a lot. He encouraged me to read. Grandpa was always hungry, just like me. We used to have our secret "meetings" in the kitchen—always an excuse to raid the refrigerator. This is probably the first and only time I recall my mom being genuinely happy. Or at least she seemed happy. Christmas at Grandpa's was wonderful. We didn't really get presents, but I didn't care. We sang songs, and Grandpa and Mom told us stories. I remember him reading us the Christmas story from the Bible. It is my first really good memory.

Then one day, we were pulled out of school—a school I actually liked—and put into a car with two strangers. No explanation was given. Claire and I were dropped off at a convent. The two strangers who took us told us our mom had gotten into trouble and wasn't allowed to be our mom anymore. It was all so sad and confusing. Claire was always the one who helped me. She was the one who encouraged me. She was the one who always told me things would be alright. But the night of the kidnapping (that's what Claire and I called the night we were taken to the so-called convent), Claire was just as sad, scared, and confused as I was. I remember both of us crying ourselves to sleep.

All of the memories I have of the convent are horrible. The nuns were so mean and hateful. There was no love there. I remember going to the Chapel and learning about Jesus. My grandpa had told us about Jesus before. He told us that God was a loving and forgiving God. He taught us to pray when we were sad or lonely. I remember how he would constantly remind us that even if we think we have no one else, we always have God. The nuns taught us the same things, but their actions were so different from what they taught. I questioned who this God and this Jesus really were. Were they real?

All of the "Love thy neighbor as thyself...," "...the Fruit of the Spirit... kindness, patience, love, joy, gentleness, self-control, and faithfulness;" none of these were visible in the nuns or the convent.

"For God so loved the world that He gave His only begotten Son that whosoever believes in Him will have everlasting life" (John 3:16, KJV). According to the nuns, that was the most important verse. One day, when they were teaching on this verse, I raised my hand, and the nun asked me to speak. I then told her, "If this is life, I don't want to live everlasting." In response to my comment, she hit me with a ruler while the other kids erupted in laughter.

The nuns were just mean. I have so many awful memories of that convent. Too many to list. The time when I put worms on the altar, worms that I had because I was sick, mind you, I got such a beating on my hands that I am pretty sure some of my fingers were broken. They battered my ears so badly that it gave me permanent hearing loss in my right ear. One time, I think they knew they had gone too far, so they kept me in the infirmary for over a week so my hands would heal. They didn't want anyone to know how badly they beat me. The nun who gave me the beating was soon gone. Probably transferred to another convent to torment other girls. It was during that stay in the infirmary that another nun molested me. She tried to be really nice to me, and I was happy for the positive attention. Then one day, I woke up with her hands on me. Her fingers were down in my panties. She wanted me to touch her, but I vehemently refused. She said that if I told anyone about what happened, she would make sure I regretted it. I never told a soul. When I got out of the infirmary, I promised myself I would never be alone with any of those nuns ever again.

The nuns used to say that I was the devil and Claire was the angel. They always said that they couldn't believe that we were sisters. It wasn't Claire's fault that everyone loved her and not me. Claire was perfect, and I was far from it. Claire tried her best to help me, but I was just me. I couldn't change. I tried it sometimes, but I just found it frustrating. Even when I tried, I felt that I fell short. I did not enjoy other people. They always seemed to disappoint me. Claire would always say, "How can people like you if you don't let them in?" She asked me one time if I wanted people to like me, or if I even wanted friends.

After I thought about it for a minute, I told her no. I told her I didn't think I wanted friends.

I thought if people got too close, they would just find something out about me that they wouldn't like. I decided that I didn't really like myself, so why should anyone else like me?

Claire was a very good student. She loved to learn. The nuns told me I was dumb. One day, during Bible class, I told the nun that I didn't believe in God. She slapped me so hard across the face that her hand was imprinted there for a week.

How could I believe in God? The words taught about Him did not match what I saw. If there truly was a loving God, why was all this happening? Claire told me that if I didn't believe in God, I would go to Hell. Well... I didn't care much because in my view, we were already in hell.

In the beginning, our mother wrote to us regularly. Claire and I both looked forward to the letters. It was the first thing we asked about every morning. The letters would tell us how much Mom missed us and that she was working on getting us home. She told us that she was sorry for everything and let us know that our dad's mom was behind it all. "I will continue to fight until you girls are back in my arms. I love you both so much." I believed her. The letters started getting less frequent, and then one day they just stopped altogether.

When my aunt Claudette came to see us at the convent, I couldn't believe that she was a nun. Aunt Claudette was so pretty, nice, and kind. I finally decided to confide in her some of the things that had happened. I thought that since she was a nun, she could rescue us. When I told her about the beatings and other things (I never told her about the molestation. I was too embarrassed), she told me that she would talk to the Mother Superior. The next thing I knew, she was gone. We never saw her again. So much for family. Just another disappointment.

Finally, one day, Tweet Martin showed up. He was one of the only people whom I remembered as being nice. I couldn't believe it when he said he was taking us home. I was so excited. As we got closer to home, I became less excited and more nervous. I had racing thoughts with a consistent theme of, *What if our mother didn't want us anymore?* I asked Tweet if he was going to stay with us. I still had visions of a happy family. Tweet and Mom could get married, and everything would be perfect. I was sad, confused, and disappointed when Tweet ended up leaving the day after we got home.

After Tweet left, things went downhill. My mom was aloof. She acted like Claire and I were only there to help with Diane and Ricky. For the first few weeks, she seemed kind of happy to see us. Then, I don't know what happened, but all of a sudden, we were in the way. Even Claire felt it. I tried to stay out of her way, but it honestly felt like she was always looking for a fight.

Although she did slap me once or twice, she never really beat me. It wasn't like it was in the convent. Mom's method was mental abuse. She was just downright mean. I wondered if it had anything to do with Tweet Martin. I thought maybe Mom wanted more from Tweet than he wanted.

But Claire said it was the other way around. She said she heard them fighting the night before Tweet left. Claire said Tweet wanted Mom to marry him, and she said no. This made me so angry. After I found out, I blamed her for ruining my fantasy of a perfect family.

I have always had these voices in my head that would tell me I was ugly. The voices told me I was dumb. They said I was unlovable, awkward, unworthy. It was a constant struggle just not to hear the voices. I hated myself. I woke up every day with dread. It was a struggle just to leave the bed. I really just wanted to go to sleep and not wake up. I prayed that I would just die in my sleep, but God didn't hear me... He never hears me.

When I left after our horrific fight, I had every intention of going to Lewiston and finding Tweet Martin, but then I started to get scared. The voices told me that Tweet would turn me away. They told me he only pretended to be nice because he wanted my mom. All of these thoughts went through my head. I couldn't stand another rejection. That was how I ended up on the streets of Bar Harbor. Now, here I am in Lewiston. I have no idea what will happen, but I know it has to be better here than it was with my mom.

CHAPTER 16
A New Beginning

TWEET:

The day after I got back to Lewiston with Martha, I called Imogene. She told me that Martha had made her decision, so she would have to live with it.

Exasperated, I replied, "You know, Imogene, it's funny you say that. I remember you telling me that your mother said the same thing about you. Martha is only fifteen years old. Do you not care what happens to her?"

"You know, Tweet, Martha has problems, and I just don't want to deal with them," she said, sounding tired and uninterested.

"Imogene, I really don't know who you are anymore. I'm worried about the other kids. How are they?"

"They are none of your concern, Tweet. I'm glad Martha found you. I know you will take good care of her."

"Please don't call me again," she added firmly and hung up.

I couldn't believe my ears, and when I told Donna about our conversation, she couldn't believe it either.

"Maybe I should call her."

"It won't do any good. The Imogene we knew is no longer with us."

That Friday, I was heading back to Booth Bay Harbor. I usually spent Wednesday and Thursday in Lewiston. Between traveling to Bar Harbor and back and staying to confer with Donna about the situation with Martha, this time I had been gone for over a week. I asked Martha to come with me to Booth Bay Harbor, and she agreed.

On the drive, Martha was quiet. I told her about Elise, and she asked if Elise was my girlfriend. I said, "Actually, Elise is my wife." Martha became greatly distressed and started to cry. I asked her why, and she said, "I still had hopes of you marrying my mom and being my dad. I know that's stupid, but I was really hopeful." I pulled the car over and gave her a hug.

"Martha, I am so sorry that you have been so hurt and disappointed. You are going to love Elise, I promise." As we traveled along the coastline, Martha remarked on how beautiful it was. I was hoping that this would distract her from her obvious anxiety.

"Who else will be there this weekend?" she asked as she nervously fidgeted with her fingers.

"Well, we have Elise's sons and the rest of the extended family."

"Do I really have to come with you?" she asked, staring into the space.

I explained that she didn't have to come, but I thought it would be a change for her and a chance to get to know people who were very important to me.

"Why is that important when you are just going to send me back to my mom?" Martha asked anxiously.

I hadn't expected that and didn't know what to say. After some thought, I asked Martha if she wanted to go back to her mom.

She looked at me and said, "What do you think? My mom doesn't want me, and I don't want to go back."

"It's settled then. You don't have to go back."

Immediately, I could see her body relax until she asked, "What are you going to do with me? I know Elise probably won't like me." After some thought again, I replied, "I am sure she will love you as much as I do. What am I going to do with you? I am going to keep you safe. That is what I am going to do."

Martha looked me in the eyes, stared for a moment, and then smiled happily.

I hadn't seen her smile since she came.

Martha marveled at the beauty of Booth Bay Harbor. As we got closer, she asked about the smell, "It smells different here."

"That is the smell of the ocean," I said.

Martha smiled and said, "I like it."

Elise was waiting for us at the house with a big smile and a yummy lunch.

Even now, I still get butterflies when I see Elise. My love for her and the excitement at seeing her bring me to my knees every time. And this time, I was so happy to see her and wanted to sweep her in my arms, but at the same time, I didn't want to rattle Martha. Elise knew all about Martha's situation, and she handled it with so much sensitivity, and I was so grateful. Elise made sure that she was the only one to welcome us. Giving me a kiss on the cheek, she whispered that the boys were at Ross and Daniella's house and would be home later.

Martha didn't say much during lunch, except about the food. Lots of things had changed about Martha, but not her love for food. It was one of the main things I remember. She was always hungry. I smiled at the memory, but then couldn't help but be sad as I realized that the fact that she was so thin, reinforced that she was definitely malnourished.

Martha told Elise that she was a very good cook and asked about each dish. It was a simple but very yummy lunch of clam chowder and salad with homemade ranch dressing. After lunch, Elise asked if Martha wanted to go for a walk on the beach. Martha asked if I was coming. I was honored that she asked.

Along the walk, Elise pointed out where Jana, her mother-in-law, and Margie lived and where Ross and Daniella lived. Martha didn't say much other than to let us know she had never been to a beach and didn't know how to swim. She said she was scared of the water.

It was a beautiful day. Even on beautiful days, though, the Atlantic Ocean can look menacing. The huge waves were fiercely crashing, and Martha was obviously frightened. We tried to distract her by pointing out the different shells on the beach. She seemed fascinated by the different sizes, shapes, and colors of them. She picked up a large conch shell and marveled at its size. Then asked if she could keep it. Elise told her that there was actually a sea animal living inside. She abruptly put the shell down quickly and made a face, which made all three of us laugh.

All of a sudden, Margie and Hardy came bounding over. "Hi, Elise! Hi, Tweet. What are you doing, and who is this? Can I walk with you?"

Martha was scared of Hardy and started to panic. "Please get that dog back. Please! I don't like dogs."

I immediately took hold of Hardy, who by the way, wouldn't hurt a flea. He was more likely to lick you to death.

"Don't like dogs? said Margie. Why? Why don't you like dogs?" She was certainly confused and cocked her head to one side, and the dog followed suit. Both were now staring at Martha.

"I'm scared of them. I just don't like them."

"Do you know any dogs?" asked Margie, placing her hand on her hip. "I bet you don't even know any dogs."

"Not right now, but I knew a mean dog when I was in the convent. He was a guard dog, and he would bite you if you went out of bounds." At that, she quickly lifted her pant leg and showed what looked to be a scar.

"What's a convent? What's a guard dog, and what does out of bounds mean?" Margie lowered her hand from her hip. Now she was looking curious.

"A convent is where they put girls whose parents don't want

them," said Martha sadly. "Guard dogs are mean dogs, and out of bounds means... well, I don't know how to explain it. You ask a lot of questions," she said, shaking her head.

Elise and I snickered. I thought, *Good ole Margie. Just what Martha needs.*

"Well, you will like Hardy. He is a nice doggie. "Aren't you, boy? He won't hurt you. Isn't that right, boy?" Hardy wagged his tail happily.

I asked Margie to go and get Hardy's leash so they could walk with us. The further we walked, the more questions Margie had. Since Margie was a little difficult to understand sometimes, I was amazed that Martha had no problem deciphering them. Martha was polite, and I think a little amused.

"Who are you? Where do you come from? Is Tweet your dad? How old are you? Why are you walking so funny?" Martha was trying to navigate the sand for the very first time in her life and was walking kind of funny. The question that brought everything to a halt was, "Do you have Jesus in your heart?" There was a stretch of silence after she asked that.

Then Martha replied, "I don't believe in Jesus. I don't believe in God."

This stunned Margie, and she hollered, "WHAT? What are you saying? You know you are going to hell if you say that." Elise tried to step in and save the day by changing the subject, but Margie was having none of it.

"I don't understand how you don't believe in God. Do you know the verse, John 3:16? Who do you think made you, if not God? On Sunday, you are coming to church with me, young lady."

Martha snickered and said, "I don't think so."

And Margie firmly replied, pointing her finger, "I do think so."

"Margie, I think your mom is calling you. You and Hardy had better head home. We will see you at Daniella and Ross's house for dinner," I interjected.

"Well, I don't hear her calling, but I know you're trying to get rid of me, so come on, Hardy boy. Let's go. I'll see you later, Martha. You and I are gonna be great friends."

Martha smiled, and so did I. I had no doubt that would be true. When Margie left, Martha said, "There is something different about her. How old is she?" We explained that Margie was thirty years old and had Down Syndrome. Elise said, "Margie is special. God gave her more love in her heart than the average person. Margie doesn't understand hate. She loves everyone and thinks everyone will love her too. Usually, she is right."

"I thought she was about twelve. She looks really young. No wonder she is so pushy. I guess she is my elder," she laughed.

I thought, *Yup. Margie is just what Martha needs.*

The boys were home when we got back from our walk. Elise and John had done a wonderful job with them. Isaac looked just like John, and from the pictures I had seen, Johnathan looked just like his mother. The boys were very polite to Martha. Elise had told them that Martha was a very shy and scared young girl. She didn't give them details about her past, but she let them know that it wasn't a happy one. They only knew that Martha was a friend of mine. Both of them shook Martha's hand and told her that they were happy to meet her.

Without looking either of them in the eye, her head down and eyes to the floor, she said, "Thank you." We had already decided that Isaac and Johnathan would stay at their grandmother's house. Jana and Margie had plenty of room. (Jana's husband, who was their grandfather, died before the boys were born). The thought was that Martha would be more comfortable if the boys were not there. Isaac and Johnathan readily agreed, and Margie, of course, was thrilled. Our house (what used to be John and Elise's house) wasn't big, but it had three bedrooms. The boys had always roomed together, and the third room was a guest room.

Martha would stay in there. The boys gathered their things and proceeded to their grandmom's house. Martha was pleased with the living arrangements, but transitions were tough. When it came time for us to go to Daniella and Ross's house for dinner, panic set in. Elise wisely redirected the conversation to food. As we were walking to their house, she started telling Martha what we were having for dinner, and I could tell that it calmed her down.

Daniella met us at the door, along with the glorious aroma of a home-cooked meal, and she immediately embraced Martha. Martha quickly stiffened, and I could tell she was very uncomfortable by the unfamiliar touch. After Daniella, Martha was greeted by Jana, who took the cue and didn't go in for a hug. Martha still couldn't look new people in the eye and slouched, as if trying to disappear. When she finally looked up and past the hair covering her eyes, she asked if Elise and Daniella were twins.

"We get that a lot," and they both chuckled.

Jana told Martha how happy she was to meet her. She said, "Welcome to the family." I could tell Martha was touched by this. Ross shook Martha's hand and handed her a freshly squeezed lemonade. Isaac and Johnathan went into the living room with Hardy. Margie came running out of the kitchen. She excitedly said, "Did you meet my new friend? Did you meet Martha? She is afraid of dogs and doesn't believe in God. She also can't swim and has never seen the ocean until today. Can you believe it? We have lots to teach her."

"Margie," Jana cautioned, "what did we talk about?"

"I know. I know. I can't tell her she is going to hell. Even though the Bible says she is."

While all the rest of us were looking a little mortified, Isaac and Johnathan burst out laughing.

"What's so funny?" Margie asks confusingly.

Martha just stood there. She looked shocked and embarrassed for a minute, and then I detected a little smile peeking out from the corners of her mouth.

Jana explained to Martha that Margie means well, but just doesn't know how to filter her words.

Martha laughed, "It's okay. I've been told I have the same problem. She's kinda cute and very funny. I like her."

When we sat down to dinner, it was the usual chaos, with everyone passing around the plates and talking at once. After our prayer, things got a little quieter as everyone was eating. All Martha did was talk about how good the food was—homemade biscuits with apple butter, fried chicken, coleslaw, corn on the cob with gobs of real butter, green beans in Jana's yummy oil, and fresh, juicy tomatoes dressed in just the right amount of mayonnaise, salt, and pepper. Martha ate ferociously. Every time she tried a bite of anything, she licked her lips and said that it was the best she had ever eaten.

Everything was "the best." For a small girl, she sure could put away the food. We all enjoyed watching her. I had never seen anyone enjoy a meal so much. Finally, Margie whispered, "Mom, don't you think Martha had better slow down?" Margie's whisper was more like a soft yell. To Martha, she said, "You know, there is strawberry pie for dessert. Daniella makes the best strawberry pie. The way you are going at this food, Martha, you will be too full to eat dessert." We all just snickered.

Martha looked around the table and said, "Oh... I am so sorry. But seriously, this is the best meal I've ever had."

After the last piece of chicken had been gobbled up from Martha's plate. Elise served the strawberry pie. Martha's eyes were as round as saucers as she again licked her lips and preyed upon the large piece that was laid before her.

As Martha took a bite of the pie, she couldn't help but exclaim, "Oh my God, this is incredible!" It was truly love at first taste! Margie was taken aback and exclaimed, "WHAT? We don't say that! You can't say that. That is taking the Lord's name in vain. You have to say 'oh my goodness' or 'oh goodness gracious.' Never that!"

"Okay, Margie, I'll try to remember," said Martha politely as the rest of us just snickered.

Ross had been very sick as a boy, and he and Daniella couldn't have children. They loved Isaac and Johnathan and treated them as if they were their own. I loved watching the boys interact with them. The whole family was very tight. When Elise and I married, I worried that I wouldn't fit into this tight family, but they welcomed me with open arms. I had no doubt that they would do the same for Martha.

Family dinners were always fun. Everyone was talking at once and sharing what was going on in their life, and meals always consisted of a prayer before eating. When I was growing up, we prayed at mealtime. But after Mom died, we kind of just stopped. To be honest, I stopped praying altogether. I always felt that there was a void in my life. I thought I was missing a person. After I married Elise, I remembered how good it felt to reconnect with God. I realized not only had I been missing something, I had been missing God. Elise helped me get back to having a personal relationship with Him. It was amazing how it changed my life.

When Imogene rejected me, I thought it was the end of the world. After weeks of me moping around, Donna finally told me that I needed to snap out of it. She had said, "You just wait, Tweet, God has a better plan for you. You'll see!" Boy, was she right! I couldn't help but think of all these things while I looked around at all of these wonderful people.

After lunch on Saturday, Elise and I took Martha around Booth Bay Harbor. We showed her where the school was, where our church was, the post office, the police station, the marina, and the boardwalk. Booth Bay isn't large, but it was starting to become a weekend vacation spot for some of the wealthy people living within an hour or two. This was great because it meant new restaurants, hotels, and bed and breakfast inns were popping up all the time. There was a boardwalk that stretched along the shore. Stores started emerging there, too. The sardine and lobster cannery provided many local jobs, but the main source of living was still fishing, clamming, and lobstering.

As we were driving around showing Martha the sights of Booth Bay Harbor, I started remembering how I was introduced to the area and how my life had changed since...

Before marrying Elise, I was a hunter. I didn't have much experience with fishing or really any type of water sports. I knew how to swim, but that was about all. Shortly after we married, I realized that if I was going to be part of the Pine family, I needed to learn to fish. Elise's boys loved to fish, and they helped their Uncle Ross with his business on the weekends and in the summer. I started to go along with them and fell in love with it. It could be hard work, but it was also fun.

My first catch was so exciting. Every time I caught a fish, I would get a rush. But clamming, shrimping, and lobstering were even better. It's like going on a treasure hunt every time. Lobster season is year-round, but the main time is from June to December. Part of the challenge is finding the best places to set your pots and traps. There are several different types of clams. The small soft-shelled clams with a tail are called steamers and are much sandier than the other ones, which are called littlenecks. Clamming is year-round, but the high season is from May to October. I could make a meal out of clams with warm drawn butter. The clams in Booth Bay Harbor are sweet and tasty. Just give me a beer and three or four dozen steamed clams with drawn butter, and I'm in heaven.

As we passed the marina, *insurance money* raced across my thoughts...

The insurance money for the boat finally came through, and I could tell that a weight was lifted off Ross's shoulders. For Elise, it seemed bittersweet. She was very emotional, and I think that while she was happy, she was also sad because it closed a chapter in her life that she was reluctant to end. The death of her beloved John was finally real to her. Now, though, in a way, she was able to move forward. Ross bought a brand new boat, and it was bigger than the old one. Ross was thrilled with it. Maine has a

proud history of building fishing boats, and apparently Ross's
new boat was a gem. A lot of other fishermen were envious.

The only thing that would keep Ross from the water was
really bad weather. In the winter, when the boys were in school,
he hired a deckhand named Luke. He was a super nice guy who
loved to have his summers and weekends off. It worked out well
for both of them. After what happened to John, Daniella made
Ross promise never to go out alone again. Isaac and Johnathan
worked on the boat in the summer and on weekends. Sometimes,
if the boys had something else that they wanted to do on the week-
ends, like baseball or hockey, I'd help Ross on the boat. I really
don't know how much help I was, but at least Ross had a wing
man. I couldn't help thinking about all of this as we drove.

We continued showing Martha around, and although she tried to
seem disinterested (I have learned this is her defense mechanism), she
asked many questions, especially about the school. The questions were
endless, but we listened to them all. "Does the whole town go there?
How many students does it have? Do Isaac and Johnathan go there?"

When we passed our church, she commented that it was small. She
was interested in the boardwalk and said she'd like to take a walk on it.
So, we parked the car, strolled, and watched the fishermen fish off the
pier. Martha commented that it was very relaxing. The drive around
town was encouraging. I thought maybe Martha would be okay.
Maybe she would like it here.

That night, the boys came home for dinner, and Elise made lobster
stew with homemade cornbread. Martha had three helpings. She just
couldn't get enough of it. Isaac and Johnathan went back to Jana and
Margie's to sleep.

The next morning was church. Our service started at 9:30 a.m.
Martha had told us the night before that she didn't want to go to
church. Elise and I felt that we should let her do what she wanted for
the time being. Before we left, Elise asked Martha if she was sure she

didn't want to come with us, to which she confidently responded, "No, thank you."

The church was close enough for us to walk. Ross and Daniella usually drove with Margie and Jana. The boys met us out front and walked with us.

"Martha wouldn't come?" asked Isaac.

"I figured that she wouldn't. Sounds like she had a rough time in that so-called convent in Canada," said Johnathan.

"How do you know about that?" I asked.

"She told us after dinner last night. She didn't go into detail, but she did say that she didn't believe in church and that the nuns at the convent were mean to her."

"It's such a shame," said Elise.

When we got to church, Ross and the crew were already there. Margie yells out, "Where is Martha? You have to go back and get her. She has to come to church." I saw Jana shush her, and Margie wasn't happy.

Our church was small. There were maybe twenty-five congregants on a good Sunday. Christmas and Easter, maybe thirty-five. Pastor Mark was a super nice, Godly man with a sweet little family. He grew up in Booth Bay Harbor and started the church about ten years ago. Many of the parishioners were reformed Catholics who, for whatever reason, had become disillusioned with the Catholic Church and started coming to our church. It has a small-town vibe, and everyone seems like family. At the end of each service, Pastor Mark asked for prayer requests. I knew Margie was just itching for an opportunity to talk about Martha. Pastor Mark didn't get the words out of his mouth before Margie was on her feet, waving her hands. Everyone knew and loved Margie. She almost always had something to say. Today was no different. Just a little more frantic. "We need to pray for my good friend, Martha LeBlanc. She needs to have Jesus in her heart. She says she doesn't believe in God. She is also afraid of dogs and water. Please put her on our prayer list."

When we got home, Margie was already in our living room talking to Martha. As we were walking in, I heard her say, "Next Sunday, you are coming to church."

Martha laughed and said, "I don't think so."

"Margie, it's time for you to go home. We will be over in a little while for lunch." This was our routine on Sundays. "I'm sure your mom could use your help."

Margie turns as she's leaving, and softly but sternly says to Martha, "We will talk about this later, young lady."

A little later, Martha asked, "Tweet, when are we going back to Lewiston?"

"I go back on Tuesday night and spend Wednesday and Thursday in my office there. Then I come back here Thursday evening to work in the office here on Friday, Monday, and Tuesday."

"So, we will be here until Tuesday night?"

"That's correct."

"Will I be coming back and forth with you?"

"For now, yes, but we haven't worked all that out yet. I thought maybe we could talk about it on the way back to Lewiston."

The week had begun and Monday turned out to be a very long day. After sundown, the town was settling and a stillness etched its way through the streets. Families were nestling into their normal nightly routines in their homes. Sitting on the edge of the bed, Elise asked me what the plan was.

"I would love to have Martha live with us, but with the boys, it would be a little difficult and uncomfortable. You know she is not that much younger than them. I just think that we would be taking a risk."

"What kind of risk are you talking about?"

"Come on, Tweet. You are not that naive. Boys! Girls! Besides, Martha has a lot of issues. I'm not sure I am equipped to handle them.

I have no experience with teenage girls. My friend, Leona, who has three of them, says girls are a huge handful with lots of drama. I just don't know."

"Listen, Elise, I hear what you are saying, but I think you are borrowing trouble. I don't know what the answer is, but we can't just abandon her."

"Well, of course not. I'm not suggesting that we abandon her. What about Donna and Phillip? Lewiston is a much larger city and might have better resources for helping Martha."

"Donna and Phillip have the same situation as us. Their twins, Robert and Benjamin, are teenage boys too. I don't know how they would feel about it. For now, let's pray about it, and maybe a solution will find us. But again, I can't just abandon her."

"Her mother should be shot. How can a mother do this to her child? It makes me so angry. God gave Imogene four children. It's just not fair."

Tuesday evening came, and we headed back to Lewiston. I tried to figure out Martha's disposition towards both locations. I asked her what she thought about Booth Bay Harbor, and she said she liked it. I asked her what she thought about living there. To that, she answered that she doesn't know.

Finally, after a brief silence, she said, "I feel like I am an outsider. I feel like I don't belong anywhere. I see Elise and her family, and I wish she were my mom. I wish you were my dad. I just feel such disappointment, an emptiness in my life. I miss my sisters and brother. The whole time we were in Booth Bay Harbor, I thought about them and wished they were there. I just really feel like I have no one."

"Martha, you do realize that none of this is your fault, don't you? You haven't done anything wrong. Unfortunately, you are a victim of circumstance. I'm not sure what is going on with your mom. She changed over time. I think she is a victim of circumstance, too. Let's just follow my routine for the next few weeks and see what happens. How does that sound?"

"Okay. That sounds okay, I guess." Back in Lewiston, Donna wanted to know everything. I told her about my conversation with Elise.

"Tweet, you can't blame Elise for being apprehensive. She makes some great points."

"What do you suggest?"

"I suggest you keep doing what you are doing. Take her back and forth with you for the summer. In the fall, you will have to make a decision. She has to be enrolled in school."

"I don't think I am going to have anything to do with the decision. I think Martha will have to decide. I think Elise will have to agree with it, or you will. The way I look at it, she will either be living here with you, Phillip, Ben, and Robert, or in Booth Bay Harbor with us."

"It will work out, Tweet. Remember, God is in control."

The next day, while I was working. Donna stayed home with Martha.

As the two of them folded clothes together, Donna started asking questions. "How did you like Booth Bay Harbor?"

"It was nice."

"Don't you just love Elise? She is the sweetest person... and Margie! What did you think about her?"

"Elise is very nice. Margie is so funny." Martha said, laughing, "That girl just says what she thinks. I wish when I say what I think, people would react to me like they do to her. I just get in trouble, though."

"Yes, Margie is funny. Very innocent."

"Honestly, Donna, I really liked everyone. Tweet is very lucky to have two great families."

"You're part of it now, Martha. We just have to figure out how it will all work. How about you let the adults worry about it for now? It's not that we all don't care what you want or that we don't want your opinion. It's just that it is a lot to put on you. Give it to God. Ask Him for help."

"That's never worked in the past. I don't know why I should think it would work now."

"Well, just think about it. For now, come on into the kitchen. We can make Tweet lunch and take it to him at his office."

As Martha strolled into my office, she took in a huge breath. It looked like she was going to pass out. In a panic, she whispered, "I've been here before. I have a vague memory of this place."

"Yes, Martha. You were here when you lived in Lewiston. Before you moved to Canada. I hope it is not a bad memory."

"No. It's not bad. It's just weird. You know how people say... umm, what do they call it?"

"Deja vu?"

"Yes, that's it. I feel like I am looking down at myself and seeing a younger me. Super weird." She shrugged.

"Is it a good feeling or a bad feeling?"

"I don't know. It's just weird."

"Well, I can tell you this, you were a cute little girl. I have very fond memories of you and your family."

"I wish I did," she sadly replied, hanging her head low.

CHAPTER 17

Family Ties

Over the next few weeks, life moved along as usual. Elise was still unsure of what to do. Then one weekend, out of the blue, Elise excitedly tells me she has a plan.

"Jana and I have talked. Jana wants Martha to live with her and Margie."

"Wow. How did that come about?"

Crying, Elise went on to tell me that Jana had reminded her of how she had felt and looked when she first came to Booth Bay Harbor and had met John.

"Jana said Martha reminded her of me. She said that when I first got here, I was so lost. I couldn't look anyone in the eye. I had no self-confidence. I had turned away from God. All of the things we are seeing in Martha. I broke down and realized that Jana was right. Martha was acting exactly how I did. Martha is broken, and I know the Pine family can help her just like they did me. Jana was instrumental in my comeback. I know she will be great with Martha."

I wrapped my arms around Elise. Although I already knew all about the past, it hurt my heart to hear. She was a broken woman back then. I could not even begin to know the pain she had been through. I heard many stories over the last few years about the Pine family and how they adopted Elise as their own. The plan for Martha to live at Jana's made perfect sense. Why hadn't I thought of it?

"Tweet, there is no one better for Martha than Jana. Of course, Margie is a bonus," Elise smiled in between her tears.

Within a few weeks, Martha and Jana had become very close. She spent a lot of time over at Jana's place. Consequently, she and Margie became close. After the second week of traveling back and forth with me to and from Lewiston, Martha started staying at Jana's house full-time so that Isaac and Johnathan could come home. I thought the whole arrangement was brilliant.

Martha was no longer traveling back and forth with me. She preferred to stay in Booth Bay Harbor. She seemed more and more comfortable every day. Now we just had to find out what Martha thought about living with Jana.

After discussing it, we decided that I should be the one to broach the subject with Martha. That was the plan anyway. But before I could get to it, Martha asked me if she could talk to me.

"Tweet, I hope this doesn't hurt your feelings, but is it okay if I live with Jana and Margie? I love you and Elise, and I love Donna and Phillip, but I really want to live at Jana's." What a relief that was.

It was settled. Our quiet, organized, and wonderful life could get back to normal with the wonderful addition of Martha LeBlanc. No more complications. Martha settled in permanently, and we began making plans to enroll her in school. She tested very well and was slated to be a junior in September.

Several weeks later, on a Friday morning, while I was working in my office in Booth Bay Harbor, Donna called and told me I needed to come back to Lewiston right away. She sounded pretty frantic.

"What's going on, Donna?"

"You just need to come back. Martha's sisters and brother are here."

I couldn't believe it. I immediately hopped in the car and headed to Lewiston. I could only imagine what had precipitated this. All kinds of things were going through my mind. *What on earth could have happened? How did they get to Lewiston? Where was Imogene?* I had no idea what I was coming back to. What a roller coaster!

As I walked into Donna's living room, I saw Claire, Diane, and Ricky already seated together. I had given myself a pep talk during the ride over, reminding myself how to approach this situation. I knew it was best to let them do the talking and take the lead. I was more familiar with Claire than I was with Diane and Ricky, and I recognized her as a very sharp young lady. As I took a moment to gather my thoughts, I tried to recall their ages. I was fairly certain that Claire was sixteen, while Diane and Ricky were probably around thirteen and twelve, respectively.

"My goodness, Claire. How did you all get here?"

"I'm sorry, Tweet, but we didn't have anywhere else to go. It's a long story."

"Don't be sorry. Are you all okay? Are you hungry?"

"No, Donna fed us already. Thank you," Claire said.

"Okay, so tell me what's going on."

Claire looked apprehensive and gave a side glance at Diane and Ricky that let me know she preferred to tell me without them there. So, I told her that I needed to take care of a few things at my office and asked if she would accompany me there. Donna took Diane and Ricky upstairs to see the rooms they would be staying in. The twins, Benjamin and Robert, just gave me a raised eyebrow. Phillip was at work.

Claire revealed that after Martha left, Imogene became stranger and stranger. She was angry all the time and was especially mean to Ricky.

Claire tells of the events, "One day, I had had enough of it. Mom and I got into a huge fight. I told her she was a terrible mother. I told her she needed mental help. Poor Ricky did nothing to cause Mom's wrath, other than look like our dad. I honestly think Mom was having a breakdown. That night we went to bed as usual. When we woke up, Mom was gone. She left a letter and some money on the dining table." Claire handed me a piece of paper with my name and address on it. At the bottom, it said "I'm sorry. Tweet Martin will help you." A few days later, we boarded the bus for Lewiston.

So, here we go again. Imogene was a piece of work. Claire said it took them three days by bus from Montreal. The bus stopped in every town from there to Lewiston. Imogene had given them enough cash to make the trip and to eat. At least she did that. They actually had some money left over when they arrived.

We settled the kids in at Donna and Phillip's. Ricky stayed in the twins' room. Claire and Diane took the guest room, while I slept on the couch. After they all went to bed. Donna, Phillip, and I went outside and had a long talk. Phillip told me that I was crazy to keep getting involved with Imogene and her children.

"You can't keep doing this, Tweet."

"Doing what? I'm not doing anything. I'm trying to mind my own business and live a good and decent life. Do you have any suggestions on what I am supposed to do? Do you want me to call and have them declared orphans?"

"They have a mother," Phillip hissed. "I want you to make her own up to her responsibilities."

"How? Ship them back? Phillip, I'm sorry. I have no idea how all this has happened, but I can't turn them away. I'm sorry that you and Donna have been dragged into it."

At this point, it was getting a little heated between Phillip and I, so Donna stepped in. "Listen, you two, stop! Just stop! Tweet is right, we can't turn them away. It sounds like Imogene is not equipped mentally to deal with her children right now. Claire said she just up and left. We don't even know where she is."

"My bet is that she is right back home. She waited for the kids to go and came right back to her cozy little nest," said Phillip. "She is playing you, Tweet."

At this point, Donna interjects, "Let's go to bed and talk about it tomorrow."

As you can imagine, I did not sleep a wink. I had no idea what I was going to do. It was obvious that Phillip was not on board with any of the kids staying with them. I needed to get back to Booth Bay. I just didn't know what to do. I prayed for wisdom all night long.

The next morning, I still didn't have a plan. When I had left home, I told Elise that there was some sort of emergency. I didn't tell her what. She called to find out what was going on. When I told her, she was speechless. I told her that I would be on my way back home later that day with all three of the LeBlanc kids in tow.

"You might want to give Martha a heads up for me," I added.

"Oh, my goodness. I think I'd better give everyone a heads-up, I guess. You are a good man, Tweet Martin. We will figure it out. I'll see you in a few hours."

I just loved that woman.

Donna told me that she would help in any way she could. "Don't mind Phillip. He just gets a little upset when he thinks there is an injustice. It's not you he is mad at. He thinks Imogene should be in jail."

"Thanks, Donna. I love you. I will keep you posted."

The ride to Booth Bay Harbor was quiet. I knew that the kids were frightened. That was understandable. Ricky got excited when we drove along the coast. They, like Martha, had never seen the ocean. "Wow, look at the waves. This is so cool. Do you live by the ocean?" asked Diane.

They all looked pretty happy when I told them, "Yes, we actually do live near the ocean." Claire was very concerned about Martha and wanted assurances (which I gave her) that she was okay.

We finally pulled up to the front of the house. I wasn't sure what to expect. I sat there for a moment in the car... stumped. Just then, Martha came running out. She was so happy to see her sisters and brother that tears welled up in her eyes. Claire was crying too. It was at that point that I knew we would somehow make it work so the kids could all stay. There was so much crying, laughing, and chattering. I had no idea what was being said. I just stood back and watched, and had an assurance in my heart that we could make it work.

Elise came out and hugged me. "I love you, Tweet Martin."

A few minutes later, Jana, Margie, and Hardy came running over. "Is this them? Margie asked, "Is this Martha's brother and sisters? Wow, that's a lot of sisters and brothers. What on earth are we going to do with all of them?" Elise and I just snickered. *Good ole Margie.*

Isaac and Johnathan came out to meet everyone, also. Isaac gave me a punch in the arm and quietly said, "Are you gonna keep doing this?" he laughed. I just shook my head. The introductions were made, and we were all invited to have dinner together at Daniella and Ross's house. Elise said they had the sleeping arrangements all figured out. For now, Claire was to stay with Martha at Jana's. Diane and Ricky would stay with us. Ricky could sleep with the boys, and Diane could have the guest room.

Much needed to be discussed, but for now, this seemed like a good plan. Well, it was the only plan. Margie had tons of questions for everyone. She always seemed to lighten the mood. We got everyone settled in, and we all headed over to Ross and Daniella's.

Seeing Martha and Claire and the way they were with each other was heartwarming. They obviously missed and loved each other very much. Martha had tons of questions for Claire and vice versa. They kept chattering nonstop. Ricky and Diane were quieter, but Margie was trying to engage them. She just kept saying I can't believe that you guys are all Martha's sisters and her brother. She made sure to tell them, "You know I am Martha's best friend."

When it was time to eat, Margie announced that she would be praying. "Dear Lord, thank you for bringing all of these people together. Thank you for Martha, Claire, Diane, and Ricky. I pray that you bless them and keep them safe. If they don't know You yet, I pray they will find You, so they don't all go to hell. Help me to be a blessing to them. Now I pray that you bless our food and our bodies. Thank you for Mom, Elise, Daniella, and the hands that prepared the meal. Amen! Now you can dig in."

As Margie was praying, I couldn't help but peek at the kids. For the most part, they all kept their heads bowed and eyes closed. Smiles appeared on their faces, and they all looked at each other when Margie finished.

Dinner, as always, was wonderful. The LeBlanc kids all ate abundantly. Like Martha, they were very complimentary. Jana commented that it was a pleasure to cook for such appreciative eaters. Claire was asking a lot of questions about Booth Bay Harbor.

"This looks like such a beautiful area. I know that in front of the house is the Gulf of Maine, part of the Atlantic Ocean. When we were driving, I noticed lots of other waterways. What are they?"

"Booth Bay Harbor is surrounded by water. We have Penobscot Bay and the Sheepscot River, which both flow into the Gulf. We also have lots of little coves like Grimes Cove. You are right, Claire. It is a very picturesque area. Obviously, you have to love the water to live here. Almost everyone here makes a living working with boats, water, or fish in some way, shape, or form. I've lived here my whole life and can't imagine living anywhere else." Jana responded by giving a summary of what life in Booth Bay felt like. Watching and listening to Jana talk about her home reinforced what I already knew. Jana loved her home and her family.

I already made arrangements to stay in Booth Bay for the next two weeks. I basically just closed my office in Lewiston. Anyone who really needed me knew they could reach me through Donna. Several nights after the kids arrived, Elise asked me what we were going to do about school. We had already enrolled Martha in the Booth Bay Harbor School. She only had two more years before she graduated. Even though Johnathan was a year older than Martha, he would be in the same school year.

Isaac graduated the previous year, and he would be working with Ross full-time until he decided what he wanted to do. He really wanted to play hockey. Ross told him he could have weekends off so he could play on the Booth Bay recreation team. The National Hockey League was founded in Montreal in 1917 and initially included three Canadian teams. In 1924, the first U.S.A. team, the Boston Bruins, joined the league. In 1926, Chicago, Detroit, and New York added teams to the league. Hockey was starting to take off in the United States, but getting selected for a team was highly competitive. Isaac was good, but so were many other guys. He was playing on the local team, trying to hone his skills for an eventual major league tryout.

Claire would be entering school as a senior, and Martha would be a junior. Diane would be in the ninth grade, and Ricky in the eighth. School was starting in less than six weeks, and there was a lot to think about.

Ricky loved going out on the boat with Ross. He wanted to go every day. The early hours didn't bother him. He was up and ready before anyone else. When he got home, he would talk nonstop about how his day went. Diane enjoyed hanging out with Margie and Hardy. They spent hours on the beach. It was really a great summer. The only one who seemed a little lost was Claire. She liked the beach and would walk for hours collecting seashells, but otherwise she seemed lonely and bored.

Martha told me that Claire was very involved in school when they were in Canada. She said even at the convent, Claire got involved in everything available, which wasn't much. Apparently, Claire always had a bunch of friends. Here, she didn't have that. Elise and Daniella

tried their best to keep Claire busy. She liked to cook, so she helped out
a lot in the kitchen. But Claire's main passion was reading and writing.
I was starting to worry that she was spending too much time alone in
her room. One week, when I was going back to Lewiston for my
regular work week, Claire asked if she could come with me, which I
agreed to. On the way, I tried to engage her in a conversation. "How are
you doing, Claire? Are you happy? Are you settling in fine?"

"You know, Tweet, it is so different from what I'm used to. I'll be
okay, though."

That was it. She didn't say anything else during the trip. Claire
went back and forth to Lewiston with me for the next few weeks.
During our time in Lewiston, Donna spent a lot of time with Claire
and showed her around Lewiston. She took her shopping. They went
out to lunch after they both worked for me in the office in the
mornings.

Claire was very interested in the schools. Lewiston was much
bigger than Booth Bay. Claire liked the big city and definitely preferred
the larger schools that they had in Lewiston.

Benjamin and Robert were a year older than Claire. Donna had
kept them home an extra year when they were slated to start first grade,
so they would also be seniors this year. Claire got along well with them.
One night, they were going to the movies with a group of their friends
and invited Claire to come. She jumped at the chance. While they were
gone, Donna said to me, "See? Tweet, I told you everything would
work out."

"Yes, I think it is working out. Jana said she is happy to have Claire
stay with her. Daniella has approached Elise with the proposal for
Ricky and Diane to come and live with her and Ross. Ricky would
definitely be up for that. But I'm not sure about Diane. She seems to
like it with us."

"Tweet, sometimes I think you are oblivious to what is going on
around you. Can't you see that Claire wants to stay in Lewiston? Men!
I swear you have no clue."

"What are you talking about? Has Claire told you she wants to stay here?"

"Not in so many words, but it is as clear as the nose on your face. Booth Bay Harbor is too small for Claire. She likes the city. The school is too small, and there is nothing else for her in Booth Bay Harbor."

"Well, I don't think she will want to leave her brother and sisters. Anyway, Phillip made it clear that he didn't want to get involved in this mess."

"Don't worry about Phillip. He will do what I want. I would love to have Claire here. She is a wonderful young lady. I still don't understand Imogene, though. How could she just turn her back on these kids? Unbelievably, all of them seem to have turned out great."

"What about Benjamin and Robert?"

"What about them? I don't see a problem."

"Alright, Donna! I'll let you handle it. See what Claire says."

As Donna predicted, Claire loved the idea. She was concerned about her brother and sisters, especially Martha, but she knew that they would be well taken care of. The next week, when I went back to Lewiston, Claire remained there and didn't return to Booth Bay Harbor with me. She told me and Elise that she wanted to go to college. She said she just didn't think that the school in Booth Bay Harbor would allow her that opportunity. It was obvious that Claire was smart. Elise and I told her she has our complete support.

Once the final decision had been made, Martha felt a deep sadness over the loss of her sister once more, yet she couldn't help but feel happy for Claire. They made a pact that once a month, either Martha would go to Lewiston or Claire would come to Booth Bay Harbor. Donna immediately enrolled Claire in Lewiston High School. She would start in the fall. Donna said that Phillip actually wasn't surprised at the arrangement and readily agreed.

The summer was a beautiful one. All of the LeBlanc kids seemed to be thriving. Ricky just couldn't get enough of being on the water. He told Ross that he wasn't "... gonna go back to school."

"I just want to work with you. I don't need school. I want to be a lobsterman like you."

"Hahaha...," Ross laughed. "While I understand your love for lobstering, you have to keep going to school until you are at least sixteen years old."

"Why? I don't understand why," said Ricky.

Ross explained that it was the law. "If you don't go to school, the State of Maine could fine us twenty dollars or maybe put us in jail. They could also take you and place you in an institution. That was the law since the 1930s."

"So, you are telling me I have to go to school for more than four more years."

"Yep, unless the law changes," said Ross.

"That's stupid," said Ricky incredulously.

By the end of the summer, Ricky had practically moved in with Ross and Daniella, and all of the kids were enrolled in the Booth Bay school. Ricky, noticing how the family had grown, laughingly says, "Man, that school is small. I think our family will take up the whole place."

Elise and I couldn't get over the change in Martha. After her brother and sister got here, they started attending church with us. Martha still bucked the idea, but while we were at church every Sunday, she prepared Jana's house for the Sunday meal. Elise tried a few times to bring up the subject and was rebuked by Martha. She just wasn't ready. One Sunday when Jana and Margie came home from church early, they found Martha in the kitchen singing with gusto. She was singing an old favorite hymn titled "Just a Closer Walk with Thee."

> *"Just a closer walk with Thee,*
> *Grant it Jesus is my plea,*
> *Daily walking close to thee,*
> *Let it be, dear Lord, let it be.*
> *I am weak but Thou art strong;*

Jesus, keep me from all wrong;
I'll be satisfied as long,
As I walk, let me walk close to thee."

As they approached, Margie's eyes bulged in surprise. "Listen, mama. Do you hear what Martha is singing?" She wasn't just singing. She was singing beautifully. Jana had to hold Margie back. She knew that this was an opportunity that needed to be maneuvered very carefully.

"Margie," said Jana, "don't say anything about this to Martha right now. Let me handle it, please."

"But Mama, Martha can join the choir. She sings beautifully."

"I know, but just let me handle it, Margie. Please!" They let Martha finish the song and then entered the house. Everything was ready for Sunday lunch. Jana had started the roast in the oven before church. It smelled wonderful. Martha had prepared mashed potatoes, peas, and coleslaw. The table was set and ready.

"Thank you, Martha, for taking care of everything. It all looks wonderful," Jana said. As she was speaking, she heard Margie humming "Just a Closer Walk with Thee." *Good ole Margie.* Martha looked at Margie and shook her head, and Jana couldn't help but smile.

CHAPTER 18
Secrets and Wonders

MARTHA:

When my brother and sisters showed up at Elise and Tweet's house, I couldn't believe it. I was so happy. So much had happened since I had last seen them in Canada. Looking back in my journal, I couldn't believe how many life-changing experiences I had gone through. Even more, I couldn't believe I had survived it all. My horrific experience in Bar Harbor (which I was trying to forget), going to Lewiston with Tweet and meeting his sister and her family there; moving to Booth Bay Harbor, and gaining a new, wonderful family there. Looking back, I was so grateful. I had seen and done things I could have never imagined before (swimming in the ocean, fishing, and lobstering). Finally, I got to see my sisters and my brother, Ricky. I had missed them and had worried about them so much.

After lots of hugs, kisses, and tears, Claire explained to me how and why they had traveled from Canada to Lewiston. I know it sounds dumb, but I was worried about our mom. I kept asking Claire over and over, "How could she just disappear?"

Claire wanted to know all about what happened with me after I left them. I told her, and she wept.

"I am so sorry, Martha. I remember in the convent we said that no matter what, we would always have each other. I'm sorry I let you down." I reassured Claire that I loved her and that she didn't let me down. Claire is the only person I ever told about the man in Bar Harbor who tried to rape me. I had told Tweet about him, but I didn't give him any details.

As the weeks went on, I could tell that Claire wasn't happy in Booth Bay Harbor. She loved the people, but she had nothing to do. She spent a lot of time in our room, reading and writing in her journal. One day, she asked if I would be okay with her going to Lewiston with Tweet the next time he went. Of course, I was okay with it. Claire went back and forth for the next several weeks. She always came back happy and brimming with information.

Finally, she very reluctantly asked me if I wouldn't mind if she moved to Lewiston and lived with Donna and Phillip. I kind of knew this was coming, but I was still sad. Claire, my wonderful sister, was always so positive. The one I always went to for advice and support was no longer going to be there. It wasn't like I hadn't already experienced that after I left Canada, but it did make me sad. Despite all that, I knew that Claire wasn't happy, and I wanted her to be happy. She deserved happiness as much, if not more than I did.

"Look, Claire, you have always been there for me. Now that you are here, I want you to stay here. But I know that you can't. I will miss you terribly, but you need to do what is right for you. It has been obvious that you are not happy in Booth Bay Harbor. It has made me sad to see you so unhappy.

Tweet and Elise are great. Truthfully, the whole family is wonderful. I am happier than I have ever been. I love it here, but it is not for everyone. I need you to know that I love you. You will always be my big sister. Booth Bay Harbor and Lewiston are not that far apart. It's time for us both to grow up."We both burst into tears. Claire promised she would always come if I needed her. The next week, she left with Tweet for good.

After that, I knew I had to pull myself together. I still had many demons in my head. As happy as I was being with Tweet and all of Elise's family in Booth Bay Harbor, my thoughts were still of bad times. I still harbored so much resentment towards my mom. I had awful nightmares of the days in the convent and on the streets in Bar Harbor. One day, Margie asked me why I cried so much in my sleep. I couldn't tell her. Finally, she said, "You need to talk to Elise. She used to have nightmares and cried in her sleep, too."

I didn't know much about the history between Elise and Tweet. I was unaware of how they first crossed paths or any details about Elise's other husband, except that he was Ross's brother, who tragically died in a boating accident. I didn't even know that Isaac and Johnathan were not Elise's biological children.

"Elise was a lot like you when she came here," Margie said. I became curious, so I began asking Margie questions because I really didn't know how to approach Elise about it. Margie had a wealth of information, as usual. The problem was that I didn't know how much of it was true and how much wasn't. Margie tended to embellish things. She never intentionally lied, but sometimes she just got the information wrong. Also, when she didn't know the answer to some-thing, she would make something up in her head. For her, it was true, though. I just loved her and her innocence. Finally, one day, she said, "Martha, to be honest. I don't know anything. Ask Elise." I knew at that point she was tired of answering my questions.

Diane and I decided to make a trip to Lewiston with Tweet one week to shop for school clothes. Claire was already waiting for us when we got there. She was so excited to see me and Diane. The three of us camped out in her room and got caught up on what was going on with each other. Diane fell asleep pretty quickly. This gave Claire and me an opportunity to talk. We had lots of things to share with each other.

At one point during the conversation, Claire asked, "Did you know that Elise was married to our father?"

"John Pine? He was not our father."

"No," said Claire. "Elise was married to OUR DAD before she married John Pine. She was married to him before Mom was." Claire went on to tell me that Elise had fled our dad and his family, just like our Mom had. I just couldn't wrap my mind around any of it.

"So, does Mom know Elise?"

"No. Elise met Tweet when he was helping Mom in the custody battle between her and our grandparents. Elise was going to testify in court so that Dad's mom couldn't take us away. She never got the chance, though, because mom fled to Canada before the case even began. She never met Mom. Only Tweet."

"This is unbelievable."

"Yeah! I was pretty shocked too."

When Diane and I were leaving to go back to Booth Bay Harbor, all three of us wept. We were going to miss Claire so much and had such a fun time with her in Lewiston. I knew that Claire was going to miss us, too. But I also knew that she had already made a life with Donna and her family. We met some of Claire's friends and knew that she already had a crowd. Benjamin and Robert were great about including her in their group. I was a little envious, but I knew that even if I moved to Lewiston, I wouldn't have the same life as Claire. We were just so different. Claire loved to be with people. I did not.

On the way home, I wanted to talk to Tweet about what Claire had told me, but I didn't want to do it in front of Diane. The only thing I said was, "Donna told Claire how you and Elise met. That's a very interesting story." When we got back to Booth Bay Harbor, Tweet said, "Let's find a good time for you, me, and Elise to sit down and have a talk, okay?"

The next day, when Diane was off playing with Margie and Hardy, Tweet and Elise came over and asked me to walk on the beach with them. I could tell that they were both nervous and uncomfortable. They didn't know what to say. Finally, Tweet broke the silence, "What exactly did Claire tell you?"

This started a torrent of information that totally astounded me. They told me all about the LeBlancs and how mean they were to Elise. I wasn't too surprised by this, but I was surprised to learn how mean my father was. I learned that he was a monster. Mom didn't share a lot of details about her life with him. She only talked about my dad's parents and how awful they were to her. She never really talked about our dad. I also learned that Isaac and Johnathan were not Elise's biological children. Elise never treated the boys in any way that led me to believe that she was not their real mother. I felt betrayed in a way. I didn't understand why Claire found out about all of this before me.

"Why am I just finding out about all this now? I don't understand why you hid this from me," I said as my eyes were burning with tears.

"It's not that we hid it from you. We just didn't want to add any more confusion or heartache. You have been through a lot. We were planning on telling you everything when we felt you would be ready to hear it," replied Elise.

"I wish you had told me. I feel like this is just another betrayal."

"We are so sorry, Martha. We didn't mean to hurt you. We were trying to protect you," said Elise.

"I need some time alone to process all of this, excuse me," I said as I ran back to the house.

I couldn't figure out what part of the story upset me the most. Was it that my father was some kind of a monster, or was it the fact that I felt that Tweet and Elise had been lying to me all this time? Once again, I felt unworthy all over again. I felt like no one could trust me with the truth. Disappointment and people seemed to go hand in hand. I couldn't think of many people in my life, other than Claire, who had not disappointed me.

At mid-afternoon, Margie came and knocked on my door. I told her that I couldn't talk to her at the moment.

"Why Martha?" she asked.

"I just don't feel like talking at the moment."

"Okay, let me know when I can come in."

Two hours later, I opened my door, and there was Margie sitting on the floor outside my room.

"What are you doing here?" I asked.

"I'm waiting to come in," she said.

"Have you been out here waiting this whole time?"

"Well, not the whole time. I had to use the bathroom once."

I couldn't help but to snicker at that as I invited her in. Margie sat down on the bed and asked if I had been crying and why. I told her I hadn't been crying, but yes, I was upset.

"Why?" she asked.

"Everyone has been lying to me."

"Lying? Who? Who is lying? That's a sin, you know. Jesus said you shouldn't lie." I couldn't explain it all to Margie. Her innocent spirit would never understand my tormented one. I just told her that I was finding out a lot of information that I didn't know. I told her that Tweet and Elise had left me out of a lot of information about my family. After which, I asked her to leave as I would like to be alone. Hanging her head, Margie dejectedly left the room.

Later that day, Jana came up to get me for dinner. I was starving, but I didn't want to go downstairs.

"I will bring you a plate, Martha," Jana said.

When she came back a little later, she asked if it was okay if she sat on my bed while I ate. I nodded yes, and we began to talk.

"Martha, one thing I have learned over the years is that you have choices in everything. You can choose happiness or sorrow. You can choose forgiveness or spite. You can choose to live in the past or choose to move on to the future. I've also learned that people will always disappoint you. Not because they try to, but because they are human. We as humans are not perfect. Everyone makes mistakes. The only perfect one is God."

Jana went on to tell me about Elise. "When we first met Elise, she was angry. She had just come through a terrible time. I thought she would never get over it. Margie and I were both so worried about her. Then one day, she seemed to just snap out of it. I didn't know what had happened, but then Elise told me that one Sunday at church, the pastor spoke about forgiveness. The pastor reminded all of us of how much Jesus had suffered for our sins. If Jesus went through all of that, then it was our duty to forgive others as Jesus forgave us. After that, Elise seemed to be a new person." Jana paused to see if I had something to say. When she noticed I was speechless, she continued.

"I know that you had a terrible time at that convent, and because of that, and other disappointments in your life, you have turned your back on God. I also know that God will never turn His back on you. I find that when I have no one to talk to, God is always there for me and He listens to me."

She went ahead to wrap me in her arms, kissed me on my forehead, and said, "Elise and Tweet love you. Anything that they did or didn't do is because they love you. You might want to cut them some slack," she concluded as she stood up to leave the room. For the rest of that night, I stayed in my room, brooding, and for the first time in a long time, I prayed to God. In tears, I asked Him for help. This was also the first time in a long time that I cried, really cried.

The next morning, I walked over to Tweet and Elise's house. Tweet wasn't home, but Elise met me at the door. She looked at me and burst into tears. "I am so sorry I hurt you, Martha. It was never my intent. Can you ever forgive me?"

In tears, I apologized to Elise too. I told her that I knew that she was just trying to protect me.

"From now on, I am going to choose to live in today. I am not going to think about the past. You, Tweet, and the whole Pine family have been so good to me. Whatever you have done, I know you did it out of love. Thank you for being so patient with me."

Eventually, Elise told me everything that happened with my father and his family. It made me sad, but I was happy to know the truth. All of it made me love and respect Elise, Tweet, and the Pine family even more.

School started in September. I was nervous. Once again, I would have to "make friends." Ugh! I felt it was all an awful dance. Small talk and fake smiles. I hated it. Everyone was pretty interested in me, "the new girl."

Even though I felt I had turned a corner in my life, I was still Martha. Friendships would always be hard. Having Johnathan, Diane, and Ricky at school helped a whole lot.

Isaac was busy working for Ross and getting ready for hockey season, which was from October to April. He and Johnathan were very nice boys. The girls at school really liked Johnny, as they called him. He was cute, smart, and funny. Isaac was more reserved. Most of his friends were from his hockey team. I told him that when he started this winter, I wanted to come and watch. I didn't know much about hockey and had never seen a game, but it sounded very fun and interesting. Johnathan played baseball and basketball. Our school really didn't have any sports teams, but there were recreational leagues for baseball, basketball, and hockey.

The family that owned the cannery had four sons. They donated money to have a large recreation facility built on the property that they owned. They built a skate rink, a basketball court, and a baseball field. All of these sports had different seasons. Baseball in the summer, basketball in the fall, and hockey in the winter. The winters in Maine are long. Generally, the cold started in mid-October and lasted through to the end of March. Sometimes, it even started in late September and lasted until the end of April. The Pine and Martin families were busy with one sport or another all the time.

Booth Bay Harbor School had a choir, and I always loved to sing, so I decided to join. Diane did too. Every day after school, we had choir practice. The teacher in charge of it was a woman named Mrs. Lolly, and she was really nice. She was a small, petite woman who seemed to be about Elise's age. She took an interest in me and told me that I had a lovely voice. There were only eight of us in the choir, with only two of those being boys. We were of all ages, but I think Diane was the youngest. We were practicing for a holiday program to be held between Thanksgiving and Christmas. After practice one day, not long after I signed up, Mrs. Lolly approached me about singing a solo. She wanted me to sing "Oh, Holy Night."

"Martha, you have a beautiful voice. Would you please think about singing "Oh, Holy Night" as a solo for our program? I think you would do a wonderful job." I was taken aback. Me? A soloist. I didn't think I could do that. It terrified me. A week later, she asked me if I had decided yet.

"Mrs. Lolly, you are very nice to think of me, but singing by myself in front of people terrifies me. I just really don't think I can do it."

"Why? Why does that terrify you?"

"I don't really know. It just does."

"How about we do this," said Mrs. Lolly as she laid out the plan. "You can sing just for me for a few weeks, and then we will see how you feel. Don't say no yet. If, after you practice with me, you still don't want to do it, then you certainly don't have to. How does that sound?"

The next several weeks after the regular rehearsals, I practiced with just Mrs. Lolly. Each time, I felt more and more confident. Finally, I agreed to do it. At the next practice, Mrs. Lolly announced that I would be singing a solo for "Oh, Holy Night."

"Martha, why don't you come on up here and let's hear it?" I got up in front of everyone. The music began, and I felt really nervous until I started singing. Initially, my voice was weak, but as the song progressed, I sang louder and louder. When I finished, all of my choir mates applauded. It felt so good. On the way home, Diane just kept going on and on about how good it was. And for the first time in my life, I was proud of myself.

As it moved into hockey season, I started going to the rink with Isaac on Saturdays. I loved watching the boys practice and play. Hockey was so exciting. I understood why Isaac loved it so much. All the guys were nice to me. The coach asked if I would like to keep the "stats." I didn't know what that meant, but I told him I was willing if he would show me what to do. I soon learned that it involved noting down goals scored, who scored them, saves made, and shots on goal. Since I was already captivated by the game and hung on every moment, I knew I could manage this task easily.

While I was keeping the stats, I realized how good Isaac was. He played center, and he, by far, had the most goals and the most shots on the goal. I couldn't believe how fast and maneuverable he was on the ice. He could turn on a dime.

The team was scheduled to travel to Lewiston to play the Lewiston hockey team. We didn't have a "team" bus or anything. Our team played on a shoestring budget. Everyone had to find their own trans-portation. Tweet, of course, would take Isaac and a few other team members. I told Elise I would love to go, and she assured me that she would see to that.

Despite our promise to each other, this was the first time Claire and I would see each other since school started. I couldn't wait to see her, but also couldn't wait to see a "real" hockey game, so with great anticipation, I loaded up with the boys and went to the game.

The Lewiston rink, like everything else in Lewiston, was bigger and better than the one in Booth Bay Harbor. The boys had all played there before, during other seasons. It was a first for me, though, and I was in awe. Claire, Donna, Benjamin, and Robert were all at the arena. Tweet looked at Donna with a sad face and expressed his regret that Phillip couldn't be there. "He would have loved this macho hockey stuff so much," he laughed. As always, I was going to keep the stats.

Isaac had told me that the Lewiston team was really good. As soon as they started playing, I saw what he meant. Within the first period, the Lewiston team got two goals. Isaac was playing well and had a few shots on goal. It seemed like Lewiston had Isaac double-teamed.

Hockey games are played over three periods, each lasting twenty minutes, with two intermissions that typically range from fifteen to eighteen minutes. After the first period, the coach gathered all the players for a pep talk.

"You guys have to be more aggressive. They are running all over you. Stop acting like you are gonna hurt their feelings if you steal the puck. They are not your friends. They don't want to be your friends. We are here to win. Now, get out there and win!" he said as he slapped their helmets.

He glanced around as though in search of someone, "Isaac, where are you? You look like you're at a dance or something. Stop playing like a girl." I was offended for Isaac. I couldn't believe that the coach had singled him out and would talk to him that way. I had never heard him talk to any of the players like that before. I thought it was mean. At the time, no one but the coach knew that there were two scouts in the bleachers. One from Boston and one from Chicago. Scouts are people who recruit for the Major Hockey League. The coach was well aware of Isaac's talent. He knew that if anyone on his team had a chance at the majors, it was Isaac.

The coach told us later that during the first quarter, he had signaled to the scouts that Isaac was the one to watch. He went on to say that he didn't want to tell Isaac because he thought it would make him too nervous. After that first period, our team came out to win. The second period saw two goals by us. Both were scored by Isaac. The game was all tied up. Tweet and all the rest of the family were cheering. I was so proud. Isaac looked like a pro. During the second intermission, the coach told the team not to let up.

"Don't think just because you got two goals, you're gonna win. We have a tied game right now. They have just as good a chance of getting the next goal as we do. Lewiston is a great team... but we are better. Isaac, I need you to play like your life depends on it. Now, get out there and win." I still didn't understand why the coach was putting so much pressure on Isaac.

The third period was so exciting. Lewiston scored a goal with only five minutes left in the game. Then, in the last minute, Isaac scored, sending the game into overtime. I could tell that all the boys were exhausted. But Isaac looked exhilarated. He was ready for overtime. The only words coming from both coaches' mouths were, "Kill them!" For me, the game seemed to be playing in slow motion. Everything seemed dramatic. What a thrill.

Overtime is five minutes long. If no one scores, it goes into second overtime, then third. Basically, there is never a tie in hockey. Someone always wins the game. This time, I was praying it would be us.

As the first overtime started, Isaac had the puck. He was maneuvering down the ice like a pro. Just before he was to make the shot, a Lewiston player tripped him. He flew down on the ice. The referees called a penalty, but at that point, the whole Booth Bay team was on the ice. Everyone was pushing and shoving and throwing punches. The refs were trying to break it all up. I couldn't see Isaac. I didn't know if he ever got off the ground.

When the ice finally cleared, I saw that Isaac, thankfully, was on the sidelines with the rest of the team. The referees penalized the Lewiston player who tripped Isaac, sending him to the penalty box. In addition, they handed out penalties to two more Lewiston players and two of our own for fighting. All of these penalties were for five minutes, meaning those players were out for the rest of the game, or at least the remainder of the overtime period. Lewiston was down three players for the remainder of the overtime, while we were down two players. Although there were several shots on goal by both teams, there was no score in the first overtime.

The second overtime began with all players exhausted, except the five who had been in the penalty box. They came out for blood. At one point, I thought there was going to be another brawl. It actually made me excited. Everyone, including me, was on the edge of their seats. Isaac made two shots on goal and finally, in the last minute, scored the winning goal for our team. Everyone was jumping up and down, hugging and kissing Isaac, who was always extremely humble, but now was more excited than I had ever seen him. Tweet, Donna, and the boys were hugging and congratulating him. Some of the guys on the Lewiston team came over to shake his hand. It was all just so exciting.

As we were leaving the ice, the coach came over to us and said, "Isaac, there are two scouts here, and both of them would like an opportunity to talk to you. I'll be waiting for you outside the locker room. Do you think you have a few minutes to talk to the scouts?"

"Man, do I!" Isaac said as he looked up to the heavens, whispered thank you, and made the sign of the cross. I had never seen Isaac so happy.

The scouts interviewed Isaac, and both of them offered him a position on their team. Isaac asked if he could have a few days to think about it. The atmosphere was so thick with joy. I had never witnessed such a level of excitement. The game was unbelievable.

That's the day I became hooked on hockey. Adding to all that excitement were the pro offers for Isaac. Such a wonderful opportunity.

After a big celebration in Lewiston, we headed back to Booth Bay Harbor. When we got home, Tweet shared all of the exciting news with Elise. She said that she hated missing it. She immediately knew that Isaac was leaving. It was just a question as to whether he was going to

Boston or to Chicago. Both teams wanted him to join the team immediately. He had a week to make his decision. During that week, Isaac,
Tweet, and Ross spent a lot of time behind closed doors with their
heads together. Elise was a nervous wreck. She confided in me that she
was okay with Isaac going to Boston, but Chicago was a "world away."

Isaac finally made his announcement at our regular family Sunday
dinner. Tapping his glass, he stood and announced, "After much
thought and prayer, I have decided that I will play for the Boston
Bruins. Although the Chicago Blackhawks offered more money, I
don't want to be that far away from you guys. I will be leaving one
week from tomorrow."

Elise covered her mouth and started sobbing with relief while Isaac
wrapped his arms around her. I was relieved too, but I regretted that it
wasn't me going to play hockey in Boston.

That week, Elise and Tweet had a big party for Isaac, and all of his
teammates came. Practically all of Booth Bay Harbor was there to send
off their new "Hockey Star." It was a really joyous occasion. At the
party, the coach approached me and asked if I would still come to the
practices and keep the stats.

"You know, Martha, it really helps me out a lot." I was so happy he
asked, and I readily agreed.

The night was coming to an end, and out of the corner of my eye, I
spotted Johnathan sitting all alone and looking sad. I realized that I
hadn't really thought about how he was feeling about all this. Isaac is to
Johnathan as Claire is to me. I could feel his pain.

After everyone left, I saw Isaac and Johnathan talking. I knew
exactly what the conversation centered on.

It was about memories and love. I knew that they would both be
okay.

On the last Sunday before Isaac left, he asked me to please come to
church with the family. Despite all my conversations with Jana and
Elise and the pressure from Margie, I still had not been to church. At
this point, how could I refuse Isaac? The message at church was about

family. The pastor talked about Jesus's family and how they had to let Him go.

"Mary and Joseph knew what Jesus was called to do. Jesus had a whole extended family that had to endure the heartache of His departure. Our families mirror the biblical family of Jesus. Jesus, with the help of his earthly family, took years to get ready to do His Father's work. As long as we raise our children with the Bible and Godly values, they will be ready for whatever comes their way. Unfortunately, that way may be somewhere else," the pastor concluded.

Many in the congregation were moved to tears, and everyone was giving well-wishes. It was a happy and a sad day. Isaac left the next day, on Monday, November 7, 1938.

I really missed Isaac after he left. Johnathan adjusted more easily than I thought he would. Elise was the most lost. She told me that she couldn't believe how much she missed him.

"Every day when I wake up, I think of him. I want to know what he is doing. I miss his beautiful smile and encouraging words. I just miss him so much."

I felt bad for her. I continued to attend the hockey practices and games to keep the stats. It was the highlight of my week.

Without Isaac, Thanksgiving was tough for everyone. He called, and I was able to say hello. He sounded happy and well. Elise and Johnathan talked with him for a long time, and they both seemed happy when they got off the phone.

"It makes it easier when you know your kids are happy. I think he might have a girl," Elise announced. Although Isaac was popular with girls and had many "dates" when he lived in Booth Bay Harbor, he never had anyone special. I couldn't help but hope he did have a girl. I know he would be a great catch for someone.

Since hockey season was from October to April, I knew Isaac would not be coming home anytime soon. I usually didn't ask a lot of questions, but one day, when I was alone with Johnathan, I asked him, "So what is going on with Isaac? Does he have a girlfriend?"

"It sounds like it. It sounds like he has a pretty serious girlfriend."

"What did he say?" I probed further.

"He just said he met a girl that he likes. Her name is Evelyn, and she is the daughter of one of the team coaches."

"He'd better be careful. If he breaks her heart, he will be off the team," I said jokingly.

"Good point," laughed Johnathan.

The holiday music program was right after Thanksgiving and had approached faster than I had expected. Diane and I were both really excited and nervous at the same time. All of a sudden, the big night was upon us. Donna and Claire traveled up from Lewiston to watch. The program went really well, and when it was time for me to sing my solo, despite my nerves, I sang my heart out. When I finished, everyone stood and applauded. It felt really good. I loved singing and being in the choir. I was so happy. After the event ended, Mrs. Lolly walked up to me, hugged me, and said, "Oh, Holy Night" never sounded better.

Claire and Donna spent the night with us in Booth Bay. Claire said that she was proud of me and glad to see how happy I was. I knew she was happy too. She said that she loved living in Lewiston. She was involved in many of the school's clubs and had lots of friends. I asked her if she had a guy, and she said that she didn't. She told me that there are lots of cute guys, but that they're just platonic friends.

"I'm trying to concentrate on school so I can get a scholarship to college. A boyfriend would only complicate that," she laughed.

Christmas was right around the corner. It would be my first Christmas in Booth Bay Harbor. Other than the Christmas in Canada with my grandpa, I didn't have a lot of good memories of Christmas, but I knew it was meant to be a special time. I was optimistic that this Christmas might be a good one.

After Isaac left, I continued to go to church each Sunday with the family. Margie was so excited. Every Sunday, she would say, "See, I told you that you were going to go to church." I laughed about it every time. It did feel good being with the family and getting back to God. I was finally optimistic about my future.

Early in the morning on Christmas Day, Margie was already in my room shaking me to wake up.

Her face radiated joy, like that of a little kid who had just seen something amazing.

"Get up, Martha. You have to get up and see if Santa came. There is snow. It snowed during the night. You have to look out the window, it is beautiful."

"Margie, it's still dark out."

"I know. That's the best time to see it."

True to her words, it was actually a very beautiful sight to behold. The snow across the ocean during the night looked like a million glistening stars. The reflection from the water made it appear as a never-ending starry sky. So stunning! I was mesmerized. I just wanted to sit there and look at it until it disappeared. The sand was white instead of brown, and it sparkled like clouds with jewels in them.

Margie still believed in Santa, and everyone was under strict orders not to break the spell. We all planned to celebrate at Tweet and Elise's house. Although each house had its own tree, all the presents were at Tweet and Elise's. But our stockings were here at our house. Margie knew that Santa brought only stockings to "old people." No presents. The presents were only for little children. We were all supposed to meet at Tweet and Elise's for breakfast and to exchange our presents. Dinner was planned for later at our house.

At this point, Ricky was living with Ross and Daniella, and Diane was living with Tweet and Elise. Everyone had their place and seemed

to be happy. All of our houses were close together, and we really oper-
ated as one big family.

Margie ran downstairs to get our stockings. Jana was still asleep. I
got so much joy watching Margie marvel at every small thing. She was
really enthralled with the little hummingbird ornament that she got.
She just kept talking about how Santa got exactly what she wanted and
how beautiful it was.

I was touched by what was in my stocking. There was some really
nice-smelling soap, a beautiful necklace made of shells, a pen, a little
notepad, and some candy. I wanted to cry. I was moved by the thought-
fulness of whoever put this together for me. Jana finally woke up and
came upstairs to see our goodies. Margie showed her each thing and
spent a good amount of time telling her how much she loved them all.
I was so thankful for this wonderful family. Christmas was wonderful.
I will always remember it as one of the happiest days of my life.

CHAPTER 19

Settling In

After the new year, I continued at Booth Bay School. I still enjoyed the choir and loved attending hockey practice and games on weekends. I also began to take a drawing class. We had a new art teacher. She was a really good artist, and she specialized in drawing seashells. I was amazed at what she could draw. I started experimenting with drawing myself. I had gotten a sketch pad as a Christmas present from Elise. She said that she had noticed the doodles in my schoolbooks and thought I might enjoy drawing. I really had never thought of it before, but it sounded like something I would like to try. Elise was right. I really enjoyed it and was pretty good at it. I especially liked drawing houses and other structures. Boats were my specialty.

Looking at all of us—the LeBlanc kids—I can honestly say we were all doing fine. We all spoke English and French. Elise encouraged us, and Donna encouraged Claire to keep using French so we wouldn't forget it. Despite everything we had been through, it seemed like we would be okay.

Ricky was so happy. Ross and Daniella never had kids of their own, and they just loved Ricky. They made sure that he had everything he needed and wanted. Any chance Ricky got, he was out on the boat with Ross. He still insisted that when he turned sixteen, he would give up school so he could be a "lobsterman."

Johnathan encouraged Ricky to take up baseball during the spring. Ricky loved that he had an older "brother" to hang out with. The girls at school loved Ricky, but he wasn't interested quite yet. He had some guy friends, but mainly he liked hanging out with "Johnny" and his friends. Johnathan didn't seem to mind. Ricky never asked about our mom. He seemed to have forgotten about her altogether.

Diane was happy-go-lucky. She missed Mom the most, but she also didn't appear to be as scarred by everything that had happened as the rest of us. To me, she seemed the least affected. She and Margie had a sweet bond.

Every day when we got home from school, Margie was waiting for us. Diane was always patient, loving, and kind towards Margie, and Margie listened to all of Diane's stories while Diane, in turn, patiently listened to everything Margie had to say. They spent a lot of time in Diane's room playing with make-up and styling each other's hair. I had been replaced as Margie's "new best friend" by Diane. I didn't mind. I loved watching their friendship. Diane was popular in school, especially with the boys. She was pretty and bubbly, always had a smile for everyone, and enjoyed any kind of social activity.

Because she was so sociable, her studies suffered. Claire and I had the advantage of a strict Catholic education. We were both above grade level in our respective schools, but Diane struggled. Part of that had to do with the fact that she really didn't care. She loved boys. Every week, she had a new "boyfriend." Both Ricky and Johnathan would just roll their eyes when she would go on and on about her latest love. Johnathan said she was "boy crazy," which she probably was.

Claire, of course, was thriving. Tweet saw her every week when he was in Lewiston. He said that they were testing Claire's IQ because she was so smart. She would graduate this year and was trying to figure out where she wanted to attend college and how she would pay for it. Bates College in Lewiston had a good English curriculum and was one of the first colleges to accept women into its programs. Claire said she hoped one day to be a teacher and writer. The good thing about Bates was that she could stay living with Donna and Phillip. If Claire's IQ was high (above 130), and she got good scores on her essay and admission tests, she would more than likely get a scholarship to anywhere that she chose. Tweet also mentioned that Claire works in his office after school two days a week.

She was basically just answering the phone and greeting anyone who came by. He said she seemed really happy, and everyone liked her.

My life was better than I could have ever hoped. I tried very hard to fight the demons that still tormented me sometimes. Although they did seem to be appearing less and less, I still struggled. I loved choir, school was tolerable, and I loved my job of keeping the stats for the local hockey league. Living with Jana and Margie was great. We three "girls" had a lot of fun, and we had mutual respect for each other.

Tweet asked me what my plans were after graduation. Honestly, I had no idea what I wanted to do or where I pictured myself. He reassured me that I had plenty of time to figure it all out and that there was no rush to make a decision right away. Since I still had another year of school ahead, I felt a bit more at ease. However, I was pretty sure that college wasn't in my future.

School was not my favorite thing, and college would mean moving to a new place and making new friends again, which was my least favorite thing in the world. The problem was, I really wanted to stay in Booth Bay Harbor, but I didn't know what I was going to do there. Not a lot of opportunities for a young woman. It seemed to me like all the women from here graduated from high school and got married. My prospect of that was zero! I was glad that I had a little bit of time to think about what I wanted for my future.

Out of the blue, Tweet returned home from Lewiston one day, excitement radiating from him as he announced he had a big surprise for me. He was grinning from ear to ear, and like an eager little kid, he said, "Take a guess! Just take a guess at what it is," while playfully hiding something behind his back. After I laughed and told him I had no idea, he revealed that he had gotten tickets to one of Isaac's games in Boston. He said that he, Johnathan, Elise, and I were going. I couldn't believe it. I was so excited. We were to drive to Lewiston, then take a train from Lewiston to Portland and another train from Portland to Boston. The whole trip would take two days. Tweet said that Isaac didn't know we were coming. He had somehow gotten in touch with the team coach, who had arranged for the tickets. We would be staying in Boston for two nights. I was so excited. The Bruins would be playing the Chicago Blackhawks, and I couldn't wait.

FRIDAY AT 11:00 A.M.

The trip to Boston was long and exhausting for all of us, but it didn't take away from the enjoyment of being together and the excitement we were all feeling. When we finally got to Boston, we found our quaint little hotel across the street from the Boston Garden Arena and settled into our two rooms with a bathroom in between. I couldn't help but think about Claire and how much she would have loved this. It was probably the first time she was actually jealous of me.

Elise was as excited about this trip as I was. The difference was that she was excited to see her son. I was excited to see Isaac, too, but I was even more excited to be at a real, live pro hockey game. We checked into the hotel and decided to explore a bit of Boston. We had not eaten since we had left Portland, so we were all starving. We discovered that there was an A&W Root Beer around the corner from the hotel, so we walked there to grab a bite to eat. Boston was amazing. I had thought that Lewiston was a big city. I found out that Lewiston cannot be compared to Boston. I couldn't believe the amount of traffic on the streets. Everywhere I looked, there was hustle and bustle. People were shopping and eating, and there were more cars and noise than I had ever seen or heard.

Finally, pre-game time had arrived. I had never seen such a crowd. When we finally reached the ticket booth, the man asked Tweet to hold on. I was worried that there was something wrong with our tickets. A few minutes later, a young, petite, pretty girl came over to escort us to our seats. She introduced herself as Evelyn and explained that there were special reserved seats for families of the players.

They were some of the best seats in the house. I will never forget my first time there. As we were being seated, suddenly I felt dizzy, and thoughts were racing through my mind. My adrenaline was blazing through my body. *Such a huge rink. Bigger than anything I have ever seen. Look at those flags. There's the American flag and yep, the Canadian flag... Oh, wow, there's the teams, and what's that smell? Hmmm, popcorn and ummm pretzels. That's it! Is this for real? Am I really here?* I had to pinch myself.

In my excitement, I didn't realize that the girl sitting with us was Isaac's girlfriend. Johnathan knew, though. He poked me in the ribs and whispered, "That's her. That's Isaac's gal." At that point, I was too excited about seeing the game to care. It was obvious that Elise and Tweet had no idea who Evelyn was, either. Since Evelyn sat down next to Elise, I assumed she was going to watch the game with us.

The arena was huge and modern. I just couldn't believe I was actually there live. The sound of the crowd when the teams entered the ice was deafening! After lining up and shaking hands, each team went to its respective bench. Then they introduced each player one by one. When they said Isaac's name, we all got to our feet and cheered. He still had no idea we were there.

A guy behind us laughingly said, "... and this must be Isaac's family."

Tweet responded, "However did you know?" They both laughed.

When they started playing the National Anthem, I was so proud. The big, beautiful American flag, along with the Canadian flag, was on full display in Boston Garden Arena. The whole thing brought tears to my eyes. Looking around, it seemed as though it brought tears to a lot of eyes.

When the game started, we were all on the edge of our seats. That's one thing about hockey: there is never a moment when you are not on the edge of your seat.

After the first period, although there had been ten shots on goal and many made by Isaac, there was no score. As we waited for the second period to begin, Elise started making small talk and asking Evelyn questions about how she was connected with the Bruins. Evelyn explained that the coach was her father. Elise asked if she knew Isaac. To this she replied, "Yes, very well."

Just then, the second period began. Elise became distracted by the game. Johnathan just snickered and whispered, "Very well! This is going to be interesting." I elbowed him in the ribs.

The second period was exciting. Isaac was right there in the thick of things. He made several shots that were checked and deflected. I loved watching him play. You could tell that he was totally invested in winning. He was playing his heart out. Just as the period was about to end, one of the Blackhawk players scored a goal. The Blackhawks were now in charge.

Intermissions in hockey are short, but they gave Elise more time to drill Evelyn. I think that during the second period, Elise's mind had been reeling. The dancing conversation between her and Evelyn was amusing. Elise asked Evelyn if Isaac knew we were there, to which she said no.

"Actually, my father wants everyone to come to dinner at our house this evening. I hope that's okay," Evelyn says with a small voice and eyebrows raised.

"If that's what Isaac wants, Elise responded, we would love to meet Isaac's coach."

I then noticed Elise nudge Tweet in the ribs with her elbow. Completely oblivious to the gesture, Tweet turned to her, taken aback, and asked why she had done that, all while pretending to be injured by her touch. Elise simply smiled at Evelyn, who tentatively returned the smile. My heart went out to her, even though she appeared unfazed by the situation. In fact, she seemed remarkably confident and comfortably at ease.

During the third and final period, every second was exciting. At one point, when Isaac was taking a water break, he looked up and noticed us. I think it was the first time he realized that we were there. I gave a little wave, and he smiled. He was back in the game pretty quickly and almost immediately scored a goal to tie it up.

A few minutes later, Isaac scored another goal, putting the Bruins up two to one. Both Evelyn and Elise seemed to be distracted during the third period. I think that both of their brains were going a mile a minute. Despite the excitement, Elise seemed to have lost all interest in the game. Tweet was loving every minute. He was cheering and jumping up and down when Isaac scored again.

"Martha, now I understand why you love watching hockey so much. This is the most excitement I've experienced since watching Donna's twins play football," Tweet said.

"Thanks a lot, Tweet. You don't think my basketball is exciting?" Johnathan chipped in with a playful tone.

Tweet just shrugged in response, and Johnathan said, "I'm just kidding. Hockey is way more exciting than basketball." They both smiled, clearly enjoying the banter.

Both goals were on point. There were a few more shots on goal by both teams, but there were no more scores. The Bruins won two to one. We were all hooping and hollering. Isaac looked up at us again and gave a huge smile. I could tell he was happy to see us in the stands and happy that they won. Evelyn excused herself and said that we should meet her and Isaac outside the Bruins' locker room.

As soon as she left, Elise was all over Tweet. "I think that she is Isaac's girlfriend. I just know she is. She is the coach's daughter. Oh my goodness. I just don't know about this."

"She is adorable, Elise. What's the problem?" Tweet said.

"I don't know. I just don't know. She seems very nice, I guess. But it's Isaac we are talking about. I just figured he was down here playing hockey and having fun. Now we are meeting this girl's family. That sounds serious. Johnathan, what do you know about this?"

"I don't know anything. I know he has a girlfriend and her name is Evelyn... so that's probably her."

"Ya think!" I laughed as Johnathan squirmed.

"What did Isaac say about her?" inquired Elise, quizzing Johnathan further.

"Nothing. We only talked one time, and that was before Christmas. He said he had a girl, and her name was Evelyn. She was the coach's daughter, and he liked her a lot."

"You knew all this? Why didn't you tell me?"

"I just did," Jonathan responded.

"Oh, never mind. You men never communicate. You never get details, and you never report your information. Why is the mother the last to know?"

"I didn't know anything about it until just now. I don't know why you're getting so upset," Tweet said.

"Because! I wanted to spend time with Isaac. Now we have to go to dinner at a stranger's house."

Tweet hugged Elise and told her to snap out of it. "We aren't going back to Lewiston until Sunday night. You will have plenty of time with Isaac," he said.

When Isaac finally emerged from the locker room, he was ecstatic. "I can't believe you guys are here. How did this happen?"

Tweet explained how he was able to get tickets. We all hugged him. He looked so good. He had put on a little weight, which was definitely muscle, not fat. His smile was so genuine, and it looked beautiful against his tanned skin. How he was tan in Boston in January was beyond me, but he was. Even his voice had changed. It somehow sounded deeper.

"How did you all pull off this surprise?" he asked again, still in disbelief.

"Elise was missing you so much, I knew I had to get her down here. Martha couldn't wait to see a pro game. She kept throwing hints at me about getting tickets. So, I finally contacted your coach. He graciously provided me with four tickets, and here we are."

While we were huddled around talking, I could see Isaac getting distracted. He kept looking above us. Finally, he said, "Evelyn, did you know about this?" She walked over, nodding and grinning from ear to ear. Isaac extended his arms and wrapped her in a warm hug. "You little stinker. What a great surprise. Thank you."

"Dad has invited you and your family for dinner. Mom said to come directly after the game. A car is waiting out front."

Wow! A car was waiting out front. That sounded so special. After a twenty-minute ride to Coach Reader's home in Beacon Hill, we rolled up to a beautiful, all-brick, Federal-style house with a small walk-up stairway and white framed windows. The streets in this quaint neighborhood were made of cobblestones.

Upon stepping inside, the home seemed to extend far beyond what we had anticipated, stretching all the way from front to back and rising three stories high. I would describe the interior as truly elegant. I'd never been anywhere so fancy. Mrs. Reader, who was a small, pretty woman like Evelyn, met us as we entered. She gave Isaac a nice hug, took our coats, and directed us to a large sitting room. Coach Reader was a large but fit man. He had a baritone voice that demanded attention.

Everyone was shaking hands and introducing themselves. There was much small talk, like: "How was your trip? Have you ever been to Boston before? Your dress is lovely. What a beautiful home you have." Blah Blah! Blah! I hated it.

I think Evelyn could tell I was uncomfortable, so she asked me if I wanted to see the rest of the house.

As we walked together, the small talk changed to real talk. "I am so happy to finally meet you, Martha. Isaac is very fond of you and says that you know everything there is to know about hockey."

"Well, I don't know about that. But I do love it," I said with a smile.

"Isaac says you kept the stats for the Booth Bay Harbor team. When I was younger, I used to try to keep the stats for my dad. It was hard. He finally fired me because I couldn't keep up with the game," she laughed. "To be honest, I was very distracted by anything and everything. Especially all the cute hockey players. The game itself was not exactly a priority," she winked.

"I'm still keeping the stats for Booth Bay. I love it. I miss Isaac, though. It was definitely more fun when he was there. Isaac and I talked a lot about hockey. I don't really have anyone else in the family to talk game with, you know. He is a great player and knows so much. We always had interesting conversations. I miss that."

"Yes, he is. I'm hoping we can be friends. I am very fond of Isaac, and I know he thinks of you as a sister," Evelyn said. That made me feel good. Just then, Mrs. Reader announced that dinner was served.

The dinner was lovely. Mrs. Reader was a wonderful cook.

Isaac and Evelyn sat next to each other, with Elise sitting beside Isaac. Tweet, Johnathan, and I sat across from them, while Coach and Mrs. Reader sat on the ends.

Coach Reader asked what we thought of the game, and Tweet was just beaming over it as he spoke. "It was the most exciting thing I had ever seen. You know, I used to like hockey, mainly because Isaac played. Now I think I love it."

"It's easy to get hooked on," said Coach Reader. "Martha, I heard you are a real expert. I heard you follow all the teams and can give us stats for almost all the players. Do you have a favorite American player?"

"It's hard to say, since I only get to read about the teams in the paper and hear them play on the radio sometimes. Based on that, I think the best player is Cecil Dillion. He plays right wing for the New

York Rangers. He has the best stats. My favorite player is Isaac, of course." At this, everyone laughed.

"Great Choice! Do you have a favorite goalie, Martha?"

"Well, the best goalie is one of your players, Frank Brimsek." His stats are unbelievable. I guess I would say he is my favorite. Obviously, I am a Boston Bruins fan."

"I sure hope so," said Isaac, laughing.

"Who is your favorite Canadian player?"

"That would have to be Maurice Richard, of the Montreal Canadians. They don't call him "the Rocket" for nothing. Someday, I would love to see him play. He sounds like a really exciting player to watch." Tweet was taking it all in and looking amazed.

"Okay, enough hockey. Elise, I want to hear about Booth Bay Harbor. From how Isaac has described it, I think it sounds lovely," Mrs. Reader finally interjected.

The rest of the dinner was spent talking about our families and theirs. Tweet and Coach Reader retreated to the back garden to smoke cigars. I don't know how they did that. It was freezing outside. But apparently, smoking in the house was not allowed. Elise asked if she could help Mrs. Reader in the kitchen, and they headed that way. It looked like everyone was getting along well. Elise seemed to have warmed up, and Tweet was his usual lovable self.

When it was just the four of us young people, it was obvious that Isaac and Evelyn were a couple. Isaac talked about how much he loved living in Boston. How wonderful the Reader family was to him. He said he didn't know what he would have done without Evelyn.

"I was so lonely when I first got here, I almost regretted coming. I think the Coach was worried about me, so he had Evelyn show me around the city. One thing led to another, and now here we are. I couldn't be happier."

Evelyn was looking at Isaac with so much admiration and love.

I could tell that something beautiful was going to come from all of this.

CHAPTER 20

Propositions

I always knew they were destined to be together. So, it didn't surprise me when, four months later, after the Boston Bruins defeated the Toronto Maple Leafs to clinch the Stanley Cup, they announced their engagement. I could see that Isaac was finally ready to settle down. He had told me before he left Booth Bay Harbor that after he was settled in Boston and secure on the team, he would start looking for "a gal." He said he knew that the single party life of an athlete was not for him.

Tweet and I traveled back to Boston for the playoffs, which were in April. Isaac was allotted only two tickets for two of the seven games. We decided that we wanted to be at games four and five. Mainly because if the Stanley Cup ended at game five, we would miss out if we picked game six and seven. Both Elise and Johnathan said that Tweet and I should go. They agreed that we would enjoy it the most. I was so grateful.

The excitement in Boston during game season was palpable! Coach and Mrs. Reader insisted that we stay at their home. We didn't really see much of Coach Reader or Isaac. They were both busy with the team. When we weren't at the games, Evelyn and Mrs. Reader graciously showed us around Boston. We visited Old North Church, which is the oldest church building in Boston, Faneuil Hall, and the Paul Revere House. There is so much history in that city. I couldn't help but think of Claire and how much she would have enjoyed being there with us. She not only loved big cities, but also anything related to history.

As always, the hockey games were exciting, even more so because it was the Stanley Cup. When it was all over, the Bruins won it in five games.

Isaac scored two goals; one in the fourth game and one in the fifth. He played effortlessly. At the end, the stands emptied onto the ice. Security couldn't control any of it. I was so excited to be there for it. I couldn't imagine anything ever topping this. There was a big celebration afterwards that lasted well into the night and the next morning. It seemed to include the whole city of Boston. It was the craziest thing I'd ever seen. Tweet kept reminding me to stay close to him, saying, "Anything can happen in celebrations like this."

Before we left the next day, Isaac asked Tweet if he could talk to him privately. I'm sure it was then that he told Tweet he was going to ask Evelyn to marry him. Isaac also asked me if we could have a word.

"Martha, would you be interested in working for the Bruins and keeping their stats? It doesn't pay much, but you could live with the Readers, so that you wouldn't have many expenses.

"Are you kidding me? Is this a joke? I have one more year of school, you know."

"No, I'm dead serious. After you were here in January, the Coach couldn't stop talking about how impressed he was with you and your hockey knowledge. He said you are the smartest and most mature young lady he has ever met. Last week, he asked me what I thought about the idea of you coming to work for the team next season. You could finish your school here. Mrs. Reader was a teacher before she decided to stay home with Evelyn. She could get your schooling done this summer."

"This is crazy! I don't know. I have to think about this. I just don't know."

As we were getting in the car to go to the train station, Coach Reader whispered, "I hope you really give the offer Isaac mentioned some thought. We would love to have you as part of the team. At some point, I would like to talk to you further about it." It felt so great to be thought of as "part of the team." Wow! Isaac told me that Coach Reader thought I was "smart and mature." It wasn't often that someone complimented me. I was beaming with pride.

Riding home on the train, Tweet asked, "Well, what did you think?"

"Think about what?"

"About the game and the whole weekend. Was it everything you anticipated it would be?"

"Of course. It was even better. I just loved watching. I wish we lived closer so I could go to every game. Listening on the radio just can't compare."

"I heard that Coach Reader might be offering you a job. Then you would be there for every game."

"Isaac did mention something to me. I just don't know if I can do it. Moving to Boston is a big move. I have another year of school, you know."

"Yes. There is a lot to think about. Anyway, tonight Isaac is going to ask the Reader's if he can marry Evelyn. They are going to dinner, and after that, he will ask for her hand."

"I figured. What do you think Elise will say?"

"I think she has been waiting for it. After we were there in January, she had said that she thinks we just met our future in-laws."

"Will she be happy then?"

"Not happy, but not sad. It's just the circle of life. She knows it. Isaac is no longer hers. Moms have been going through this since the beginning of time."

"What do you think I should do, Tweet? Do you think I should take the job and move to Boston?"

"I think you should do what you want to. But I also think that if you don't take it, you will regret it. Look, you can always come back home if you don't like it."

"The sad truth is, I don't really have a home. That really is the sad truth."

"Not true at all, and it makes me sad to hear you say that. I've told you before, Booth Bay Harbor is your home. It makes me upset to know you don't think of it that way."

"Well, it is my favorite place. Does that make you feel any better? I do love Booth Bay Harbor, and I love your family. You are the closest thing I've had to a dad, and Elise and Jana have been more like mothers to me than my own mom. It's that I feel like I just got settled, and now I might be leaving again. Boston is huge. I just don't know if I am ready for it."

"I would never push you. I love you as a daughter and would love for you to stay in Booth Bay Harbor. Maybe they would let you finish school and then move to Boston for the job. That would give you another year to get ready."

"That wasn't the offer."

"I know, but they might consider it. When do you have to give them an answer?"

"Isaac didn't say, but I wouldn't want to keep them hanging for too long."

"All of it is very exciting, no matter what you decide. Elise and I will support anything you want to do."

"Did Isaac say when he will marry?"

"Not exactly. But I got the impression it would be before the next season starts in October."

When we got back to Booth Bay Harbor, I was happy to be home. *Home!* That was exactly what I thought. Maybe Tweet was right. Booth Bay Harbor was my home.

Elise, Johnathan, Jana, and the rest of the family wanted to hear all about the trip. Neither Tweet nor I told them about Isaac or about my offer. Those were conversations that needed to be had in private with Elise first.

It ended up that Elise was actually happy about Isaac's upcoming wedding. She said that she thought it was good for Isaac. "Evelyn and her family seem like wonderful people, even if they are Catholic."

Tweet just smiled, "Remember, Elise, I was Catholic when you met me."

"You weren't really Catholic. You didn't go to church. You were just pretending."

"Pretending! That's an interesting way to put it. Besides, there are plenty of good Catholics. You just got caught up with the wrong ones."

Tweet asked me if I wanted to tell Elise about my job offer by myself or if I wanted him to be with me. I opted for the second option. Jana had also invited Diane to come to dinner one night so Tweet, Elise, and I could talk privately.

When I told Elise about the offer in Boston, she emphatically said, "No! You can't do that! You have a year of school left." I told her that Mrs. Reader was going to give me my classes this summer so I could graduate before the hockey season began.

"I think that is a terrible idea. Elise said. I absolutely don't want you to go. Why can't they wait until next year? I think they are taking away my whole family. First Isaac and now you." She was getting very upset and teary-eyed. I really didn't know what to say, but secretly I was so happy. Elise didn't want me to go. Finally, someone wanted me. I ran to her and gave her the best hug.

"Thank you. You are the best. I don't know what I am going to do, but the fact that you want me to stay here means the world to me." At that point, we were both crying. Tweet just sat and smiled and finally said, "For the record, I don't want you to go either, but I will understand if you do."

Two weeks later, Isaac called. First, he wanted to talk to Elise. He told her that Evelyn had accepted his proposal and they were getting married in Boston on Saturday, August 19. Evelyn then got on the phone with Elise, and they had a short but nice chat. Elise said that Evelyn assured her that she would take care of Isaac and would be the best wife ever. She also asked if it would be possible for them to come and visit with us in Booth Bay Harbor this summer. She really wanted to see where Isaac grew up and meet the rest of the family. Elise was ecstatic.

After that, Elise gave the phone to Johnathan. Isaac asked him if he would be his best man in the wedding. Of course, Johnathan said yes. He then handed the phone to me. Isaac asked, "Have you decided anything about coming to Boston?" I told him that I really wanted to come but could not this year. After I graduate, I hope they will consider hiring me. Then I asked, "Is Coach Reader available to talk?"

After a brief hold, Coach Reader's booming voice echoed through the phone, "Martha, so nice to hear from you. Have you decided anything about my offer?"

"Thank you so much for this offer. I feel so honored. I just don't think I am ready to leave home yet." The word home lasted longer than the others, and it warmed me inside to say it. I was home. I continued by smiling and saying, "If that position is open next year after I graduate, I hope you will give me another chance."

He thanked me and told me I am such a special young lady. "Martha, if that job is open next year, it's yours. I'll see you at the wedding. Looks like we are going to be family."

Tweet and Elise were both standing there listening. Elise started crying again, and Tweet said, "I am so proud of you. I am so glad you are not leaving home yet."

"I don't know what that was all about, Martha, but I'm glad you're not leaving home yet, too," Jonathan added.

Over the next two months, we planned for Isaac and Evelyn's arrival. Elise wanted everything to be perfect. Elise was a bit nervous and kept perseverating on the differences in the family homes. "You didn't see their house. Ours is so little and drab compared to theirs," she told Jana and Daniella. We were all getting a little tired of the negative commentary on Booth Bay Harbor and our homes that Elise was spouting.

Jana finally got mad and said incredulously, "What are you talking about? Do they live on the Atlantic Ocean? Do they open their door every morning to the sound of waves crashing on the shore and seagulls cawing? Did they build their home with their own hands? Do they live next door to a loving family? I didn't realize you thought so little of our houses, our family, and Booth Bay Harbor."

"Oh, Jana, I'm sorry. That's not what I mean. It's just that they come from a different world. I want to make a good impression."

"If you need to make a good impression for this girl by putting on airs, then I guarantee she is not the girl for Isaac. From what I hear, she is lovely. You aren't making her seem that way, though. I'm going home. You know where I am if you need me," Jana said as she left in a huff.

A little while later, Margie came over with Hardy.

"Boy! Elise, you sure did make Mom mad. What did you say? What does pretentious mean? She said she didn't know that you weren't happy in Booth Bay Harbor. She said she didn't realize that you were ashamed of us. Are you ashamed of us and unhappy here? She said God doesn't like it when we covet what someone else has. She said—"

"Okay, Margie, that's enough. I know your mom is mad. I'll go over and smooth things out."

"Can I come?"

Elise stopped Margie in her tracks. "NO!"

Elise eventually went to see Jana and admitted that she had been right all along. "Who am I to judge how Evelyn is going to judge us? If Evelyn were a pretentious, snooty person, Isaac would never have been attracted to her. Besides, I do love my house, our family, and I do love Booth Bay Harbor. We are going to just be ourselves and have a good ole Booth Bay Harbor clam bake. How does that sound?"

With a big hug, Jana said, "That sounds perfect. I think Isaac and his gal will love it."

Isaac and Evelyn were to arrive in two weeks, and everyone was so excited about their trip. The Booth Bay hockey team was planning on a big homecoming for Isaac and Evelyn. Isaac was a hometown hero when it came to hockey. They were set to arrive on Friday, June 23, and they would be staying through the weekend. The team had arranged a game for Friday night. Saturday was the clam bake. Sunday was church and our family dinner. It was going to be a packed couple of days. I was pretty sure the whole town would be there for the clam bake. Ross, Ricky, Johnathan, and Tweet were in charge of getting all the fish and seafood together.

Everyone was anxious about the weather. Our clam bakes were always held outside on the beach in front of the houses. If the weather were bad, it would make it difficult. For clam bakes, we dig a large hole (about four feet deep and five feet square) in the sand and line it with flat rocks. Then we light a big fire on top and let it burn out so that the rocks are good and hot. Then we shovel off the ashes, layer seaweed on top, and load it up with lobster, clams, mussels, oysters, corn, sausage, potatoes, and fish. Next, we cover it with more seaweed, cover that with a large burlap tarp and sand, and wait. Since the potatoes and sausage take longer than the rest of the food, they are pre-cooked until almost done.

When it is ready, we serve up the most delicious tasting fish and seafood that you could ever dream of. Dip it in drawn butter, and you will feel like you have died and gone to heaven.

Jana was going to make her wonderful coleslaw, while Elise and I would make corn bread. Daniella was in charge of dessert.

Margie kept bugging her about what she was making. "You have to decide, Daniella. What are you going to make for dessert? Dessert is the best part of the meal."

"What do you want me to make, Margie?"

"Strawberry pie! It's my favorite."

"Good idea. Strawberry season has just started. I will have to make a lot of pies to feed all the people."

"How many people? Who is coming? I'm so excited. I can help," Margie said. Margie always loved a good party.

"The better question is who is not coming? I'm pretty sure from what I can gather, the whole town is coming," Daniella replied. "Maybe the lady who does the pies at church can help, and we can add blueberry pie to the menu."

Once Daniella mentioned all of this, I felt a wave of nervousness wash over me. As I realized that the whole town would be present, my stomach began to turn; however, I tried to stay involved in their conversation.

"Margie, you've had a lot of good ideas today," Daniella said. With that, the whole menu was complete.

Donna, Phillip, Claire, and the twins were coming for the clam-bake. Even though they would only be around for a day, they insisted that they wouldn't miss it for anything in the world. I couldn't wait to see them. Claire and I had a lot to talk about, and I was excited for us to get caught up.

She had gotten a scholarship to Bates College in Lewiston and would start in September, majoring in English and History. I was so happy for her. She would still be able to live with Donna and Phillip, and Tweet would keep her working in his office part-time. Even though I was excited to see Claire and the rest of Tweet's family, I was still anxious about it all. I still hated being around a lot of people. I still hated small talk and social pressures. Oh, how I wished I could be more like Margie.

As the day got closer, I got increasingly anxious. I kept thinking of ways to stay in my room and just avoid the event altogether. Just the thought of it made me sick to my belly. I was supposed to help Elise make the cornbread, but the thought of cornbread, or any food for that matter, only made me panic all the more. The day before Isaac and Evelyn were to arrive, Jana finally noticed something was wrong with me and decided to find out what it was.

"Are you sick?"

"I just don't feel well. My stomach is upset. I think I'm getting sick."

"Oh, Martha! Are you sure it is not just anxiety over the upcoming festivities?"

"I don't know. I do feel anxious, and my stomach is in knots."

"It sounds like social anxiety to me. We've talked about this before. Remember when you were scheduled to go to Boston to watch Isaac play? You told me then that you were sick and could not attend. I convinced you to go, and everything was great. This happens to you. Every time there is something new or you are going to be around a lot of strangers, you get anxious, and it upsets your stomach. Then once you get there, you are fine. Drink some ginger ale to settle your stomach and go over and help Elise with the cornbread. It will take your mind off it."

Jana was right. This happened all the time. I just didn't know how to stop it, and it was so disheartening.

CHAPTER 21

Celebration

Isaac and Evelyn arrived in a fancy, new car at around noon on Friday. It was a sunny, beautiful day. The hockey game wasn't until 6:00 p.m. Evelyn couldn't stop talking about how pretty the whole area was, and I was happy we had a little time to talk.

"Isaac," she laughed, "I can't believe that this is where you grew up. Man, you must really love hockey if you moved away from here. To me, it looks like paradise."

Elise was beaming, and Isaac looked extremely proud. "As beautiful as it is here, Evelyn, Booth Bay Harbor was not what made the decision to leave hard." Hugging Elise, he went on to say, "Leaving my family... that's what made it hard."

We had a flagpole in front of the house, which always proudly displayed the American flag. The day before Isaac arrived, Tweet had added the Boston Bruins flag to it. Isaac immediately noticed and appreciated it. He hugged Tweet, "Great addition. Thank you." Isaac settled into his old room with Johnathan, while Evelyn took Diane's room, and Diane stayed with us. Elise was excited to spend as much time with Isaac and Evelyn as possible. Evelyn was eager to share all of the details of the upcoming wedding, and from the sound of it, the wedding was going to be the event of the century. Ugh!

Margie was so excited to see Isaac and meet Evelyn. She kept asking Evelyn lots of questions, and her speech was so fast. She does that when she is nervous. I could tell that Evelyn could hardly understand what Margie was saying and was very uncomfortable. I wondered if she had ever been around anyone like Margie before. If not, I could see how it might be uncomfortable for her. Jana finally came to Evelyn's rescue by telling everyone lunch was ready at Daniella and Ross's house.

That evening, we all piled over to the hockey arena. The boys from the team were on top of Isaac like bees on honey. They wanted to know everything about the Boston Bruins and Isaac's teammates. Isaac was his happy-go-lucky self and was eager to answer all of their questions. Evelyn said how "quaint" the arena was. "I think this is what my father calls working on a shoestring," she laughed. It didn't settle well with me the way she said it, but I kept it to myself.

Isaac was loving being right in there on the ice with all of his old buddies. I could tell he was trying not to be a "hotdog." That's what they always call the guys who hog the puck. It was just a fun night all the way around. Isaac is very humble and not really an attention seeker. That was one of the reasons everyone liked him.

Evelyn seemed content on the bleachers. Although she commented several times about how uncomfortable they were. I was in awe of how easily she worked a crowd. At Daniella's, she didn't seem the least bit uncomfortable at lunch. She laughed and talked to everyone effortlessly. Now, at the arena, there were plenty of strangers that she was meeting, and it didn't seem to faze her. I didn't know how she did it, but I liked it. I wish I had the same magic as her. The only time she appeared to squirm was around Margie.

At the end of the game, everyone said that they couldn't wait for tomorrow's clambake, especially since the weather was supposed to be glorious.

Tweet, Ross, Johnathan, and Ricky got up before dawn to get everything prepared on the beach. Isaac was right there in the thick of it, lugging logs and rocks to the pit. All the rest of us were running around like crazy people. Evelyn kept asking what she could do to help, but no one knew what to tell her.

"You guys move fast around here," she said. We had brought our picnic tables out to the beach to put all the food on. There were coolers full of ice, water, beer, and soda lined up. There was a little breeze off the ocean to make for a perfect day. The road in front of the house was cordoned off. We had games of volleyball and badminton set up. It was going to be a fun day for sure.

Finally, Donna, Phillip, Claire, and the twins arrived. More introductions were made. As always, Evelyn handled it like a movie star. She was just the most unflappable thing I had ever met.

"Isaac, you have the most wonderful family. We are going to have to make it a point to come back here more often. Maybe Mom and Dad could come one time. They would love it."

As the whole town started to arrive, I could see that Elise was getting nervous. I heard her tell Tweet that she didn't think there would be enough food. Tweet just laughed. I looked around and thought Elise might be right. Almost everyone brought chairs and blankets to sit on. And some brought coolers of food too. The whole beach was full of people. Tweet told Isaac that this was a testament to his character. I heard him say to Isaac, "You, my boy, are obviously missed and well-loved."

Jana came over and asked me how I was doing. She was always so thoughtful about my anxiety, and I always appreciated her understanding. I remember my mom never understood. She just always told me to "snap out of it." She blamed me and said I was just "awkward." Today, although anxious, I was okay because I was hanging out with Claire, Diane, and Margie.

"Well, what do you think of her?" asked Claire.

"Evelyn? She's nice. I think she and Isaac make a good couple."

"I think she is elegant," said Diane.

"I don't think she likes me," said Margie.

"I don't think that's true," I said. "I think she is just having a hard time understanding what you are saying, and that makes her uncomfortable. Sometimes you talk very fast, and if people aren't used to it, it can be hard to follow what you are saying." This seemed to appease Margie for the time being.

Later on, I overheard Margie apologizing to Evelyn.

"What on earth are you sorry for, Margie?" Evelyn asked, obviously in shock.

Very slowly, Margie said, "I'm... sorry... for... talking... so... fast... that... you... can't... understand... me."

With a smile on her face, Evelyn said, "Thank you for saying you are sorry, but you don't have to be sorry. I just have to get used to it. It is hard to understand when you talk fast, though."

With a big hug, Margie followed up quickly with, "I'll do better. I promise."

Finally, Tweet announced that the food was ready and introduced our pastor to say the blessing, which was short and sweet. We all laughed later about how brief the prayers were, clearly a sign that the pastor was quite hungry.

Everyone lined up to fill their plates. It almost felt like the Bible story about the five loaves and two fish in the Book of Mathew. The food just seemed to multiply, and boy, was it good!

Claire wanted to know all about Boston, and I wanted to know all about Bates College. We talked non-stop. Finally, when Diane and Margie were occupied elsewhere, I asked Claire if she had heard anything about our mom. She said she hadn't.

"Don't you think it is the oddest thing? How could she just disappear like that?" I said with worry, written all over my face.

"At this point, we don't know that she disappeared. She could be right back home. She obviously wasn't worried about us, so I'm not going to worry about her. Do Diane or Ricky ask about her?"

"Diane mentioned something the other day. She said, 'I wish Mom were here. She is really missing out.' I personally think we all really should thank her for being such a crappy mom. After all, we wouldn't be here if she hadn't pretty much abandoned us. It's quite ironic that both our mom and our dad turned out to be not such nice human beings, but the four of us turned out great. I found our dad's death notice a few weeks ago. Do you know that it didn't mention anything about us? It said nothing about him having four kids. How do you just ignore that in a death notice?"

"Well, that would have been a product of his mother, I'm sure. How did you find it?"

"I was snooping, and Elise had it in a drawer. In fairness, I wasn't really snooping. I was looking for a pencil."

"Yeah, sure you were," laughed Claire, as she nudged me. She obviously wasn't as bothered by the death notice as I was. She changed the subject, saying that she really wanted to come to the wedding in August.

"Do you think we will be invited?"

"From what I gather, the whole world will be invited. It is going to be the event of the century," I said, rolling my eyes.

Claire smiled, "You don't sound too thrilled."

"I am thrilled for Isaac. He is super happy, and none of this could have happened to a nicer guy. I just wish he had picked someone who was not so social. Someone quieter... like me," I smiled and then burst into laughter.

"What are you gonna do when you move to Boston next year for that job? It sounds like that will require lots of social interactions."

"I don't know if I will move to Boston. I haven't decided yet, and I don't know if there will be a job still available. If I do move, though, I have observed that when I have a job to do, the social anxiety doesn't seem to bother me so much. It is funny, but when I was with

Evelyn's family at dinner and we were talking hockey, I was very comfortable."

"Good. Maybe you are outgrowing it."

"I think I'm grown already, but maybe it will get better though," I laughed. "What about you, Claire? Are you happy staying in Lewiston?"

"For the time being, I am. Eventually, I'd like to move to a bigger city. Right now, Lewiston works for me. Donna and Phillip are great, and I get along with the twins really well. I like working in Tweet's office, but I'm looking forward to starting college in September."

We talked about Ricky and how well he was doing with Ross and Daniella.

"He never talks about Mom or asks about her. It's almost as if he doesn't even remember life before moving here."

"That may not be a bad thing," said Claire.

Claire had to head out much sooner than I wished. The drive back to Lewiston was always quite a stretch. We embraced tightly, and I let her know I was looking forward to seeing her in Boston for the wedding.

The weekend went by quickly. Everyone seemed to love Evelyn, and she fit in great with the rest of us. On Monday, when they were leaving, Elise cried. Isaac told her that he would see her in August.

Isaac consoled his mother. "It seems like a long way away, but it is only two months." When you are part of a family that works on the water in Maine two months during the summer goes by pretty quickly.

Evelyn gave everyone a hug and told them how much she enjoyed everything. "I can't wait to get home and tell mom and dad how much fun we had and what a wonderful family I am marrying into. Thanks for everything."

CHAPTER 22
The Scare

A month before the wedding, Elise suggested that all the girls take a trip to Portland and shop for dresses. We caught the bus to Lewiston, spent the night at Donna's place, and then headed to Portland the following day. Claire and Donna were also joining us for the Portland adventure.

Margie and Diane were enthralled by everything. They chattered on and on about any new thing that they saw. Congress Street in Portland was alive with shoppers, and the J.R. Libby department store had everything we could possibly need. It was packed with people, and the excitement was palpable as we all set out to find our perfect dresses.

Evelyn had told Elise that the wedding would be semi-formal. According to her, we could wear "nice church clothes," whatever that meant. Elise, Daniella, Jana, and Donna were contemplating getting chic long dresses. Donna said that since the wedding would be in the evening, long dresses would be preferred. The rest of us were being more practical. Margie was hard to fit, because she was so short and stout. Jana promised to tailor Margie's dress just to suit her. Jana was a master at sewing and had made most of Margie's clothes. We finally found a beautiful red dress. Red was Margie's favorite color. It would have to be hemmed, but otherwise fit her perfectly. Everyone was rushing all around, going from rack to rack and trying to figure out sizing. Claire and I took Diane to see what we could find for her. After she tried on several pretty dresses, she decided on a sweet powder-blue tea-length dress that looked beautiful with her golden hair and blue eyes. Diane was very happy with it. Claire and I both found lovely dresses for ourselves as well. Mine was a tea-length yellow dress with a pretty orange and yellow sash at the waist, while Claire chose a blue dress like Diane's, but it was more of a light, navy color.

Elise was having the hardest time. She couldn't make up her mind between two dresses. One was navy blue, and the other was a pretty pink. In the middle of her contemplations, Jana said, "You can't wear navy. You are the mother of the groom. If you wear navy, everyone will think it is black. The pink is beautiful, and it shows off your beautiful olive skin and lovely brown hair. Get the pink."

Everyone else agreed, but Elise finally decided to get them both. "I need one for the pre-wedding dinner. The blue one will be good for that."

Finally, after several hours, we all had picked out our dresses and were ready to check out. Standing there around the counter with our purchases, I heard Jana ask, "Diane, Martha, where is Margie?"

"I don't know. I thought she was with you," Diane responded. Everybody turned to look at me as if hoping to get an answer. "I don't know either, Jana."

She had Margie's dress in her hand, but Margie was nowhere to be found. We all looked around. A few seconds later, when we realized that no one knew where Margie was, panic set in. The girl at the check-out counter asked what Margie looked like and how old she was. Jana described Margie as having light brown hair and blue eyes, and added, "She is short and stout and is wearing blue shorts and a white shirt." When Jana told the girl that Margie was thirty, she was taken aback until we further explained the situation.

"Thirty," the girl said, "oh my goodness. I thought we were looking for a child. I'm sure she is around here. When was the last time you saw her?" We all looked at each other. It seemed that each of us thought that Margie was with one of us. Diane, Claire, and I thought she was with Jana and Elise, while Elise, Jana, Daniella, and Donna thought she was with us.

After we explained to the salesgirl that Margie had the mind of a six-year-old, she got more serious. She called for security, and we described Margie to him. He suggested that we all spread out and look everywhere in the store.

"Check the dressing rooms. Check upstairs and downstairs. Can Margie talk? Will she be frightened when she realizes she doesn't see any of you? Will she know to ask for help?"

Jana was so upset she couldn't answer, so Elise took over. "We had been in the store for almost two hours shopping. The last anyone remembered seeing Margie was in the dressing room, trying on dresses. That was at least an hour and a half ago. Once we picked her dress out, no one knew where she went.

Finally, the store security called the police. Several hours had gone by, and we were all certain that Margie was not in the store. This had everyone frantic. It was getting late, and we were supposed to catch our train back to Lewiston at 6:00 p.m.

The police had gotten all of the information that they could. Donna had called Phillip, who spoke to the Portland Chief of Police concerning the case. The police knew that they were looking at a dire situation. Poor innocent Margie. None of us could imagine where she was or what had happened. Margie was so friendly that she could have gone with someone. Jana said that she had talked to Margie about strangers, but it had been a long time since they had that discussion. After all, there really are no strangers in Booth Bay Harbor.

"I should have had her with me every second. Margie has no idea about cities. She's so trusting. She would never think that anyone would do her harm. This is all my fault," Jana said as she broke down in tears.

As 6:00 p.m. drew closer and we still hadn't found Margie, we knew we weren't leaving Portland that night. The police had a "Be On The Lookout" alert in effect, and every cop on the street was looking for Margie. Portland, like all cities, had its share of crime. There were hobos, hoodlums, and flimflam men. There were the good and bad sections.

Donna finally said, "We all need to pray. Right now, that is the best thing that we can do." So that's what we did. We went from frantically crying and yelling to almost complete silence as we were all processing what was happening in our own minds. Just as we were trying to decide where to spend the night, a police officer came over to Jana and said, "Can you please follow me, Ma'am?" We became alert immediately. The officer took Jana outside to one of the patrol cars. In the backseat of the car was Margie, fast asleep.

Jana's whole body went limp. "Where did you find her?"

"Apparently, she was in the cafe just down the street from J.R. Libby's, curled up in a booth. The staff said she had eaten and was waiting for her family. They thought that she had left until they were closing the restaurant and found her. They called us right away because they had heard about the missing girl."

Even though we were all relieved, we all wanted to give Margie a piece of our mind. It was late and we were all exhausted, but we decided to catch the midnight train back to Lewiston anyway. Phillip and Tweet, who had driven down to Lewiston from Booth Bay when he heard what was happening, were waiting for us when we got there. Margie slept like a baby the whole way home with her head in Jana's lap. I think the one who was the maddest was Diane. She started lecturing Margie as soon as the train stopped and Margie woke up, but Elise stopped her. Margie looked sad and honestly didn't seem to understand what all the hullabaloo was about.

"I'm sorry, Diane. You guys were all busy, and I was so hungry. I kept saying I was hungry, but no one was listening to me. I didn't mean to do anything wrong."

The next day, Tweet drove Elise, Jana, and Margie back to Booth Bay while Daniella, Diane, and I took the bus. Elise and Jana had the "stranger-danger" talk with Margie again. She assured them that she understood.

On the bus to Booth Bay Harbor, we were all still so tired that we slept most of the way. The excitement of our trip to Portland and finding our beautiful dresses would always be overshadowed by the fact that we thought we had lost our precious Margie. I think it made all of us realize, even more than ever, how much we all loved her and how important she was in our lives.

In the summer of 1939, the situation in Europe was heating up. Radio broadcasts were full of news of the escalating crisis and Adolph Hitler's annexation of Czechoslovakia, the Sudetenland, and Austria. Even with that, there still was not a shot fired yet. It seemed like Hitler was just marching in and taking over, but the threat of war was looming. Both Great Britain and France had threatened war against Hitler's Germany. So far, President Roosevelt has been advocating for neutrality.

I was irritated by all this talk of war, as it was interrupting the baseball season on the radio. We couldn't listen to one whole game without it being sidetracked by war news. Europe, Germany, and Hitler seemed worlds away. I just didn't care and didn't want to hear about it. I was more interested in the fact that there was talk of commercial television being available to the general public. The radio reported that RCA was getting ready to mass-produce television sets.

They said that sporting events would be one of the first things to be put on television. I was so excited. I could just imagine sitting down and being able to watch my favorite teams and players. I was already trying to sell it to Elise or Jana. "You'll be able to watch Isaac. Every game, you'll be able to watch every game."

"How much will they cost? I bet a lot." Jana said.

"They haven't mentioned that yet." I hoped that the price wouldn't be too high. I really wanted a television set. I was pretty sure that Tweet was on board with it. He loved all the sports as much as I did.

August 19 was approaching quickly. Tweet suggested that we arrive in Boston on Thursday, August 17, to give us some time to settle in before the pre-wedding dinner, which was to happen on Friday night. He had coordinated with Donna so that she, Phillip, Claire, and the boys would stay at the same hotel. They weren't arriving until Friday evening and weren't invited to the pre-wedding dinner anyway, so that worked out fine. I was sad that Claire would not be at the dinner, but we had to follow the rules that were laid down.

CHAPTER 23

Pre-Wedding Party

The dinner was to be held at the elegant Parker House. All of Isaac and Evelyn's family would be attending, along with the bridal party and close friends of the Reader family. Johnathan was Isaac's best man, and three of his teammates would be groomsmen. Evelyn's bridesmaids were high school friends, and her maid of honor was a cousin.

The wedding reception was to be held at a restaurant across the street from the church. Since it had an outdoor courtyard, we had all been praying about the weather for weeks. So far, although hot, it looked like it was going to be a perfect weekend. Elise said that she thought that there were going to be two hundred people at the wedding. Tweet whistled and said, "I can only imagine how much this is costing."

We were all staying at the same small, quaint hotel we had stayed in the first time we came to Boston. Nothing fancy, but certainly nice enough. Between Donna's family and ours, we took up practically the whole place.

On Friday evening, as we all gathered in the lobby of our hotel, in our elegant rehearsal dinner finery, I couldn't help but feel proud. I was proud to be with such a good-looking group of people. Family: this was my family. We definitely turned some heads as we waited for our taxis to take us to the ball. I really did feel like Cinderella. The wedding rehearsal took place that afternoon at the church. Johnathan, Isaac's best man, was meeting us at the Parker House.

The Parker House was situated right on the Freedom Trail in downtown Boston. Pulling up out front, our taxis were met by men in tuxedos. The opulence and ostentatiousness were obvious and somewhat unsettling. My stomach started hurting. The doormen asked if we were there for the Reader-Pine wedding dinner and pointed us to the elevators. The dinner would be held in the rooftop ballroom overlooking the city. The hotel had been renovated in 1927. The original five-story hotel was now fifteen stories, with the 15th-floor rooftop ballroom being the Pièce de Résistance. The ballroom provided a panoramic view of the city. At night, it was just breathtaking.

Coming up the elevator, I really thought I was going to throw up. Jana noticed and took my hand. "You'll be fine. Just breathe." As soon as the doors to the elevator opened, I saw that the ballroom was decorated with everything ice hockey. It was great. In the middle of all the luxury of this hotel, there was ice hockey. I loved it, and my stomach immediately settled down. Most of the guests were dressed casually. The groomsmen, Isaac and Coach Reader in particular. They were dressed in their uniforms. I couldn't help but smile. It endeared me to the Reader family even more than I had been the first two times I met them. Isaac and Evelyn saw us come in and immediately came and gave us welcoming hugs. Evelyn was dressed to the hilt. She wore a lovely, passion pink evening gown that showcased her petite, flawless figure.

For the first time, I noticed that even though she was little, she was pretty buxom. Isaac was grinning from ear to ear. Tweet was snickering, "You guys don't really match, you know."

To this, Isaac said, "We know! Isn't it fun? Martha, what do you think about the hockey theme? When we were putting it all together, I couldn't help but think of you."

"Are you kidding? I love it." There were only about thirty to forty people at the dinner. That suited me just fine. I had met about half of them before, so I was feeling better and better by the minute.

All of the table decorations were brown and gold (the Boston Bruins' colors). It was beautiful. The tablecloths were a soft, light brown. The flower arrangements were tastefully spray-painted gold, and the silverware was gold with the napkins being gold and brown. The whole ballroom was shimmering. Everyone had an assigned seat that was displayed on a mirror at the entrance. I was happy and relieved to be sitting with the Pine family.

They were serving canapés that looked like hockey pucks and sticks. They were actually latkes and chicken drums which tasted superb. Everyone was milling around, making small talk. For me, this was always the worst part of any event. As I was standing there looking lost, Coach Reader came over and greeted me. "Martha, what do you think? Do you like the decor? Isaac and Evelyn were especially excited for you to see it."

"I love it, Coach Reader. So creative and so beautiful."

"Come and see the cake." The cake looked like a hockey rink. The icing looked like real glass.

"Now there is a creative baker," I commented.

"Did you see the ice sculpture? It looks like the Stanley Cup."

"Oh, how beautiful," I said, "I wonder how they do these things. Obviously, the people who do this must take years to hone their craft."

"I'm still disappointed that you won't be joining the Bruins in the fall. I hope you haven't ruled it out for next year. You would be an asset."

"Thank you, Sir. I am honored that you think so highly of me. I will definitely give it serious consideration after I finish school."

"Good. Now go get yourself a drink and relax." Just then, a maître d' came over and whispered something in the coach's ear. "I'll talk to you later, Martha. Have a wonderful time," said Coach Reader as he took his leave.

After he walked away, Mrs. Reader approached me. "Martha, so lovely to see you. You look stunning."

"Thanks. So do you, Mrs. Reader. I know that you have been working so hard to put all of this together for Evelyn and Isaac. Everything looks perfect."

"Thank you, but this is all Evelyn and Isaac's doing. I wasn't really thrilled with the hockey theme... but I have to say it turned out beautifully. Tomorrow, you can compliment me on the wedding and reception. I worked tirelessly on that," she laughed. "Coach told me that you couldn't take the job with the Bruins this year, but maybe next year? I hope you will. The offer to live with us will still be open. Evelyn will be gone, and I would love to have another young lady in the house."

"That's very kind of you. I haven't ruled it out for next year."

Just then, I heard a glass clinking. That apparently meant we needed to pay attention to something. Everyone got quiet as Coach Reader got up to thank everyone for coming. "You all are the most important people in Evelyn and Isaac's lives. Our family is so honored to have you here. Please find your seats so we can pray and eat."

The rest of the night was filled with food and speeches. Johnathan, as Isaac's best man, got up and gave a very heartfelt, although funny speech. He talked about how Isaac was the best brother anyone could ask for, but he told Evelyn that he was going to pray for her because she was getting one messy roommate. He talked about the time that Isaac got his head stuck in a bucket, and his dad had to cut it off him... "He kept begging me to go and get Dad. It took me an hour to get up the courage. By that time, Isaac had almost suffocated. He was so mad at me, he didn't talk to me for a week." Everyone was laughing while listening to the story.

Evelyn's cousin gave a speech saying how much she had admired

Evelyn all their lives. She went on to say things like, "She is the nicest, kindest, and best cousin anyone could ever ask for." It was very sweet.

Tweet talked about how kind, thoughtful, and funny Isaac was. Coach Reader stood, and he got choked up as he said, "I could not have asked for a better husband for my little girl. There is not an ounce of reservation about this marriage. Isaac and his family are exactly what my wife and I have prayed for since Evelyn was a little girl. Tomorrow will be a glorious day." Everyone clapped and raised their glasses in another toast.

After dinner, there was dancing to a live orchestra. I was sitting there talking to Margie and Diane when a very nice-looking boy came over and asked me to dance. I was so stunned.

"No! No, thank you," I said emphatically. As he was walking away dejected, Margie asked, "Are you crazy, Martha? Wait! Me! I will dance with you," she stuttered. A huge smile appeared on his face as he bowed and looked in my direction. He said, "It would be an honor." The next thing I saw was Margie out on the dance floor with this dashing young man. They were both smiling and laughing. When she was facing my direction, she stuck her tongue out at me. Diane laughed and said, "I guess she showed you." I felt like an idiot. If Margie could interact with people, dance, and have fun, why couldn't I?

"That was mean," said Margie when she returned. "You hurt his feelings. He was nice and cute, too. Why would you be so mean?" Then, she walked away. On the ride back to the hotel, Margie said, "That boy was really nice, Martha. Why wouldn't you dance with him? You know he plays hockey with Isaac."

"No, Margie, I didn't know," I replied, acting disinterested.

"He was cute, too. Didn't you think he was cute?"

"I didn't really notice," I lied.

Everyone was listening to our conversation. I didn't know what to say. I was feeling embarrassed again by my social awkwardness. Why couldn't I fit in? Tomorrow was going to be unbearable. I could tell.

We got back to the hotel so late that the only thing to do was to go to sleep. Claire, Donna, and the rest of them were already settled into their rooms and fast asleep. Given how I was feeling, I thought I would be tossing and turning all night, worrying about what tomorrow would bring. Luckily, that wasn't the case at all. As soon as my head hit the pillow, I drifted off to sleep.

CHAPTER 24

Great Matches

Saturday was a beautiful summer day. Just perfect for a wedding. The Cathedral of the Holy Cross is a beautiful church that was built in 1875. Although truly beautiful, it is a huge and intimidating structure. As the largest Roman Catholic Church in Boston, it could hold up to 1700 people on Sundays for Mass. For the wedding, the church was elegantly decorated. There were beautiful arrays of flowers everywhere. The flowers were a brilliant combination of the Massachusetts state flower, the Mayflower, and Maine's state flower, the White Pinecone. These two were combined with perfect bright pink roses. The Mayflower is a sweet, delicate pink-ish-white lavender color and went beautifully with the roses. The White Pinecone was artfully displayed in the midst of the other two more prominent components of the arrangements.

As the family of the groom, we were seated at the front of the church. Since the Readers had so many more guests than we did, Evelyn had wisely decided that she didn't want to split the sides by bride and groom, as was traditional. Elise and Jana, who both looked stunning, were escorted to the front by Johnathan, who was extremely handsome in his tuxedo. The rest of us were escorted by one of the ushers, or Tweet or Ross. When it was my turn to enter the sanctuary, I looked up and was mortified to see that the usher who was escorting me was the young man who had asked me to dance the night before. He looked even more dashing in his tuxedo.

"Well, well, we meet again," he said, smiling.

I couldn't say a word. I was so tongue-tied and embarrassed. I'm sure my face was the color of a tomato.

As we were walking arm in arm, he whispered, "It's okay. I don't bite, you know." Depositing me in my pew, he said, "You look lovely. I'm looking forward to seeing you at the reception." I couldn't even look at him.

Isaac finally came through the side door and stood at the front of the church where Johnathan and the other groomsmen were waiting for him. Tall and handsome Isaac and Johnathan, standing next to each other, could have been featured on a magazine cover. Although they had some opposite traits, anyone who saw them could tell they were brothers.

Finally, the introductory music ended after the bridesmaids walked down the aisle, and the wedding march began. We all stood as Evelyn and her dad came down the aisle. The gown Evelyn had chosen was simple and elegant. It had a very tasteful illusion neckline, sweet, laced, capped sleeves, and an empire waist that perfectly showed off her tiny waist and buxom top. She looked breathtaking. As a matter of fact, I'm pretty sure I heard some breaths being taken. The back of the dress was just as elegant as the front. Evelyn's hair was swept up, and there was glitter sprinkled throughout it. The hairstyle accented her long, slim neckline. Her jewelry, a sweet set of pearl earrings and a beautiful pearl necklace, and her makeup was simple and understated.

She told me later that the jewelry had been her grandmother's. She went on to say she didn't think the dress needed anything fancy to adorn it except for her bridal bouquet. I could not have agreed more. The bouquet was completely white, with a smattering of greenery.

Lovely! Coach Reader looked very regal walking her down the aisle. I felt like this could have been the wedding of a prince and a princess.

The priest was up front the whole time presiding over it all. As Coach Reader sat himself in the front, I noticed Mrs. Reader for the first time. WOW! That was the only thing I had to say. She looked like a million bucks. I just couldn't believe that I was a part of this. Me! Little, sad Martha LeBlanc.

The wedding went off without a hitch. As I looked around, I was sure that there were way more than two hundred people in attendance. To me, it looked more like three hundred. I thought to myself, *Who knows three hundred people?* The wedding was a long Catholic Mass. I was entertained watching all the older people fight falling asleep. Phillip, in particular, kept dozing off until Donna would jab him in the ribs. Both Elise, Jana, and Mrs. Reader cried. I would have been surprised if they hadn't. Despite the length, it was beautiful!

As Isaac and his new bride were walking down the aisle to get to the head of the receiving line, I started having another panic attack. I excused myself from the sanctuary and ran to the bathroom, where I immediately threw up. Jana was the groom's grandmother, so she was in the receiving line and wasn't around to calm me down and remind me to breathe. I was in the bathroom for just a few minutes when Claire came in looking for me.

"Are you okay?" She asked.

"I'm fine. Just my nerves. I don't know how I am going to get through all this."

"Come on, Martha. I promise I won't leave your side all night. You will be fine," Claire said as she hugged me.

We decided to skip the receiving line and head to the restaurant and courtyard across the street for the reception. There were a lot of people already there. Once again, everything was beautiful. Added to the flowers from the wedding were little sparkling lights and glitter. The little lights were everywhere. In the courtyard, men in white coats walked around with trays of champagne and canapés. There was a spat-

tering of high-top tables in the courtyard, but mainly people were
milling around, mingling.

"Ugh! My favorite thing to do." Claire and I grabbed one of the high-
tops. I unexpectedly started thinking about that cute boy who ushered
me down the aisle, and I started looking around for him. I couldn't
decide whether I was looking for him to avoid him or looking for him
because I wanted to see him. Finally, I found him. He was leaning against
the bar, looking very dashing as he sipped his beer. He had taken off his
jacket and tie and appeared to be flirting with a girl standing next to him.
That figures! So, I decided I would try to avoid him.

"Who are you looking for or what are you looking at?" Claire's
voice brought me back to reality.

"Who me? No one. I'm not looking at anyone."

"Oh, I see now. You're looking at that handsome guy who walked
you down the aisle at the church. He's pretty cute, you know. Was he
the one who asked you to dance at dinner last night? Margie told me all
about it," said Claire, laughing.

"Why is that funny? I don't see anything funny about it."

"Relax, Martha. I'm laughing because of the way Margie told the
story. I'm not laughing at you. You know how funny Margie is.
Anyway, why didn't you dance with him? Now that I get a good look
at him, he is pretty dreamy."

"Obviously, he has a girlfriend."

"How do you know that?"

"She is standing right next to him. Can't you see?"

"Oh, my goodness, just because he is standing next to a girl, you
assume it is his girlfriend! Martha, boys and girls can talk without being
in a romantic relationship, you know. Maybe it's his sister."

"Oh no... now he is looking this way and here he comes," I said, in
a panic.

"Good! Smile and be nice," smirked Claire.

Sure enough, he was coming right over to us.

"Hello again. Looks like we are sitting at the same table for dinner. He put out his hand and said, "I am Rhett James. Isaac and Evelyn have told me a lot about you. Martha, right?"

Now that I was looking at him close up, I saw that he was even more handsome than I thought. He had thick, curly brown hair and rich dark brown eyes. He was taller than I was by about a foot, which put him well over six feet tall. He was well-built and muscular. I was still so tongue-tied, I didn't know what to say. Finally, Claire cleared her voice and broke the awkward silence, "Martha, are you going to introduce me?"

Rhett turned to Claire and said, "I'm sorry, I should have introduced myself to you. Maybe you can be the interpreter that Martha and I need. I'm pretty sure I have yet to hear Martha say one word," he laughed. Claire laughed too. Finally, I said, "I am Martha LeBlanc, and this is my sister, Claire."

"Nice to meet you both. I'm looking forward to dining with you both. Now I must excuse myself because they want pictures of all the groomsmen and ushers. I'll see you inside." With that, he bowed and left.

"Oh, my goodness. Can we please just go back to the hotel? This is going to be so humiliating."

"Why? He seems charming," laughed Claire. Just then, a waiter came by holding a tray of champagne. I grabbed two flutes, quickly slurped them both down, and grabbed two more. Claire was watching me. With an amused look on her face, she said, "Slow down, sister. Have you ever even had any alcohol before in your life? That stuff will put you in front of the toilet on your knees, and it wouldn't be because of nerves. Give me one of those," she said as she giggled and grabbed one out of my hand.

After downing the Champagne, I immediately felt more relaxed. As we were walking into the dining room, Claire teased me, "He is super cute. If you don't want him, I'll take him." To which I replied,

"Go ahead. He is too arrogant and pushy for me." Just then, we were all summoned to the dining room for dinner.

As we settled in, Claire whispered into my ear, "It's not me he is interested in."

Sure enough, Claire and I were seated with Rhett James, two other guys from the hockey team, the twins (Benjamin and Robert), and another young lady, who was the girlfriend of another player who was also sitting at our table. I was seated between Claire and Rhett. Before Rhett got to the table, I asked Claire to switch seats with me. "Not on your life," she said, laughing.

After lots of toasts to the bride and groom, the food was served. The steak and shrimp dinner served with scalloped potatoes and green beans looked yummy, but my stomach was in knots.

"So, I hear that you are a hockey expert," said Rhett. "Coach Reader said you will be coming to Boston to keep the stats for the team next season. He says you are brilliant."

"I don't know about 'brilliant,' but I do love the game of hockey. As far as coming to Boston next year, nothing is set in stone. I told the coach that I would think about it."

"Okay. I hope you come, though. You will love Boston. I came here from Canada, and I love it."

"Canada? Where in Canada?"

"A little town in Ontario, called Kitchener. It's just west of Toronto. What do you do in Booth Bay Harbor, Martha?"

"I'm still in school, but I keep the local hockey team stats. That's how I became interested in the game. I used to attend the practices with Isaac and just fell in love with the sport. When I came to Boston for my first professional game, it was so exhilarating. After that, I just couldn't get enough of it. I listened to every game I could on the radio. I am hoping that Tweet will get us a television so we can watch the games this season. Instead of just listening to them."

"Who's your favorite team?"

"Boston, of course."

"Good answer. Favorite player?"

"Isaac, of course."

"Man, I'm trying to trip you up, and you are not falling for it," he laughed.

We talked all through dinner about hockey. I felt like I was reliving the night that I met the Readers. The other players were asking me questions about the game, and dinner seemed to fly by. By this time, my stomach had settled, and I was even able to eat. The other single hockey player at our table was seated next to Claire, and they seemed to be having a nice conversation, and Rhett James was looking better and better to me by the minute. He apparently had joined the team a little before Isaac, and according to the other players at our table, was a formidable opponent to anyone on the other side. I remembered that he played left defense.

"Who is the best team in the league?" I asked him.

"Boston, of course," he laughed. "But if I can't choose Boston, it's probably Toronto. The Maple Leafs are hard to beat. What do you think?"

"The New York Rangers will be the Stanley Cup winners this coming season," I confidently said.

"Really?" he laughed. "You sound pretty confident. Let's bet on it." At that, we shook hands.

"So, you say Toronto and I say New York?" I asked.

"No. I didn't say Toronto would win the Stanley Cup. I just said that New York would not. My money's on Boston."

"Boston is not a choice. Remember?"

"Okay, here is the bet: if Toronto wins, you come and work for the Bruins in Boston next year, and if New York loses, you come to work for the Bruins next year. Deal?"

"It's a deal." It was only later that I realized he had tricked me.

The night went on, and we retired back to the courtyard where there was a live band with a singer and people dancing. I was definitely feeling pretty tipsy from more than a few glasses of champagne. But I was having such a great time with Claire by my side.

We later learned that the other two Bruin players at our dinner table were also from Canada. Johnathan was dancing with a pretty, blonde girl and seemed to be having fun. Benjamin and Robert also seemed to be having a fun time dancing with different girls. I wasn't much of a dancer, so I just sat with Rhett and some of the other team members talking hockey. I couldn't help but notice how handsome Rhett James looked.

"Are you sure you don't want to dance?" he asked.

I shook my head, "I have two left feet."

"I could teach you. I'm pretty good at it."

"Modest too, I see," I laughed.

At some point, I looked over and saw Claire talking to an older woman who looked familiar, but I couldn't recognize who it was, so I didn't give it too much thought at that time. Claire was very social, so it wasn't anything unusual, except that it was the same woman I saw schmoozing with Elise earlier that evening. While talking to her, Elise had looked very uncomfortable and annoyed.

The party was winding down, and Tweet had come over to inform us that our ride was ready to take us all back to the hotel. Rhett asked if Claire and I could stay longer.

"Joe and I will take you and Claire back," he said. Joe was the other hockey player who had been dancing with Claire all night. "It's only nine o'clock. The night is young."

Claire and I exchanged glances, shared a smile, and she said, "Let me go tell Tweet."

A few minutes later, Margie came marching over to us. She had been watching us all night long.

"I know what goes on, you know. No hankie pankie, Mr. Hockey Players. The girls must be back at the hotel by eleven. No exceptions." At that, she stomped off, and we all laughed. A second later, she came back and said, "THAT'S 11:00 P.M. NOT A.M.! I wasn't born yesterday, you know." She looked adamant with her hand on her hip and tapping her foot. Again, we all got a kick out of it.

The rest of the night, Claire and I had a ball. Most of the hockey team joined us at a local bar for drinks and laughter. Claire and I couldn't drink because we were not old enough. That was okay with me. I had already had my limit. "Just how old are you?" asked Rhett. When I told him I was sixteen, he said, "Oh man. That could be trouble."

To which I said, "Nope. There is no trouble. I'm going back to Booth Bay Harbor, and you're going back to playing hockey."

"You know, Martha, you're a pretty smart girl for being only sixteen."

Rhett and Joe had us back at our hotel right on time. I was still very loosened up by the champagne I had consumed at the reception, and would not have minded one bit if Rhett James had tried to kiss me. That in itself was a miracle. Any other time, I would have been a basket case. In any event, it didn't matter; Rhett was a perfect gentleman. He shook my hand, bowed, and said, "This was a fun night, Martha LeBlanc. I hope we get to do it again when you move to Boston next year." As he was leaving, he turned around and asked, "When is your birthday anyway?"

"August 11."

"I'm in trouble," he screamed as he and Joe drove off.

"Wow! That was fun, Claire. I didn't want it to end."

"I'm pretty sure your Mr. Rhett James didn't want it to end either. He definitely likes you. But listen, before we go upstairs, I need to tell you something. I met our aunt tonight."

"Our aunt. What aunt? What are you talking about?"

"Aunt Claire. Our dad's sister. She somehow knows the Readers."

"Wait. Stop. I didn't even know we had an Aunt Claire. How did all this come about?"

"She came over to me and asked if she could have a word. Then she asked if I was Claire LeBlanc, and I said yes. She then introduced herself as Claire LeBlanc-Reece. She said, 'I am your father's sister.'"

"Holy cow! What did you say?"

"I was speechless. She gave me her address and phone number and said she would love to have lunch with you and me so we could catch up."

"Catch up? How do you 'catch up' with someone you didn't even know existed? Wow, that's unbelievable. Did she specifically say she wanted to have lunch with me and you... or just you?"

"Yes, she said, 'I would love to take you and Martha to lunch to catch up.'"

I wanted to talk more, but we had to be upstairs by eleven, so I didn't ask further questions.

CHAPTER 25

Decisions

The next morning, we all met downstairs to go to the Reader's house for brunch. Mr. and Mrs. Reader had invited us to brunch so we could send Isaac and Evelyn off on their honeymoon for a week in the Pocono Mountains. Tweet wanted to know where they were staying, and I heard Elise tell him that they would be staying at Mount Airy Lodge. She went on to say that Evelyn told her the hotel had heart-shaped beds and bathtubs. Tweet and Johnathan both rolled their eyes, with Johnathan sarcastically saying, "Oh, Isaac is gonna love that."

"Oh, hush," said Elise. "Just wait until you find the love of your life, you'll be happy with anything she is happy with. Isn't that right, Tweet?"

"Yes, dear," said Tweet as Elise elbowed him in the side.

The brunch was strictly for family. Claire and I were dying to talk to Elise about this Aunt Claire of ours. We just couldn't find a good time. There always seemed to be people around. Claire finally decided to leave it to me to find out and asked that I clue her in on any information I get from Elise.

The brunch was lovely but short because Evelyn and Isaac couldn't wait to get on with their honeymoon. Isaac gave each of us a separate hug and told us he hoped to see us soon. Once again, Elise was in tears. Evelyn gave her a special hug and promised again to take very good care of her wonderful son.

We all headed home later that day. After we all arrived in Lewiston, we said our goodbyes to Donna, Claire, and the others—with plenty of hugs and promises to visit more often—we finally boarded our bus to Booth Bay Harbor.

Between trains and buses and while everyone else was occupied with other things, I asked Elise about Aunt Claire. "Claire said that she met a woman at the wedding who claims to be our dad's sister. Do you know anything about that?"

Reluctantly, Elise said, "Yes, your Aunt Claire was there. I was as surprised as anyone. I had no idea she was connected to the Readers. I knew she lived in Boston, but that's all I knew. I was just sitting there, and all of a sudden, I heard someone seated next to me say, 'Hi, Elise. Do you remember me?' At first, I didn't recognize her. It had been over twenty years since I last saw her. I recognized the voice first. Then it dawned on me. It was Claire LeBlanc-Reece. I was speechless."

"What did she say?"

"She said, and I quote, 'I don't know why I didn't make this connection sooner. Isaac must be your stepson.' Once again, I was speechless and didn't know how to respond. She then went on to ask how you and Claire came to be at the wedding.

"I told her that you and Claire were staying with Tweet and me. I didn't think she needed to know details, so I didn't give her any. She then asked if your mother was at the wedding. At that point, I told her it wasn't the right time or place to have such discussions. I said, 'Imogene is not here. I am here for my son, and I am ending anymore discussion about the LeBlancs.' I then got up and walked away. Later, she came around to apologize. She said, 'I'm just confused, Elise. I'm trying to wrap my head around this. Forgive me for the intrusion.'"

"What do you think she wants? She told Claire that she wanted to take her and me to lunch and 'catch up.' What should we do?"

Just then, our bus was called.

"Let's talk about this tomorrow," Elise said as we all got up to board our bus.

The next morning, Elise asked if I wanted to go for a walk on the beach. Seems like the beach is always where we have had our serious discussions. On that day, we had a long discussion about Aunt Claire.

"Look, Martha, I really didn't know Claire very well. She was already married and gone by the time I came along. Claire and her mother, your grandmother, didn't get along very well, so no one really talked to her. Your dad didn't seem to care for her, which is why I was surprised when I found out he and your mom named Claire after her."

"Well, what do you think she wants with us?"

"Maybe she just wants to get to know her nieces. As far as I know, she doesn't have any children of her own. It's kind of uncomfortable and scary, though, because we don't know where your mom is, and we have no legal claim to you or your sisters and brother. You and Claire will be old enough to make your own way soon enough, but Diane and Ricky are still minors and will be for a little while. She could decide, as a blood relative, that she wants custody of them."

"What? No! Not another custody fight."

"I'm not saying that will happen, but it is a possibility. I can't tell you and Claire what to do, but just be aware of what could happen. It might be a good idea to lay low and see if she makes any other effort to contact you or Claire."

We left it at that until a few weeks later, when Elise said that Mrs. Reader had called her about the connection between Claire Reece and me. Mrs. Reader said that Mrs. Reece told her that she was my and Claire's aunt.

Mrs. Reader asked if that were true. Elise said that Mrs. Reader was as dumbfounded as the rest of us. Apparently, the Readers only knew Mrs. Reece through the hockey team. Her husband owned a concession company and was a sponsor of the Boston Bruins. Mrs. Reader had only met her one other time before the wedding. When Elise vaguely explained the situation, Mrs. Reader apologized for putting everyone in an obviously uncomfortable situation. "Do you have a clue what Mrs. Reece might possibly want?" Elise asked.

"I have no idea, but she asked if I could arrange a meeting with the girls. I just didn't know what to say."

After the conversation with Mrs. Reader was over, Elise dropped the phone and turned to me. "Martha, what do you want to do?"

Clearly confused, I responded, "I don't know... I will do whatever Claire wants to do."

A few weeks later, I found myself in Lewiston with Tweet, so Claire and I could meet our Aunt Claire for lunch. When we arrived at one of the only fancy lunch restaurants in Lewiston, Aunt Claire was already there, waiting for us. She was impeccably dressed, and her hair and make-up were flawless. I felt like I had met her before, but I couldn't remember. Although she greeted us warmly, I could tell that she was extremely nervous. I was so glad Claire and I were doing this together. I could not have possibly done it alone. Claire told me before we arrived that I shouldn't divulge any information to her.

"Let her do the talking. Just give short yes and no responses to her questions."

After we greeted each other, Aunt Claire began by saying that she was so happy to finally meet us. "I just want you to know that I don't expect anything from you. I just want to get to know you. When you were just babies and living at home with my mom and dad, I didn't really get to see you," she said. "You see, my mom and I didn't really get along. She didn't approve of the fact that I married outside the Catholic Church, so she cut me out of the family. My brother, your father, would contact me now and then to tell me about you guys, but he was under the thumb of my mother, so... well, I just wasn't welcome in their home. It wasn't that I didn't want to see or know you, but it was just how it was. I should have made more of an effort to find you after my brother and parents died. I'm sorry."

After she said all that, Claire and I looked at each other, and everything we had planned changed. We had a lovely lunch with Aunt Claire. We found out that she didn't have any children or other living blood relatives. She asked about our mom, and Claire took control.

"Our mom is fine. She made arrangements for us to live in the United States because she felt the education and opportunities were better here. She and Tweet were old friends, so he and Elise agreed for us to come."

"Oh wow! That is wonderful," she said.

Two hours later, we finally parted ways with hugs and the assurance that we would stay in touch. Before she left, Aunt Claire turned around and said, "Martha, I don't know if you recognize it, but you look just like I did at your age." She fumbled in her purse and withdrew a picture of herself at about my age. I was dumbfounded. "When I saw you at the wedding, I knew you had to be a LeBlanc. Claire, I only saw your mom one time, but you look just like her. She was a very beautiful woman." At that, she was gone.

Claire and I stood there for a moment. We were both in shock. This is not how we pictured this lunch going. Finally, Claire said, "Wow. What a nice lady. I'm glad we decided to give her a chance."

"Me too," I said. On the way back to Donna and Philip's, we chattered on and on about how it was such a shock.

"You know, Claire, you are a very good liar. I never knew you could tell such stories with a straight face. I'll have to be on guard," I laughed. "I really thought she was going to be a monster. Everything we know about our dad and grandparents leads me to believe she would be the same kind of trouble."

"You really do look like her," said Claire. "She is a very nice-looking lady. A picture of your future, Martha."

"Ha! Ha!" I burst into laughter. "Wait until she sees Ricky. From everything I can gather, he looks just like our dad. At least that's what Imogene always said. And Diane looks even more like Imogene than you do."

"Do you think she saw Ricky and Diane at the wedding?" Claire asked.

"If she did, she didn't mention it. She might not even know about them. By the time Ricky came along, Imogene was already in Lewiston and Diane was just a baby."

"Imogene! It is interesting that you always refer to her by her first name and never call her Mom," Claire said with raised eyebrows.

"Nothing interesting about it. She made it clear she didn't want to be my mom, so why should I call her Mom? Listen, Claire, I don't know what happened with Imogene. I don't know why she made the choices that she made, but she obviously has her own issues and problems. I decided a few months ago that I was not going to let her choices ruin my happiness. I forgive her, because if I didn't, then it would only hurt me. Forgiving and forgetting are two different things. I've tried to forget the hurt she caused me. Calling her Imogene instead of Mom helps in a way. I don't know why, but it does."

At that, Claire gave me a hug and said, "If it helps you, then good."

Over the next few years, Claire and I both kept in contact with Aunt Claire and saw her occasionally. She really was a lovely person.

As the end of 1939 approached, the war in Europe was escalating. The United States was still maintaining its neutrality, but Canada had entered the war in September 1939, the day after Great Britain's declaration of war on Germany. Once Canada entered the war, there were many in the USA who were calling for a more aggressive approach. Many others were saying we should continue to stay out of it. We were a country divided.

Regardless, the war in Europe was the primary discussion in the news and around dinner tables across the country. Elise, Tweet, Donna, and Phillip were especially on edge. I didn't understand it all, and being just a teenager, I didn't really want to hear about it. Looking back at it now, I was really a self-absorbed girl. The adults in our lives were terrified because they knew that if we entered the war, the chance of their children going off to fight was pretty high.

Between the Pines, the Martins, the Becks, and the LeBlancs, there were five young men who either were already of age or would be of age soon to enter the armed services. All the news from Europe looked like it was a bloody war with lots of casualties. It sounded like it was going to go on for a very long time. Tweet and Elise were on opposite sides of opinion. Elise said it wasn't any of our business what they did in Europe, while Tweet thought we should be taking more of an active role in the war. There were many heated dinner-time discussions. Johnathan and Ross agreed with Tweet, while Daniella and Jana agreed with Elise. The rest of us were too young or too far removed from it to have a real opinion.

The New Year's celebrations of 1940 unfolded as usual, drawing over 500,000 attendees to the traditional Times Square Ball Drop. In the United States, it felt like business as usual. However, the festivities were dampened in Europe by a tragic event: a German bomber had struck the London to Margate train. This shocking news left many on edge.

Radio coverage of the war was extensive, and people kept their radios tuned in around the clock. While there were familiar shows like Jack Benny, Amos and Andy, The Shadow, and Gunsmoke, everyone had vivid memories of the War of the Worlds broadcast in October 1938, which had caused a nationwide panic with its realistic portrayal of Martian invasions. That incident had mostly consisted of news bulletins interrupting regular programming, misleading many into thinking it was actual news.

Now, the "we interrupt this program" announcements about the war were a daily occurrence, and this time, there was nothing fictitious about it. Thankfully, sporting events carried on as usual, and just as I had predicted, the New York Rangers clinched the Stanley Cup in 1940. Not long after their victory, I was taken aback when I received a phone call from Rhett James. Elise quickly dashed over to Jana's house to inform me that a young man was on the line for me. Since all three houses shared a single phone, news traveled fast.

"A young man? What? Who? Who is it?" I bombarded her with questions as I picked up the phone.

"Hello, Martha, this is Rhett James. I hope you remember me from your brother's wedding. You are a very smart girl. The New York Rangers won."

"Rhett? How did you get this number? Oh, never mind. I'm sure Isaac gave it to you."

"You don't sound happy to hear from me. I just wanted to remind you of our deal. Are you sorry to hear from me?"

"Of course not. Just surprised."

"I'm not sure why you are surprised. We had a bet. Remember?"

"Yes, I remember. I also know that you tricked me."

"So, when are you coming to Boston?" he laughed.

"Well, I haven't decided anything yet. I still have to finish school, and Coach Reader hasn't made me another offer."

"When are you done with school?"

"I graduate in two weeks."

"Isaac and Evelyn said they are coming to Booth Bay Harbor to watch you and Isaac's brother graduate. I don't have anything going on, so I thought I might tag along with them. What do you think?"

Taken aback, I said, "It's a free country so far. So, I guess you can do what you want. But I guess you'd better ask them first."

"Oh, they said it was fine."

"Do you want me to come?"

"Like I said, do what you want."

"Okay then. I'll see you in a few weeks. Bye, Martha!"

I hung up and was flabbergasted. I hadn't heard from Rhett James since Isaac's wedding in August. Was he really coming to Booth Bay Harbor to see me? Elise had been standing behind me all along, listening to my end of the conversation. She wanted to know what that was all about.

"It seems that Isaac is bringing a friend home when he and Evelyn come for graduation. That Rhett James is coming with him," I said.

"Really? He said he was bringing a friend? Rhett James? That's very interesting. Do you like him? Cause apparently, he likes you," she smirked.

"Don't be silly. I don't even know him."

"Well, you spent some time with him at the wedding."

"Yes, and he is nice enough, I guess. I'm just not sure why he is coming to Booth Bay Harbor."

"Really, Martha. I'm sure. I know exactly why he is coming to Booth Bay Harbor."

"I have to go, Elise," I said dismissively. "I have one more test to study for. I'll see you tomorrow." I didn't sleep a wink that night. Rhett James was coming here to see me graduate. There must be more to it than that. Not that I hadn't thought about him since the wedding, but I just didn't know he had thought about me.

As the graduation approached, I was getting more anxious. I was anxious about graduation, sure... but I was more anxious about seeing Rhett James again. Graduation would be small; there were only six of us graduating. Johnathan was graduating with all honors. His teachers were encouraging him to go to college, but he wanted to join his Uncle Ross in the lobstering business and stay right here in Booth Bay Harbor. When we talked about it, he said, "I love it here. I love what I do. I love my family. Why would I want to go anywhere else or do anything else?"

"I'm sure Betty Rose doesn't have anything to do with your wanting to stay here, right?" I asked.

"Maybe. Maybe not. Anyway, I'm staying."

Betty Rose was the daughter of the family that owned the boat-building business in Booth Bay Harbor. She had a brother named Roger, who was on the Booth Bay hockey team. A very nice, religious family. Johnathan and Betty had gotten close over the last several months.

Graduation was upon us, and I still hadn't decided what I wanted to do. I also loved Booth Bay Harbor. Coach Reader hadn't reached out to me again, so I didn't know if moving to Boston was even an option. I loved to draw and had won a few state award competitions with my sketches.

Particularly with my drawings of ships and boats. Betty Rose's dad was a boat builder in Booth Bay Harbor and had commented on one of my works at a local art show. He had said that whenever I was in need of a job after graduating, I could always reach out to him as he had an opening for me. That certainly piqued my interest.

Everything was so up in the air. Tweet said if I was interested in pursuing a job with the Bruins, I should call Coach Reader. I felt like Coach Reader knew I was graduating, and if he was still interested in hiring me, he would call me. Anyway, I was lost. Elise, Jana, and Tweet said I should take my time. But I didn't want to take my time. I wanted to know what I was going to be doing, but I just couldn't arrive at a conclusion.

Just before graduation weekend, I asked Elise where Rhett James was going to be staying, and she said he would be staying with them, while Diane would stay with Jana, Margie, and me."

Claire and the crew from Lewiston were not coming, so it was just going to be us. I was anxious and a bit embarrassed that Isaac, Evelyn, and Rhett James were coming a long way for a lot of nothing.

Graduation from Booth Bay High was not a big deal, but Elise assured me that graduation was a big deal because it only happens once. She also said that in addition to coming for the graduation, they were coming to see the family. "The number of people in the graduating class does not dictate how big a deal it is," she said.

We had not seen Isaac and Evelyn since the wedding, and I was excited for that, but I kept worrying about the Rhett arrival. "Do you think that Rhett James will expect me to entertain him?" I asked Elise.

"I don't know, Martha. I don't know what Rhett James will expect," said Elise.

Jana, knowing my anxiety a little better than anyone else, was more sympathetic than Elise. "You will be fine, Martha. There will be plenty of people here to entertain that young man. Just concentrate on graduation and look at it as if Isaac were just bringing a friend home. Pretend it has nothing to do with you," she chipped in.

CHAPTER 26

Getting Acquainted

When Isaac, Evelyn, and Rhett arrived, my stomach turned so much that I thought I was going to throw up. I was having a panic attack, and thankfully, Jana noticed it and grabbed my hand. "Take a deep breath. You'll be fine."

Seeing Rhett, I was reminded of how handsome he was. I had apparently forgotten that he took my breath away. My heart skipped a beat. Isaac made the introductions, and smiling, Rhett said, "Martha, it is very nice to see you again. You look as lovely as I remember."

Evelyn ran over to where I was and gave me a big hug as she whispered into my ear, "Relax! You are as white as a sheet."

As the day progressed, I did become more relaxed. But I sure wished I had some of that champagne that we had at Isaac's wedding. The graduation was the next day. That night, Isaac asked Johnathan and me if we wanted to join him and Evelyn in showing Rhett around town. We drove to the boardwalk and parked so we could take a stroll. Rhett said that he loved our town. He said that it reminded him of the small town in Ontario where he grew up.

"Your town is more picturesque, but there are a lot of similarities. You know, Martha, I only had ten people in my graduating class. Now three of us are on the Boston Bruins hockey team," he laughed. "Hockey was the only thing we had in my town. I love a small town."

He smiled, and I thought my heart was going to melt. Rhett James was the cutest boy I've ever seen. His striking dark eyes had the longest lashes I had ever seen on a boy, and his curly brown hair, which was a little long for the times, would be the envy of anyone. When he smiles, his whole face lights up with his perfect, white set of teeth.

"Interesting!" That was all that came out of my mouth.

"When are you moving to Boston? Remember, we had a bet."

"You kind of tricked me on that one. Besides, I don't have a job offer on the table anymore. I haven't heard from Coach Reader."

"If he offers it, will you accept?"

"I don't know."

"Are you afraid of me? You act like you are. I promise, I will not bite you."

"I'm not afraid. I'm just confused. I'm not sure why exactly you are here."

"I'm here because I have thought about you a lot since August, and I wanted to see you again. Have you not thought about me at all?"

"Honestly, Rhett, no. I really hadn't thought about you until you called." I blurted the lie as I struggled to swallow the lump forming in my throat.

"Wow! Okay. I must have gotten it wrong. I thought that we made a connection in Boston."

"I'm sorry. It's just that Boston is such a long distance from here, and August was a long time ago. We had a great time at the wedding, but I didn't think there was any way it was anything more than just a fun night."

"You are a tough one. How about this, Martha? I like you. I'm here for a few days. Would it be possible for us to hang out to see if maybe you like me even just a little? I did come a pretty long way."

"I do like you. I just never dreamed that this would happen."

"So, do we have another deal? Of course, I won't mention that you are trying to welch on the first deal," he laughed.

"I'm not welching on anything... and yes, we have a deal. We can hang out."

"If that's the best you can do, I'll take it. Now relax and let's just have fun. I promise no harm will come to you," he laughed. "Graduation from high school is a pretty big deal, you know. You should be having fun. Not stressing over some guy," he rolled his eyes and laughed again. He sure was cute.

At that, he turned around and hollered at Isaac, "What have you done with the bubbly? I think we should celebrate Martha and Johnathan." Isaac, Johnathan, and Rhett ran back to the car where they had stowed a few blankets, two bottles of champagne, and five fluted glasses. They were only gone for a minute or two, but it was long enough for Evelyn to tell me her dad was ready for me to come join the team whenever I was ready. My heart skipped a beat.

"Martha, you made quite an impression on Rhett at the wedding. He couldn't talk about anything but you for weeks. Do you like him?" I just smiled and shrugged my shoulders.

Rhett came back with a small bunch of daisies for me. "For the lady," he said, with a smile. Those smiles were going to be the death of me for sure.

We laid out the blankets, and Isaac popped the first bottle of champagne.

"Here is a toast to Martha and Jonathan. May you both find success, love, and laughter, and may love, laughter, and success find you," said Isaac.

"Here, here," said Rhett as we all raised our glasses.

"Johnathan, Elise says you are planning on staying here after graduation. She says you will be working with your Uncle Ross. I certainly can see why you would want to stay here. It is such a beautiful place. Is there a special girl to make you stay too?" asked Evelyn.

"Evelyn, don't be so nosy," said Isaac playfully.

"It's okay, Isaac," said Johnathan. "Yes. As a matter of fact, there is a girl here that I am quite fond of. She is a year younger and won't graduate until next year. Her family owns the boat-building business in town."

"Betty Rose!" said Isaac incredulously. "Last time I saw her, she was a funny-looking little girl with braces and glasses."

"I know. She doesn't have either anymore," laughed Jonathan. "You'll meet her again tomorrow. Just be warned, you probably won't recognize her."

"How long has this been going on?" Isaac asked.

"Now look who is being nosey," laughed Evelyn.

"He's my brother. I want to know what's going on. Jeez! Johnathan, you never mentioned her on the phone or at my wedding. This is the first time I'm hearing about a serious girlfriend. And it's Betty Rose of all people. Betty used to follow her older brother, Roger, around at the skate rink. It used to drive him crazy."

"We had just started seeing each other right before your wedding. It wasn't anything serious. But I really like her."

"Is it serious now?"

I could tell that Johnathan was getting embarrassed. "Why don't you guys talk about this later? Looks like Isaac wants details, which might be better discussed brother to brother," I interjected, coming to his aid.

"Thank you, Martha," said Johnathan.

For a minute, there was a loud silence as we each tried to think about what to say next. Then Evelyn said, "Martha has a big decision to make. Will you stay here or go to Boston? Dad has said that all she has to do is say the word, and he has a spot on the team for her."

"Really, Evelyn?" Rhett said as he raised his eyebrows. "When did this happen?" he asked accusingly.

"He told us to relay the message to Martha just before we left."

"I just found out also, Rhett," I said quickly.

"Martha, that is wonderful! I know how much you love hockey

and how smart you are about it. Besides that, you also loved Boston when we were there. Are you going to call him?" Johnathan queried.

I was a little irked at this whole conversation. I had just learned about it thirty minutes ago, and now everyone was already looking at me for an answer. Additionally, Rhett James seemed to be questioning my honesty. He acted like I knew about it before he and I talked. That bothered me. Irritated, I said, "Look, everyone, I just found out about this a few minutes ago, and I haven't had time to process it yet. I need another glass of champagne. Can we please talk about something else?"

"Yes, please pass the champagne," encouraged Rhett, "How about we talk about hockey? Since you are obviously a soothsayer, Martha, tell us who will win the Stanley Cup for the 1940-41 season."

"Are you making fun of me?"

"Not at all. I think you have a good handle on the game and appreciate your knowledgeable opinion. I would never make fun of you."

"Since the season doesn't start for a few months, and I don't really know what changes the teams will make. I have no idea who will win the Stanley Cup next year. I haven't any, as you say, 'knowledgeable opinions' right now."

"What if nothing changes? Who do you pick?"

"Boston. In a pinch, I always choose Boston."

"See, I knew you were smart," Rhett laughed.

I was impressed by how Rhett was able to change the subject to one I was comfortable with. The night continued with more hockey talk and more champagne, and I felt better by the minute. Finally, Evelyn decided to change the topic. "Okay, enough hockey. Rhett, are you going back to Ontario at all this summer?"

"Hopefully, for a week or so before summer practice begins. The coach wasn't very happy that we didn't make the play-offs this season. I think he wants to start practice early. Eddie and Georgie are going home. I'll probably join them. My dad wants me to enlist in the Royal Canadian Air Force to help the cause over in Europe. He thinks that playing hockey is a sin against God and creation since there is so much death and destruction in Europe. Eddie and Georgie are already talking about enlisting."

"What do you think?" I waited patiently for the answer as Rhett pondered for a while.

"I don't want to enlist, but if it gets much worse, I will. We all need to do our part."

"Do you think America should get involved?" asked Johnathan.

"Yes. If the United States enters the war, it will end more quickly." It had been almost a year since Canada had entered the war. The United States was still sitting on the fence.

Evelyn shook her head and said, "I wanted to stop talking about hockey, but I don't want to talk about the war. That is all we hear about on the radio these days... war, war, war. I personally hope we stay out of it. Can we talk about something less depressing?"

"Yes, please," I said. "How long will it take you to get home, Rhett?"

"It's over two thousand five hundred miles, but it depends on the trains. Even if we get a non-stop, it will still take at least three days to get there and three days to travel back. We need a full two weeks off to go. Six days travel and a week at home."

"Wow!" Johnathan whistled.

"I know! That's why we never go home. If the coach wants to start practice early, we might not go home this year either."

"Oh, that's sad," said Evelyn. "I'm sure Dad can make some accommodations for you guys."

After an uncomfortable silence, Rhett looked at me and asked, "What else do you guys do in Booth Bay Harbor for fun?"

I said, "In the summer, we have the beach, obviously. Johnathan, tell Rhett what we do for fun. I just can't think right now."

"Fun? Well, we work pretty hard up here in Maine. There is not a whole lot of time for fun. But we do have recreation leagues for basketball, baseball, and hockey. Almost all the boys start working on the water in some capacity at a young age. The girls, well, I don't know what they do," he laughed and continued. "We have bonfires and beach parties, which usually are clam and lobster bakes. Mostly when we have free time, we hang out on the boardwalk or on the beach when the weather is good. The winters are long, though."

"And you are gonna stay here? You must really like lobstering."

"It gets in your blood. I just like being on the water. I can't imagine not living on the coast and not being able to go out on the boat every day. I do love it."

"What about you, Martha. What kinds of things do you like to do here?"

Everyone was looking at me, waiting for an answer. "I like hockey, baseball, and basketball. I go to any recreation game that I can. Of course, hockey is my favorite." At this point, my words were starting to slur a little.

"Do they have any girls' leagues?"

"You're funny, Rhett. No!"

"Some places do, you know? What else then?" asked Rhett.

"I love the lobster and clam bakes. I like to cook and bake to get ready for them, and then I like to eat."

"When Martha first came to Booth Bay Harbor, we all joked that she had a hollow leg. For a skinny little thing, she sure could put the food away."

"Oh, you hush, Isaac."

"Martha is a really good artist," said Johnathan.

"Really?" asked Rhett in amusement.

"Yes, I forgot I do like to draw a bit."

"Now you are being modest," Johnathan said. "Martha has won some awards for some of her drawings. She is especially good at drawing structures, like buildings, houses, boats, and ships. Betty's dad thinks she is very talented and could have a future in drafting boat and ship designs and plans."

"How about some more champagne?" I asked.

"Good idea. Give the lady some more champagne," laughed Rhett.

I was definitely feeling a little tipsy.

"I am a pretty good drawer, even if I do say so myself. Betty's dad said that if I wanted a job after graduation, he would have one for me. I just can't decide if I like drawing or hockey more. Or Booth Bay Harbor or Boston more."

"Oh, you definitely like hockey more," said Rhett, smiling. "And the people in Boston are a whole lot more interesting, especially the men! Right?"

"I don't know, there are some cute men here in Booth Bay Harbor. Betty's brother, Roger, is pretty interesting and cute."

"Gippy, little Gippy Rose?" Isaac spit out his champagne in laughter, "She is pulling your leg, Rhett. Roger, they call him Gippy, and he still has braces and glasses. His sister might have outgrown them, but he didn't," he said.

"Isaac Pine, you haven't seen Roger Rose in a while. He is looking pretty cute these days," I said, smiling.

"Has he grown too? Last I saw, he was hardly taller than five feet."

"You are exaggerating. Roger is just as tall as I am."

Now, Rhett was smiling and snickering. "Okay. Good. That means I have nothing to worry about. I think you like Boston better."

"Okay, Mr. Boston, maybe!" I smiled.

The rest of the night went on with a lot of banter and a whole lot of flirting between Rhett and me. When we got back to Tweet and Elise's place, Rhett asked if he could walk me home.

"Sure, I guess so. I only live right there, you know," I said, laughing and pointing to Jana's house.

"I do know, and it is going to be hard sleeping tonight knowing you are right next door. Are you feeling any better about me? Have I proven that I am not some cad coming to do you harm?" he asked with all seriousness.

I was the one laughing now. "Yes. I like you, Rhett James," I said as I gave him a kiss on the cheek. "Gotta go, though. I'll see you tomorrow. I hope there will be champagne at the graduation."

"Goodnight, Martha. I hope so too," he laughed.

"Goodnight, Boston."

I ran inside, happy that Margie wasn't up to interrogate me. As soon as I walked a bit further, Jana's voice greeted me: "Did you have fun? That Rhett James is a pretty cute guy."

"Yup! Gotta go to bed. Tomorrow is an important day. Good night." I said in a rush, slipping away before she could notice I was tipsy.

I got up to my room, closed the door, and dropped onto the bed in a swoon. My heart was in my throat, and I felt like it would pound out of my chest. Yes, I really did like Rhett James. I couldn't stop smiling. I knew I was not going to get a wink of sleep. I also knew what I was going to do after graduation.

CHAPTER 27
Small-Town Graduation

Graduation was nice. It was held at a cute little restaurant on the boardwalk. When you have a class of only six graduates, it isn't hard to accommodate everyone anywhere. After lunch, Johnathan, being the valedictorian, gave a wonderful speech.

He talked about several things, but the gist of it was, "If you have God, family, and friends, you have everything." Everyone applauded. When each of the six of us went up front to receive our diplomas, there was a round of applause. Betty was there to see Johnathan graduate. After Johnathan's speech, she came over and hugged him, and they stood there holding hands while all the well-wishers approached. I was reminded of what a good-looking couple they were. Johnathan was a handsome, robust guy. Everyone said he looked like his mom. She must have been a very beautiful woman. Betty was also a very nice-looking young lady; they complemented each other well.

Isaac came to give his well-wishes and told Betty how lovely she turned out. "You certainly are not the little girl with braces and glasses that I remember." Betty smiled politely.

Both Tweet and Elise told me how proud they were of me. "You have risen above all the turmoil of your youth. I could not love you more if you were my own daughter," said Tweet. "No matter what you decide to do, I know you will be successful."

Elise began crying again. "You are the daughter I never was able to have. Thank you." At that, I was crying too. I looked over and saw Rhett walking over with two glasses of champagne in his hand, waiting to talk to me.

"I think this calls for a toast, Martha."

"You know, Rhett, she is still only sixteen," said Elise.

"I thought maybe since it is a special day..." Rhett looked down, hoping for a good response.

Elise smiled and gave a nod of approval.

"To the future," said Rhett.

My knees were weak again. He had that effect every time I was around him. I thought to myself, *I'd better get over this, or I'm gonna be drinking champagne every day for the rest of my life.* Margie gave me a big hug and told me that she and God were proud of me. Then she turned to Rhett and said, "I knew you would come looking for her. You two are gonna get married someday."

Rhett smiled and asked, "Margie, do you have inside information that we don't know about?" She just smiled back and nodded her head, "Yes, they say I have a direct line, ya know!"

The rest of the day was free, and I planned to make the best of it because Isaac, Evelyn, and Rhett were leaving the next day. It was a beautiful evening, and so Rhett and I wandered down to the beach. We threw down a blanket and sat and watched the surf.

"This is very relaxing," said Rhett. "Are you going to miss it when you move to Boston?"

"Probably so," I said.

"Really! Are you really serious?" Rhett said as he grabbed me in his arms and hugged me.

"I'm going to call Coach Reader on Monday. If he still wants me to come... I'm going to Boston. Can I ask you something, though? Why did you really come to Booth Bay?"

"Why do you think? I came to see you. I told you. I really like you, Martha."

"How many girls have you had, Rhett? Am I just another?"

"Honestly, I've dated some, but nothing serious. You are probably the first girl in a few years that I really feel a connection with. I had a serious girl in Canada before I moved to the States. Once I moved here, it was over. What about you, Martha? Any serious relationships before me?"

Laughing, I said, "Before you? That is pretty presumptuous of you. Are we having a serious relationship?"

"I hope so," he said as he reached out and drew me to him. "I really do hope so. Do you mind if I kiss you?"

Looking into those big, beautiful eyes, I couldn't do anything but nod. We kissed, and it was the most glorious thing I had ever experienced. My knees got weak, and my whole body went limp. There was a little bug inside that started squirming from my thighs to my bosom.

"You know, Rhett, I've never kissed a boy before."

"You're kidding, right?"

"No. Not in the least."

"Well, you are pretty good at it. Let's try it again."

I still remember that night as one of the best nights of my life. I could have stayed wrapped in his arms with my lips locked to his for the rest of my life, and I'm sure I would have been happy.

Three weeks later, after much talk and planning, I was on my way to Boston. Elise and Tweet went with me to get me settled. They were so wonderful and supportive.

"Martha, if it doesn't work out, you always have a home with us. You are family now. Anything you need, we will be there for you."

Coach and Mrs. Reader opened their home to me. Mrs. Reader

was particularly happy. "I have another young lady in the house. I have been so lonely since Evelyn left. I thought I would die."

Tweet and Elise were happy to see Isaac and Evelyn again and to know where they lived. I felt like Elise was envious of Mrs. Reader having them nearby. But I also knew that she was happy to have someone close by for them if they needed anything. Rhett came over to the Reader's home shortly after I arrived. He had a bouquet of daisies for me. That would always be our flower.

"Well, hello, Boston," I grinned. And that would always be my "pet name" for him.

CHAPTER 28

Torn Apart

As it turned out, Rhett and his two friends never got to go home that summer. The coach had them working overtime to prepare for the 1940-41 season. Although I had a week to settle in before starting my commitment to the team, I actually started two days after arriving since there wasn't much to settle in and Rhett was at the rink all day anyway.

The coach had me keeping stats on every team I could get info on. It really was a daunting job, but I loved every bit of it. I was at the rink every day watching the team, listening to the radio, and reading the newspapers. Little did we know that this would be the last "normal" season for a while. Neither Rhett nor I had a whole lot of free time, but when we did, we made the most of it and spent it together.

The season started with a bang. The Bruins were on fire. They were undefeated for four games. When the team traveled, I traveled with them. My relationship with Rhett continued to blossom. I was quite sure I was falling in love with him. He was a great guy, and I thought he was falling for me, too. However, I could tell he was growing increasingly anxious about the war.

The United States remained neutral, but Canada was all in. They weren't one of the major Allies, but they had people from each branch of their armed forces fighting in Europe. Canada was providing lots of support. One night, we had a heated discussion about it.

"I don't understand why your country won't take a stand about this war," he said. "Roosevelt needs to get off the fence."

"I don't want us to go to war, Rhett. Europe is way over there. It has nothing to do with us."

"You're wrong, Martha. It has everything to do with you and the rest of the world. If you saw someone getting bullied or beaten up and you could stop it, wouldn't you do something?"

"Of course. You know I would."

"Well, that is what is happening. This man, Hitler, is marching into these small countries, which have no defense, and just taking them over. He is a bully. I have no doubt that once he conquers Europe, he will try to conquer North America. That means Canada, the United States, and Mexico."

"Surely that war won't come here."

"I think it will. And sooner rather than later. The more time that passes, the more I'm thinking I need to be doing something. Hockey seems frivolous to me while the world is going to hell."

"Rhett, you can't possibly be thinking of enlisting!" He shrugged his shoulders, shook his head, and said, "Morally, I think I have to."

For my seventeenth birthday in August, Rhett bought me seventeen daisies. He took me to A&W Root Beer (one of my favorite places) for dinner and then to the rooftop bar where Isaac and Evelyn had their rehearsal dinner. We laughed about our encounter that night, drank Champagne, and danced.

"Little did I know at the time that I just needed to give you a few glasses of champagne before I asked you to dance," Rhett said as we both laughed.

As 1940 turned into 1941, things were getting increasingly heated. Hitler was obviously a lunatic. Italy's Mussolini and Japan's Prime Minister, Tojo, were equally crazy. The major Axis powers were

Germany, Italy, and Japan. The Allies were the United Kingdom (under Winston Churchill), the Soviet Union (under Joseph Stalin), France (under Charles De Gaulle), and China (under Chiang Kai-shek). Although the United States, Canada, and Mexico were a world away from Europe, people were getting anxious. Canada was involved in the war because they were still tied to England. The Canadian hockey players, living here in the United States, where there were quite a few, were under increasing pressure to return home and do their part for the "Motherland."

It finally came to a head in January 1941. Rhett told me we needed to meet as he wanted to discuss some things with me. I made time for us the next day, but there was dread in my heart.

"I have to go home," he began. "All of us: me, Georgie, and Eddie are all heading home at the end of the month to enlist." With tears in his eyes, he said, "I love you, Martha. If things were different, I would ask you to marry me. I have never felt this way about a girl before. I hope you will wait for me to come back. Were it not for the thought of not seeing your beautiful face each day, I'd go home gladly and fight. I will miss you more than words can say."

At that moment, he looked like an innocent, beautiful little boy to me.

"No!" I said. "I don't understand why. WAIT! WAIT! Did you say you love me and would marry me? YES! My answer is yes." At this point, we were both in tears, saying how much we loved each other.

"When this war is over, I am coming back for you, Martha LeBlanc. We are going to have the best life anyone could have. You, me, a white picket fence, and three beautiful kids: two boys and a girl. All of them will look like you, and all of them will play hockey. Even little Martha." We embraced and passionately kissed.

"Little Martha?" I laughed.

Over the next several weeks, we came very close to consummating our relationship. It was so hard for both of us to restrain ourselves. One time, Rhett said, "We might never see each other again after I leave

Martha. Please let's do this!" Then, quickly realizing his words, he said. "I'm sorry, I shouldn't pressure you. We will wait until you are completely ready. It will make it even better."

Two weeks later, after we had spent every possible minute together, he was gone, and I was completely shattered. I regretted not making love to him before he left. I locked myself in my room and cried for two days straight. Eventually, Mr. and Mrs. Reader came up and coaxed me out.

The team was decimated, and everyone was walking around in a fog. Every day when I woke up, I didn't want to get out of bed. My heart ached so badly. Rhett entered the Royal Canadian Air Force. At first, he was stationed in Canada for training. While he was in Canada, I got letters from him at least once a week. I wrote to him daily. But in September 1941, he was deployed to England. After he was moved to England, the letters became less frequent. Every day, there was news of more Canadians killed and wounded. I didn't want to hear the news, but I had to. One day, Mrs. Reader said, "Oh, Martha, turn it off. You are going to drive yourself crazy if you keep listening." I had never met Rhett's parents, so I didn't have an inside source. I only knew what I heard on the radio.

Despite all odds, Boston won the Stanley Cup that year. The celebration was hardly a celebration. How could anyone possibly celebrate when the world was in turmoil? That stupid war had ruined everything. The Bruins and all of the other teams were having trouble getting players for the 1941-42 season. The Canadian league was barely operating. Some Americans were going to Canada to join the fight, while others were going to Canada to play hockey in the Canadian league.

In the early hours of Sunday, December 7, 1941, the unthinkable happened. The Japanese bombed Pearl Harbor, taking over 2,400 American lives. War had come to the United States. In the months leading up to the Pearl Harbor attack, the United States and Japan were involved in heated diplomatic discussions and economic conflict.

The Japanese were not happy after the USA imposed economic sanctions and an oil embargo against them in response to Japan's aggression against Indochina.

The Pearl Harbor attack virtually shut down sports for a short period. No one knew what to do. Many young athletes were enlisting. Our country was angry. How could this happen? Everyone wanted to do their part to avenge such a horrible injustice. Finally, President Roosevelt made an announcement, proclaiming the need for sports to continue. He stated that continuing sporting events would be beneficial for our country. He specifically mentioned baseball, the "All-American" sport. The letter was known as the "Green Light Letter." He went on to say that America needed recreation to take their minds off the war. Baseball and hockey would continue, albeit in a different form. On December 11, 1941, Germany and Italy both declared war on the United States. Things just kept getting worse and worse.

Shortly after the Pearl Harbor attack and the declaration of war by Germany and Italy, Tweet, Johnathan, and Ross came to Boston to meet with Isaac. Isaac had been making noise about enlisting, and Evelyn was beside herself with worry. She had just announced her pregnancy a week before the attack on Pearl Harbor. Benjamin, one of Donna and Phillip's twins, had already announced that he was enlisting in the army. Robert wanted to go too, but Benjamin talked him out of it.

"We can't both go. It will kill Mom. You are more established in your job here than I am, and as a fireman, you are technically already serving. I'm still trying to figure out what I want to do with my life. You stay, and I will go to represent our family in this war."

Behind closed doors, it was decided that Johnathan would go to war and represent the Pine family while Isaac stayed home with his wife and his soon-to-be child. No one ever said, but I was sure that Evelyn had called Tweet and asked him to come and talk to Isaac. However it happened, Isaac was a mess. He wanted to serve his country and felt guilty for not enlisting. So many of his teammates were already enlisted, and now Johnathan was going. Scenes like this were playing out all over the country. Families were struggling to make decisions about who should go and who should stay.

There were no exemptions for multiple family members serving; if you were physically fit, you were expected to serve. In September 1940, the United States instituted the peacetime draft. If you were a man between the ages of twenty-one and forty-five, you had to register. When the war started, Johnathan was not yet twenty-one, and neither was Benjamin nor Robert. Issac was, but because he was married and his wife was with child, he was exempt. Later in the war, this exemption was lifted.

When Tweet and the boys returned home and told Elise about the plan, she and Jana were devastated. They understood the need for everyone to pull together and everyone to make sacrifices, but Elise couldn't help but say, "If anything happens to that boy, I will die." When Ricky found out, he said he was going to enlist, too.

"Sorry, buddy, you can't enlist until you are at least seventeen. You've got two more years. Besides, with Johnathan gone, I will need you on the boat," said Ross.

"Thank God," said Daniella as she heaved a sigh of relief.

Within a month of the attack on Pearl Harbor, roughly 134,000 men had enlisted to fight the "Japs." The attack sparked a surge of patriotism that had never been seen before or since. Johnathan enlisted in the Marines and was sent immediately to Paris Island, South Carolina. Benjamin enlisted in the army and was going somewhere in Maryland. It happened so fast for both that no one really had a chance to say goodbye. By the first week in January, they were both gone.

A few weeks after Pearl Harbor, I got a letter from Rhett.

Dear Martha,

Welcome to the war. The Jap's really screwed up when they bombed Pearl Harbor. I'm hoping that the United States will shut this damn war down. I miss you so much. Every day I think about you first. Thoughts of you are what get me through the day. Don't worry about me. I am really in a pretty safe, though vital, job. I am on an antisubmarine warship that they call a corvette. We escort merchant ships, whose cargo is vital to Great Britain, through the Atlantic Ocean. Compared to some of my mates, I have it good.

I know before I left, we talked about getting married. I still want that white picket fence and three kids. I hope you still want it too. I've picked out names for our kids that I hope you will approve of. Our little girl will be named Daisy. I know we said Little Martha, but I'm sure you know why I love the name Daisy. I hope you love it too. I've also decided that we will have twin boys. I want them to be named Buddy and Bobby. I like those names. I think they are pretty fun. When I get out of this hellhole, I want FUN. You and I are going to have a FUN life. I hope you like the names, but if not, we can change them.

I hope you are keeping the team together in Boston. Please don't let this war get you down. I try to catch games on the radio now and then, and the games always make me and my shipmates smile and laugh. Lots of new players. I don't even want to know who is leaving the team now to fight.

I'm sure there will be a lot leaving now that the U.S. is fighting too. I hope you still love me like I love you. I am praying for us every day.

Forever Yours,
Boston

I cherished his letters. In my letter back to him, I told Rhett about Johnathan and Benjamin. They were still in basic training but would be deployed somewhere soon. I told Rhett that Isaac wanted to fight, but since Evelyn was going to have a baby, everyone talked him out of it.

Dear Boston,

I got your latest letter and am happy to hear that you are relatively safe. I pray for you every morning and every night. I miss you so much that my heart hurts. I wish I could count the days until we could be together again because then I would know that there will be an end to this awful war. I really am lost without you.

I love the name Daisy. I like it a lot better than the name Martha. I have never been too keen on my name. We might have to talk about the twin thing, though. You do know that God is the one to decide who has twins, right? I keep trying out my new name in front of the mirror. Martha James! It sounds wonderful. Silly, I know, but it's little things like that that keep me sane.

Anyway, things are different here, and everyone is on edge. Hockey is struggling. There is talk of many teams closing their doors. Coach Reader puts on a good face, but I can tell he is worried. I think that if the New York (Brooklyn) Americans lose one more player, they won't have enough to continue. Many other clubs are in the same tough spot. The Bruins haven't had the best year and probably won't be in the playoffs.

Watching everyone play, it seems to me that no one has a heart for the game like before.

As I'm sure you have predicted, the war has ravaged our family. Johnathan is in the Marines, and Benjamin is in the Navy. Isaac is angry and depressed. He told me he feels "useless." Since he's married and Evelyn is expecting a baby, everyone has talked him out of enlisting. If this awful war lasts long enough, my bet is he will eventually enlist, too. I am praying the war ends before Johnathan and Benjamin are sent overseas.

I'm going home to Booth Bay Harbor for the summer. Please send your letters to me there. I run to the mailbox every day to see if you have written. I will cherish your letters forever.

I love you, Boston!

Yours Always,
Martha

The war progressed, and hockey continued. Toronto beat Detroit to win the Stanley Cup, but no one really cared. The Bruins had a terrible season, and truthfully, were never the same even after the war.

Just after the Battle at Midway, Johnathan and Benjamin were shipped overseas to places unknown to us. The Battle of Midway saw the United States Navy decisively defeat the Imperial Japanese Navy. Over 3,000 Japanese lives were lost. It was looked at as a huge victory even though the United States lost almost 350 men. I was doubtful that the families of the men who were lost saw it as a victory.

In June, I went home to Booth Bay Harbor. Isn't it funny that I could finally call somewhere "home." I really did feel like it was home.

After Rhett left Boston, I was really homesick. I missed the Pine family as well as Diane and Ricky. I missed the beach and my small town. I missed our little beach church and my spiritual talks with Margie. When I got home for the summer, I was pretty sure I wasn't going back. I think Mrs. Reader and the Coach realized it, too. When we said goodbye, it felt like it was final. Evelyn and Isaac's baby was due in late July. Mrs. Reader would be occupied with being a grandmother. This made my leaving much easier for her. I appreciated everything that they had done for me and told them that I would always remember their kindness.

CHAPTER 29

Secrets

Several weeks after I arrived home, Tweet came back from his weekly trip to Lewiston looking distressed. He had gotten a call from the Royal Canadian Mounted Police. It seems that they had found the body of a woman, whom they believed to be Imogene. Hunters found her less than a quarter mile from the home we had lived in. Her father's home, in Canada. Although the body was in bad shape, they were able to determine that the cause of death was blunt trauma to the head. The police were investigating it as a murder. They couldn't definitively say it was Imogene, but all indications were that it was.

"They want to come and interview you, your sisters, and your brother," said Tweet.

"Interview us? Why?" I asked.

"I'm sure they want to know if you remember anything that might help them solve your mother's murder."

"They said that they are not even sure it is her. I mean, it's been over four years. She was out there for over four years? I would think a positive identification would be hard at this point," I sighed.

"Not necessarily. It's been four years since you saw her. That doesn't mean she has been dead for four years. Besides, there might be clothing or other things that could identify her. That's probably why they want to talk to you—to see if you can help them with the identification."

"Can't they tell how long the body was there? Can't they tell how long a body has been dead?"

"They can estimate, but there is nothing precise. They know that she has been out there for a long time."

"I need you, Diane, and Ricky to come with me to Lewiston next week. They are going to meet us at my office on Wednesday."

"How did they know to contact you?"

"I referred your mom to an attorney many years ago when you were in the convent. He told them about me."

"What did Claire say?"

"She seemed pretty shocked, and said she didn't know how any of you would be able to help."

"I'm not shocked. I thought she was probably dead somewhere. It was always surprising to me that she just walked away, never to be heard from again. Imogene was pretty crazy, but even for her, that would have been shocking."

At this point, I was actually thankful for this little diversion to take my mind off what was happening in Europe. It would also give me an excuse to see Claire. We hadn't seen each other since the day we had met our Aunt Claire for lunch. It seemed like ages ago. It was odd, but I wasn't the least bit sad about my mom. I wasn't surprised either.

Diane and Ricky took the news pretty well. Diane actually said, "This makes more sense to me than Mom just walking out the door and never coming back. I never believed that."

Ricky said, "None of it makes sense to me. None of it."

When we arrived in Lewiston, Claire was waiting for us. She was off from college for the summer and looked great. I could tell she was happy. She still worked for Tweet, manning the office when he was in Booth Bay Harbor. In college, she was majoring in English and

History, which she loved. She was the brilliant one in the family. I still didn't know who she had gotten her brains from.

We were to meet the Canadian investigators the next morning at Tweet's office. That night, he and Phillip sat us all down and asked us if we were alright, which we all answered yes to. Tweet said to just answer their questions and tell them anything that we remembered, which might be helpful.

"Are you nervous?" he asked.

We all shook our heads no. Then, Diane shockingly said, "I know who killed her. It was that guy she was seeing. That guy named George."

"What are you talking about?" shouted Claire. "You can't go about making accusations like that. How do you know?"

"Well, it just makes sense. Who else would have done it?"

"So, you are just guessing about this?" asked Tweet.

"Well, I don't know for sure, but if I had to guess, yes, I would guess him."

"Okay, Diane, don't make statements like that to the police," said Phillip. "If they ask you if your mom had any friends or boyfriends, you can tell them what you know, but don't say you know who killed her," he said, shaking his head.

"Listen, all of you, just answer their questions to the best of your ability. Don't make conjectures. Tweet said, "Phillip and I will be right there with you, and if the questioning gets too harsh, one of us will step in and help. Okay? Now let's all go to bed and get a good night's sleep."

Claire and I stayed outside on the porch talking for a while. We talked about our lives.

"I can't believe you are not going back to Boston. I thought you loved it there. What have you got in Booth Bay Harbor?" Claire said incredulously.

Sadly, I replied, "I loved Boston when Rhett was there, and hockey was normal. Now, nothing is normal, and I miss Rhett terribly.

Between that and homesickness, I am always depressed. Before Rhett left, I was getting a handle on my anxiety. After he left, it came back. I just want to be back in Booth Bay Harbor, where it is comfortable for me."

"What do you think about all this stuff with Mom?" Claire asked, raising her eyebrows.

"I don't really think anything. I'm not sad, and I'm not surprised. I have no information to give the police. I find it all very interesting, though," I responded.

Claire questioned, "You're not surprised or sad at all?"

"Nope!" I said.

"Do you have any good memories about our mom? Any at all?" asked Claire.

"Not really. The truth is, I hardly remember anything from before we went to the orphanage. What do you think about what Diane said?" I asked Claire.

"I think it is just Diane running her mouth about something she knows nothing about. I hope she doesn't do that tomorrow. Allegations like that could ruin a man's life... not to mention his marriage."

"Did you know Imogene was seeing him?" I asked.

"Yes, Mom was head over heels for him. That's why she turned Tweet away. He was married, though. There was no future there."

"Maybe he did kill her to keep her from telling his wife. I can't think of anyone else who would have done it. She didn't really know anyone else. Did she?" I asked.

"Martha, now you sound like Diane. We have no idea what Mom did every day while we were at school. She certainly wasn't home being Susie Homemaker."

"True. Tomorrow should be interesting."

"I just hope Diane keeps her speculations to herself," said Claire.

"I'm sure Tweet will keep her in line," I said.

The next morning, we all headed to Tweet's office. Everyone was quiet on the way. Pulling up, we could see the Canadian police waiting outside for us. After introductions, we entered the office, which was much more sunny and inviting than I had remembered from the past.

"Gentleman, can we speak to you privately before you interview the kids?" asked Phillip.

Promptly, Tweet, the two investigators, and Phillip went behind closed doors into Tweet's "library."

That's what we called the room with all the law books and dictionaries. Tweet said later that he told the officers that we had been through a lot with our mom. He said that he explained how Imogene had all but abandoned us. Although he didn't say it to us, I'm sure he told them that Imogene had some mental problems. When they came out, they called us all in together. Tweet said that he did not want us to be interrogated separately, as we were all still too fragile about the past.

The officers were very nice. They spoke calmly and asked basic questions. When they showed us pictures of some clothing and a ring, we knew that it was Imogene and were able to verify it for the police.

When they asked if we knew anyone who would want to harm our mom, we all looked at Diane. "Mom had a boyfriend. I know he was married." Then she said, "I don't think he would hurt her, though."

The officers asked, "Are you talking about George Jenkins?"

"Yes, George." Claire continued, "George was always nice. I don't think he is involved in this. Let me ask you this: you said that our mom was killed with blunt force trauma. How do you know that she didn't just fall and hit her head?"

"That is a very good question, young lady. We know because someone tried to bury her. If she had fallen and hit her head, that probably would not be the case."

"Claire, do you remember the last time you saw your mom?" they asked, staring blankly at Claire.

Matter of factly, she said, "I don't know the date, but I know we went to bed one night, and when we got up the next morning, she wasn't there. She left me a note and some cash."

Tweet was able to give them a better idea of dates.

"Do you still have the note?"

"No, but it just said for me to call Tweet, and he would take care of us. His name, address, and phone number were on the note."

"Did you call him?"

"No. We just showed up here in Lewiston."

"How much money did she leave?"

"A few hundred dollars. Enough to get us here to the states, and then some."

"When did you leave, Claire?"

"We left that day."

"So you don't know if your mother ever came back to your house after you left?"

"No."

"Did any of you ever go back?"

"No."

"Martha, is it true you left prior to this?"

"Yes. About a month before."

"Did your mom have any other friends or people that she was in contact with regularly?"

Claire spoke up and said, "Honestly, we don't know. Mom used to work taking care of George Jenkins' mom. We don't know when that ended, but when it did, we had no idea what our mom did all day."

I chimed in, "Mom didn't have any friends as far as we knew."

Claire asked, "Did you talk to George Jenkins? What did he say?"

"I can't really talk about that with you, Claire, as it is an ongoing investigation."

"Is Mr. Jenkins a suspect?" Tweet asked.

"We haven't ruled him out."

"See," said Diane, "I knew he was involved."

"Diane!" said Tweet in a warning tone. "You don't know anything of the sort. Gentlemen, I think the LeBlanc kids have told you everything that they know. Can you tell us anything about the house and any other assets she might have had?"

"We don't handle that, but attorney Carr is handling her estate stuff. You might want to give him a call. Just one more thing, we found some blood on the porch at the house. Old, of course, but did anything happen before you left that would have left blood on the porch outside?"

Claire, looking shocked, shook her head no.

"Diane and Ricky?" They also shook their heads no.

When the officers left, Claire was mad at Diane.

"Diane, why would you cast suspicion on George Jenkins? You don't know anything about this. Why would you want to insert yourself in it and cast blame on an innocent man?"

"How do you know he is innocent?" retorted Diane.

"Well, I don't, but you don't know that he is guilty. We have a system here that people are innocent until proven guilty. I'm pretty sure it is the same in Canada."

"George Jenkins is the only one with a motive as far as I can tell," said Diane defensively.

"Oh, shut up, Diane. You're always running your mouth about things you don't know anything about."

"You shut up, Claire."

Tweet intervened, saying, "Okay, girls. Let's allow the Canadian authorities to handle this. You all did fine. I'm proud that you were able to speak with the investigators. I know it was hard hearing about your mom and all. Now I have to get back to Booth Bay Harbor, so let's go."

I turned toward Tweet. "Hey, Tweet, if it's okay with Donna and Phillip, can I stay with them and Claire until next week? I'd like to catch up with Claire some more."

"That's fine with us," replied Phillip. "I know Donna would love to have you."

Tweet left with Diane and Ricky, and I stayed with Claire. Man, was Claire mad at Diane. "What is wrong with her? Why would she so wantonly throw out George Jenkins as Mom's murderer?"

"You know, Diane. She loves drama. I'm sure she has it all played out in her head. "George killed Imogene in a fit of rage because he was afraid she was going to tell his wife about the two of them. Then he buried her in the woods. That is exactly how her mind works. She is already writing a book about it." I laughed, trying to lighten Claire up.

"Well, her mind is pretty scary then."

"She is a romantic. In her mind, the whole thing is a love story. I don't think she means any harm."

"Martha, that's sick."

"Maybe... but I'm telling you that is how Diane thinks."

"You know her better than I do these days."

"What do you think happened, Claire?"

"I honestly don't know."

As the week went on, Claire and I continued to talk about what we thought had happened and discussed our family and our new lives. I asked, "What do you make of the blood outside? I think Imogene must have gone back home after you left, and something happened there. It seems to me that George Jenkins is a very good suspect. Ricky certainly was quiet during it all."

"Ricky was quiet because he doesn't know anything and is smarter than Diane. He knows not to open his mouth about things he knows nothing about. For heaven's sake, he was only eleven years old."

"Claire, he never talks about Imogene or life before we came here. It kinda worries me. It's almost as if he has blocked it all out."

"If he has, good for him. I wish I could block a lot of things out. You don't talk about anything either. We all have different ways of coping. I think Ricky is fine."

I shook my head and said, "I just don't think it is healthy. I'm hoping it doesn't all come to a head one day. He says next year he is quitting school so he can work full time on the water with Ross."

"I hope he doesn't quit school. If he does, I'm sure he will regret it. What do Ross and Tweet have to say to that?" asked Claire.

"Tweet just says, 'We will cross that bridge when we come to it.' I think Ricky might change his mind."

"Ricky is so cute," said Claire. "Does he have any girlfriends?"

"No, but he is a big flirt. All the girls like him."

"What about Diane? Any boyfriends yet?"

"A different one each week. I have never seen anyone so boy crazy. Every time I turn around, she is "in love" with someone new," I laughed.

"See! She worries me. I think she is a loose cannon."

"I think you, for some reason, have a bias against Diane. She is a typical teenager. What about you, Claire? Any special guys yet?"

"Not really. I mean, there is one guy who I think is pretty special. But he is way out of my league, though."

"Why? Why is he out of your league?"

"He is older and works at the college."

"Works there? Doing what?

"He is one of the professors. He is super smart. He teaches micro-biology."

"Yeah, that sounds pretty smart. How much older is he?"

"Maybe ten years. I don't know exactly."

"That sounds risky. He isn't married, is he?"

"Of course not!"

"Have you been "seeing" him?"

"Not officially. The school has rules about professors and students dating."

"I see. What's his name?"

"Please don't tell anyone else about this. You are the only one I am sharing this with. Dr. Port. His name is Melvin Port."

"Even his name sounds smart," I said, laughing. "Now, tell me everything."

Claire went on to tell me that she and this professor had been "seeing each other secretly." She said that he is the only man she has ever been able to have a really good and interesting conversation with.

"Most of the boys I have dated in the past have wanted one thing. It's not like that with me and Melvin. He is so smart. We have discussions about history, science, geography, and just life in general. He thinks that this war is ridiculous and said he would never "volunteer" to go to war. He doesn't believe in war."

Skeptically, I asked, "What do you mean he doesn't 'believe in war?' I don't think anyone believes in war, but sometimes there are things you can't just turn a blind eye to."

"Well, I agree with him. We should have stayed out of it. A bunch of people dying for nothing."

That was unbelievable. I was shocked and mad that Claire would say such a thing. "For nothing! I think you and this Port man need to listen to what's going on if you think people are dying for nothing. I guarantee that the men who died did not die for 'nothing,' as you say. I can also tell you that Benjamin, Johnathan, and Rhett are not over in Europe fighting for nothing."

"We don't mean it like that. It's just that we think there could have been a more diplomatic way."

"Are you kidding me? Have you never heard of Pearl Harbor? I don't want to talk about this anymore. You are a smart girl, Claire. Smarter than I could ever hope to be, but you are wrong about this. If this "professor" is filling your head with this garbage, I think you have the wrong man. He sounds dangerous."

"Dangerous! He has never made any inappropriate advances towards me. I feel safe with him."

"That's not what I mean, and you know it. Where do you go when you date?" I asked.

"We can't be seen together, so I don't even know if I would call what we are doing dating. I go to his place, or we see each other at school in the library or in his office. We have never even kissed. We just talk a lot."

"Has he said that he is attracted to you?"

"Oh, yes. We have talked about a future together."

"It all sounds a little strange, Claire."

Exasperated Claire said, "Well, never mind. I shouldn't have told you. I just thought that you, of all people, would understand and support me."

"I'm sorry. I didn't mean to hurt your feelings. It's just that without a real date or any physical touch, I don't know how you can have conversations about having a future together."

"I said, never mind. Just forget I told you."

The rest of the week was a little chilly between us. The morning before I left, Claire said, "Please don't tell anyone about me and Melvin."

"I won't. Why would I? But I seriously think you should reevaluate that whole situation. He doesn't sound like he is right for you."

"Maybe you should reevaluate your relationship with Rhett James. I don't think he is right for you," she huffed.

"Let's not fight, Claire. I just want you to be happy. I don't know how you can be happy if you have to hide in the dark."

After I was home for a few days, I guess Tweet and Elise noticed my short responses to their inquiries about my week with Claire, so they asked me if something had happened between us. "We grew up," I responded. "We just grew up. That's all," I said.

The investigation into Imogene's death was still ongoing in Canada. Tweet said that a source Phillip knew indicated they were close to making an arrest.

"Phillip thinks they are going to arrest George Jenkins." He also said that Claire was very upset about the whole thing.

"How well did you know George Jenkins?" Tweet asked me.

"I didn't know him at all. I actually had no idea that there was a thing between Imogene and anyone until just before I left Canada. Claire told me that George was the reason things didn't work out between you and Imogene. You know, Tweet, I was busy trying to survive in that house. I didn't have a clue about my mother's "love life." I think I met George Jenkins one time, and that was at a local diner when we were with you."

"Claire seems to have known him well. She certainly seems to be very protective of him."

"I know. It is baffling. If he did it, I hope they arrest him," I said.

As the summer went on, so did the war, and so did life. Letters from Rhett became fewer and fewer. Letters sent would take four to six weeks to get to the troops, depending on where they were stationed. In one letter, he said that he hadn't heard from me for so long, he was beginning to wonder if I was still waiting for him. I had written him every week, never failing. Tweet said he thought the mail just wasn't getting through. It made me cry to think that, on top of everything else he had to deal with, he was worrying about my loyalty. Finally, letters started arriving home by V-mail. I was hoping the same was happening going outbound. Rhett's letters told me about the conditions on the ship and about some of his mates.

"One guy has never gotten one letter. It is so sad. Please get someone to write to him. I feel so bad for him every time the mail comes in. His name is Loyd Nixon. Just a few sentences would be great. I just feel so bad for him." So, I got Diane to start writing to him, and she was glad to do it. It was her and Margie's weekly project.

CHAPTER 30

Secrets Unraveling

In August, Walt Disney released the animated movie "Bambi," and Tweet proposed that we all travel to Lewiston to see it.

"Let's go and spend the weekend. Maybe it will take our minds off this war for a few minutes. We don't all have to stay at Donna's. I will splurge for a hotel, unless you and Diane want to stay there so you can visit with Claire."

"I'd kinda like to stay in the hotel," I said.

"Okay. Whatever you want," said Tweet.

Off we went to Lewiston. Diane decided she wanted to stay in the hotel too. Ross and Ricky stayed behind in Booth Bay Harbor to work. This was the first time I was seeing Claire since our harsh words about the war and her so-called "boyfriend." She and Donna met us at the theater. As usual, Phillip was working, and so was Robert. Robert had moved out of the family home into an apartment close to the firehouse. Donna said she didn't understand why he had to have his own apartment, since he was on call most of the time, and he almost always sleeps at the firehouse.

Claire and I greeted each other coldly. I was sure that everyone took note and was preparing to answer their questions later. Then I realized she seemed to greet everyone coldly like that. Margie was not having it. "What's wrong with you, Claire? Why are you looking so mad?"

"I'm sorry, Margie. I'm not mad. Just a bit preoccupied with getting ready to start school again."

"I'm excited to see this movie. It's about a deer, you know. About a deer and his family," said Margie.

"I'm excited too," said Diane. "I've never been to the movies before. I wish they would get a theater in Booth Bay Harbor."

"Tweet, how does it feel to be surrounded by all these women? You are a real sport taking us all to see an animated movie about a deer," laughed Donna.

"It is my pleasure. I'm used to being surrounded by women, and I love deer. I used to hunt them. Remember?" he laughed. "Besides, we all need a little distraction from the war."

"I'll say," said Claire. That's all everyone ever talks about anymore. Personally, I don't want to hear about that stupid war."

"Is that so?" I asked with my hand on my hip. "I'm sure all those boys over there are really worried about you, and what you do or don't want to hear about, as they are losing life and limb in, as you call it, 'that stupid war.'"

Claire threw me a dirty look.

Clearing his throat, Tweet said, "Let's hurry up and go in so we can get our seats. It looks like it is filling up."

As it happened, Claire and I were seated next to each other. Margie was on the other side of me, with Diane on the other side of Claire.

"Did you hear that they were going to arrest George Jenkins?" Claire whispered to me.

"I heard that they might, and it's about time."

"Why do you say that? You don't know that he is guilty," defended Claire.

"No, but that is what trials are for," I said.

"He is guilty," chimed in Diane.

"Oh, shut up, Diane. You have no idea about anything. You just like to run your mouth," said Claire.

"You shut up, Claire. If he isn't guilty, who is? If you know who did it, then why don't you say so?" said Diane.

"You all need to shut up so I can hear the movie," Margie yelled.

Half the theater turned and gave us dirty looks. Jana swatted Margie on the leg, but it shut us all up.

During the film's intermission, Claire whispered, "Meet me in the lobby."

In the lobby, Claire asked me almost accusingly if I had told anyone about her and Melvin.

"Of course not. Why would I?"

"I don't know, but he abruptly broke things off with me shortly after you left. He didn't give any explanation other than his job."

"I'm sorry, Claire, but it has nothing to do with me."

"Anyway, how have you been?" asked Claire.

"Just peachy. I spend my days worrying about Rhett, Johnathan, and Benjamin. Other than that, life is just dandy."

"What do you think about George Jenkins?"

"Like I said, I hope they arrest him so we can get this all over with."

"Arrest an innocent man?"

"You talk as if you know for a fact he didn't do it. How do you know?"

"Never mind. I guess you're right. That's what trials are for. Let's go back in. The movie is getting ready to start again."

It turned out that "Bambi" was not the uplifting movie we had thought it would be. When we left the theater, we were all crying, especially Margie.

"They killed Bambi's mom. How could they do that?" Margie asked, with tears running down her cheeks.

"Anyone want to grab a bite to eat?" asked Tweet, trying to change the subject.

Margie, who never turned down food, all of a sudden forgot all about Bambi.

"I'm not hungry," said Claire. "I think I'll head back home."

"I'll go with you," said Donna. "I'm not hungry either."

We parted ways with them and didn't see either of them before we left to go back to Booth Bay Harbor.

A few weeks later, they arrested George Jenkins. The news was all over Canada and the United States. Headlines read:

"Prominent Montreal man arrested in Murder of Mistress."

"Woman's Murderer Arrested After a Four-Year Hunt."

It was apparently going to be the trial of the century.

"The Canadian Authorities will probably want you and your sisters and brother to come to Montreal and testify at the trial," said Tweet. I really didn't want to go back there, but I knew that he was right. We all would have to go back.

CHAPTER 31
The News

Isaac and Evelyn's baby girl came "screaming into the world" on August 8, 1942. She was eight pounds seven ounces. I was secretly hoping that the baby would wait until August 11 so we could share a birthday. Isaac called Elise, and she said he was obviously "beaming with pride."

"You could hear his smile through the phone," Elise laughed.

He excitedly told us about the baby. "She has the thickest, darkest, curliest hair you have ever seen. Evelyn did great, but said she is never doing it again," he laughed.

"She'll change her mind," said Jana. She added, "God has a way of making women forget the pains of childbirth. It sounds like the baby looks like Isaac. What are they going to name her?"

With tears in her eyes, Elise said, "Jana-Marie! They are naming her after you, Jana, and my middle name, Marie."

Tweet, Jana, and Elise finally traveled to Boston in November to meet their new granddaughter and great-granddaughter. They came back excited to tell us all about their visit...

"Isaac says that they can't come for the holidays, but maybe they will plan a trip here in the summer."

The holidays weren't very merry this year. But with Margie, we had to put on a happy face and celebrate. At one point, Margie overheard Elise say, "With the war and everything going on, maybe we should skip Christmas this year."

"What?" hollered Margie. "Skip Christmas? We can't skip Christmas! Christmas is Jesus' birthday! I don't think He would like it if we skipped His birthday. We are having Christmas." Margie was the only person I knew who seemed unaffected by the war. She knew we were at war, and she prayed every day for the safety of Johnathan, Benjamin, and Rhett, but I was kind of envious of her innocence. The word worry did not seem to be in her vocabulary.

We did have Christmas. However, it was a scaled-down version. On the morning of Christmas, Margie said while we were eating, "I think Santa Claus is not happy about this war either."

Just after Christmas, I got a beautiful letter from Rhett:

My Dearest Martha,

I miss you so much that my stomach hurts. It's probably my heart, not my stomach, though. Thoughts of you are the only thing that keeps me going. I have pictures of you in my wallet and on the board above my bunk. All the guys are jealous. They say that you are too pretty to wait for an ugly guy like me. Ha! Ha!

It is so exciting to hear that Isaac and Evelyn have a new baby girl. I love the name that they picked out. I still like the name Daisy for us. I wish I could give you a bunch of daisies right now.

I'm so sorry that Isaac still wants to enlist. Tell him I wish I hadn't and hope he doesn't. What do you hear from Johnathan and Benjamin? That battle in Sicily was a doozy. I hope they are safe. The Americans are taking big hits everywhere, but it sounds like they are killing a lot of Krauts and Japs, too.

Anyway, I love you more than anything and can't wait to get home. I know I asked already, but WILL YOU MARRY ME? We need to do this as soon as I get home. I already told my mom and dad that they would be getting a daughter-in-law. If you say no, don't tell me until after this crappy war.

Love Always,
Boston

I wrote back immediately...

Dear Boston,

I love your nickname. Should we keep it, because I love your real name too? I mean, who doesn't love the name Rhett after seeing the movie "Gone With the Wind?" Clark Gable is dreamy... but you are even dreamier.

Before I forget... YES! The answer is still yes. I would marry you today if you were here. I am afraid of meeting your parents, though. What if they don't like me?

Johnathan and Benjamin are still okay as far as we know. They are not as faithful about writing as you are. Johnathan writes to Elise and to Betty. That's the girl he was dating just before he left. I work for her family at their boat-building business. She is a really nice girl, and I think she likes Johnathan a lot. She gets maybe one letter a month. I know she writes to him regularly.

They have arrested a man named George Jenkins for the murder of Imogene. I know, shocking, isn't it? His trial is to start just after the new year.

I am eagerly awaiting your return.

Love Always,
Martha

CHAPTER 32

Pressure

As 1942 turned to 1943, there was much talk about the Battle of Stalingrad. Thankfully, our troops were not on the Eastern Front. Thank God. The Battle of Stalingrad was fought between the Red Army (Soviet Union) and Nazi Germany. That battle lasted from July 1942 to February 1943, with around 19,000 deaths per day. It was the bloodiest battle in history. I was thankful that our boys were not over there. The Soviets eventually prevailed, forcing the German troops to surrender. Additionally, there were speculations about the mass murders of Jewish people in Lithuania, Latvia, and Poland. In December 1942, the Raczynski Note, a report from the exiled Polish government, raised suspicion about Nazi atrocities. At the time, most of this information was withheld from the general public.

In July 1943, the Allies invaded Sicily. That same month, the evil dictator, Mussolini, was voted out by his own Grand Council and was arrested as he left the meeting. The Sicily invasion saw the United States 7th Army lose over 2,200 soldiers, over 4,900 were injured, and almost 600 were captured. Italy, with Sicily practically decimated by the invasion and the loss of its fearless leader, finally surrendered to the Allies in September 1943.

Although Isaac continued to play hockey during the 1942-43 season, I could tell that his heart wasn't in it, especially after the invasion of Sicily. Isaac again started making noise about enlisting, so Tweet and Elise made another trip to Boston to try to calm him down and talk some sense into him.

"Isaac, you have a wife and a baby. They need you." After much argument and discussion, Isaac relented again, though he was not too happy about it. Elise came home beaming about the baby. I was so happy that little Jana-Marie was helping everyone think about something other than war.

I was still getting letters from Rhett, but I could tell he was getting disheartened. "Does anyone even remember that we are over here?" he wrote at one point. "It looks like I will spend another Christmas alone." It broke my heart. I tried to send him little gifts with each of my packages. It was hard to tell if he was even getting them.

As the 1943 holidays approached, we finally heard from the authorities in Montreal. It seemed that the trial of George Jenkins was to start on November 1. The Crown's Attorney told Tweet that he would need all of us—Claire, Diane, Ricky, and me. We were to travel across Canada to meet with him. Tweet explained to the Crown Attorney that it wouldn't be easy to travel back and forth, so they would have to get everything they needed from us in one meeting. Claire, Diane, and Ricky had school, I was working at the boat factory, and Tweet had an office to maintain. The Crown Attorney said that he would try his best to get what he needed, but he couldn't guarantee that we wouldn't have to go back.

"Can they make us go?" I asked.

"No. They can't make you go, but they have requested you come. Other than the inconvenience of it, is there any reason for you not to go?" asked Tweet.

"It just brings back a lot of memories that I was hoping to forget. I also worried about Ricky. You know he never talks about Canada. He never talks about Imogene. He acts as if he didn't have a life before moving here. He hasn't said one word about the fact that his mother was found dead. I don't think that is normal. Do you?" I asked.

"I don't know. We all deal with things differently. I guess I could tell the Canadian authorities that we are not willing to travel to Canada, but we are willing to give written statements of fact. But I honestly thought you might want to go up there and see what is left of your old home. The home belongs to all of you. I thought it might give us an opportunity to try to sell it or something."

"I have no desire to ever set foot in that house again. I don't want any part of it."

"Let me see what Claire says when I am in Lewiston next week," said Tweet. After Tweet talked to Claire, we decided that we would give the Canadian courts anything they needed in writing. They would send Tweet the questions, and we would fill out a sworn written statement of fact. The Crown Attorney agreed to this, but said he might need one of us or all of us to testify when the time comes. "We will cross that bridge when we come to it," said Tweet. "You still can't compel them to testify. You can request it, but we can deny the request," Tweet told them.

The questions came, and with Tweet's help, we each filled out our own statements. Tweet told me that Ricky couldn't remember anything after the time I left Canada for Maine.

"I don't know whether he is blocking it out or what, but he has no memory of anything after you left. That was a whole month. I believe him, too. I really think he doesn't remember."

"All I can say is that things must have gotten pretty bad in that house. What about Diane? What does she remember?" I probed further.

"She just says that your mom wasn't there a lot and that Claire took care of everything. She said that when Imogene was around, she and Claire fought. She was vague on the last time she saw your mom."

"What about Claire?"

"Claire says that your mom walked out the door and never came back. She left an envelope with a note, my information, and money inside. Claire says she just packed up Diane and Ricky, and they all left."

"Martha, I think you have the least information since you left a month before Imogene went missing. I doubt that they will want you to testify. Is there anything that you can think of that might shed some light on this and would make them want you to testify?"

"No, like I said, I didn't even know this man."

"I'm going to go up there and talk to the Crown Attorney. George Jenkins' defense attorney has requested to talk with Claire specifically. I want to know what he wants. I also want to meet with the attorney handling your mom's probate so we can get that moving. Maybe if I go up there, I can make some sense of all this."

Tweet was gone for a whole week. When he came back, he was pretty quiet about what the authorities in Canada had to say. "Martha, you don't need to worry about anything. They won't need any other information from you. The other three are a different story. The defense attorney and the Crown's Attorney are pushing for them to come and testify in person. The defense attorney wants to postpone the trial until that happens."

"Will they postpone it?"

"Yes, probably." Tweet went on to say, "On another note, the house and land are for sale. Since there are no issues with the estate, when the property sells, you and your sisters and brother will get the proceeds. After the Crown takes its share, of course."

"I'm gonna talk to Claire again. I think maybe they all should just go up there and get this over with," declared Tweet.

"Well, I don't want any part of it."

"Martha, do you have any good memories of your mom? She really was a wonderful person before you and Claire went to the convent. She was a good mother and loved all of her children. She was fighting to keep you. I don't know what would have happened if she had stayed in Lewiston instead of going to Canada. It is another "what-if." We can't live on what-ifs, though. I believe she had some mental health issues that didn't manifest themselves until she reached a certain age. I just wish you weren't so hard on her."

"I wish I had some good memories, but the truth is, I don't."

Sure enough, they postponed the trial. Now, it looked like it wouldn't start until January.

Thanksgiving and Christmas came and went. We all tried our best to celebrate family and the birth of our Savior, Jesus Christ, but our hearts were heavy. I was really beginning to think that this war would never end, and I would never see Rhett again.

The trial in Canada finally began on January 11, 1944. Tweet was following it closely. One day, when Tweet was in Lewiston, Elise warily approached me, saying, "I need to tell you something. George Jenkins's attorney is alleging that Claire killed your mom and then covered it up. Tweet is doing his best to protect Claire, but they are really pressing for her to go back up there. He doesn't want to tell you because you said you don't want any part of it. I think he could use your insight, though."

"What? Claire! That's ridiculous! Do they have any evidence, or is this just a guilty man grasping at straws?"

"I don't know. This all happened over the past two days. Tweet will be home tomorrow. Hopefully, he can shed some light on this for us."

When Tweet got home the next day, he looked like he hadn't slept in a week. I think he had aged by ten years since I saw him three days ago. Elise suggested that we give Tweet some space and not bug him for details. Tweet, saying he was exhausted, went directly to his room and slept for at least twelve hours.

The next day, Jana came to my room and said, "Tweet wants to talk to you."

I walked over to Tweet and Elise's house, and they were sitting at the kitchen table. Diane was at school, so we had the house to ourselves.

"Martha, how much do you want to know about what is going on regarding your mom's death?" asked Tweet. "I know you already mentioned that you didn't want any part of any of it. Is that still the case?"

"Yes, but no. I mean, I don't want any part of it, but it sounds like my sister is getting dragged way into it. I need to be there for her. What does she say?"

"Right now, she has refused to say anything. Claire said that she already told me everything she knows and has nothing else to add."

"Why can't that be the end of it then?" I asked with a poignant look.

"What do you think? Do you think that is the end? I have to talk to Diane and Ricky again. If something happened between your mom and Claire, we need to find out about it."

"Why? Why can't we just let it alone? You said that they can't compel any of us to go back up there."

Angrily Tweet said, "Why? You want to know why? Because George Jenkins might be innocent. He might go to jail for the rest of his life for something he didn't do. Would you be okay with that, because I wouldn't be?" Tweet was exasperated.

"Okay, let's just calm down. Do you think that Claire would talk to you, Martha?" asked Elise.

"A year ago, maybe, but not now. It sounds like you think Claire might be involved, Tweet. Do you?"

"I don't know. I just get a weird feeling about it all. If you want to stay out of it all, I would understand," said Tweet exhaustedly. "If not, then I could really use your help with Diane and Ricky."

"Of course I will help. What do you need?"

"I just need you to be with me when I talk to them. I think they would feel better if you were there."

Later that afternoon, when Diane and Ricky got home from

school, we met again in Elise and Tweet's kitchen. My little sister and brother both looked so young and innocent sitting there. I knew this was going to be hard. We had discussed talking to them separately, but decided we would talk to them together. Diane was barely twelve and Ricky was just shy of eleven when they last saw Imogene in 1938. It was now 1944. Almost six years had passed, and a lot had happened. Ricky was sixteen and Diane was seventeen now.

Tweet started the conversation by saying that the trial of George Jenkins had started. Do you two have any questions about the trial or anything that you want to know or think that the authorities in Canada should know?" They both shook their heads no. "What do you remember about the day you left with Claire?"

"I just remember Claire saying that Mom was gone and we were going to America to find you. I asked her where Mom went, and she said she didn't know. Ricky was crying, and Claire looked frightened," sputters Diane.

"Do you remember when you had seen your mom prior to that?"

"I hadn't seen her that morning. Claire sent me off to school. Ricky was sick, so he was staying home, and Claire was with him. I think the last time I saw her was the night before at dinner."

"Ricky was staying home sick? This is the first time I am hearing this. Is that right, Ricky? Did you stay home that day?" asked Tweet.

"I don't remember," said Ricky. "I don't remember anything," he stuttered.

"Ricky, you were almost eleven. It's not like you were a little boy. You have to remember something!" Tweet demanded.

"I told you. I don't remember!" Ricky said angrily, wringing his hands and shuffling in his chair. "Can I go now?"

I stepped in, "Ricky, what is the last thing you remember about Mom? Can you tell us that?"

"The last thing I remember is you and her fighting. I remember you left, and Mom went in a rage. She said some nasty things about you and the rest of us. That is the last picture I have of her."

"Do both of you remember George Jenkins?" asked Tweet.

"I do," said Diane. "He was really nice."

"Ricky?"

"Yes. I remember him. Mom spent a lot of time with him before Claire and Martha came home. That's all I know. Can I go now?" asked Ricky dejectedly.

"Yes, Ricky," said Elise as she gave Tweet a warning look and hugged Ricky. Ricky hurriedly left the room.

"Diane, after Martha left, how did your mother seem?"

"I don't know," she shrugged. "She just seemed depressed and angry all the time."

"How do you know she was depressed and angry?"

"She just was. She was always yelling at Ricky and always fighting with Claire. Claire was really angry at Mom, and Mom seemed to just stay away. She was never home."

"Did George Jenkins ever come to the house?"

"Not after Claire and Martha came home. I heard Mom tell Claire that it was her fault that George broke up with her. She said, 'If it weren't for you and your sister, George Jenkins would still be around.'"

"Was this after Martha left?"

"Yes."

"What did Claire say?"

"I don't remember exactly, but I know she got really mad. I do remember her saying, 'Martha was right, you are a horrible mom, and you would have been happier if we had stayed at the convent, and so would we.' Then mom slapped her."

"Where was Ricky when this happened?"

"It was late, so he was probably in bed. I really don't remember."

"That's okay, Diane. Is there anything else you do remember?" asked Tweet.

"I can't think of anything. I'm pretty tired. Do you mind if I go to my room now?"

"Yes. I think we are through for the time being. Thank you, Diane. I know this is hard," Tweet said as he hugged her.

After she left, Tweet, Elise, and I went out to the front porch and sat. Although the weather was very cold, it gave us a nice feeling.

"What do you think, Martha?" asked Tweet.

"I think I need to talk to Claire." I had an awful feeling in the pit of my stomach. "After I left Canada, I think something really bad happened in that house."

CHAPTER 33

Surprising Events

The next day, Tweet and I left for Lewiston. When we arrived, Claire was at school. Donna said that Claire had been "distant." Tweet suggested that I speak to Claire alone, so when she got home, Donna and Tweet made themselves scarce.

Initially, Claire said she didn't want to talk about it. "What is there to talk about?" she asked. "I have already told the authorities everything that I know."

"Did something happen between you and Mom? Something that got out of control?" I asked.

"Now you want to call her 'Mom' all of a sudden," Claire said angrily. "You left, Martha. I had to stay and take care of Diane and Ricky. Mom was missing in action. She was never there, and when she was, she was using Ricky as the new target child."

"So, what happened? Did you and Mom get into a fight? Was it an accident? Tell me, Claire. Tell me what happened!"

Slamming her fist on the table, with clenched teeth and tears in her eyes, Claire declared, "I can't. I can't tell you!"

"Why? Why can't you tell me? What if I promise not to tell?"

With a look of resignation, Claire barely whispered, "Martha, I did not kill Mom."

As soon as she said it, I knew what had happened. "Oh, my God. Ricky did it, didn't he?"

Claire paused for what seemed like an eternity. "It was an accident. He and Mom were fighting on the porch. Mom was really bullying him. She was calling him names and telling him he would never amount to anything. You know sweet Ricky. He always took a lot and never got mad or lost his temper. I came outside to intervene, and Mom started in on me. I don't know what had happened that day to set her off. Ricky asked her to shut up, and then he pushed her. She fell off the porch and hit her head on the rail. He didn't mean it. Ricky was so distraught. He was crying and telling Mom he was sorry. He kept begging her to wake up. I knew almost immediately that she was dead. Martha, you know Ricky wouldn't intentionally hurt a fly. It was just an accident."

"Claire, that's exactly right. It was an accident. You have to tell Tweet. Ricky was just a kid. They will understand."

"No! I can't. I would rather say I did it. He is much too fragile. I tried to talk to him about it, and he really doesn't remember. I don't want him to remember."

"All the more reason we have to tell. Ricky needs help. One day, it will all come back to him, and he will explode somehow. Besides, they are going to convict George Jenkins. An innocent man will go to jail."

"If he gets convicted, I will come forward."

"Please, Claire! You and I can talk to Tweet and Phillip together. We have to."

When Donna and Tweet got home, I told them that Claire and I needed to talk to him and Phillip. We told them what happened. Neither Tweet nor Phillip showed any emotion until it got to the part where Ricky pushed Mom. Tweet looked at Phillip and took an almost inaudible gasp. I think until that point, they both thought that Claire did it. Claire was crying and gasping for air herself.

"It was an accident, Tweet," she said. "Ricky never meant to hurt her. He just wanted her to shut up. Please, we have to protect Ricky."

"Claire, you have carried this burden long enough. Let Phillip and me handle it. I promise we will not let anything happen to Ricky. Phillip quietly asks, What did you do after that?"

"Ricky and I carried Mom as far as we could. Then we dragged her and tried to bury her."

"Where was Diane during all of this?" asked Tweet.

"She was asleep. The next morning, she went to school as usual, while Ricky and I finished burying Mom and cleaning up outside. Diane came home from school, and we just told her that Mom wasn't home. There was nothing unusual about that, so she didn't question it. We all went to bed, and the following morning, I showed her Mom's note, and we left for Lewiston."

"Where did you get the money to travel to Maine?" asked Tweet.

"Mom really did leave a note and money. I found it in her room. I think she was planning on leaving soon. I didn't know if she was planning on leaving with George or not. Since then, I have decided probably not. She had gotten more and more bizarre over the weeks after Martha left. Now, I'm not so sure she wasn't going to kill herself."

Ricky and I had agreed that we would never talk about what happened ever again, and we have never talked about it since we left Canada. I think, for Ricky, it is as if it never happened. I've tried to talk to him once about it, and he acted like he didn't know what I was talking about. I really believe he doesn't remember."

Hugging her, Tweet said, "Claire, like I said, Phillip and I will handle it from here. You are a very brave young woman. Don't talk to anyone else about this."

"What do you think is going to happen?" sobbed Claire.

"It was an accident. We will tell the truth to the authorities in Canada, and I don't think anything will happen. They will drop the charges, and Imogene's death will be ruled an accident. At least that is what I think should happen."

CHAPTER 34

Closure

Weeks had passed. Mom's death was ruled accidental, and George Jenkins was released. I'm sure life for him was never the same. I know it was never the same for us. Daniella and Ross tried to get Ricky into counseling, but he refused. Soon after everything came to light, Ricky enlisted in the Navy. He was only sixteen, but the navy took him anyway. A nice, willing, healthy, strong young man was not to be turned away during wartime. Daniella was distraught! Ricky left in the middle of the night, leaving a note that read:

THANK YOU, EVERYONE, FOR TAKING CARE OF ME AND LOVING ME. I'LL BE FINE. I WILL BE AT BASIC TRAINING IN NORTH CAROLINA.

LOVE,
RICKY

So now we had one in the Army, one in the Navy, and one in the Marines, not to mention Rhett in the Royal Canadian Air Force. I hated this war. I hated Germany. I hated Japan. I prayed every night that the war would come to an end. If we got out of this war with all our boys alive, it would be a miracle. I prayed that God would give us a miracle.

Despite my prayers, the war continued. We had no idea where any of the boys were. I knew Rhett was still escorting merchant ships in the Atlantic Ocean. Where Benjamin, Johnathan, and Ricky were was anyone's guess. I just knew they weren't in the U.S.A.

As 1944 drew to a close, the war was still in full swing. Betty Rose's brother, Roger, was killed in action. I remember sitting at the desk in the drafting room at the boat factory when two fully dressed soldiers came to break the news to the family. Before they had a chance to tell Mrs. Rose about Roger, she fell to her knees and wept. Mr. Rose, who was a man of great faith, tried to be strong and console her, but she was clearly inconsolable.

Betty cried, and so did I. I knew she was terribly sad about her brother, but I also knew in the back of her mind she was also thinking about Johnathan, just as I was thinking about Rhett. We hugged and cried together. The war had always been "real" to me, but the fact that I now knew someone who had died made it even more real.

Booth Bay Harbor had the funeral of all funerals for "Gippy" Rose. He actually came home in one piece and was buried in full dress uniform. He apparently had the back of his head blown off, but no one could see that. Mrs. Rose was still so distraught that she could barely make it through the service. After it was over, no one saw her for weeks. I couldn't help but wonder again if this war would ever be over. At the funeral, I heard Margie ask Jana if Gippy was in heaven. Jana told her that she was sure Roger was in heaven. Jana explained, "He believed in Jesus, just like us. We will see him again."

Gippy was buried at the cemetery up on the hill with his grandparents. Betty visited his grave every Sunday. She spent several hours there telling him all about what was happening in Booth Bay Harbor.

Just after his funeral, I heard Margie ask Jana if Hardy was going to heaven when he died. Margie's dog, Hardy, was getting up there in years. He still seemed pretty spry, but we all knew his days were numbered. A few days later, I heard Margie telling Jana that Hardy was ready to die.

Jana responded, "I really don't know. He still seems to be pretty peppy."

"No, he is gonna die soon. God told me so."

"What do you mean God told you so?"

"In a dream. God told me that Hardy-boy was ready to go to heaven. He said that Hardy would be waiting for me when I got there." Jana just raised her eyebrows, looked at me, and shrugged her shoulders. I mean, what are you supposed to say to something like that? Sure enough, two days later, Hardy was dead. He had died peacefully in his sleep. Margie didn't cry. She simply said it was his time, and she would see him again in heaven. We buried Hardy's twelve-year-old body in Jana's backyard.

Soon after the death of Hardy, I heard Margie tell Elise, "God is not ready for Johnathan or Ricky yet. He won't be ready for them for a long time. I've been praying every day for them, and they are coming home soon."

"I hope you're right," said Elise, turning to Margie with a worried look on her face and confirming, "We all know that it is God's time, not ours. God decides when He takes us up to heaven."

"But Elise, I do know. I know because God told me in a dream. He said that Johnathan and Ricky would be okay."

"Margie, we all have dreams. Sometimes they come true, and sometimes they don't. I pray that your dream about Johnathan and Ricky is true." Elise breathed deeply.

"Well, I know it is true. I am a faithful prayer, and God is faithful to me."

I wanted to ask Margie about Rhett and Benjamin, but I was too afraid.

The next Sunday, while we were at church, the police chief came in and motioned for Tweet to come outside. My heart was in my throat. I knew if the chief was interrupting church and beaconing Tweet outside, it had to be something urgent. All of us looked at each other with dread. Elise followed right behind Tweet. I could only imagine what she was thinking.

We all thought it was about Johnathan. Betty Rose looked at me with a face of dread. I said a silent prayer that it would not be Johnathan.

Yes, it was urgent, but it wasn't Johnathan. It was Phillip. He had been shot in the line of duty by a crazy, drunk person while trying to calm a domestic dispute in Lewiston. He was in a very serious condition and not expected to live. Tweet and Elise immediately left to be with Phillip and Donna.

What next? It seemed like every time things had settled down, some other tragedy would happen. We were all in Booth Bay Harbor waiting for news about Phillip when Margie shocked us all. She said, "God isn't ready for Phillip yet. He still has important jobs for Phillip to do. I have been praying about it." Once again, no one knew what to say in response to what Margie had said, so we just listened.

Phillip was in the hospital for two weeks. During the first week, he failed to regain consciousness. Then on the seventh day, he finally opened his eyes. He couldn't talk yet, but we knew he could hear and understand. The doctor said that it was a miracle. A week after he gained consciousness, he was released. The doctor said he expected Phillip to make a full recovery. According to Elise, the doctor had said, "I don't know who you have praying out there, but they have a direct line." It was funny because that's what Margie always said. Donna, Tweet, and Elise all looked at each other knowingly. The doctor went on to say, "If you had asked me when he was brought into the hospital if he was going to make it, I would have emphatically told you no. Granted, he needs to take it easy for a few weeks, but if everything goes as it has so far, he will be back to work and back to normal before you know it."

Maybe Margie did have a "direct line." I certainly didn't know anyone who was more faithful with prayers than she was. My bedroom was next to hers, and I heard her praying for people every night. Her night prayers lasted an hour. I often told people that she was the most Christlike person that I knew. The faith of a child. The Bible says that God honors that.

The next time I saw Phillip, although he seemed like he was back to "normal," I could tell that he was different. His speech was slower, and he walked with a slight left-leaning gait. He was still Phillip, but somehow seemed softer. He was still always a man's man. After all, he was a police officer. Now, though, he seemed to be more caring. I don't know how to describe it. I just liked him better this way. He was fully instated into the police department. Donna wanted him to be relegated to desk jobs, but Phillip was having no part of that.

According to him, if he can't be a "real police officer," then he doesn't want to be one at all. He was back on the streets of Lewiston within two months of his release from the hospital. Donna confided in Tweet that she cried every time he left for his shift. She just wanted him to retire or quit.

Tweet tried to reassure and comfort Donna, "This was his once. It's like lightning; it doesn't strike the same target twice."

CHAPTER 35

Coming Home

The war finally came to an end in September 1945. Our boys would finally be coming home. However, sadly, over 400,000 of our soldiers, and 4,500 Canadian soldiers would never be coming home. They had left home to do a job, to protect the world from some deranged lunatics, but never made it back. Despite that, life went on. Although everyone knew it would never be the same.

Claire had moved on to grad school in Boston. She and I never had the same close relationship we once had. I loved my sister dearly, but we had different views of the world. She never reconnected with that professor, thank God. Instead, she went on to marry a different professor. He was also a few years older than her. Claire finished her education and became a professor herself. That was quite a feat for a woman back then. She moved as far away from Maine as she could, and I think she had a great life. She and her husband had two children, a boy and a girl. Although we lost touch, I prayed that she had a full, wonderful life.

Diane married young. A husband and children were always all she ever wanted. Her husband was a great guy who seemed to love her deeply. She finally met him after sending him a letter every week during the war. Yes, he was that serviceman, Loyd Nixon, that Rhett asked her to write to. When he got home, he couldn't find her fast enough. I believe it was love at first sight for both of them. He stayed in the Canadian military as a career. They got married, and Diane moved back to Canada with him. She always loved to sew and cook and was really good at both. Diane was a positive, bubbly light to those who knew her. She loved being a wife and mother, and she loved enter- taining the military brass. She had three children, two boys and a girl, and was happiest when she was taking care of them. The older she got, the more she looked like Imogene. Looks are deceiving, though, because she was nothing like her.

Ricky came home from the war, and the first thing I noticed was that the spark in his eyes was gone. He was no longer the happy-go- lucky kid I knew. Although Ross told him that he would always have a job on the boat with him, Ricky decided to pursue a career in the mili- tary. I worried for a while that he had a death wish, especially before the war ended. He never spoke about what happened that night on the porch of our house in Canada.

Daniella and Ross were, for all intents and purposes, his parents. He loved them, and they loved him and were there for every important moment in his life. He married a woman he met in Washington, D.C., who was a few years older than him. Unfortunately, it was not a happy marriage. Ricky didn't talk about it, but I always thought that she was as mentally abusive to him as Imogene was. They never had any chil- dren, which was probably a good thing.

Finally, they divorced, and Ricky seemed happier. He still makes the trip back to Booth Bay Harbor whenever he can. For him, it is home. I have often wondered if he wished he had stayed and worked on the boat with Johnathan and Ross. Another one of those "what-ifs." I asked him one time if he was happy. He said, "I think I am as happy as I can be, Martha." I understood what he meant, because I felt the exact same way.

Benjamin came home from the war with lots of terrible memories that tormented both his waking and sleeping hours. He struggled with depression and a deep and frightening anger for a year, until finally it got the better of him. Phillip found him dead from a gunshot to the head.

Benjamin had used Phillip's police service revolver. He didn't leave a note or anything. He didn't need to. We all knew how hard each day was for him. He never talked about his demons. He never told us the things he had seen or done overseas. Donna and Phillip were devastated, and so was Robert.

For a while, Robert was so depressed that Donna was worried he would have the same fate as Benjamin. Phillip was so distraught and felt so guilty because Benjamin had used his service weapon. Both Tweet and Donna tried to tell Phillip that it wasn't his fault. "If he hadn't used your gun, he would have found another way. You can't blame yourself."

Donna asked Tweet to talk to Robert. Tweet told Robert that it was his duty to have a great life. He told him that Benjamin would want him to be happy. "You need to be happy enough for both of you. Benjamin gave his life for all of us. He didn't kill himself. The war killed him. We owe it to him to be happy." Robert eventually did find happiness. He fell in love with a great girl and stayed in Lewiston working as a fireman. He had two boys. The first one was named Benjamin.

Unfortunately for Phillip, it was a different story. He started drinking heavily and was perpetually angry and distraught. Nothing anyone could say seemed to help. He died peacefully in his sleep two years after Benjamin. Donna swears he died of a broken heart, and maybe he did.

Johnathan came home from the war and married Betty Rose. He continued to work on the water with Ross. Johnathan and Betty had two little girls—Helen and Joan—who grew into beautiful young women. I was very close to both of them. Joan was a tomboy who loved every sport imaginable. Helen was the complete opposite. She was as girlie-girl as you could get. They reminded me of Claire and me when we were much younger. Although they are two years apart, they were as close as twins. I hoped that their relationship would never splinter like Claire's and mine had.

Betty, Jonathan's wife, and I became best friends. She was a wonderful wife to Johnathan. He had his demons from the war, just like most of the soldiers who returned, but being able to work on the water and do what he loved helped him deal with his depression. Betty knew just the right thing to say when the demons started to rear their ugly head. She had a calming effect on Johnathan.

Truth be told, she had a calming effect on me, too. Whenever I thought I just couldn't cope, she knew how to get me out of my funk. Betty reminded me a lot of Jana. She was probably the smartest person I knew when it came to Bible scripture. Whenever there was a problem, she knew a verse that spoke to it. She didn't even have to look one up. She just knew them. I was always amazed.

Isaac and Evelyn went on to have three more beautiful children after Jana-Marie. Two more girls, Florence and Dorothy (we called them Flo and Doe), and a boy named Jacob. I laughingly told Elise, "I guess Jana was right when she said that God has a way of making women forget the pains of childbirth." All of Isaac's children were beautiful and smart, but when Jacob started school, Evelyn realized that he was struggling to keep up with his classmates. He had difficulty reading and writing. Everything was difficult for him. All three girls had been smart, easy learners. Some of Jacob's teachers said that Jacob was lazy, but Evelyn and Isaac never saw that. One teacher even told Evelyn she thought Jacob was dumb.

"He tries so hard. I don't think he is lazy or dumb. I just don't know what to do," cried Evelyn. Jacob was becoming increasingly frustrated and angry with school. Finally, when he was ten years old, his teacher requested a conference with Isaac and Evelyn. Evelyn was dreading it. *Just another teacher telling us about Jacob's hopelessness*, she thought. This teacher was different, though. She told them that she thought that Jacob was dyslexic.

"Dyslexic? What on earth is that?" they asked. The teacher explained that she thought Jacob saw letters and numbers either backwards or upside down, making reading and writing quite difficult.

"Now things are making sense," Evelyn said. "That's why when he was learning to write his name, he always wrote it backwards. Jacob is not stupid or lazy. I knew he wasn't."

After that, Isaac and Evelyn researched different teaching methods and got Jacob a tutor. Although he still struggled and had to work twice as hard as everyone else, he was able to overcome the disorder. He would always be dyslexic, but now he knew how to deal with it.

Jacob went on to graduate from high school, college, and medical school. He became a child psychologist specializing in helping children with learning disorders, particularly those with dyslexia. Jacob is one of the smartest and hardest-working people I have ever known. He was asked to speak and give lectures about dyslexia to teachers around the country. Jacob said, "I never want another child to be told they are dumb or lazy because they have dyslexia. If we can educate teachers about dyslexia, then they will not make that mistake." Everyone was very proud of him.

Isaac followed in Coach Reader's footsteps and became a hockey coach and part-owner of the Boston Bruins. He and Evelyn stayed madly in love and had a wonderful life in Boston.

Rhett came back home and, true to his word, he asked me to marry him... again. I don't know why, but I just couldn't bring myself to commit. I had been so excited for him to come home, but when he got here, I felt like we were strangers again. Despite all the love we had expressed through letters, when it came to reality, I just didn't know anymore. Rhett didn't understand, and neither did I. He was a wonderful man. The homecoming that we had both planned was not the homecoming that happened. Nothing was as I had pictured it. Rhett was persistent, though. "I love you, Martha. I will always love you and will wait as long as I need to." He told me this over and over again.

Tweet finally came to me and wanted to know what I was thinking. I told him I was just confused and scared. I shared that I didn't know if I loved Rhett. Tweet ever the wise man said, "Martha, don't make the mistakes that your mother made. I think you are afraid to be happy. I always thought that Imogene was her own worst enemy. She over-thought things. She was so afraid of being hurt, especially after what happened between her and your father, that she would never commit to anything that might have a future. Rhett is a great guy who obvi-ously loves you, and I think you love him too. I think it is YOU that you don't love. Don't wait too long to give him an answer. If you do, I fear you will regret it for the rest of your life."

At first, I was angry at Tweet. How dare he compare me to Imogene? But then again, I knew he was right. When I looked at this situation with Rhett and me, and what had happened so long ago between my mom and Tweet, I realized that I was doing exactly what Imogene did. What on earth was I thinking?

Rhett was living back in Boston again. Trying to make another go at hockey. A lot of time had passed, though, and he just couldn't compete with the younger guys who had been on the ice while he was fighting a war. He had made some connections when he lived in Boston before, and a sporting goods company hired him to handle their advertising and promotions. He continued to pursue me with deliveries of daisies, letters, and phone calls. He always said he would never give up on us.

Finally, he did give up. The letters, daisies, and phone calls all stopped abruptly. It left me devastated. I had planned on telling Rhett that I would marry him the next time he called, but he never called again. Tweet and Elise knew I was sorry and worried that I had blown it. In the depths of my misery one day, Tweet came to the house to see me. "I told you if you waited too long, it would be too late. If you want Rhett James, I think you'd better get yourself to Boston and tell him."

The next day, I hopped the train to Boston, and after buying a small bouquet of daisies, I went directly to his apartment. Working through my anxiety, I knocked on the door. When Rhett opened it, I handed him the flowers and said with tears in my eyes, "Boston, if it's not too late, I hope you will still marry me."

I was terrified that he would turn me away. Instead, he grabbed me in his arms, and we kissed the deepest kiss I had ever had. The tingling was back. My heart was thumping so hard that I thought it would come out of my chest. Tweet was right. I did love Rhett. It was me I didn't love. I had this idea that I didn't deserve to be happy. But when I thought about what made me happy, I realized that Rhett made me very happy.

"Martha, I have been praying for this day," he said with so much excitement in his voice and on his face. Yes! Let's get married. I promise I will make you the happiest woman in the world."

A few weeks later, we had a small ceremony at our church in Booth Bay Harbor. Rhett said he wanted a clam bake after the ceremony. I loved the idea, and I loved that it was what **he** wanted. He expressed, "I've heard so much about clam bakes, and I still haven't been to one. I can't think of anything that would be better."

"I can't either." I was happy, but just didn't want it to be chaotic. "Can it be small, though? Just us and the family?"

"Whatever you say, Martha. My family probably can't come. It's way too far. Someday, we will get back to Canada so they can meet you."

CHAPTER 36
Going Home

J ust before Tweet walked me down the aisle, I had a major panic attack. As always, Jana was there to lift me out of it. "Breathe! Just breathe!" At the moment I said my vows, I felt God's presence more than I ever had in my life. I knew that my life with Rhett was going to be great. I was happy. Truly happy.

After our marriage, we moved back to Boston. I was sad to leave Booth Bay Harbor, but Rhett's job was in Boston. I was back working for the Bruins and loving my job again. Rhett brought me daisies every day when he came home from work. He said, "I am bringing you daisies every day until we have our own beautiful Daisy." I just laughed.

Our Daisy was born exactly twelve months and one day after our wedding. She was and is the light of our lives. She has the tender heart and easy smile of her father. She is witty and smart. Ironically, she had no interest in hockey, and Rhett and I continued to laugh and tease her about that to this day.

Shortly after Daisy had been born, I became homesick and depressed. I had stopped working and was at home all day with her. I felt isolated and guilty for being depressed. I had everything I could ever want, and I still wasn't happy. I didn't know what was wrong with me. These days, they have a name for what I was experiencing. It's called postpartum depression. Back then, though, everyone just told me to "get over it."

Rhett came home from work one day and found me crying. "What is wrong?" he asked with concern in his voice.

"I miss home. I miss Tweet. I miss Elise, Margie, Jana, and the rest."

"Well, come on then. I can get off work for a few days, and we will make the trip. I know all of them would love to see Daisy." I didn't have the heart to tell him that a weekend trip was not going to cure what I had. He seemed to know it, though. After our short stay in Booth Bay Harbor, on the way back to Boston, we stopped at one of my favorite places, Ken's Place. It was just a little walk-up place between Booth Bay Harbor and Portland, and had the best fried clams on the planet. As we were enjoying the clams, Rhett interrupted the silence. "Martha, do you want to move back to Booth Bay Harbor?"

"Yes!" I said, without thinking twice. I didn't know how we could even contemplate that, as his job was in Boston.

"Martha, I am in sales and promotions. If you don't mind me traveling occasionally, I think I can work anywhere. When we get back, I'll talk to the boss and see what my options are."

Sure enough, a position was available for a sales manager in the Northeast region of the U.S.A. and Canada. The company loved Rhett and gave him approval to move to Booth Bay Harbor, provided he spent one week a month in Boston. Most of what he did was on the phone, and he could do that from anywhere. He was the boss of four other sales representatives. It was perfect.

A month later, we were moving back to Booth Bay Harbor. Elise, Tweet, and Jana were thrilled. Jana offered for us to live with her and Margie until we could find a permanent home. Elise confided that she and Tweet would love to have us live with them, but she said that Jana's health was faltering and she felt we could be a big help with Margie. I hadn't realized that there were health problems involving Jana.

"No one is sure what's wrong, but something is. Daniella is taking her to Portland for some tests," Elise said. We were all praying that it was nothing serious. Jana was only sixty-two years old. No one was telling Margie anything about Jana's issues, although she definitely noticed changes.

"Why is Mom always tired and forgetting everything?" she asked me.

"I think the older we get, the more tired and forgetful we become," I replied. Margie seemed to accept this.

Several weeks after Jana and Daniella got back from Portland, the test results came back. They did not look good. It appears that Jana had a growth in her brain. A tumor that was inoperable. There was nothing they could do. The doctors said that she would lose her eyesight first and then other functions such as speech and memory. Daniella asked how much time Jana had, to which the doctor replied, "It's hard to tell. It could be as little as a few months or up to a year. To be honest, the quicker the better in cases like this. It can be a slow and painful death or a quick and quiet one."

Jana took the news like a trooper. "I have had a wonderful life. I know where I am going, and I am not afraid. The only regret I have is that I won't be here to see any more great-grandchildren born," she tenderly said. Jana said she wanted to tell Margie herself.

It seemed like Margie was not surprised by the news. "I know, Mom. I have been praying, and I know that Jesus is waiting for you. I'll be coming to heaven soon, too, so be sure that you wait for me at the gate. I can't wait to see Dad and John. I know they are waiting for us."

Before Jana died, she called a meeting and confided that her one worry was about Margie. "Please make sure you all take care of her. I don't even want to choose who. You all can argue over who will be blessed enough to be the primary caretaker. Whoever it is will be lucky."

That was the God's honest truth, too. Whoever took Margie in would be lucky. Jana did not have a slow and painful death. Three months after the news of her tumor, she died in her sleep. She had not even lost her eyesight yet.

The funeral was a private family event, which was what she requested. Jana was a humble lady and specifically said she didn't want a whole lot of "fuss" made. Isaac and Evelyn came home for it, and so did Ricky and Diane. Jana was laid to rest in the cemetery on the hill overlooking the bay that she loved so much. Her husband and son, John, were already there.

I still visit her grave at least once a week. I will never forget how kind and understanding she was of my anxiety when I first arrived in Booth Bay Harbor and every time after. I promised myself that when she died, I would always honor her memory. Rhett and I stayed living in Jana's house with Margie. She helped with Daisy, and we were blessed to have her.

Four years after we had Daisy and three years after Jana's death, Rhett Junior was born. We called him RJ to make it easier. RJ is a replica of his father. He has an easy smile and is kind and smart. He loves hockey, and I love watching him and his dad play together.

Our Ricky was born two years after RJ. He, like his namesake, loves the water and would fish 24/7 if he could. Ricky is soft-spoken, shy, and sensitive. Like me, he is guarded when it comes to people. I love all my children, but Ricky needs more love than the other two, so I try to give him a bit more attention. Rhett and I are very careful with his heart.

Although Ricky tried to love hockey and other sports, he just didn't find them interesting. He likes drawing, reading, and fishing. I am thankful that Rhett understands Ricky and takes extra care with him. It would be easy for Rhett to spend more time with RJ and less with Ricky, because they are more alike, but he told me one day, "Ricky is like you, Martha. I adore spending time with him just like I adore spending time with you."

Surprisingly, I did not have any depression after Rhett Junior and Ricky were born. Maybe my previous experience after Daisy's birth had more to do with being homesick than anything else. Whatever the reason, I was happy to be able to enjoy my infants. The fact that Margie was a big help with all the kids also helped. Her sweet spirit and positive attitude were a breath of fresh air.

All three of our kids are a mixture of Rhett and me in the looks department. Over the years, many people have told us that Rhett and I look like we could have been brother and sister rather than husband and wife. I didn't see it before, but as Rhett and I got older, I could see what they meant.

Rhett loved living in Booth Bay Harbor. He was gone one week each month, and that was hard, but other than that, he didn't have to travel much. He had other people to do the traveling. It was only when there was a problem that he had to go and handle it. Rhett was a great dad. He was just the right combination of playful and strict. When he was home and not working, he spent every minute he could with one or all of the kids. I often thought that our kids were getting the life that I wished I had as a kid, and that made me smile.

Tweet and Elise were aging gracefully. They were enjoying a new phase filled with grandchildren. Tweet closed his office in Lewiston and stayed full-time in Booth Bay Harbor. He still practiced law occasionally, but mostly went fishing with Ross, who said he would never retire.

Tweet Martin is one heck of a guy. He is one of those people who is great at keeping relationships. He is the rock that holds us all together. My mother... yes, I can finally say, "mother," missed out on one great guy. I will never know what motivated her to do the things that she did. Tweet was probably right when he said that she was her own worst enemy. Maybe she just didn't think she deserved happiness, so she sabotaged it at every turn. No one will ever know. I do know now that there are names and diagnoses for mental illnesses that they didn't have or know about back then. Bipolar or manic-depressive are illnesses that might fit my mom's symptoms. If she had been treated for it, she might have been okay... but they didn't have the knowledge back then that they have now. Anyway, things might have been different if my mom had married Tweet, but maybe not. She might have brought him down, too. I'm kind of glad we will never know. My life after Canada has been great. We can always say, "if only," but for me, my if only was exactly as it should have been.

After Jana died, Margie's health deteriorated. Despite her brave face, I think that she really was heartbroken. Before I met Margie, I didn't know anyone with Down Syndrome. I found out later that they put people like her in institutions. I was aghast at this. I couldn't imagine sweet Margie in an institution. The average life expectancy for Down Syndrome was twelve years old. I couldn't believe it! Margie always had health issues, but now she was middle-aged. Would other people like her have lived longer if they weren't institutionalized? Margie had low vision and always had a slow reaction to everything. Her speech was sometimes hard to decipher, and she moved slowly and was easily winded. She needed help with some basic functions, such as showering, dressing, and occasionally with potty issues. Nothing that would have made her life shorter. She was a joy, and no one minded helping her with whatever she needed. But for the first time ever, Margie was depressed.

I asked her about it, and she said she was just tired. Rhett and I finally brought home a dog, thinking that it would lift Margie's spirits, and it did for a time. We wanted to get her up, walking, and exercising. The dog looked just like Hardy. Margie excitedly said, "I'm gonna name this doggie Hardy Junior, and we will call him HJ." We all liked it. HJ helped for a little while, but eventually Margie went back to staying in her room most of the time, which left us all worried.

One day, she told me that she was ready to see Jesus "face to face." I didn't think much of it because she was always talking about Jesus and God. She hadn't told us about any other visions since Jana passed. I just chalked it up to Margie just being Margie. Sure enough, she died a few days later. We woke up, and she never came downstairs. I went up to check on her, and she had died during the night. The doctors said it was her heart. Her heart had just stopped working. When I found her, she looked so calm and peaceful. She had a smile on her face, and I knew she was looking at the faces of all the people she loved who had gone before her. I cried so hard. Not for her. I knew she was happy. I cried for all the times that I knew I would miss her. I would miss her hugs, her smiles, and her bossiness. I would miss her wonderful, Godly advice and her sense of humor. I would miss watching her with our children. There was just nothing I wouldn't miss about Margie.

I remembered that when Jana died, Margie had told me, "When I die, I want a big funeral. I want everyone to come. I want the preacher to preach about heaven and hell. I want him to tell everyone how to get to heaven, so they don't go to hell. I want him to tell everyone about John 3:16, and then I want Clara Carson to sing, "Amazing Grace" and "When the Roll is Called up Yonder." Clara is the best singer, and I love both of those hymns. When that's over, I want to be buried on the hill with my momma, daddy, and my brother, John."

We made sure that every one of Margie's wishes was followed. The town came out in full force, and so did our family. Our small church was overflowing and not big enough to handle the crowd. People were lined up outside and in the parking lot. Clara sang the best "Amazing Grace" I had ever heard. While she sang, "When the Roll is Called up Yonder," everyone was crying. I'm sure everyone was picturing Margie up in heaven next to her Jesus. It was a very emotional event, with many tears shed by all. Our Daisy had gotten especially close to Margie, and during Margie's burial, she looked up to me and asked, "Mom, how are we ever going to live without her?"

This was a question I had no answer to.

Epilogue

Life after Margie was indeed difficult. The joy that she brought, that flicker of daily light was burned out. My anxiety had come back with a vengeance. I hated going anywhere where there would be a lot of people. I stopped going to church altogether. Thankfully, we lived in Booth Bay Harbor, so there were not many other social obligations besides church, but Booth Bay Harbor was growing. As the kids got older, there were more social things that, as a mother, I was required to participate in. Even though I still loved hockey, RJ's hockey games were difficult for me. Rhett was the coach of the team, and I needed to not only be at the games, but as the coach's wife, I needed to be there to help with practices. The schools had gotten bigger, and the older the kids got, the more involved they were. Ricky was not as socially involved as Daisy and RJ, but he played the piano, and he loved going to every event to cheer on his brother and sister.

Besides being a cheerleader, Daisy loved the choir, and they had performances several times a year. RJ not only played hockey, but he also played basketball and baseball. He was a star at them all. Getting to all their events was a daunting task. It was like climbing Mount Everest.

Rhett was very understanding, but I know that he got frustrated with me at times. These days, I think they would say I was agoraphobic. That is exactly how I felt.

The feeling escalated as time went on, and it finally left me paralyzed. It was so debilitating that I couldn't leave the house. Back then, there was no name for it, and so people just thought I was odd. Those close to me would tell me to "just get over it." I missed Jana so much during those times. Where my disorder or anxiety came from, I didn't know. I didn't know how to control it, either.

Although the kids were always wonderful to me, I knew that they just couldn't understand what was wrong with their mom. It was the same with Rhett. I was so thankful that God sent him to me. I honestly don't think there was another man on the planet who would have put up with it.

Every week, he still sent or delivered daisies to me. He was quick with a compliment and never hesitated to say he was sorry for any perceived wrong towards me. He was simply the best husband and father I could have ever asked for. I was happy. Or maybe I should say that I was happy as long as I could stay home and not have to deal with anyone. I finally told Rhett. He didn't really understand, but he told me he wouldn't make me go anywhere I did not want to go. He said that I should always just remember that the kids love their mom and want her at their "stuff."

One day, after I had been behind closed doors for a few weeks, Johnathan's wife visited me. Betty knew my situation. I looked at her and could see nothing but compassion in her eyes. She asked to pray with me, which I obliged to. She prayed for mercy and peace for me. She especially prayed that I would find a way to get through my anxiety. She asked for wisdom and understanding for my family and friends to help me cope with whatever was stopping me from enjoying the life that God had given me. When she finished, I felt true peace. Betty told me that if I asked God, He would be with me. She reminded me about what God's word said, "I will never leave you, nor forsake you," and that, "... His grace is sufficient for me and his power is perfected in my weakness."

She told me that anytime I am fearful and anxious, I could try to find a word from the Bible to help me through it. Psalm 27:1 states, "The Lord is my light and salvation, whom shall I fear?"

Every time Jonathan felt PTSD, she said he always recited that verse. And she didn't fail to drum it into my ears that the Lord is with me ALWAYS, and all I needed to do was to let Him in.

I tried, and it helped a lot, but I still missed so many things. When it became time for Daisy to graduate high school, she sympathized with me. "Mom, it's okay if you don't come to my graduation. I know it is hard for you."

It broke my heart. She was graduating from high school in a few weeks, and so I started praying. Even though I was already anxious about it, I was not going to miss it. In that moment, I promised myself that I would not miss another important event in my children's lives, and I didn't. From then on, I relied on this verse, "The Lord is my light and my salvation, whom shall I fear?" (Psalm 27:1, KJV).

Author Notes

This book has been a labor of love. Although it is a work of fiction, I have drawn inspiration from several people in my life to create some of my characters.

The star of the book, Martha, as mentioned in the introduction, is loosely based on my mother's life. There really was a custody battle between her mother and her father's family when she was very young. It left her and her older sister in a convent in Canada for almost four years, until they were able to come home to Lewiston, Maine, to live with their mom. My mom did not have many good memories about the convent or the nuns. Many of the convent incidents in this book were told to me by my mother. My mom did try to commit suicide when she was in her late twenties. That was before she married.

Martha had many "what-ifs" in her life. I chose to write the version of her life that I think she wished for. Unfortunately, her life was not as happy as this one. My mom loved ice hockey, baseball, and football, just like the Martha character. She also knew every player and even knew their stats. She would have loved to have had a career in sports.

Because we lived in a suburb of Philadelphia called Levittown, my mom's favorite teams were the Philadelphia Flyers, the Phillies, and the

Eagles. My friends would often joke that the voice coming from the family room was like a recording, as my mom would cheer on her favorite teams as it replayed over and over every time we watched the games at my house. I also had no idea she played basketball or softball, and certainly didn't know she loved to sketch.

After she married my father and became a mom, it was as if the Martha of her youth didn't exist anymore. Unfortunately, my mother didn't have a Rhett or a Tweet in her life. My father was not Rhett, and their marriage was not good, and her father died when she was too young to remember him. There was no Tweet to replace him. The part in the book about Martha finding her father's obituary is true. His obituary says nothing about his wife and children. My mother rarely spoke of him or his family. I find that ultimately sad.

I wish I had been more sympathetic to my mom's struggles. I was one of those people who thought, "Why can't she just get over it?" I looked at her as weak, and now I regret that so much. My youngest daughter, Peyton, is a lot like her Nana (that is what she called my mom). While there are many differences between them, Peyton has the same gift and love of art, although that's not touched on in the book. With a master's degree in architecture, she is an accomplished designer. Thankfully, like the Martha in this book, Peyton has a wonderful support system, to include a great husband and father. I know her Nana would be so proud of her.

I hope this book will pay homage to my mom. I pray she is looking down, reading it, and smiling.

Imogene is also a fictional character. I didn't know my grandmother very well. Everything that I do know tells me she was nothing like Imogene. Her character in the book is more for interest's sake than anything else. In real life, she raised four children alone during the Great Depression and the two World Wars. That alone is a feat.

Lovable, funny, smart Margie is based on my daughter, Whitney, who has Down Syndrome. I often tell people that Whitney is the most Christlike person I know. She loves Jesus, and she is not afraid to tell anyone she meets about Him. Whitney prays faithfully, and we have seen many of her prayers answered. Some of those answered prayers can only be described as miracles. I am convinced that it's because she has the faith of a child. God honors that. When my friends are in need of prayer, they always ask me to "get Whitney on it." We often say, "Whitney has a direct line."

In the 1930s and 1940s, they called people with Down Syndrome mongoloid. I refused to use that derogatory term in this book. Back then, the life expectancy for people with Down Syndrome was only twelve years old. That's because they placed these wonderful people in institutions and waited for them to die. I am so happy that we, as a people, have become more compassionate, smart, and caring. Many have asked me to write a book about Whitney. Maybe one day I will.

The wonderful and illustrious Tweet Martin is based on my dear husband, Brian. He is the glue that holds our family together. Steady and always the voice of encouragement and reason. Like Tweet, Brian excels at building relationships. He is a great husband, a great father, a great son, a great uncle, and a great brother. He is the one that everyone turns to for advice. We started dating when I was eighteen and he was nineteen. We dated for seven years before we married and have been happily married since 1983. I sometimes think of my "what ifs," and I am happy I chose the right path.

All of the other characters in the book are fictional.

I hope you have enjoyed reading *MARTHA* as much as I have enjoyed writing it.

A Taste of
New England

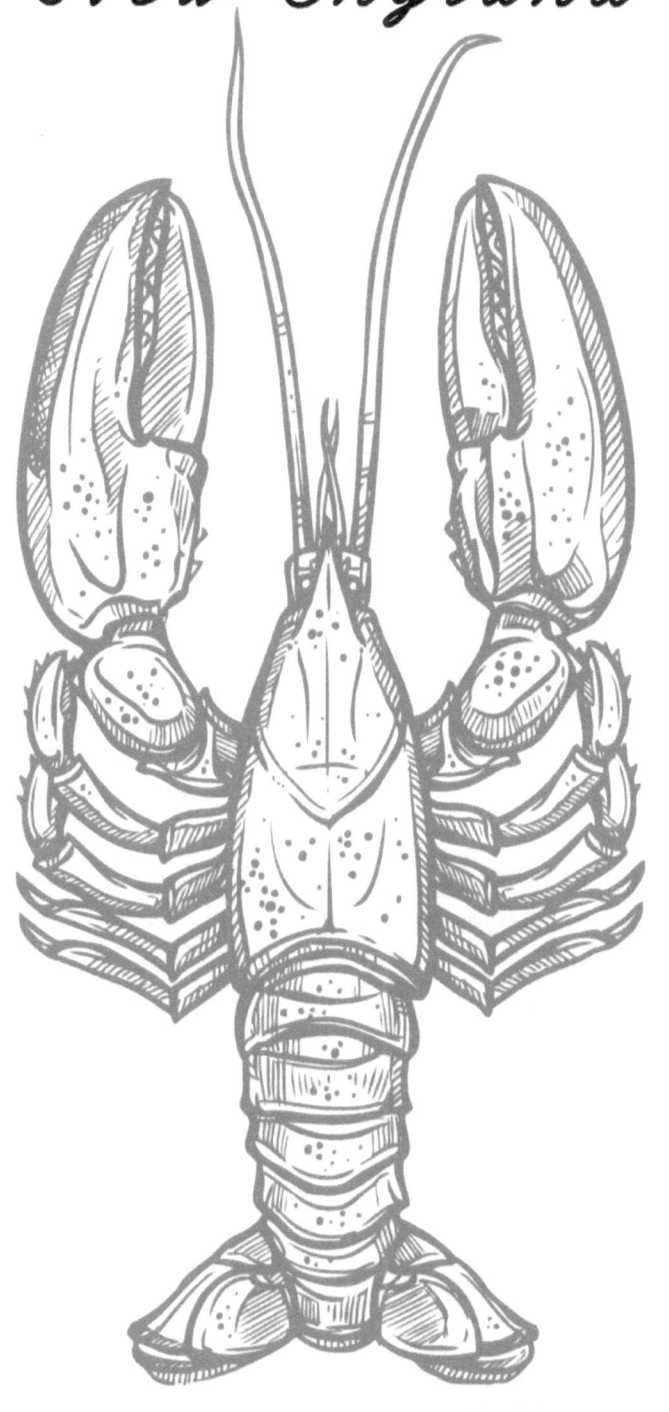

Lobster Stew

6 Tbsp. of Butter
1/2 Cup of Flour
2 Tsp. of Old Bay Seasoning
2 Cups of Seafood Stock (homemade recipe on next page)
6 Cups of Milk
2 Tbsp. of Tomato Paste
Sea Salt & Pepper
1 Pound or more of Lobster, torn into 1/2 Inch pieces
1/2 Cup of Heavy Cream

Melt butter in a saucepan on medium heat. Whisk in flour and Old Bay and continue to cook for one minute. Add seafood stock and continue to whisk over medium heat until smooth. Add the milk and tomato paste and cook for ten minutes or until the soup starts to thicken, stirring periodically so it doesn't burn. Lower the heat and continue to cook until the desired thickness. Season with salt and pepper to your preferred taste. Add lobster and heavy cream. If desired, garnish with a dash of Old Bay and a drizzle of heavy cream.

Homemade Seafood Stock

1 1/2 Cup of Water
2 1/2 Pounds of Seafood Shells (Lobster, Shrimp, Crab)
Black Peppercorns
Sea Salt
Large Onion, quartered
Whole Garlic Head, cut in half

In a large pot of water, boil all ingredients for 30 minutes until reduced. Season to taste with peppercorns and sea salt. Strain and keep the liquid.

Oyster Stew

8 Ounces of Bacon, cut into pieces
1 Tbsp. of Butter
3 Medium Onions, finely chopped
2 Tbsp. of Minced Shallots
1/4 Cup Flour
1 Pint or more of Oysters (the plumper the better!)
1 Tsp. of Salt & 1/2 Tsp. of Pepper
1 Bay Leaf
A Pinch of Thyme
2 Cups of Half & Half

Fry bacon in butter until crisp. Add onions and shallots. Sauté until tender. Stir in flour and add oysters. Cook until the edges curl (about 4 minutes). Stir in salt, pepper, bay leaf, and thyme, then add half-and-half. Heat stirring until smooth and thickened. Discard bay leaf and sprinkle with paprika or chives if desired.

Easy Popovers

2 Eggs, beaten
1 Cup Milk
1 Tbsp. Vegetable Oil
1 Cup Flour

Liberally grease 6: 6-ounce custard cups with Crisco shortening and place on a baking sheet. Put the baking sheet in the oven and preheat to 450 degrees. Meanwhile, mix all the ingredients in a 4-cup glass liquid measuring cup. Add 1/2 tsp of salt. Beat until smooth. Remove pan from oven and pour batter into hot cups until 1/2 full. Return to oven and bake undisturbed for 20 minutes. Reduce oven to 350 degrees and bake for 15 to 20 more minutes. Prick each popover with a fork to let the steam escape. Serve with a generous amount of butter and enjoy.

Corn Bread

1 Box of Corn Bread Mix (I like Krusteaz)
2 Tbsp. of Sugar
2 Large Eggs
3/4 Cup of Sour Cream
1/2 Cup of Buttermilk
1 Cup of Sharp Cheddar Cheese, grated
2 Small Jalapeno Peppers, if desired

Set oven to 425 degrees. Add 8 tbsp of unsalted butter to a 10-inch cast iron skillet and place on the middle rack of the oven. Melt the butter and allow it to brown a bit. Then remove from the oven and pour most of the butter into a heat-proof measuring cup, leaving about a tbsp in the skillet. Put the corn bread mix in a bowl and make a well in the center. If using jalapeno core and seed, chop one pepper. Crack eggs in another bowl and add the sour cream and buttermilk, and whisk together. Slowly pour and whisk the butter into the egg mixture. Pour the egg mixture into the corn bread mix well, and still just until moistened. Gently mix in the shredded cheese and jalapenos. Pour batter into skillet and smooth out the surface if needed. Put sliced jalapenos on top if desired.

Bake for 15 minutes and check for doneness. If not done, bake for 5 more minutes. Eat hot with butter and honey as desired.

Simple New England Clam Chowder

1- 16 Ounce Can Minced Clams
1- 10 Ounce Can of Whole Clams
4 Ounces of Salt Pork, diced
4 Medium Potatoes, peeled and diced
1/2 Cup Onion, chopped
2 1/2 Cups Whole Milk
1 Cup Light Cream
3 Tbsp. All-Purpose Flour
1/2 Tsp. Worcestershire Sauce

Drain clams, reserving liquid. Add enough water to the reserved clam juice to measure 2 cups; set aside. Fry salt pork until crisp in a large saucepan. Remove and set aside. Add reserve liquid, potatoes, and onion to the fat in a saucepan. Cook covered for 15 minutes or until potatoes are tender. Stir in the clams and 2 cups of milk and the light cream. Stir the remaining ½ cup of milk into the flour and make a slurry. Stir this into the chowder. Cook and stir until bubbly plus 1 minute. Add Worcestershire, 3/4 tsp salt, and a dash of pepper. Sprinkle chives or parsley on top and enjoy. (serves 4 to 6, depending on appetites). Pairs great with Popovers!

Acknowledgements

Writing this book has been one of the most rewarding yet challenging things I have ever done. Through research, whether personal family research, geographic, or historical, I learned something new at every turn. I found the whole process daunting yet exhilarating. There are so many people to thank, and I hope I don't leave anyone out. In no particular order, the following people were instrumental in achieving my lifelong dream:

Kathleen Branks for reading my very rough first draft and giving me the encouragement I needed to continue.

Elisa Lawrence for her photography,
social media knowledge and skills.

My local book club friends who continually
encouraged me along the way.

Lisa Carsten for helping me with all the technical challenges. I come from the generation of cursive writing and hand-written journaling. I don't know what I would have done without the help
and the patience of Lisa.

My husband Brian and my two daughters, Whitney and Peyton,
for just being who they are and loving me through this process.

My wonderful publishers at **PipStones Publishing, Abby, Debby,** and also one of the editors, **Elizabeth**. I could not have done this without you. Your patience, insight, and attention to detail have made my book come alive. I cannot thank you enough.

Most of all, I thank my Lord Jesus for all the ideas He woke me up with in the middle of the night when I thought I had nothing else to say.

About the Author

Elle Hess was born and raised in Levittown, Pennsylvania. After graduating from high school, she attended Temple University in Philadelphia, where she graduated with a degree in Business Law and Economics. After college, she worked at the start-up airline, People Express, as a Training Manager. This began her stint in technical writing and teaching. Elle married her high school sweetheart, Brian, in 1983. Upon his graduation from Rutgers Law School, the two moved to Panama City Beach, Florida, where they began their family, raising two girls, Whitney and Peyton. When the girls were grown, Elle was finally able to channel her love of books and creative writing. *Martha*, which was two years in the making, is her debut novel. Her second novel is in the works.

–

__Follow Elle's social media for more book news and upcoming works:__

www.Facebook.com/authorellebhess
www.Instagram.com/authorellebhess

About the Publisher

"Weavers of Tales and Tellers of Truth"

Mission Statement:

Our mission is to publish unique and refreshing works of various authors and genres; to present and highlight literary endeavors in an ever-changing marketplace.

Services:

Editing, Formatting, Illustrating, Publishing, Distributing, Local & Social Marketing, Author Coaching

Note to an Author:

Our goal is to walk with you through every step of your publishing journey.

Reach out for a free author consultation:
https://www.pipstones.com/booking-calendar

Enhance your Publishing Journey
with Our Book:

Now What?:
The 7 Vital Steps to Self-Publish your Manuscript

Now What? Book

Follow our social media for more book
news and information:

www.Facebook.com/pipstonespublishing
www.TikTok.com/pipstonespublishing
www.Instagram.com/pipstones
www.x.com/pip_stones
www.pipstones.com